MW01076118

Slaying the Vampire Conqueror

SLAYING THE VAMPIRE CONQUEROR

A CROWNS OF NYAXIA NOVEL

CARISSA BROADBENT

BRAMBLE

TOR PUBLISHING GROUP · NEW YORK

SLAYING THE VAMPIRE CONQUEROR

Map by Rhys Davies

A Bramble Book
Published by Tom Doherty Associates / Tor Publishing Group
120 Broadway
New York, NY 10271

www.torpublishinggroup.com

Bramble™ is a trademark of Macmillan Publishing Group, LLC.

The Library of Congress Cataloging-in-Publication Data is available upon request.

ISBN 978-1-250-36892-8 (hardcover)
ISBN 978-1-250-40649-1 (international, sold outside the U.S., subject to rights availability)
ISBN 978-1-250-38862-9 (signed)

Our books may be purchased in bulk for promotional, educational, or business use. Please contact your local bookseller or the Macmillan Corporate and Premium Sales Department at 1-800-221-7945, extension 5442, or by email at MacmillanSpecialMarkets@macmillan.com.

Previously self-published by the author in April 2023
First Bramble Edition: 2025

Printed in the United States of America

0 9 8 7 6 5 4 3 2 1

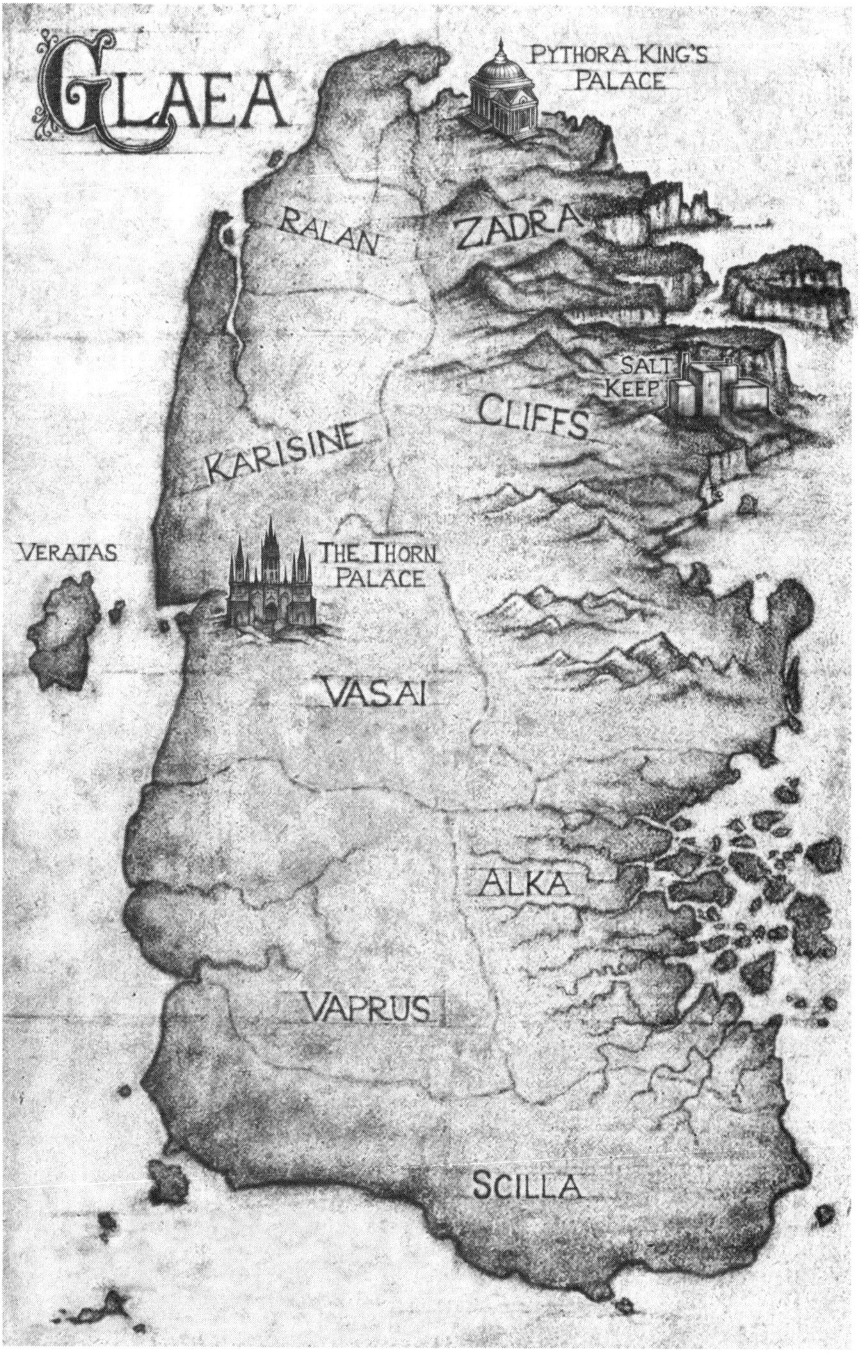
GLAEA
PYTHORA KING'S PALACE
RALAN
ZADRA
SALT KEEP
CLIFFS
KARISINE
VERATAS
THE THORN PALACE
VASAI
ALKA
VAPRUS
SCILLA

SLAYING THE VAMPIRE CONQUEROR

CHAPTER ONE

I didn't miss sight anymore. Sight was an inefficient way to perceive the world around you. It was a crutch. What I was given instead was far more useful.

Take this moment, for example—this moment when my back was pressed to the wall, dagger in my hand, as I waited to kill the man on the other side.

If I were relying on sight alone, I would have to crane my neck around the doorframe. I would have to risk being seen. I'd have to go by whatever I could make out of him and his lover in the darkness, squint into that writhing mass of flesh, and figure out the best way to make my move.

Inefficient. Room for error. A terrible way to work.

Instead, I *felt*. I *sensed*. Through the magic of the threads, I could still perceive the boundaries of the physical world—the color and shape of the scenery, the planes of a face, the absence or existence of light—but I had so much more than that, too. Crucial, in my work.

My target was a young nobleman. Six months ago, his father died. Within weeks of him receiving the keys to his father's significant cityscape, he began using all that newfound wealth and power to steal from his people and build more wealth for the Pythora King.

His essence now was slick with desire. The Arachessen could not read minds, not truly, but I didn't need to see his thoughts. What use were his thoughts when I saw his heart?

"More," a female voice moaned. "Please, more."

He mumbled something in response, the words buried in her hair. Her desire was genuine. Her soul shivered and throbbed with it—her pleasure spiking as he shifted angles, pushing her down to the bed. For the briefest of moments, I couldn't help being jealous that this snake had better sex than I did.

But I drove that thought away quickly. Arachessen were not supposed to mourn the things we gave up in the name of our goddess—Acaeja, the Weaver of Fates, the Keeper of the Unknown, the Mother of Sorcery. We could not mourn the eyesight, the autonomy, the pieces of our flesh carved away in sacrifice. And no, we could not mourn the sex, either.

I wished they'd hurry up.

I pressed my back to the wall and let out a frustrated breath through my teeth. I blinked, my lashes tickling the fabric of my blindfold.

{Now?}

Raeth's voice was very quiet in the back of my head—she was nearly out of Threadwhisper range, all the way downstairs, near the entrance of the beach house. When she spoke into my mind, I could sense a faint echo of the ocean wind as it caressed her face.

{Not yet,} I answered.

I felt Raeth's irritation.

{I don't know how much longer we have. He's distracted, isn't he? Take him and go before he starts to pay attention.}

Oh, he was distracted, alright. His woman wasn't the only vocal one now, his grunts echoing against the wall behind me.

I didn't answer right away.

{Sylina—} Raeth started.

{I want to wait until the girl is gone.}

As I knew she would, Raeth scoffed at this. {Wait until the girl is gone? If you wait that long, someone will notice that something is off.}

I clenched my jaw and did not answer, letting her Threadwhispers fade beneath the sounds of our target's enthusiastic climax.

Threadwhispers were very useful. Communication that couldn't be overheard, that could transcend sound the same way we transcended sight. It was a gift from the Weaver, one for which I was very grateful.

. . . But I hated that it meant I could never pretend I hadn't heard something.

{Sylina!}

{She might not know,} I told her.

What he is. Who he is. What he's doing, and who he's doing it for.

I had no qualms about killing the nobleman. I would take more joy than I should in feeling his presence wither and die beneath me—and that would be my little secret, a guilty pleasure. But the girl . . .

Again, Raeth's scoff reverberated between us.

{She knows.}

{She—}

{If she's fucking him, then she knows. And if she doesn't, she has terrible taste in men. What difference does it make?}

And then I felt it.

A sudden crack through the air. Sound, yes, a distant *BANG*—but the sound was nothing compared to the sensation that ripped through the threads of life beneath the physical world, a force powerful enough to set them vibrating.

I froze.

My target and his paramour stopped.

"What was that?" the woman whispered.

But I was no longer focused on them. Not with the force of the vibrations, and Raeth's wordless panic spreading slowly across them, rolling toward me like a pool of blood.

{Raeth?}

Nothing.

{Raeth? What was that?}

Confusion. Fear. I felt it, though it was dimming because she must have been walking away from the door—then running, out into the city streets.

{Raeth!}

But she was out of range now. All I could feel from her were faint reverberations.

That is, until I heard her scream.

An Arachessen was not supposed to abandon a mission for anything, not even for the sake of saving a Sister's life. But every thought of my dutiful teachings drained from me the moment I felt her terror, visceral and human and too familiar in ways I'd never admit aloud.

I ran.

Down marble steps, across tile floors, newly slick with I-didn't-even-know-what, through the door where my Sister had been moments ago, standing watch. The air hit me, salty and ocean-sweet.

And with it came the sensation of *them*.

The vampire invaders.

Decades later, I would not forget this moment. Exactly how it felt when they made landfall. Their magic sickened me, tainted and cursed, making the air taste so thickly of blood I nearly gagged on it.

Sisters of the Arachessen are trained extensively in the magic of every god. From the time we were children, we were exposed to all magics, even when our bodies protested, even when it burned us or broke us.

This, I recognized immediately, was Nyaxia's magic. The heretic goddess. The mother of vampires.

Hundreds, perhaps thousands, of them crashed upon our shores that night.

Sound was useless, all the bangs and screams and groans of crumbling stone running together like the rush of a waterfall. For a moment, I was blinded, too, because the sensations were so much— every essence, every soul, screaming at once.

In that moment, I didn't know what was happening. I wouldn't understand exactly what I was witnessing until later. But I did know that this wasn't the work of the Pythora King. These were foreigners.

{Raeth!}

I threw the call as far down the threads as I could, flinging it toward her like a net. And there, near where the land met the sea, I felt her. Felt her running—not away from the explosions at the shore, but toward them.

No.

Idiot girl. Stupid girl. Impulsive. Impatient.

I ran for her.

{Raeth! Fall back!}

But Raeth didn't listen.

I was getting closer, dodging slabs of broken rock, dodging clusters of the strangest fire I'd ever felt—not hot, but cold, devouring trees, devouring buildings. My head pounded, my magic wailing with overexertion at having to constantly reorient myself, over and over.

But I didn't miss a single step.

Raeth was at the shore. At the docks. Many, many presences surrounded her—so many I struggled to separate them from each other. Human. Vampire. I couldn't count them. Too many. More coming. Pouring onto the shore in a wave of sea froth and magic and explosives and bloodthirsty rage that I could feel throbbing in my veins.

{Sylina!}

Asha's voice was sharp as she called to me. Even a little afraid.

I'd never felt my commander's fear before.

I'd never disobeyed her before, either.

Because in that moment, Raeth screamed. Another explosion of dark magic roared through the air, so powerful that when it faded, I was on my knees, splinters of the pier digging into my flesh.

And Raeth was simply gone.

It is difficult to describe what it feels like to sense the death of a Sister. I could not see her. I could not hear her voice. But when you're near another of the Arachessen, you can simply feel them the way that one feels the body warmth of another, all their threads connected to yours.

All that, all at once, severed.

The dead did not have threads.

Raeth's color was purple. Sometimes it was a little warmer when she was happy or excited, a glowy pink hue of delight. Sometimes it was colder when she was moody, like storm clouds at sunset.

Now it was nothing, a hole in all of us where Raeth should have been. It was strange how viscerally it reminded me of another distant memory, a memory I was no longer supposed to have, of how it felt to witness life snatched away in the unforgiving jaws of war.

Asha felt it, too. Of course she did. We would feel it everywhere.

{Let her go,} Asha said. *{Come back. We need to leave now. We'll complete our task another time.}*

Task? Who cared about that limp-dicked little nobleman now?

I had bigger game.

Because there *he* was.

Even in the sea of vampires and magic, he stood out. His presence was bigger than all of theirs, a gravitational force. All the rest of it—the countless souls, the gray of the sea-foam, the cold of the night—framed him like a throne, as if the universe simply oriented itself around him as he rose from the surf.

Even then, through the chaos, with the lack of information I had, I knew I was witnessing something deadly and incredible and horrible. I knew, from that first moment, that he was the leader.

I'd burn his presence into my soul after that. Every angle of him. Every scent that war carried across the sea breeze. Even from this distance, I could sense his appearance through the threads—that he wore fine clothes, and even finer armor over them. His hair was long and reflected the moonlight, soaked in salty tendrils around his shoulders.

And of course, there were the horns. Black as night, protruding from his upper forehead and curling back. They were like nothing I'd ever witnessed before. The product, surely, of some dark, unknown magic.

He was cursed. He was tainted. I could feel that even from here. And as he stepped right over Raeth's body, I didn't even think as I reached to my back and withdrew my bow.

I was a fantastic shot. Human eyes are fallible. But the threads are never fooled.

I had a perfect opening. A single thread stretching from me to him, straight to his heart.

{Get back here, Sylina!} Asha commanded.

{I have the shot.}

{You're too far.}

I was not too far.

I drew.

{We can't sacrifice another Sister here!} Asha roared—so strong her words made me lurch, my head splitting.

He stepped onto the shore. The thread between us stretched tight. I felt his head turn. Felt his gaze fall to me. Felt his toxic magic shiver down the connection.

{Sylina, the Sightmother commands *that you come back.}*

I could make it.

I could make it.

My hands shook. Every shred of my focus went toward cutting through all these sensations, falling only on him. Nothing else existed.

But the Sightmother's stare was on me, too. A Sister did not disobey the Sightmother.

I lowered my bow and backed away, fleeing into the chaotic night. By the time I reached Asha, I had so overexerted my magic and my senses that I was stumbling over rocks in the road. I knew I had a punishment waiting for me at the Keep, but I didn't care.

It was punishment enough. That moment.

The moment I let him go.

I'd think about that moment for a long, long time.

CHAPTER TWO

When they take your eyes, they take them slow—an offering given in pieces every day, rather than all at once. The Sightmother told me then that it meant more to Acaeja that way. A single act can be made in impulse. It can be rash. It can be regretted. But it can never be rash to decide every day for one year to give your goddess your eyes, and mean it each time.

It was a fair trade. The Arachessen, after all, saved me.

I was ten years old. Older than most. I was acutely aware of that then and would remain aware of it forever after—those ten years of life that separated me from my Sisters. Most of them barely recalled the process of their initiations, nor did they remember the lives they had before coming here. The Arachessen and the Salt Keep were all they knew. Sometimes I pitied them, because they would love this place even more if they understood what it had been like to live beyond it.

I did. I remembered it all.

I was old enough to remember the way each drop of Marathine extract burned going into my eyes. I was old enough to remember the visions that came after, visions that would leave me jerking awake at night with tears crusted on my face. And above all, I was old enough to remember that even that pain was an embrace compared to the outside world.

People thought that we were so isolated, that we did not hear the things they said about us. Foolish. We heard everything. I knew that people talked about us like we're insane—as if we'd made some unimaginable sacrifice. It was not a sacrifice. It was an exchange: *Close your eyes, child, and you will see an entire world.*

Contrary to what people thought, we were not blind. The threads of life that ran through our world, and our mastery over them, told us everything we needed to know. Everything and more.

The first time, it was the Sightmother herself who leaned over me, pinning my arms to the stone table. I was frightened, then, though I was smart enough to know that I shouldn't be. I hadn't yet gotten used to the sight of the Arachessen and their covered eyes. As the Sightmother leaned over me, I didn't know where to look, so I stared into the deep crimson silk of her blindfold. She was the kind of woman who defied markers of time. The faint lines around her mouth and nose did little to dull the uncanny appearance of her youth.

"You must be very still, child," she said. "Even in the face of great pain. Do you remember how?"

I liked the Sightmother's voice. It was smooth and gentle. She spoke to me like she respected both my vulnerability and my intelligence, which was very rare among adults. The moment I met her, I knew I would do anything for her. Secretly, I imagined the goddess Acaeja with her face.

"Do you understand, Sylina?" she said, when I did not answer.

It was the first time she'd called me by that new name. It felt good to hear it, like I'd just been let into an open door.

I nodded, my mouth dry. "Yes. I understand."

I knew, even then, that this was another test. I'd been tested before they allowed me into the Salt Keep. The ability to withstand pain was a non-negotiable skill. I was good at withstanding pain. I showed the Sisters so, and I had the broken fingers to prove it. Decades later, I would still feel a bit of pride when I touched my left hand.

The Sightmother had smiled at me, and then nodded to the Sister at my side.

When it was done, tears streamed down my face, and blood pooled in the back of my throat—from my tongue, which I had bitten so hard I couldn't eat solids for a week.

It was worth it, though. They told me later I was the only recruit that didn't make a sound.

I NO LONGER noticed the Sightmother's blindfold because I, like all my Sisters, had my own. Tonight, I wore my red one, the same shade that the Sightmother had donned when she leaned over me that day, fifteen years ago. An accidental coincidence, and I only thought of it now, as I sat at the gathering table with my Sisters, my fingertips in the gritty pile of salt that had been spread along the large, circular table. Forty of us gathered here, each pressing our hands to the salt—our grounding connection to each other, and to the Weaver, the Lady of Fate, the goddess Acaeja, to whom we had all sworn our unending loyalty.

But I was acutely aware of the empty chairs. More empty still since our last meeting, when Asha and I returned from the south the day the invasion began.

It was impossible not to feel their absence. The breaks in the chain, the expanses of salt left untouched.

Raeth was lost in their initial landfall. And then, later, Vima was lost in Breles. Another city conquered by our invaders, another lost Sister.

The vampires moved quickly. They didn't waste time. It was clear that their goal was to take over all of Glaea—why else would they start at the southernmost shores and then move slowly north?

So, it was not a surprise to me when the Sightmother cleared her throat and said, "The vampires have taken Vaprus."

Utter silence. But we all felt the ripple of fear, of grief, through the threads.

I tilted my head to the third empty chair. I didn't need to ask to know the truth. But a young Sister, Yylene, said weakly, "Amara?"

The Sightmother let out a long exhale. We all sensed her sadness before her words came. "She has been lost."

Yylene bit her lip and sagged over the table. She was only seventeen. Loss still hit her deep. But then, I supposed it hit us all deep. We just learned how to cover the wounds with other things. Stitch it up with the threads of our next task.

My jaw tightened, and I tried to exhale my frustration before anyone else could sense it. My whole life, I had never felt more seen, more accepted, than I was here at this table—connected to all my Sisters, to my Sightmother, to the goddess Acaeja herself.

But these last few weeks, what had once felt like connection had started to feel stifling, as it grew harder and harder for me to strangle the shameful thoughts I was not supposed to feel.

"Do we have any further insight into what they want, Sightmother?" Asha asked. I found it slightly satisfying that I could hear, could feel, the tinge of anger in her words, too.

"I assume," the Sightmother said mildly, "they want to conquer."

"The Obitraens have never conquered a human nation before."

Obitraens—those of the continent of Obitraes, the home of vampires and the domain of Nyaxia, the heretic goddess. Obitraes consisted of three kingdoms: the House of Shadow, the House of Night, and the House of Blood. They squabbled among themselves, but had never been known to venture forth into human nations—at least, certainly not as a coordinated act. And this? This was nothing if not coordinated. This was an army.

"We know that the House of Blood is the most unpredictable of the vampire nations," the Sightmother said. "It's impossible now to say why they have moved."

"Has there not been a formal declaration?" Asha asked.

"No. The king of the House of Blood has offered no declaration of war."

"Then this man . . . this commander . . . could he be acting independently?"

"We can't say."

There was a certain weakness in the Sightmother's voice at that—a helplessness from a woman who was never helpless. I hated hearing it.

Everyone was silent for a long moment.

"Perhaps it's all a mercy," Asha said softly, at last. "Let them destroy each other. Maybe it will thin the herds."

My head snapped toward Asha. I couldn't choke down the sudden wave of indignation at that statement.

I bit my tongue, right over the raised ridge of scar tissue from when I was ten years old, until the pain supplanted the anger.

Too late, though. I could feel the Sightmother's gaze on me.

"What do you wish to say, Sylina?"

"Nothing, Sightmother."

"No lies are spoken here."

The refrain was uttered frequently around this table, as we pressed our fingertips to the salt—and maybe it was true, because we were never more exposed to each other than we were around this table, but it didn't mean that there weren't thoughts that were unacceptable to express. To even feel.

I shouldn't have answered at all.

But before I could stop myself, I said, "There could be a high human cost to letting that happen."

"I would think that you, of all people, Sylina, would know this," Asha said, in a pitying tone that made me want to leap across the table and slap her. "We act on the will of Acaeja alone. Not our personal feelings."

Yes. True. The Pythora King had ravaged our country, leaving Glaea in a state of perpetual war since he tore his own ruthless conquering path, two decades ago. But even that would not be enough to make the Arachessen act. The Arachessen didn't make decisions based on morality—some made-up measure of right and wrong, though of course, by any measure, the Pythora King was wrong. Worse, the Weaver had shown us that the Pythora King disrupted the natural order. His actions moved our world away from its course.

That is the measure of an enemy of the Arachessen. Acaeja's will. Balance. Not evil or righteousness.

But this . . . it felt . . .

"Acaeja has no hatred for Nyaxia's children," Asha reminded me. "She may support this. Sometimes, gods deem a purge necessary."

I choked out, too angry to stop myself, "A *purge*?"

"No progress comes without a cost."

My temper had been short lately. Too short. Especially with

Asha. Sometimes, when I heard her voice, I could only hear how it had sounded as she commanded me to stand down.

I could have taken the shot. These seats would not be empty.

And yet, I knew that she was right. Nyaxia, the mother of vampires, was an enemy of the White Pantheon of human gods. Two thousand years ago, when she was just a young, lesser god, she had fallen in love with and married Alarus, the god of death. But their relationship was forbidden by the rest of the White Pantheon, ultimately resulting in Alarus's execution. Enraged and grieving, Nyaxia had broken away from the other gods and created vampires—a society to rule all on her own. Now, the gods of the White Pantheon despised her. Acaeja was the only exception—the only god who tolerated Nyaxia and the vampire society she had created.

It was not up to us to judge our conqueror.

But I wanted to. I wanted to judge him. I wanted to judge anyone who made a city look like that, feel like that, just as my own home had felt so many years ago.

That made me a poor Sister. I was, at least, self-aware.

It would be one thing to control a facial expression. But like sight, facial expressions are shallow indicators of the truth. I could control every muscle in my body, including those on my face—it was much harder to control the shifts of my aura, more visible than ever here before my Sisters.

Right now, it seethed with anger. Anger with our conqueror. Anger with Asha for daring to claim his killing could be for the greater good.

And—who was I kidding?—anger with Asha for not letting me take that shot.

{Is there something more you want to say, Sylina?} Asha Threadwhispered, and I was so close to snapping back—

{Enough!}

"*Enough!*"

The Sightmother spoke in both places simultaneously—her voice ripping through the air and the threads.

We all went silent. I collected myself.

The Sightmother said, "Sylina is right."

Beneath my blindfold, my brows twitched in surprise.

And satisfaction.

"We know better than any that evil can wear many different faces," she went on. "Yes, the Pythora King is our enemy. But that doesn't mean that all his enemies must be our friends. This conqueror is troubling indeed."

Troubling might seem, to any other, to be a mild word. Coming from the Sightmother, it might as well be damnation.

"Has the Weaver spoken to you, Sightmother?" Yylene asked tentatively.

The Sightmother did not answer for a long moment. Then she rose, her palms pressed to the salt. "It is too early to say what the Weaver believes. But we all must be ready for dark times ahead. That, daughters, is true. We must look inward. So go now and prepare for evening recitations."

In unified movements, we each drew our flattened hands in a single sweep across the table before us, scattering the salt. Then we rose. I went to follow my Sisters from the room, but the Sightmother said, *{Not you, Sylina. You're coming with me.}*

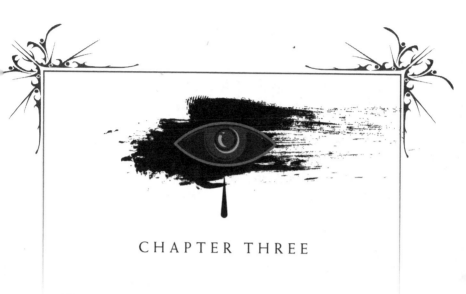

CHAPTER THREE

The Salt Keep earned its name due to its location in the mountains of eastern Glaea, a notoriously inaccessible piece of land. The mountains that surrounded the Keep were tall, treacherous, dense, and incredibly effective at keeping outsiders away. Even if one managed to locate the Keep—difficult on its own, given the Arachessen's unmatched ability to keep secrets— the journey over the mountains on foot would mean almost certain death. The mountain range was so dense that even most magical travel—already very rare—was impossible over such a distance, and dangerous. Unless your coordinates were very, very accurate, you had a significant chance of throwing yourself into a ravine. Which did indeed happen once, about a century back, when some poor love-struck sorcerer tried to follow the object of his affections back to the Keep.

Yes, there were many practical reasons why the Salt Keep was built here, right where the mountains met the sea, isolated from the rest of the world. None of them were its aesthetics.

Still, it was beautiful.

When I saw it for the first time as a child, I'd never felt smaller in my life—like I was caught between two godly realms, the mountains to one side and the sea to the other, massive forces that rendered me nothing but inconsequential flesh and bones. It cemented the Arachessen, in my mind, as a power greater than the sum of its members—something greater than all of us. Of course, I reasoned, the Salt Keep would be the only thing that could exist here, at the apex of these two worlds.

I no longer could see the view as I did then, of course. Not that I didn't see it in my own way—not that I didn't still experience it, maybe even more deeply than I did that day. I now *felt* the world around me in every sense, the presence of the world wrapping me up from all angles. Every jagged plane of the rocky cliffs (gray), the roll of the surf (green), the dusty, dry, shin-tickling grass (dim gold).

I had nothing to mourn. I had gained more than I had lost. This is what I would tell anyone who asked me.

But secretly, in a part of myself I tried not to acknowledge, I missed being able to *see* it. Sometimes, when I'd come out here, I'd try to conjure that memory—the memory of sight, from when I was ten years old.

"You're distracted, Sylina," the Sightmother said, and I snapped my head forward. We walked through the rocky paths along the cliffs, pulling our cloaks tight against the salty wind that stung our cheeks.

She was right. I was distracted.

"I apologize."

I heard the warm smile in her voice. "You don't need to apologize. Ascensions are difficult. And I know Raeth's has been especially so for you."

This was what I had always appreciated about the Sightmother, from the time I was a child. She was foreboding, powerful, strict— yes. But she was also kind, warm, present. I had so needed that when I met her. I still felt that I needed it.

For this reason, I didn't bother trying to lie to her.

"I've struggled with it," I admitted.

"Raeth is more alive than she has ever been. But I know that you know that."

"Yes."

Ascension, not death. Never death. Arachessen didn't believe in death, only change. Just as the loss of our eyes didn't mean the loss of sight, the loss of a heartbeat didn't mean the loss of life.

Still, it was hard not to mourn someone who existed now only as air and earth and water, which had no room for the memories or thoughts or experiences that made a human a human.

"What's so troubling to you, Sylina?" the Sightmother asked.

I didn't answer, and she laughed softly. "You were always ever the mysterious one. Even when we found you."

"I—" I chose my words carefully. "I felt that Raeth's fate was avoidable, and I've carried bitterness about that. That is my weight to carry, not Asha's."

"It isn't just about Raeth."

I didn't answer. I couldn't think of a way to do so without sounding resentful. Maybe because I was.

"Weaver's name, Sylina, just speak your mind." The Sightmother nudged my shoulder affectionately, shaking her head. "It's no interrogation."

"I don't like to give voice to thoughts that don't deserve it."

"And I'm sure Acaeja is grateful for your piousness. But humor me."

My teeth ground, just as they always did, involuntarily, whenever I thought about the shot I was so close to taking and didn't.

"I could have ended it then," I said, after a long moment. "I had a clear shot to him. I was going to take it."

"Why didn't you?"

I disliked when the Sightmother did this—asked questions she already knew the answer to, just to make us say the answers aloud.

"Because Asha commanded that I return."

"Is that really why you didn't?"

I paused. The Sightmother kept on walking.

"Keep going," she said. "Why did Asha tell you to return?"

"She felt we were running out of time to flee."

"That isn't the only reason." Now, the Sightmother stopped, too, and turned to me. "The Arachessen only exist to be architects of the fate the Weaver shows us. We are not judges. We are not executioners. We are followers of the goddess Acaeja's will, and followers of the unknown."

My cheeks flushed—irritated to have this explained, and embarrassed that the Sightmother, who I so admired, apparently felt it needed to be.

"I know, Sightmother. And I'm committed to that."

"Oh, I know you are, Sylina. This is why I'm telling you this. Because you're a committed Arachessen. A committed Sister of the threads. A committed daughter of the Weaver. And I know you have struggled with this. I think for reasons beyond those even you yourself understand."

"It's—there is so much suffering," I said. "It isn't just about Raeth, or Asha, it's—"

"It reminds you," the Sightmother said, "of your own past."

I was ashamed of the defensive anger that leapt up in me at that.

"With all respect, Sightmother—"

She raised a hand. The movement seemed to erect a wall between us—her presence pushing back against mine. "You do not need to agree with me or argue with me. In the end, it doesn't matter if you think I'm right or not. You have had a longer life beyond the walls of the Keep than most of the Arachessen. I know that has been difficult for you. In some ways, it has compromised your training—compromises that I'm proud to say that you've overcome."

My face was hot. I didn't like thinking about this. It had been a long time since I'd had to defend myself against the many accusations that I would never be a good Arachessen because I was so old by the time I got here.

"Your past has instilled a strong sense of justice in you. This makes you a powerful warrior, strong in your conviction. But it also means that you struggle with the reality that there is no good or evil in this world, just as there is no good or evil in us. Only what is Right by the fates."

I wished I could say she was wrong. I had tried over the years to beat that quality out of myself, the piece that was so obsessed with justice and righteousness. And I'd done a good job of it, for the most part.

There was no moral good or evil. There was only what was fated and what was not. What was Right by the threads our goddess wove, and what was a deviation of what should be. Judging which was which was not our place.

I nearly jumped as a warm hand touched my cheek. The Sightmother's caress was brief and gentle.

"You have a kind heart, Sylina," she said. "That is a gift to Acaeja, even if it is, at times, a burden to you. Temper your expectations of this world. But do not dampen your fire. You'll need it for what's ahead."

What's ahead?

I didn't need expressions to feel the shift in the Sightmother then, a solemn tinge to her presence.

"What is it?" I asked.

The Sightmother pulled away, resuming her walk. She didn't answer for a long moment.

"I peered into the darkness last night."

I faltered.

Peering into the darkness. A phrase to describe the advanced form of seering conducted by the highest ranking of the Arachessen—usually only by Sightmothers. That, then, was why the Sightmother had been absent for the last several days. Peering into the dark was a long, arduous task that left them near-dead to the world for many hours, sometimes days. But the upside was that they came as close as most humans ever would to the gods themselves.

"What did you see?" I asked.

"Acaeja showed me the conqueror. She showed me terrible consequences that would take place if he were to succeed in his task. His actions are not Right. They threaten the realm of Acaeja, and all of the White Pantheon."

My brows lurched.

That was a strong, strong accusation.

I managed, "How? Why?"

I felt her wry smile. "The Weaver, hearts thank her, is cryptic. She shows me only threads, not the tapestry. But I saw enough to understand her intentions. The conqueror needs to be stopped." Her brow twitched. "If you're still regretting that missed shot, you won't be for long."

I couldn't speak for a moment. Then, "You want me to go."

"I do."

"But I'm—"

"We need fire, child," the Sightmother said simply. "You have it. But if you don't want the task—"

"I do want it."

I spoke too fast. Too eagerly.

I had been given many missions during my time as an Arachessen. All of them I executed skillfully, accurately, quietly. I trained twice as hard to make up for my late start, to make up for everything I knew the others would always say about me. And it had been recognized. I had risen through the ranks swiftly, earning respect if not always affection.

Still, these last few weeks . . . parts of myself I thought I'd long ago discarded had started nagging at me again. I hid it the best I could, but it bothered me to know that the Sightmother had noticed.

I had seen other Sisters be cast out of the Arachessen. Our goddess demanded discipline, distance. Not emotional volatility.

I had been handed a gift in this mission. I would not squander it.

I bowed my head. "Thank you, Sightmother. I accept the task."

The Sightmother tilted my chin up, lifting my lowered face.

"All deserve another chance," she said, then looped my arm through hers as we walked together. "What do you know of the Bloodborn vampires? The House of Blood?"

Arachessen extensively studied all the continents and major kingdoms within them. It was hard to learn about the vampire Houses in much detail because they were so isolated, but we had our ways.

"I know enough of their history," I said. "I know of their position with their goddess."

Nyaxia, the mother of vampires, was notoriously protective of her people, lording singularly over the continent of Obitraes for the last two thousand years. But long ago, the House of Blood had questioned Nyaxia and, some said, perhaps even betrayed her— offending her so violently that they were cursed rather than given the gifts matching those of the other two Houses. Few details about the curse were known, only that it resulted in young, ugly deaths by vampire standards. The House of Blood was reviled not only by the human nations—who wanted nothing to do with any of the vampire kingdoms—but also the other two vampire Houses.

"Are you aware," the Sightmother said, "that they have a strong affinity for seers?"

That, I did not know.

"They don't make such information well-known, of course," she went on. "But all major military operations from the House of Blood are almost always accompanied by one seer, who typically remains very close to the leading general. Their king, apparently, has one who never leaves his side."

Strange, that a kingdom of Nyaxia would be so reliant upon seers. Nyaxia did not offer her followers any magic that could be used for peering into the future—which meant that seers would need to be human, worshipping other gods who offered magic that could be used for such things. Like Acaeja.

"Our conqueror is no exception," she went on. "He has a seer as well. Join him, infiltrate his army, and watch his movements. Should you earn his trust, your position as his seer will give you unmatched insight into his movements and intentions."

"You say he already has a seer?" I asked, and the Sightmother nodded.

"He does. For now."

She did not need to say more. I understood right away what she was telling me to do—create my own opening.

"His forces move north," she said. "I do not know what his ultimate intentions are with our country, but I know that now he moves for the Pythora King. We need to know why, and what else he intends. Accompany him. And then, when the time is right, you will kill him."

Years ago, I might have wanted to kill him immediately. But I knew now what it was to cut off the head of a snake and have two more grow in its place. It would take more than a single dagger to his heart to end this.

Perhaps it could've been that simple when he first landed. Not now, after he'd started laying roots.

"I won't lie to you, Sylina," the Sightmother said quietly. "This will be a dangerous and unpleasant task."

"All tasks are dangerous and unpleasant."

At least this one meant something.

She nodded, understanding me exactly.

"Go now," she said. "Travel through the pools. He moves to the southwest tonight."

I didn't argue. I didn't ask if I could say goodbye. The threads connected us all, anyway.

I bowed my head. "Thank you, Sightmother."

I started back to the Keep. I'd gather my things and go within an hour.

The Sightmother did not follow me.

"May she weave in your favor," she called after me, her voice lost in the ocean wind.

CHAPTER FOUR

I used to paint, sometimes.

When I came to the Salt Keep, I'd had a few of my paintings with me—little doodles I'd done in my notebook to pass the time. I did one that night, of the sea and the cliffs, the sight so beautiful I couldn't resist capturing it however my little hands could.

The Sightmother had found it the next day, as the Sisters went through my belongings before I began my tests. She had held that notebook for a long time, staring down at the paper with her blindfolded gaze.

"What is this?" she asked me.

"It's the ocean," I said.

"No," she said. "It is paper."

Her magic shredded the parchment in seconds. I hadn't known then that the sight of those shards of paper swept away into the ocean was one of the last things I would see with my eyes alone. Maybe that was why I still dreamed of it, sometimes—those painted scraps of color, fluttering away like butterfly wings, so easily consumed by the world.

Nothing but paper, just like the Sightmother had said.

I CAME OUT of the water gasping. The rush of cold air was a slap across the face, making what was already disorienting a shock to all senses at once.

Some Sisters claimed that they didn't mind the sensation, but I was sure they had to be lying. After fifteen years of traveling through the pools, it still never got any less nauseating. Or maybe I just hated the way that it yanked me into my past in the moments between threads.

I took a moment to right myself against the rocks. I dragged my fingers through my hair, pushing it away from my face. I rose on shaky legs and tried to take stock of my senses.

It was hard because there were *so many of them*.

Crowds could be difficult for those of the Arachessen. With eyes, one could only take in so much information at once. Without them, we had no such limitation. We felt everything at the same time. And here, it was overwhelming.

The Sightmother's instruction had been remarkably accurate. I had arrived not far from their encampment. I was several miles north of their last target, Vaprus. Since much of Glaea's land was harsh and the Pythora King's warlords were more than happy to hoard resources for themselves, civilization tended to cluster in city-states with long stretches of empty wastelands between them. In the south, that land consisted of rocky, barren plains.

I followed the sensation of the crowd. I crept to the edge of the rocks, where cliffs began to give way to flat earth.

Just beyond the rugged stone, the conqueror's encampment spread out before me.

There were so many of them that for a moment, the sudden existence of so many auras overwhelmed me. How many—hundreds, thousands? *Thousands*, I settled on. Every one of them vampires. They *felt* different than humans, like a chord struck at a different tone, a minor note against a major, every shade of color just a little off.

Immediately, I knew the encampment was extensive. I reached through the threads to examine it and found tents that were elaborate and firmly rooted to the ground, meal carts that had been spread out, soldiers that appeared to be quite content to stay where they were. Their exhaustion was obvious, even from this distance, as they continued to erect tents at the edges of the camp.

They'd only just gotten here. And it seemed like they intended to stay, at least for a few days. Why they would do so here instead of remaining in whatever city they had last taken over was beyond me, but I was grateful for the time. I needed to find this seer, remove them, and insert myself.

I crept down closer to the encampment, remaining in the rocks for cover. Vampires had fantastic eyesight and even better senses of smell, so I was careful to stay far enough to avoid either my movements or my scent giving me away. Still, I managed to get close enough to map out the boundaries of the camp.

While all individual presences were unique, in such a large group the warriors' all blended together, more similar to each other than they were different. I sensed the same emotions across them all—determination, exhaustion. All familiar feelings. I'd been around a lot of soldiers over the years. It was actually a little strange that these ones felt so similar to their human counterparts. Then again, maybe war was universal, no matter whether our blood ran black or red.

Halfway around the camp, I froze.

I recognized him immediately. In a sea of gray, his soul was dark, bruise-bitten red. None of his men's mundane weariness. No, his was steady, intense—*angry*. The kind of anger that knocked the breath out of my lungs.

His tent was one of the largest, near the southern edge of the encampment. He stepped out of it and straightened, looking out over his men.

And then he turned right to me.

I stopped breathing, falling back into the shadows of the rocks. One silent step backward. Two. Three. Surely I was too far for him to see or scent, even with his superior senses. And yet . . .

For a long moment, he stared into the darkness. Right at me.

Then he turned around and went back into his tent.

IT TOOK TWO days of watching and waiting to find the seer.

It was overwhelmingly likely their seer would be human—someone who drew from a god of the White Pantheon. So I kept up my watch most carefully in the daylight hours, when the vampires retreated into their thickly shrouded tents and the encampment went quiet.

On the second day, she made an appearance.

She emerged when the sun was high in the sky. She had a tent near the edge of camp, not far from the conqueror's. She was indeed, as I'd suspected, a human. Older—perhaps in her mid-sixties. Her presence was firm and aged as worn-down stone. I couldn't tell which gods she worshipped. Then again, it didn't really matter.

She carried a little bag with her. Flowers peeked out from it. I could sense the weight of wax candles in the sack, too. She was leaving to pray.

I followed her, far behind when she was closer to the camp, then venturing steadily closer, very slowly, as she grew farther and farther away from it.

Soon, we were half a mile from the camp, at the edge of a rocky lake, and I was mere strides away from her.

And then, as she started to kneel down to place her tokens, I made my move.

I envisioned an invisible thread drawn taut between us, a single thread connecting our souls, and stepped through it. The world withered around me and reformed. In half a breath, I was right behind her, my dagger halfway to her back.

Before I could strike, she turned around. It was such an abrupt movement that it made me stagger a little, repositioning in anticipation of a strike. But she didn't move for me. She just stared. Up close, I could sense the wrinkles in her face. The wisdom of her eyes.

"I see you," she said.

"Does it matter?" I replied.

She let out a vicious laugh. "Probably not. Funny, how I spent my entire life peering into the future and never thought that my end would come at the hands of one of you fucking cultists. Well, I'm not one to fight fate." Her lip curled. "But I will fight you."

I knew better than to underestimate a sorceress, even one who seemed so nonthreatening. I lurched away before she struck, the swell of light at her hands lunging for me, filling my nostrils with the burning tang from where it struck the grassy ground instead.

But magic or no, it was an easy fight. I strung threads around her, slipping through air to evade each of her attempted blows, and it only took a few minutes before I got behind her, my arms around her neck. *SNAP*, as my leg swept hers out from under her, twisting her knee until it gave. She let out a cry of pain. I didn't let her slump, holding her tight to my chest.

I shouldn't have hesitated.

And yet I couldn't help but ask, my face against her gray, wiry hair, "Why? Why are you helping him?"

She scoffed. "You'd think that a child of your goddess would understand that the world looks awfully different depending on where you stand. Or maybe they took your eyes so you wouldn't see that." She turned her head just enough to look at me. I felt her smile, poison sweet. "How old were you? Four? Five?"

I didn't answer, and perhaps my silence alone told her—or perhaps her magic found the answer my lips refused.

"Oh, you were a late one," she laughed. "No wonder you're so desp—"

I drew the blade across her throat. Her blood was warm and salty over my face. Her final breaths sounded like the burble of a rising brook.

I let her slump to the ground, the dry dirt gulping down the crimson like long-awaited rain.

CHAPTER FIVE

The vampires noticed the seer was gone right away—apparently the old woman didn't often leave on her own during the night. I watched them search for her. At first, they were irritated. My Obitraen was poor, but I could grasp fragments—profanities cursing that the old woman had been so absentminded. They thought she'd wandered away and was just late returning.

Eventually, *he* came out.

If the others were irritated by her absence, he was outright furious. When he emerged, all the others went silent. He demanded that they search for her, immediately, and not stop until she was found.

They did. A night passed.

I waited another night. Another. The search continued. The conqueror's burst of fury faded to a constant simmer, obvious even from my distant vantage point, radiating from his presence like steam off hot coals.

Days passed. They were growing anxious. They needed to move on. But he didn't want to go without her. I watched him snarl commands at his men every night, every few hours, when their search came up fruitless. But everyone knew, by now, that the seer was not coming back.

This, I decided, was the perfect level of desperation.

There was a town not far from here—or maybe "town" was a generous word. It was more like a little collection of trading posts and buildings. A single inn, a few marketplace stalls, a watering hole. At nightfall, I went there, ordered a drink, and waited.

Eventually, as I knew they would, the vampires showed up. Two of them—foot soldiers, it looked like. They came asking the businessmen about their seer, if she had passed through.

I sat there and sipped my wine, in my highly visible seat, right at the edge of the street.

Secretly, I was enjoying the wine. We didn't often have it at the Keep, considering what it did to the senses. It was what a typical traveler would be expected to be drinking, though, so it was what I drank as well. I took only the tiniest sips, barely allowing it to touch my tongue.

The barkeep was not being cooperative, which the soldiers did not appreciate. After a heated exchange that went nowhere, they released him, and he staggered back against the wall with a gasping breath. They looked at each other—I could sense their mutual frustration, and even more powerful, their dread as to what they would find when they returned to camp empty-handed.

And then I felt their eyes on me.

I took another sip of wine, seemingly oblivious to them. But I didn't move. Didn't shy away from their gaze. I let them stare right at me—me, and my blindfold, and my dress that looked so perfectly befitting a seer of Acaeja.

Remember me, soldiers, I thought, and waited until they were gone before I smiled to myself.

MOST OF THE time, my unusual appearance made things more difficult. I was, of course, happy to offer my goddess my eyes. Over the years, she's taken my little finger on my left hand, too, and etched several scars into the skin of my abdomen. All gifts that I gave her freely, and it was an honor to allow my reverence for Acaeja to mark my flesh so permanently. There's a strange sort of kinship in it, too, among my Sisters and I—we all turned ourselves into something foreign to the outside world, forever branded as Arachessen.

From a logistical perspective, though, sometimes being so prominently marked . . . had its challenges. We stood out. It was difficult to maintain any kind of disguise. The eyes, after all, usually gave it away quickly.

So, it was a nice change of pace that this time, my appearance worked in my favor. From the moment those Bloodborn soldiers saw me, they knew exactly what I was.

All I had to do was wait for them to come back for me.

I got myself a room in the inn that was the least secure place I could possibly choose—right in the front, with big windows that I left uncovered. The innkeeper didn't even try to stop my would-be captor. I didn't blame him for that. Some misguided attempt at noble chivalry wouldn't be worth laying down his life.

The vampire didn't knock before forcing open my door. Whatever he did to it made the rickety piece of wood fly open with a *BANG*, the iron knob gouging the plaster of the wall. If that was brute strength alone, I was almost impressed.

He stood in the doorway. I recognized him as one of the soldiers who had seen me the night before. He was stocky and broad, with pale skin and shaggy ash-blond hair, and a neat, trimmed beard. He wore the uniform of the Bloodborn soldiers—it had probably been a fine jacket once, dark red and double-breasted with silver buttons, but it was a bit worse for wear these days.

"You're coming with me," he said. His voice was deep and heavily accented. It echoed the same weary exhaustion I felt in his presence—spurred, I'm sure, from days of fruitless searching.

I didn't move. "I—excuse me? What are you doing here?"

My voice notched up an octave, emphasizing the depths of my shock.

"You'll come with me," he said again. "We can do this the easy way or the hard way. Up to you."

I rose, staggering a little, pressing myself against the wall like I was truly terrified of the man before me.

"I—I'm not going anywhere with you."

He heaved a dramatic sigh. Then he crossed the room in two strides and grabbed my arms.

Immediately, I struggled. Not too hard, of course. Not as hard as I could. Just enough to make it convincing. "Get your hands *off* me!"

He didn't, predictably. Instead, he dragged me across the room. Even though all of this was going exactly as I'd hoped it would, my heartbeat quickened despite myself when my captor flashed a smile at me and revealed two sharp fangs—so sharp I could practically feel them through the threads. A sudden spike of claustrophobic fear wrenched through me, reminding me far too much of decades ago, and I had to stop myself from succumbing to the instinct to slip his grasp.

Instead, I flailed like a fish on a line and let him drag me.

"Let me go!" I demanded. "Get your hands off me! *Let me go!*"

For effect, I managed to free one of my hands, then grabbed the metal candle holder from the bedside table and swung it across his face.

He spat a string of Obitraen curses. His face darkened. I'd opened a gash over his cheek, which now dripped black blood. He glared at me.

"You're trouble," he muttered. "You're not worth any of this."

Then, without hesitation, he held me tight with one arm, used the other to withdraw a dagger from his belt, and opened a long slice down my forearm.

I hissed in pain, stunned. At first I was confused—if his intention was to either subdue me or kill me, this made no sense. But moments later, as blood bubbled to the surface of the wound and dripped down my skin, I realized:

The vampires of the House of Blood used blood magic.

A slow burning sensation started at the wound, then intensified, slowly, slowly, until it left my teeth grinding and my breathing shaky. The vampire lifted his hand, and without my permission, my arm jerked closer to him—a genuinely disconcerting sensation, like my muscles were no longer under my control.

Then he flicked his fingers up, and suddenly my face was hot, and my head felt like it was splitting in two.

I had trained through worse pain than this. Experienced worse. But this—the feeling that my body was turning against itself—

I opened my mouth, but nothing came out.

"That's enough," my captor said, annoyed, as I slumped back into his arms, and everything went dark.

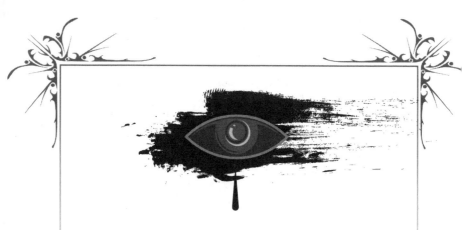

CHAPTER SIX

I awoke slowly. My head was splitting. The first thing I became aware of was the scent of snow—strange, because there was little snow in Glaea.

Voices. A language I didn't recognize at first. Then I realized, it was Obitraen.

Someone shook me, hard, and with their touch came a sickening jolt that stirred me from the inside out.

At that, the threads came alive again.

The vampire that took me from the inn leaned over me, grinning at me in a way that did far too much to highlight the sharpness of his canines.

"Good evening," he said.

I'd been trained extensively on how to retrieve my consciousness quickly. Amazing what one can do with tightly controlled breath. I quickly took stock of my surroundings. I was in a chair, slumped over. My neck ached, probably from being wrenched forward for Weaver knew how long. It cracked a little as I lifted my head, though I didn't let my grogginess or the pain show on my face.

I straightened my back, lifted my chin—

And came face-to-face with the conqueror.

He was right before me, sprawled out in a chair, one heel propped up on a box. We were in his tent, I gathered, the space small for a room but huge for a tent. Though there was another soldier here, the conqueror's aura dwarfed his, like a wave crashing over rocks.

I could kill him now.

I wouldn't, of course. It wasn't my mission. Those weren't my orders. I wouldn't disobey the Weaver's command.

But the certainty that I could, right here, *end it,* seized me and wouldn't let go.

He didn't say a word, but I could feel his stare, drinking me in from the bottom of my feet to the top of my head. It's rare that I could feel that so acutely, just as firm and invasive as hands over my body.

"Welcome," he said.

His voice was deep, but he was oddly soft-spoken. I wasn't expecting that, given the domineering force of his presence.

There were a lot of things about him, actually, that did not seem to fit together. Strange layers to his presence that seemed to vibrate in uncomfortable dissonance. Even his clothing seemed contradictory—a dissonant combination of very fine, albeit very old, clothing and battered armor. Clearly he was indeed god-touched in some way, or else he'd befallen some other very unpleasant event with a powerful magic user. Even experiencing people as I did, taking them in all at once rather than with sight, his horns were . . . disconcerting. And the horns, I could see in the threads, were not the only part of him that had been tampered with, even if he did his best to hide the other darknesses.

"Leave us," he said to his soldier, who obeyed in silence.

Leaving me alone with the conqueror.

I wouldn't admit to myself, and certainly not to him, that I was intimidated.

For a long moment, he said nothing.

I rose, carefully, keeping the movement smooth and still even though my legs felt wobbly beneath me. Whatever they'd used to drug me, it was powerful.

"That isn't necessary," he said.

"I prefer to meet death standing up."

He laughed. The sound slithered over my skin like a snake. Then he stepped closer, one step, two. The scent of snow, I realized, was him. Like he'd carried that piece of his homeland all this way, all the way across the sea. Snow and iron. A hint of salt.

"I hear that your kind can see even without your eyes," he said. "Is that true?"

"Eyes are a very inefficient way to see."

"Sounds like something a cultist would say."

"Hypocritical for one of your kind to be calling me a cultist. All of Obitraes is Nyaxia's cult, isn't it?"

He laughed again, low and rough. I felt him approaching, and yet I still had to fight hard not to flinch when his fingers brushed my cheek. They were rough and calloused, the nails a bit sharp, coaxing just a hint of pain to the surface of my skin.

"Maybe you're right," he said. "We've all made such sacrifices for our goddesses, haven't we?"

His hand ventured to my blindfold, fingers closing around the fabric, and I grabbed his wrist.

"No."

"If you get to see me so thoroughly, shouldn't I get to see you?"

"Sounds like something a conqueror would say."

He didn't laugh this time. He didn't move, either, his fingertips still warm against my cheek, pinching the silk fabric of my blindfold.

"Moral outrage from a member of the Arachessen," he said. "Interesting."

He released me and stepped back.

"I have no love for your little cult, but I don't intend to piss them off, either. Tell me where you'd like to be returned, and my second will escort you there. You'll make it there safely. You have my word."

What?

He was letting me go?

I didn't let my expression change, but internally, I cursed.

I wasn't expecting this turn. I'd miscalculated. I'd been right that my appearance as a member of the Arachessen would mark me clearly as someone who could seer—but hadn't accounted for the fact that our conqueror might be more risk-averse than I'd suspected. A little funny, actually, that he wasn't afraid of taking on the Pythora King, but the idea of tangling with the Arachessen scared him.

"It was my men's mistake that you were taken here," he went on. "My apologies."

He didn't sound all that sorry.

"I'm not a member of the Arachessen," I said. "Not anymore."

He paused. I felt his interest—and skepticism—ripple through the air.

I laughed softly. "That's so surprising to you?"

"People don't usually forsake their goddesses."

A question, in that statement. I saw the trap laid before me.

"I have no qualms with my goddess," I said.

No, he had to know I was still on good terms with the gods. Otherwise, I would be useless as a seer.

"The Arachessen, though . . ." I lifted one shoulder in a shrug. "You said it. They demand sacrifices. Take them without permission."

I could feel the little smile on his lips, something between a grimace and a smirk. "Is it really a sacrifice if it's taken instead of offered?"

It bothered me a bit that this was a reasonable point. I tilted my head, as if to concede it.

"So you're a former Arachessen. Still devoted to the gods. All by yourself." He paused, as if lining up all of these incongruent, unlikely facts. "And the Arachessen let you leave."

"I didn't give them a choice."

"You don't look strong enough to evade them."

No sarcasm, no double-speak. Surprising, but I could appreciate that.

It was a valid point. The Arachessen did not allow its members to leave their ranks. You joined for life. Death was the only escape, and they would make sure that anyone who did escape did it through that door alone.

"I've been running," I said.

"Yet you're still here in Glaea. One would think it would be smarter to get out of the country."

"*Your* invasion made it hard to leave," I snapped. "No ships out anymore. So thank you for that."

His presence shifted. Interest. He leaned forward.

"So you need protection."

I could sense him thinking. Considering. Did he need a seer so badly that he was willing to risk earning the attention of the Arachessen? Would one escaped Sister earn the same degree of attention he would have gotten from the order if he had kidnapped one of us? That had been too much risk for him, too much trouble.

But this . . . he was considering it.

It was stupid of him. If my tale had been true, the Arachessen would indeed have thrown as many resources as needed into finding and snipping that loose thread. A Sister carried many secrets. Dangerous to leave out in the world, let alone in the hands of a conqueror.

But his stupidity, at least, benefitted me now.

"Yes," I admitted, between gritted teeth—like it pained me to say aloud.

"You can seer."

"Yes."

"Fine." He raised a hand and snapped his fingers. The flap to the tent opened, and the guard returned again, grabbing my arms and wrenching them back.

I tried to pull away, to no avail.

"Get off me!" I snarled, with convincing desperation and a note of fear I was a little proud of. "Let me go!"

The conqueror stood there, his hands behind his back, watching as his men restrained me.

"No," he said. "We'll be needing your services."

"I don't offer any services," I spat.

"You will help us," he said, "or we will kill you. That's the only choice I offer you."

He stated it flatly. No dressing up, no games. I knew he meant it.

"But," he went on, "I'm fair."

"Fair?"

"You need protection. You'll have it. And you want to leave Glaea. You'll have that, too, once we're done with you."

I scoffed. "You expect me to believe that you won't simply kill me when you're done with me?"

It was almost funny to me that he was even pretending otherwise. Even if he had completed his task, it would be stupid to let me go.

Just like it was stupid of him to keep me here, knowing the Arachessen wanted me.

He seemed offended that I'd question his truthfulness. "I don't lie."

"Everyone lies."

"Not me." He stepped closer, closer, until he stood right in front of me again, the scent of salt and iron thick in my nostrils. "Don't be foolish. Maybe I haven't been in this country long, but I already see it isn't different from mine in any way that matters. You won't outlast the Arachessen another month without me. Don't spit in the face of your protector. Accept a gift when it's offered to you."

My mouth twisted into a sneer—this one too easy to fake. I wondered if he had convinced himself he was this country's savior, too. "So *benevolent* of you."

I jumped a little, startled, as he touched my cheek, the rough pad brushing a strand of my hair behind my ear.

"You're lucky," he said, "that I have a soft spot for caged birds."

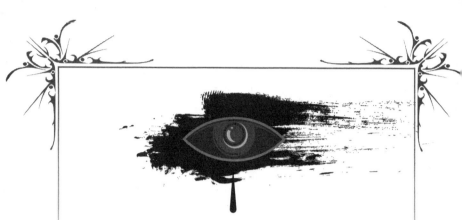

CHAPTER SEVEN

I was brought to my own tent. My wrists were shackled, and I was chained to the center post. At least, in a small show of mercy, the restraints were long enough that I was given some room to move around. There, I was left alone for hours.

Eventually, I leaned against the post and reached through the threads that connected me with the others here. If I guessed correctly, it would be past midnight by now, and the camp was abuzz with activity. The tent's fabric was thick, making it difficult to make out the specifics of what was being said outside, but I caught fragments of grumbled conversations about exhaustion or hunger, and pieces of orders shouted at slacking young soldiers in Obitraen.

I knew better than most that all people were, more or less, the same. Yet, even I might've expected something . . . less mundane, from an army of cursed vampire warriors. It was almost funny that the way they spoke was so similar to what I'd heard from human soldiers as a child.

I let myself fall further into the world around me, my awareness of my body loosening. The threads tied tight around me, growing taut as they stretched further, further, forming connections between me and the countless vampires outside.

Sometimes young Arachessen asked me, on the verge of tears, whether it ever stopped hurting. They always looked and felt so utterly hopeless—exhausted by the sudden stress of their new way of experiencing the world, their minds and bodies strained with the sudden weight of it all.

In those moments, I had the shameful desire to hold them, stroke their hair, and lie to them. *It's hard now,* I so wanted to tell them, *but it won't hurt anymore later.*

I didn't tell them that, of course. That was too easy and dishonest of a comfort.

What I offered them instead was, *One day, the pain won't matter anymore, and the power it grants you will matter immensely.*

That, at least, was true. No, it never stopped hurting, but pain grew inconsequential as it simply became another bodily constant.

Still, even for me and all my years of experience, the weight of the camp and the thousands of souls that surrounded me stretched me to my limits. With every forced nudge of my subconscious further into those outside, my headache grew more intense, sweat pooling at the small of my back.

Captains, generals, foot soldiers. Equal parts men and women—very different from Glaean armies, which rarely contained women. All ages, from young teenagers to seasoned warriors.

I tucked these little pieces of information away.

Enough of facts. Now I wanted emotions.

Exhaustion. Hunger. *I haven't eaten in three fucking days.* But also, resolve. Satisfaction. *Vaprus was a solid victory. Long way to go, but we've come far.*

The conqueror. *Show me what they think of—*

"Hey! *Seer!*"

Someone shook me hard by the shoulders, sending the world crashing back down around me. My body responded before I told it to, jumping to my feet and reaching for the sword that I, of course, did not have.

I stopped myself halfway through the movement, bracing against the pillar.

The floor tilted. The room spun. Vomit made it partway up my throat before I forced it down.

Center.

My threads dangled wildly, still leaving me partially connected to the world beyond. I reeled them in carefully, drawing my attention back to the room around me.

It was dangerous to yank an Arachessen from a Threadwalking session so abruptly. If I'd been doing anything deeper, such an interruption could have killed me.

"I . . . sorry."

The accented voice was gruff and stilted. One of the conqueror's soldiers—the man who had dragged me from the inn—stood before me. He took a few steps back, like he was nervous to be so close to me.

"You wouldn't wake up," he said, half-apologetically, half-defensively.

"I was fine," I said stiffly.

Not that he needed to know what I was actually doing.

He held up a plate. On it was a single, messily cut turkey leg.

"I brought you, uh, food. If you want it. From him." He glanced at the plate, then at me. "It's—"

"I know what it is."

"It's cooked."

"I can see that."

The man seemed unsettled by this, giving me a skeptical stare I was certain he didn't realize I saw.

I slid down the post and sat down, legs crossed.

"Thank you," I said. "I am hungry."

"Don't thank me," he grumbled, before setting the plate down in front of me. He sat on the ground, watching me. His fingers played at the cut on his cheek—the one I had given him at the inn. Vampires really did have incredible healing abilities. The gash was barely there.

"That already seems a lot better," I said.

"What?"

"Your cheek."

After a moment of hesitation, I bit into the turkey. It was incredibly bland and overcooked and cold, like someone had carted this back from the nearest town. I supposed I couldn't fault them for not really understanding what humans ate.

"So you really can see, huh?" He was openly skeptical. "Despite the eyes."

"Yes."

"How many fingers am I holding up?" he said, not moving.

"None," I replied.

He muttered, "Damn," which sounded like either respect or disapproval, or probably both.

I took another bite. It was awful, but I was hungry.

"So you're here to supervise me?" I said.

"Something like that. At least until we know you aren't running."

I jangled a chain and smiled. "Clearly I'm not going anywhere."

The soldier did not smile back. "My commander has a high opinion of your cult. Thought it would be foolish to rely on iron to keep you."

Ah, maybe he was wiser than I'd thought. He was right. If I'd wanted to be gone, the chains would be the last thing keeping me here.

"Very flattering," I said. Then, "What's your name?"

"Erekkus."

"It's a pleasure to finally meet you formally." I took another bite, then said pointedly, "Mine is Sylina."

Since no one had bothered to ask.

Erekkus just stared at me like I was a show animal, unblinking, rubbing his beard.

I gave him a bemused smirk. "Is there something more you'd like to ask me, Erekkus?"

"No."

A lie. There were all kinds of questions he wanted to ask me.

Then he said, after a moment, "Atrius is giving you a very good deal. I hope you know that."

Ah. There it was. No question mark there, but the question was clear all the same. He was wondering why his commander was taking this risk for me.

"Atrius," I said, rolling the name slow over my tongue. "It's good to put a name to a face."

It suited him, I had to admit. Felt a little uncomfortable on your lips. The Arachessen believed strongly in the power of names. Mine was given to me after three days of meditation by the Sightmother.

"If you know what's good for you," Erekkus said, "you'll cooperate with him. If the Arachessen are half as brutal as Atrius seems to think they are, you won't make it another month out there on your own."

"So you expect me to take the word of the man who's conquering my country."

Expect me to take the word of the man who killed my Sister.

I closed my jaw hard at the end of that sentence—because it was too truthful, too real. I stuffed those emotions down before they could threaten to reveal themselves.

"Ah, so you are some great loyalist of the Pythora King?" Erekkus said snidely. "Unlike your king, my commander keeps his word. If he promises you protection, he will give you protection. If he promises you freedom, he will give you freedom."

"And how do you know this?"

Just the right amount of defiance to keep him talking. I wanted to know how this Atrius's men thought of him.

"I've been fighting under his command for centuries," Erekkus said. "He's earned my trust."

"How?"

He scoffed. "I don't think that's any of your business."

"It is, if it's intended to make me trust him, too."

"I don't need to make you trust him. I'd just as well dump you in the next river and find some other seer who's far less trouble."

"I appreciate the honesty."

I took one more bite of the turkey before deciding it wasn't worth it anymore.

"I have to ask," I said, wiping my hands on the edge of my skirt—useless, since I was filthy. "What, exactly, do you intend to do here? In Glaea?"

Erekkus laughed, like I'd just said something very foolish.

"Conquer, of course."

So blasé. So careless. Like we were just fruit to be plucked.

I didn't let even a hint of anger slip through my mask.

"But what use does the House of Blood have for a human country half a world away?"

The remnants of Erekkus's smile faded. His presence went suddenly cold.

"You know nothing about our home," he said, rising and turning away. "Atrius will be in to see you tomorrow. Prepare yourself for him."

MY MENTION OF the House of Blood had apparently so offended Erekkus that he chose to spend the next several hours standing guard outside my tent instead of inside. The sounds of the camp quieted as dawn approached and the Bloodborn slipped back into their dwellings. I did, eventually, allow myself to get some sleep, too. I'd been given a bedroll and more than enough slack in my shackles to rest in it comfortably. I must have been exhausted from the activity of the last two days, because sleep took me more swiftly than I'd been expecting, washing me into a river of dreamless dark.

When I woke up, Atrius was in my tent.

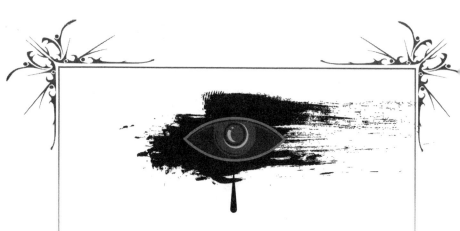

CHAPTER EIGHT

I shook away sleep fast, sitting up immediately. Atrius didn't move. He didn't blink. He stood just within the entrance of the tent, staring at me. I had no idea how long he had been there.

"I didn't mean to startle you, Sylina," he said.

"You didn't," I lied. I didn't react to either his presence or his use of my name. I'd show him nothing.

I rose, drawing myself up to my full height. Even with Atrius across the room, it was clear that he loomed over me. I didn't like how small I felt around him.

I still could not quite make sense of his presence. Alone in a room with him, it was overwhelming all over again—contradictions that I had never before experienced within a soul, and all of them roiling constantly. This was a man that was never at peace, and yet was so steadfast in his singular cause that he managed to force it all into a tightly controlled box. I had met few people who could hide the truth of their presence so well, even Arachessen.

He approached me, and I had to remind myself not to move away. My instinct was to cringe as he reached out, but his touch against my wrist was gentle and nonthreatening. He unlocked one shackle, then the other.

This close, I could sense his features more clearly. They were rigid and strong, as if carved out of stone, albeit imperfectly—his nose slightly crooked, as if it had been broken and poorly set once, his brow low over deep-set eyes, mouth thin and serious. The scent of snow was overwhelming.

He dropped to his knees. I stiffened as he lifted my skirt and slid his hands up my calf. Mission or no, I'd kick him in the face if he—

"I'm not going to rape you," he said flatly. "I prefer my partners willing."

He said that, but I'm sure he saved that for the teenage daughters of the homes he burned when he conquered. I'd experienced war before. I knew what it was like.

With him kneeling, his horns were right in front of me. They were black and ridged, curving toward the back of his head, stark against the smooth silver of his long hair. I carefully reached for them with a thread of magic, testing them. They felt foreign and unnatural, like they weren't of this world. My line of work had exposed me to many curiosities, but none quite like these. How, I wondered, had he gotten them?

He finished unlocking the shackles on my ankles. Then he rose again and offered me his hand.

"Come."

I didn't take it.

"I'll follow," I said, and took only a step before he grabbed my arm, hard enough that his fingernails—sharp, black claws—dug into my wrist.

"I know the Arachessen are skilled," he said, "but I have lived your lifetime six times over, and I've spent all that time becoming better at killing. If you run or fight, it won't end well for you."

His stare was unyielding, hard, cold. When most people stared at me, they seemed to just look at my blindfold, where my eyes would be. But Atrius's went deeper than that, like he was grabbing my soul itself and turning it to him, making sure I understood.

I didn't like that. It felt like a challenge, and I, petty as I was, disliked being challenged. Another flaw the Sightmother frequently pointed out.

We held that stare for a long, long moment, a silent battle of wills playing out in the inches between our faces.

"Fine," I said primly. "You don't rape me, and I don't attack you."

The sound he made was something between a grunt and a scoff. "Did the Arachessen like that sense of humor?"

He took my arm and I decided not to fight him this time. His touch was barely there, light over my sleeve. He led us to the tent door and opened it.

The moment we stepped outside, the camp went silent. Attention was unblinkingly, unwaveringly on us. I could feel all those threads of presence wrapped around our throats as clearly as I could feel Atrius's hand on my arm. Their curiosity. Intrigue.

And . . . hunger. Unmistakable hunger.

The hairs rose on the back of my neck. These were vampires, after all. Blood drinkers. Corpses of drained deer had been piled along the outskirts of camp, but I knew that human blood was the most enticing to them.

Atrius didn't address anyone, and no one addressed us, as we walked through the camp. When we reached the outskirts, he leaned down and murmured in my ear, "Never leave your tent without permission and me or Erekkus with you. Understood?"

I wondered if he sensed what I had. The hungry intrigue.

"So I don't get eaten?" I asked. "You don't train your men to have better discipline than that?"

His lip twitched with distaste. "My men have impeccable discipline. But there will be difficult times in this war, and is there any amount of discipline that will stop you from crawling to water in the desert?"

I was the water in this metaphor. But did that mean that Glaea, a country populated by many humans, was the desert? That didn't make any sense.

He took me far beyond the outskirts of camp, out into the rocky plains, where the grass was so tall that it tickled my thighs. The ground beneath it was rocky and uneven. "Watch for that," he muttered, pointing out a particularly rough patch of gravel and guiding me around it.

"I know," I said, stepping around it easily, and felt his stare grow a little more intense.

He was interested in me.

That was good—to capture curiosity. It couldn't keep me alive forever, but it would keep me here long enough to earn his trust.

Maybe curiosity was the real reason why he was willing to take the risk of having me join him.

It was a powerful thing.

He led me down a steep incline through narrow openings in the rocks, the grass now gone in favor of jagged stone. I knew this area—I'd killed his last seer not far from here. He brought me to the edge of a lake, all the way down to where the water lapped at shores of gritty sand.

At last, he released my arm and leaned against a sheer stretch of rock. "I need you to seer for me."

Atrius, I was already certain, was not a man who liked to have things handed to him easily. If I wanted to earn his trust later, and make him believe that he had earned mine, I would need to make him work for it. People did not believe in the value of what was too freely given, and I needed him to believe in me.

So I said, "What makes you think I will?"

He let out a rough exhale, almost a laugh. Then he stared out over the lake.

"Can you see this?" he said.

"In all the ways that matter."

"What does that mean?"

"It means that I know the water is still and flat. I can sense that there are no ripples in it. I know that there are rocks on the other side, more on the west, and grass on the eastern edge."

"Those are facts. That's not the same as seeing it."

"In what way?"

"When you see the moon rise, some might say there's something more to it than coordinates in the sky."

For some reason, I found myself unwillingly thinking of my little painting of the sea.

It's the ocean.

No, it is paper.

The memory hit me with an uncomfortable pang I didn't want to look at too closely. I shrugged it away.

"Why are you asking me this?"

"Just wondering if you're smart enough to know the value of things that can't be quantified. Like the value of the offer I made you."

"I don't think it was an offer. Offers can be accepted or rejected."

"You can reject it."

"But you'll kill me after."

He didn't say anything. Just gave me a grim little half smile.

"I don't like forcing people to do things," he said. "Bad way to earn loyalty. And I do require your loyalty, and your services. I can take them permanently, or you can offer them temporarily. I can get them by your fear or your choice. I'd rather the latter, but I'll do either."

"So why do you care?"

He shrugged. "Seems a shame for my generosity to go unappreciated."

I was silent for a long moment. I let him believe it was because I was considering his words, but instead, I was considering how much I should let him win now.

I should give him something. Not all of it—that would be too easy. Plus, the thought of rolling over for him . . .

It made me think of his entry on our shores. Raeth's body beneath his armies.

I was supposed to be the good actress, the perfect spy, playing my role without complaint. My personal feelings shouldn't matter. And yet . . . I couldn't shake that anger when I considered the possibility of complete acquiescence.

No. Not yet.

But I'd give him something.

"The Arachessen are more effective and persuasive than you can possibly know," I said haltingly.

"I've had plenty of experience with cults."

I hated how dismissively he called us a cult.

"They're worse," I bit out. "Worse than you can imagine. They see everything. As long as I remain in Glaea, it's only a matter of time before they find me."

"I already told you that—"

"You can't protect me from them."

He laughed.

Outright *laughed*, from deep in his chest, like what I'd just said was the funniest thing he'd ever heard. The sound was rough and unpracticed, like he did it very rarely.

I was a bit offended on behalf of my Sisterhood.

"You laugh because you don't know them," I said.

"I laugh because you don't know me."

He straightened, crossing his arms over his chest. "I told you, Sylina, I do not lie. If I say it, it is true. I protect my people. If you're one of mine, the Arachessen will not touch you."

Such hubris. And yet, he didn't say any of it with the boastfulness of a bragging commander. He said it as if it was nothing more than fact, and his presence radiated not cocky showmanship but steady truth.

He *believed* it.

That was strange to me, that a man who recognized the power of the Arachessen—recognized their ability to make trouble for him— would still be willing to cross them on my behalf.

It was confusing.

I let out a sigh, showing him all my reluctant consideration, carefully measured. "I don't understand how you can make that promise."

"You don't have to understand. You just have to seer."

He stepped away from the rock, extending his hand, the question silent but obvious: *Deal?*

I drew my lips thinly together. The thought of taking his hand sickened me.

But those were the feelings of Sylina, Arachessen spy. Not Sylina, desperate fugitive.

I took it. His grip was rough and calloused.

"Good," he said firmly. Like that was that.

He released my hand, and I felt his skin burning against my palm long after. He leaned against the rock again, arms crossed, taking me in.

"Now," he said, "about the seering."

ATRIUS'S ARMY WAS, apparently, so active right now because they were preparing to leave and continue on their conquering path. He told me this flatly, in simple fact. He withdrew a crumpled piece of parchment from his pocket and flattened it as best he could against the smooth side of the rock, revealing a map of Glaea. He pointed to a city-state just north of here: Alka.

"You know it?"

"Of course."

I didn't bother hiding my distaste. It was a bleak, dark place. The Pythora King had given most city-states to his cronies to rule over in absolute power, and the one that held Alka was a warlord, Aaves, who was among the worst of them. Like most of the Pythora King's followers, he kept his population drugged and starving and his warriors drugged and strong. Worse, most of the city was built directly into the stone and sea, so the whole place was constructed of narrow tunnels and rickety bridges over brackish, pest-infested waters. I'd been sent on several missions there over the years, and all of them had been miserable.

I could understand why Atrius was concerned about taking Alka. It was so decentralized and so difficult to navigate that numbers alone wouldn't be enough to hand him victory.

I told him this, and his brow lowered as he inclined his chin.

"You're right. That's why we have you."

"You expect a seer to get you out of this situation."

He smiled faintly. He said nothing, but his presence said, *Yes*.

Even if the Bloodborn liked to make use of seers, it was strange to use them in this way—for something so specific. Visions were cryptic and unpredictable. They weren't instructions or even guideposts—nothing concrete. The images were often difficult to make out and even harder to make sense of. The best seers in the world might have strong enough connections to the gods to be able to ask specific questions and get specific answers—or something close—but I certainly wasn't one of them. In fact, I didn't like seering much. Too abstract. I didn't like to relinquish that much control.

"If I ask the gods how you can conquer Alka," I said, "they aren't going to just respond by giving you a map and a set of instructions."

"I know," he replied simply.

That was all. He just waited, expectant.

"I gave you an order," he said.

"Now? And you'll stand here and watch me?"

"Yes."

It felt wrong, to seer with him just staring at me, like I was doing something intimate with a very unpleasant audience. But while I was willing to put up a little bit of a fight just to make him trust his victories, I also knew which fights weren't worth having, and this was one of them.

I sighed.

"Fine," I said. "Help me build the fire."

IT TOOK A significant amount of preparation to seer to Acaeja. She was a goddess that placed great value on ritual—she lorded over the unknown, after all, and tapping into the unknown took significant focus.

Atrius helped me without complaint, following my commands with surprising amiability. We built a fire on the beach, feeding it until it was a roaring blaze. I tended it with elements of the earth—a handful of sand, a sprinkle of flower petals, the roots of tall grass. When it was time to get the blood sacrifice, Atrius turned away and started walking, before I stopped him.

"What are you doing?"

"Getting the creature for you."

"I can hunt."

His presence shifted in the first hint of annoyance I'd seen all night. "We don't have time to waste."

That was almost sweet. Weaver bless him.

"Give me that," I said, motioning to his bow.

I thought he might hesitate, thinking I'd shoot him with it, but he handed it over immediately. He really did underestimate me.

Animals were active at night. When I reached for the threads, I felt them everywhere, lurking in the rocks, in the tall grass. I settled on a rabbit, which crouched in the sparse greenery. If I were relying on eyes alone, I wouldn't have a sightline to it. But I wasn't.

One shot, and the rabbit was dead.

I retrieved it, yanked the arrow from its guts, and returned to Atrius. If he was surprised or impressed, he didn't show it.

"Here." I gave him back his bow, then opened my hand. "Your knife."

He gave it to me, and I crouched before the fire, heat nipping at my nose as I sliced open the rabbit's throat.

My goddess Acaeja, Weaver of Fates, Keeper of the Unknown, I silently incanted. *I give you this gift of life. Open your doors to me.*

The rabbit's blood dripped into the fire. I rubbed some of it over my hands, using my thumb to draw it across my face—two lines, one under each eye, just beneath my blindfold. Then I cast the corpse into the flames.

The blaze surged and roared in a sudden burst, making Atrius take a half step backward. Good. That meant it was working.

I dragged my bare toes in a circle, all the way around the fire, until I returned to my starting position. Then I sat down before the fire, so close that sweat now trickled down the back of my neck.

"Be back soon," I said to Atrius, closed my eyes, and fell back.

And back.

And back.

Into darkness.

CHAPTER NINE

My feet touched glass water, perching on the top but
not breaking through. It was dark. Mist surrounded
me. A single silver line stretched out before me, flush
to the smooth surface of the water, disappearing into the mist.

I walked forward, heel to toe, remaining on the silver line. It
was shockingly cold against my bare feet, and a little painful, as if
it was sharp.

The mist grew thicker, and then dissipated.

Now cliffs surrounded me, stretching endlessly into the sky. The
water rippled and shifted. The air was thick with the scent of blood.
It trickled, too, down the faces of the cliffs, pooling in the water. The
path before me narrowed, narrowed, narrowed, until stone squeezed
my shoulders.

I knew this place. This was Alka.

Good. The right path.

Give me something more, Weaver, I whispered.

I reached out my presence in all directions. My palms pressed to
the stone, searching for cracks and weaknesses.

Another step.

My left hand pushed through the stone. *Blink,* and the rock gave
way to thick, soupy mist. The threads split before me—one continuing
forward through the cliffs, another veering off into mist.

I changed courses, following the second thread.

Blink, as the cliffs shattered and fell away.

Before me was a moon, full as a silver coin. *Step*, and red and black dripped down its surface, trickling into the water. The distant cliffs of Alka drowned in it.

Show me another.

Another thread before me. I stepped off my path and onto this one. *Shift*, and the moon became a crescent, clear in the sky, bloodless. The cliffs loomed beneath it. Ivy slowly crawled up their sides, rising from the water, red-black flowers blooming over the stone.

I kept walking, and time shifted, moonlight falling over the stone. Bodies tumbled from the cliffs and into the sea.

More, I whispered.

Another thread before me. I stepped onto it. The cliffs fell away. I saw a man before me, dripping in opulent silks, kneeling in a pile of bones. He looked up at me and smiled, blood spilling from between his teeth. He collapsed beneath the crescent moon.

In the midst of a seering, you couldn't question what you saw. Your ability to think critically ceased—you could only absorb and observe.

I thought of Atrius. Thought of the Bloodborn.

Show me something more, Weaver, I asked the goddess.

You are not looking in the right direction, she whispered.

I stopped short.

It was rare that I heard the Weaver's voice in my sessions. Her voice sounded like little more than a distant echoing breeze. Yet, it drew my entire body still, a chill rising to my skin.

Slowly, I turned around.

Darkness. The same thread, running backward, extended into mist.

I walked this path.

The mist didn't dissipate. It just grew thicker, and thicker. Each of my steps grew labored, painful. The thread here was sharper than ever, as if I walked on the polished edge of a blade. My bloody footprints remained perfectly formed in the water behind me.

It was cold, and growing colder, and colder, until my breaths came in little silver puffs, my bare arms covered in goose bumps. The sky had gotten inky dark. Stars surrounded me, so bright and bulging I felt like I could reach out and grab them.

I was now walking uphill, though the surface of the water remained perfectly still. The mist cleared enough to reveal jagged, snow-capped peaks, stained red.

These did not look like the mountains of Alka. It was warm there, and the mountains weren't tall enough for snow.

No, everything about what I was seeing seemed . . . foreign. Like I was peering into a world a universe away from my own.

The mountains shifted, encircling me. The stars grew larger. The moon, full and round, slowly rose from beyond the horizon line, so big it stretched across my vision, a shadow falling across it with each step I took.

An eclipse.

Blood slicked my feet now. I was fighting hard to go so deep into the threads. But I had the overwhelming sense that I was seeing something important. I would not turn back.

Another step, and I crested the peak of the mountain. The moon was now a glowing, black circle, monstrously large, unavoidable as an all-seeing eye.

And there, right in the center of that circle, was Atrius.

I recognized him immediately, even from this distance. He was younger, yes, and his back was turned to me, but his presence was unmistakable—even though that, too, was a little different. Brighter, maybe. More hopeful. His hair was a bit shorter, flying out behind him against whips of wind. He had no horns.

Beside him was another man who wore matching armor to his, though more ornate, and a circlet upon a head of silver-streaked, ash-blond hair. I wasn't close enough to hear what they were saying, or see what they were looking at beyond the ridge of stone.

I forged ahead and nearly stumbled—my feet were so bloody now that I slipped on the thread. Frantically, I righted myself. When I lifted my head again, a gasp ripped from my throat.

A goddess stood before them.

She was beautiful—more than beautiful. She was a natural

phenomenon, something so entrancing, so otherworldly, that her mere existence left you changed. Her eyes were pits of star-speckled darkness, her hair long tendrils of ebony ink, her body dips and curves of silver.

My heart beat faster.

The fear set in slowly at first, sneaking in beneath the amazement until suddenly, it was as strong as the jaws of a python around a rat. It constricted, tighter, tighter.

The goddess's face was as big as the moon. She smiled, blood dripping from her lips, but it was a horrible, furious expression—the last thing one sees before death.

I was so afraid I couldn't move. Couldn't breathe. The thread cut deep into my feet, so deep I swore it touched my bones.

This was dangerous, to be stuck in a vision. Dangerous to fall from a thread. A voice screamed this at me in the back of my head, but my body wouldn't move.

I just stood there as the goddess rose into the sky, laughing down at us with cruel anger. A wave of pain, of betrayal, of grief rolled over me, so strong it left me gasping for air.

In the distance, Atrius's companion was nothing but black blood in the snow, and Atrius was on his knees beside him, bowed and broken.

Despite the distance, I still heard his voice so clearly, cracking with desperation:

Wake up, my prince, he begged. *Wake up. Wake up.*

"WAKE. UP."

I started awake, and tried to lurch upright on instinct, but couldn't because a firm grip held my shoulders down. Atrius leaned over me, serious and perhaps just a little bit annoyed. Sweat plastered my clothing to my body. The fire, nearly encroaching on my toes, blazed high, a wall of light that silhouetted Atrius's form.

"Why did you wake me?" The words came out in heaving gasps.

"I know the signs of a seering gone bad."

He released my shoulders and rose, leaving me to push myself to my hands and knees, wincing as my bare feet touched the gritty sand. The wounds were deep.

"We'll get you healing for those," he said, nodding to my feet. Then he added, after an awkward beat, "Your feet."

"I know what you meant," I said, irritated. I rubbed my temple, which throbbed viciously.

I did not mourn my eyesight. But . . . all the darkness of traditional sight made it difficult to shake away nightmares. What I had seen in the vision . . . that smiling face followed me back to the land of the mortals. I suspected it would follow me for days.

"Here."

Atrius handed me a canteen. I was so parched I didn't even question it—just grabbed it and gulped down mouthful after mouthful of water. When I was done, the canteen was empty, and I was still gasping for breath. I let the canteen fall to my lap. My hands were shaking.

I could feel Atrius's eyes on them.

"So?" he said. "What did you see?"

"Give me a moment," I muttered, rubbing my head. "I need to sort through it."

It was hard to process visions while within them, floating in a semiconscious dream state, incapable of truly questioning anything. Now, I rifled through the images and tried to string them together.

I'd seen Alka. The full moon was bloody. The crescent moon, much less so—and the bodies falling into the sea under that moon were of Alka's men, not Atrius's.

As far as visions went, it was actually a surprisingly useful one. But useful didn't help me here.

Because did I *actually* want to help Atrius conquer Alka?

No. Of course not.

I hadn't thought this far ahead. I couldn't claim that I saw nothing. That was clearly untrue, and it would mean Atrius would probably kill me and run off to go find a more useful seer.

I could make up something. Something truly nonsensical.

Or . . .

"The full moon," I said. "Move for Alka under the full moon."

It was an impulsive, risky lie. But I was not about to help Atrius kill hundreds or thousands of my kin. Besides, Alka was a difficult territory. There was a reason why Atrius was unwilling to move on it without the help of a seer. If he failed here, it could be enough to stop his progression completely.

And if he still managed a victory . . . seering was unpredictable and hard to understand. I could weave a story for him, build myself a net of reasonable doubt.

Atrius seemed dubious. "You're certain?"

"I'm certain."

"I want to know what else you saw."

Content that my single lie would be enough, I told him the rest of my journey truthfully—of the king, the rocks, the mist. I even drew what I recalled of the arrangement of the channels for him. He wrote down all of this in a beaten-up little leather notebook that he withdrew from the pocket of his jacket, often stopping me to make me repeat descriptions verbatim.

I had to appreciate his thoroughness. At least he respected the art of seering more than I expected him to—understanding that it was about general interpretations, not questions and answers.

When I got to the end of the vision about Alka, I paused and observed him. He was finishing writing the last description I had fed him, sitting cross-legged in the sand, his head bowed over his work—leaving those horns on full display.

He didn't have those in my vision.

I shivered against a breeze.

He finished writing, and his eyes flicked up to me. "And?"

A single, expectant word. He knew there was more. Nothing that I had described to him would rise to the intensity that would've left me twitching in the dirt like I was.

I could tell him that was it. I would maintain another secret card in my hand, but he would know I was lying, and I would have to deal with that mark on my trustworthiness later.

Or I could tell him what I saw and see what his reaction taught me.

"I saw one more thing," I said.

He waited.

"I saw you."

Still, no reaction.

"You were younger," I went on. "You had none of your . . . physical abnormalities. You were on a mountain, with another soldier." I thought about the scene again—with the added context of what I knew now. "Another Bloodborn vampire, I think."

Atrius's presence had gone very, very stoic. Utterly unreadable, like a wall of steel. It was rare I saw anyone capable of stilling themselves like that.

"The two of you were on a mountain peak," I said. "And you went before a goddess."

Nyaxia, I realized now. It had to be Nyaxia.

"Nyaxia," I corrected myself. "And she—"

"That's enough."

Atrius rose abruptly. The stillness of his presence shattered into cold anger.

"Never do that again," he said.

Atrius did not raise his voice. But that was only because he was not the type of man who needed to. The quiet carried his threat, and his rage. Enough to shiver up your spine like the tip of a blade.

"*Never* do that again," he repeated. "Do you understand?"

"What?" I asked. "Seer? You asked me to—"

"Do not seer about me."

And this was the stab, sharp and brutal.

"I—" I started, ready to weave my web of sweet apologies, but Atrius shoved his hands into his coat pockets and turned away.

"Erekkus will get you ready to leave," he snarled as he walked away, leaving me on my knees by the bonfire. "Don't try to run. I'll find you. Be back at camp by sunrise."

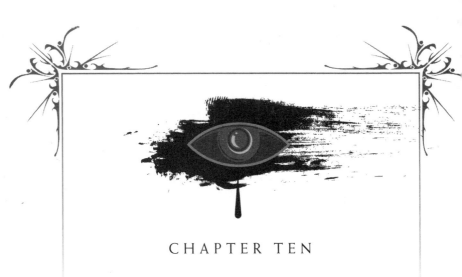

CHAPTER TEN

Doesn't that hurt?"

Erekkus cast a glance down to my bandaged feet. Atrius had been true to his word—he'd sent Erekkus to me with medicine after I made it back to camp, apparently long after he did. Erekkus had given it to me and then dutifully stepped to the other side of the room while I applied it, apparently to show his self-control in the presence of my blood. I could appreciate that.

The medicine was magic, and it worked well. Still, the wounds were tender and sore, especially since I'd been on my feet immediately the next night, called upon to help alongside everyone else with breaking down the tents. Erekkus worked with me on mine, always calling me back sharply if I wandered too close to the other soldiers.

"Stay in my sight," he said. "He'll have my head if one of them gets their hands on you."

"So that's your incentive to keep me alive," I said, returning to his side. "We'll both be equally fucked if I die."

My language must've been surprising, because Erekkus arched his brows and shook his head.

"What?" I said. "I'm religious, so I can't curse?"

He froze for a moment before resuming his work.

"That's fucking uncanny," he muttered.

I took my mission seriously . . . but I had to admit that in between all the very important work, it was fun to unnerve a Bloodborn vampire.

I liked messing with Erekkus, and it was shockingly easy to do. Atrius seemed to expect that I'd stay by Erekkus's side at all times unless I was with him, so there were plenty of opportunities for it.

After one such event, when I snapped at Erekkus for something he was doing behind my back and he palpably shuddered with discomfort, I couldn't help but laugh aloud.

"You enjoy this, witch," he muttered.

"I'd think you'd have thicker skin."

I turned and helped him haul the rolled-up tent into a carriage. The horses shifted and snorted impatiently. I sensed their unease— near constant. I wondered if these beasts had been brought with the conquerors on their ships from Obitraes, or if they had been stolen from locals here. If the latter, they still seemed very wary of their new vampire masters.

"My skin is very thick," Erekkus grumbled. "I fought the Wraiths of Slaede. Do you know what those are?"

I shook my head, amused by his seriousness. He leaned over the top of the wagon.

"Embodiments of death itself. Vampire souls tortured and mutilated until they became nothing but shells of pain and anger. I fought a thousand of those things. *A thousand.*"

"Hmm." I pushed the cart door closed, latching it. I felt Atrius before I saw him—I always felt him, as if ripples in the threads constantly flowed in his direction. He hadn't spoken to me at all since his outburst, instead occupying himself with the preparations to move camp. My awareness lingered on him as he helped some of his other soldiers disassemble tents.

I'd give him this: the man was brutally efficient. He'd been working from the moment the sun went down and had not stopped moving once for hours. He did not eat. He did not rest. He just worked.

He also had been slowly discarding his clothing over the course of the night—first jacket, then belt, then shirt, even his boots. Now he wandered around in the mud, shirtless and barefoot, his hair messily half thrown up in a leather binding that barely clung to its hold.

"And who led you in this great heroic battle against the wraiths?" I asked. "Was that Atrius?"

It was a casual prod for information, and not one that I expected to go anywhere. But Erekkus's presence immediately shifted, so abruptly that I stopped mid-movement, turning to him.

His back was to me as he tied up another tent roll, but I knew his hands had stopped moving.

I prodded his presence gently. Regret. Guilt. Sadness. But above all . . . shame. Deep, all-consuming shame. All of it clamped down, like a bandage over an old wound that never healed right.

"Yes," he said curtly.

That wasn't the whole answer.

I kept my voice light and casual. "Is he a good leader?"

Most of Erekkus's discomfort melted away. "A great leader. We're damned lucky to have him. Not often a soldier gets a commander who's just as willing to walk over coals for you as the other way around. Especially not us."

That was an interesting little addition.

"Especially not you?"

Another pause. He seemed suddenly very interested in tying down the tents.

Erekkus, I'd come to learn quickly, had a very big mouth. That would be useful to me, especially given that Atrius was about as transparent as a rock.

"Not sure if you know this," Erekkus said, at last, "but the House of Blood is not very popular in Obitraes."

I did know that, even with my scant knowledge of Obitraen society. The House of Blood was the cursed house, looked down upon by the Houses of Shadow and Night.

Of course, it would be suspicious for me to be so knowledgeable. So I just said, surprised, "Really? Why?"

"It's a long, depressing story." He waved his hand. "An old, boring, depressing story. Angry goddesses and entitled kings and vengeful curses. Your typical tragedy."

"That doesn't sound boring to me."

"It's boring if you live it."

I made a mental note to come back to that one later. Maybe sometime I could make sure he had a bit too much to drink. He struck me as someone who would be a very chatty drunk.

I cast my attention again to Atrius, who now hauled materials into the back of a cart. He was . . . bigger than he'd seemed clothed. Well-built. Muscles worked over his back and shoulders as he lifted the crates into the cart, then winced and stretched.

Then again, if the way he had worked today was any indication of his usual habits, I guessed it should be no surprise that he looked like that.

"Didn't realize blindfolded ladies could still be lecherous," Erekkus said. "Still just as unsettling as all your other tricks. Maybe I'd feel differently if I was on the receiving end, though."

"I'm not being lecherous," I said, too quickly, turning back to the cart.

"No shame in it, Sister."

"Don't call me that," I grumbled. "I'm not a Sister anymore."

He barked a laugh. "So no more chastity vow, eh? That's convenient."

"I wasn't being lecherous."

I didn't know why I said it again. I had nothing to prove.

Erekkus raised his hands. "Like I said, no shame in it. I've got no interest in the man, but even I'll admit he's a good-looking one. You wouldn't be the first. Won't be the last, either. Not that many people get lucky."

I let him pull me up to the cart. When he dusted his hands off, he gave me a lopsided grin. "But hey, maybe you'll be different. You're just his type, actually."

"His type?"

Erekkus leaned forward and gave me a conspiratorial smirk. He held out a finger with each word. "Beautiful. Mysterious. Dangerous. And an obvious, clear-as-the-fucking-moon mistake."

CHAPTER ELEVEN

Atrius's horse was certainly Obitraen. The thing just radiated otherworldly power—a big, muscular draft horse, ghostly gray with dark, dappled legs marked with pink scars. It was one of the largest horses I'd ever seen, leaving Atrius towering over those who rode beside him. Unlike many of the other horses, who were clearly uneasy about their new vampire lords and needed to be constantly shushed and calmed, this one was stable as stone. Atrius constantly wove his fingers through the beast's mane as he rode, eyes drawn out to the horizon, like he was staring a million miles away into the past or the future or both.

That little gesture—Atrius's constant stroking of his horse's mane—kept drawing my attention. It was . . . confusing. Most Glaean warriors were careful to never display weakness, ever, and such blatant affection for an animal would certainly count. I found it hard to reconcile this gesture with the man who had burst onto our shores with the vicious animosity of a wolf, ready to tear Glaea apart in his jaws.

We rode for a long time, Atrius taking up the front of the army. Erekkus and I weren't far behind him, though off to the side, isolated from most of the other soldiers who trailed behind. This, I was sure, had to have been Atrius's command—forever concerned about my safety among the other soldiers. That, too, was probably why

Erekkus was constantly at my side. He was chatty, and often about nothing in particular, which got very old very fast—worse, because being in such a big crowd for so long tended to be exhausting for Arachessen. I was starting to feel the strain of it after a few days on the road. The headache at the back of my head and behind my eyes was now a constant, sharp pain.

Unpleasant. But I'd have to deal with it. I could be spending months in this position. Maybe years. It depended on what the Sight-mother expected of me.

The Arachessen were never far from my mind. We operated independently on our missions, but given how important this one was, I'd be expected to find a way to make contact with the Sightmother soon and update her.

But I wasn't given many chances to sneak off on my own. I thought that the first sunrise on the road would be my opportunity, but we didn't even set up a proper camp that day, just enough to keep the vampires packed together and sheltered from the sunlight. With Erekkus two feet away from me, I wasn't willing to risk sneaking out, especially not since I quickly learned the man basically didn't sleep.

Finally, after a week of travel, we came to a wide, flat grassy patch of land. It was easy to defend, and spacious, and Atrius seemed conscious of the fact that his soldiers were growing weary after a week of nonstop travel and little rest. He had us erect real tents again, a camp that wasn't as expansive as the one I'd been initially dragged into, but close.

That meant privacy. Room to move around without attracting attention.

My tent was placed on the outer edge of the encampment again, far from all the others except for Erekkus, who was placed right beside mine. But once the work of setting up camp was done, Erekkus seemed more than eager to go socialize with people much more pleasant than me. It was a little surprising, actually, how quickly he ran off into the rest of the camp.

I stood outside my tent for awhile, arms crossed, observing the others in the distance. A great bonfire had been lit in the center of the camp, and many of the warriors clustered around it, drinking and talking. Their presences were dim with weariness, yes, but also unusually lively. A number of deer had been hunted and dragged into camp that night, still alive and twitching while the vampires crawled over their corpses and fed on them directly, or emptied their blood into goblets that they raised in drunken toasts. I shivered as the wind shifted and I caught a glimpse of those beasts' auras—different than the acute fear I would have expected. It was there, yes, but it was dull and fuzzy, coated instead with a thick layer of euphoric docility.

Vampire venom. That was a mercy, perhaps.

This wasn't a normal night. It felt like . . . a celebration of some kind. Maybe some kind of Obitraen festival? Some religious night? I almost wished Erekkus was around to ask him about it. Almost.

Instead, I planned to take full advantage of my newfound freedom.

I crept around the outskirts of the camp, noting the layout of the tents and guard posts. I wouldn't try to sneak off until daybreak, but it couldn't hurt to at least see what I was working with now.

I kept expanding my circles, until the bonfire was a distant glow and I was beyond the final bounds of the camp. Too far—I was pushing my luck while the others were awake.

I froze, scanning the horizon.

I felt something out there, not far from me now. A presence that almost seemed familiar, but twisted from what I typically knew, that stone stillness warped into molten steel—sharper and more dangerous.

My curiosity—a dangerous quality—got the better of me.

I lingered in the shadows and clung to the rocks, and edged closer.

Atrius.

Atrius, on his hands and knees, clutching the head of a stag with bare arms, his teeth sunk deep into its throat. His shirt and jacket were discarded in a pile nearby, his bare skin covered in blood.

The beast was enormous—one of the biggest stags I'd ever seen around this area. Atrius's arms barely encircled its head, though he held it tight, muscles straining. Blood soaked the creature's neck, matting its white fur and dripping into the gritty sand.

I stilled, unable to move.

I'd witnessed predators work countless times before. But even what I had seen the rest of Atrius's men doing near the bonfire seemed . . . different than this. This was primal and foreign and yet, at the same time, deeply, innately natural. I was repulsed by it and fascinated by it and . . .

And, ever so slightly, frightened of it.

Or maybe *frightened* wasn't the right word to describe the way the hairs stood upright at the back of my neck, the shiver that ran up my spine. It was more that something had changed in the way I saw him, a mismatch between what I had thought he was and what I was witnessing now.

Atrius's eyes opened. Looked right at me. For a split second, we were both frozen there in our sudden awareness of each other. Then, in a movement so swift and oddly graceful it seemed instantaneous, he was standing, the stag twitching on the ground at his feet.

Blood ran down his chin and covered his bare chest, stark against the cold pale of his skin under the moonlight.

"What are you doing here?" He was, as always, soft-spoken, but his voice was a little hot with the anger that flickered at the center of his presence—quickly tamped down.

"Walking," I said.

He wiped the blood from his mouth with the back of his hand, though the attempt mostly just smeared it across his face.

"Go back to your tent," he said.

"Why? When everyone else seems to be celebrating?" I tilted my head, pointedly, at the stag. "Feasting?"

"Exactly why you should be away." His eyes narrowed, as if in realization. "Erekkus left you alone?"

Oh, Erekkus was going to be in trouble.

I took a step closer, curious, and Atrius lurched backward so abruptly that he nearly tripped over a cluster of rocks, as if frantic to get away from me.

That made me pause.

He collected himself fast, so fast that maybe someone else might have dismissed it, but I saw that . . . that fear. Not of me, exactly. Not quite.

I observed him closely, reaching for the presence he kept so carefully guarded. His chest rose and fell heavily. Nose twitched.

Hunger. He was hungry.

"Go back to your tent," he said. "Stay there until morning."

"What's happening tonight? Is this a . . . festival? Ritual?"

He let out an almost-laugh. "Ritual. No, only your kind do rituals."

"Then what is it?"

"It's a festival in the House of Blood, to celebrate the birth of our kingdom. It takes place every five years, under the waxing moon closest to the spring equinox."

"Every five years," I remarked. "Must be special, then." After a moment of thought, I added, "Maybe not, considering how many years your kind have in a lifetime."

"It is special," he snapped. "And they—"

He cast an unreadable glance back to the camp—the bonfire, and his warriors surrounding it. His throat bobbed, then he turned back to me. He wiped his mouth again, seeming to realize all at once how he looked—half-naked, blood-covered.

"Go back to your tent," he repeated. "That's an order."

An order? He said those words to me with such casual authority. I bristled at them without meaning to, being reminded far too clearly of the last time they were thrown at me—the night I came so close to killing the man who stood before me now.

I bowed my head, mostly hiding the sarcasm in the movement. "Very well, Commander. I'll leave you to your . . ." I tipped my chin, motioning to the stag corpse on the ground, my eyebrow twitching, ". . . meal."

I turned away. He watched me go, unmoving. Weaver, he was capable of being so very . . . still. Not just his body, but his presence, too. His inner self. I sensed that something thrashed beneath the surface of that calm, like a beast that did not so much as ripple the glass surface of the water, but I couldn't even begin to reach into those shadows.

"Beware that curiosity, seer," he called after me. "It's a dangerous thing."

I paused, turned back. Smiled at him.

And there it was—just a hint. A single wisp of smoke against the impenetrable velvet-black of his presence:

A glint of interest.

Careful, Commander.

I smiled at him. "So it is," I said, and continued on my way.

I HAD EVERY intention of obeying Atrius's command—though I admit I chafed at it a bit, on principle. But I also liked staying alive, and his advice to stay away from his horde of vampire warriors on a night dedicated to drunken, delirious feasting seemed objectively wise.

I was, however, going to take a quick detour.

I wouldn't have much time now that Atrius had caught me, and I was convinced that he would certainly have Erekkus guarding me during the daytime, so I had to be fast. I had spotted a pond not far from here when we arrived in this area—actually, it seemed more like a collection of murky standing water collected from a rainstorm, but I'd take what I could get. I could reach the Arachessen through stone if I had to, but that was a much more stubborn, unworkable element, and I'd never quite mastered it the way many of my Sisters had. The Keep was designed to sit at an apex of several powerful collections of threads throughout Glaea, stringing across key elements through-out the country. This way, a Sister could communicate with the Keep from virtually anywhere, so long as those veins of energy ran there.

I came to the pond quickly and knelt beside it, water lapping at my knees through my skirts. I hastily drew several sigils in the sand and pressed my hands into the muck, letting the cloudy water cover them.

I let myself fall forward. Forward.

Forward . . .

The threads collected here. Through the water, I could feel them extending in all directions. It was always easy to find the one that would lead me to my home—it always felt close and warm, as if vi-brating at a higher frequency.

I reached for that thread, and pulled . . .

One second passed, then two. I waited. I could feel the Keep, but it was possible no one there would be able to talk to me. I resisted the urge to bite down on a curse as seconds became a minute. I wasn't sure when I would next be able to get away like this.

But I breathed an exhale of relief when the Sightmother's face appeared before me, as if projected on the surface of the water.

"Sylina," she said. "Tell me what you see."

The Sightmother was kind and warm in person, but while we were on missions, she had no time for pleasantries. That was fine. Neither did I.

"I've made it into the conqueror's army," I told her. "I've been taken as his seer."

Normally, the means through which I accomplished this task would not be relevant to the Keep. But this detail was important to the Arachessen.

"It was difficult to get him to accept me," I went on. "He recognized me as an Arachessen, and I told him that I was an escaped Sister. He offered me protection from the Arachessen in exchange for my loyalty during his war."

The Sightmother said nothing. It was impossible to read presences through a thread this distant, but the silence held a strange tinge to it—something I couldn't read even if I had tried to.

"Good," she said, at last. "Wise. So long as he believes you."

"He believes me."

"Make sure it stays that way."

"Yes, Sightmother. He had me seer for him once already. His next target is Alka, and my Threadwalk was to help him strategize his attack."

"And did you?"

I paused, coming up with the best answer to this question. "Yes and no," I said. "I had a productive Walk. But I changed the information I gave him. Just enough."

Again, a beat of silence that I did not know how to decode.

"Why, child?" the Sightmother asked, a question that left me stunned.

Why?

"Because—of course, I can't *actually* help him conquer Alka," I said.

"Alka has few resources. It's drug-infested and weak. He can have it."

She said it so dismissively. As if she were sacrificing marbles on a game board.

Words evaded me. Or . . . no, the words were there. They were just not appropriate to say to my Sightmother.

"Sylina?"

"I—" I collected myself, choosing my response carefully. "There is a human cost to allowing him to conquer them, Sightmother."

"The state is ruled by warlords. Inhabited by a drug-addled populace. It is not our place to judge the morality of an individual act. We are playing a bigger game."

Hypocrite.

The word shot through my mind before I could stop it—a word I never thought I would think of the Arachessen. With one sentence, she damned a city-state to death as punishment for their crimes. In the next, she told us we aren't arbitrators of morality.

I kept my temper close, filtered through decades of careful training.

"I'll shed no tears for the warlords, either," I said. "But thousands of people live in that city. Many of them innocent. Children."

It was the last word that betrayed me. I knew it right away.

The Sightmother's face shifted into understanding. It was a little pitying—the way one looks at a well-meaning dog who is prone to peeing in the plants because it mistakes them for the outdoors.

I cursed myself. I hated that look. That look was the rift between me and my Arachessen Sisters. That look was directed at the gap of time that made me different from all of them.

"You will never be free, Sylina, until you let go of the hold your past has on you," she said. "The past cannot dictate the future."

"I know, Sightmother."

"We fight for what is Right. What is Right goes beyond good or evil."

I hated being lectured like this. I didn't show it. I kept my face placid. My presence calm.

"I understand, Sightmother. I'll choose differently in the future."

I glanced over my shoulder. Commotion stirred in the distance. Probably just the festival debauchery going on too long—but I was still conscious of how long I'd been gone.

"Go," the Sightmother said, as if sensing my concern. "You have our faith and our Sisterhood, Sylina."

She paused at that sentence, as if to let it sink in—as if she knew, even over this distance, that I needed to hear it. I would never admit that I did, never show her that insecurity. But of course, she saw it anyway.

I bowed my head. "Yes, Sightmother. May the threads guide you."

I severed my connection to the Keep, rose, shook off my now dirty, wet skirt, and retreated back to the camp.

CHAPTER TWELVE

The next night, the vampires were sluggish and slow to rise. Erekkus looked like a corpse when he dragged himself into my tent not long past nightfall.

I laughed the moment he revealed himself. In response, he shot me an acidic glare, punctuated with a sarcastic sneer.

"I can see that face," I said. "Don't you know that by now?"

"Oh, I know, Sister. Just like you can see my shame, too, apparently."

I made an exaggerated sound of sympathy. "Poor little thing. Overindulged? Is it the blood that makes you look like that, or the wine?"

He grumbled something wordless, then jabbed a finger at me. "You got me in a hell of a lot of trouble with Atrius, you know that? I told you to stay put."

I shrugged. "Everyone else seemed to be having fun," I said innocently. "Why can't I?"

"Because if there's one thing the Arachessen are known for," he muttered, dripping with sarcasm, "it's *fun*."

I almost chuckled at that one. He wasn't wrong. I loved my Sisters, but they could be . . . a stoic bunch.

"I'm not an Arachessen, remember. Maybe I was just so much *fun* I got myself kicked out."

Erekkus, despite his obvious misery, actually made an expression resembling a smile at that.

"I'll remember that," he said, "and challenge you to prove it the next time there's wine around."

I returned his smile despite myself. "I might be moved to accept it."

I was a little surprised to see Erekkus that day, actually. Atrius had seemed so unhappy to see me wandering around the night before that I thought he'd fire Erekkus as my bodyguard. But no— apparently Atrius still trusted Erekkus, because he remained my companion, and I had to admit I liked that. In part, because he was talkative enough to get information from. But I found I also just enjoyed the chattiness.

We packed up camp and traveled over the next week, venturing closer to Alka as the crescent moon approached. Then, several hours' travel from the city, we stopped again, shielded from the city by the rocky cliffs. Because of the steep, mountainous terrain, we were able to get quite close to the city while still remaining hidden—though no doubt Aaves, Alka's warlord king, had some inkling that Atrius was coming for him.

This was, however, the only advantage offered by Alka's terrain. The roads from here were narrow and steep, making it difficult to move thousands of soldiers at once and forcing them into a choke-point that would make them easy to target with snipers—or, more likely, a bunch of drunken maniacs with oil-fueled firebombs. Beyond the mountain passes, the city was broken up into tall, isolated islands, connected by a series of difficult-to-navigate, poorly maintained bridges.

It was challenging. But Atrius, I'd learned, didn't back down from a challenge.

Here, we stopped and waited. Erekkus was called away from me for the first time since the festival night. No matter where we went, my tent was always beside Atrius's, separated slightly from the rest of the group. With Erekkus gone, I sat against the cloth wall of my tent, on the side closest to Atrius's, and reached out for their presences.

I couldn't make out their words, but I could sense their intentions. Half a dozen people gathered in Atrius's tent, and as always, Atrius's presence overwhelmed them all. They were tense and serious. Every so often, the energy would rise—in arguments, I thought—and then would immediately fall back into quiet with a single soft-spoken word from Atrius.

They were strategizing. Determining their approach.

Hours later, Erekkus left the tent and strode back toward mine. Curiously, another presence I didn't recognize joined him. I moved away from the wall quickly, settling onto my bedroll and looking thoroughly bored by the time he opened the flap.

"You should knock," I said. "You might've seen something you didn't want to see."

A reluctant smile pinched his mouth. "Oh, I doubt that," he said, but his companion gave him a stern glance and he quickly sobered.

I cocked my head at the newcomer—a dour-looking man, older than most others I'd seen in Atrius's army. His body didn't betray his age as much as his presence did—worn, tired, beaten down.

"This is Rilo," Erekkus said. "I'm needed in the offensive, so he'll be watching over you."

"Watching over me where?" I said. "Here?"

Erekkus looked at me like I was stupid. I wondered if he'd ever really understand that I knew when he did that. "Yes."

Oh no. Absolutely not.

I straightened my back and clasped my hands. "I'd like to speak to Atrius."

Erekkus actually laughed. "Atrius is extremely busy before an imminent attack."

"I'll be quick."

"No. He's not taking uninvited visitors."

"I've had another vision. It's very important. It affects the attack."

Erekkus looked annoyed. "Bullshit. You're lying."

"Does Atrius trust you to decide that that's true? I think he'll be unhappy if he marches without this information, just because you made a unilateral decision you weren't supposed to make."

Erekkus was silent for a long moment, then cursed, turned around, and ripped the flap open.

"Stay there," he commanded. Then, over his shoulder, he added,

"I'll ask, but I'm telling you, he's not going to see you. He's got better things to do."

ATRIUS SAW ME.

He wasn't happy about it, of course. I could sense his irritation even beneath that constant, powerful calm—though I suspected that was only because he was allowing me to.

"You take up a disproportionate amount of my time, seer," he said, "considering that I have a thousand other people reporting to me."

"Call me Sylina."

I smiled. Atrius did not. It was difficult to charm him. Then again, I'd never been a very charming person.

"I would like to march with you," I said. "Let me fight with you in Alka."

Atrius didn't even look up from his desk—if the makeshift stack of crates could be called that. "No."

"I'm your seer. I'd be useful out there."

"I've never seen anyone seer on a battlefield, and if they did, I think it'd cause much more trouble than it's worth."

He had a point there.

"I'm a trained warrior," I said. "You yourself said the Arachessen are a force to be reckoned with."

He lifted a lazy hand—gesturing to the camp beyond his tent. "I have a thousand warriors, and all of them are good. I have only one seer."

It made it hard to argue with him when he was so thoroughly correct in his reasoning. I would make the same decision in his place. Any rational leader would.

I didn't have to argue with him. I could sit like an obedient little prisoner in my tent, guarded by whatever-his-name-was, and then learn about the battle afterward.

But I was here to gather information, and fast. What informa-tion was more valuable than seeing how they fought? I'd witnessed it once—it had been like a wall of water crashing over the shore, inevitable and inescapable. I had been distracted, though. This time, I needed to dissect their tactics. To do that, I had to be there. I could only learn so much after the battle ended, piecing the story together secondhand. Hyperbole and myths took hold fast.

I wanted the truth.

The challenge would be coming up with a good enough reason to be there.

I let out a long, noticeably shaky breath, clasping my hands together tight. For a long moment, I didn't speak.

It was an uncomfortably lengthy stretch before Atrius's gaze flicked up.

"What's wrong with you?"

So blunt. It was almost charming.

I ducked my head, as if embarrassed by myself.

"I—I didn't lie to Erekkus," I said, "about having another vision. But I confess I lied about the nature of it."

"I'm shocked," Atrius said blandly.

"I saw a vision about . . . myself. That the Arachessen would come for me the night of the attack." I lifted my head, straightened my back, clenched my jaw—as if trying oh-so-very-hard to collect myself. "They don't give clean deaths, Commander."

"So I've heard."

I waited, shrouding my building annoyance. Given all this talk about how important a seer was to his mission, I expected the news of my impending death to be met with a little more urgency.

"So?" I said, after a long silence passed. "I can march with you?"

He set down his pen. Raised his gaze.

People tended to assume that Arachessen, given our condition, didn't care about eye contact, but that's false. Yes, I could sense a presence without ever turning my head toward them, but I sensed plenty more with a gaze meeting mine. It's amazing what I could see when one extended a thread of their own. Most revealed more than intended.

Atrius's stare was an exception. It felt like having your chin tipped up with the point of a dagger. Not an overt threat, but never losing the potential to become one with the most minute movement.

"I'm—" I let my voice waver. "I'm ashamed to say that I'm *afraid*, Commander. That's the truth of it."

"I'm not sure that I believe that," he said.

I couldn't help it—I was a little indignant. "You don't believe that I'm afraid of the Arachessen? That's just common sense, isn't it?"

"I don't believe *that*." He jabbed his pen at me. "*That* little chin-wobbling thing. Enough of the theatrics."

My brows lurched a little.

This man. Full of surprises.

I gave him a small, conspiratorial smile, like I was letting him in on a secret joke.

"I'm sorry. A woman alone in this world sometimes needs to perform to make men take her seriously."

Only a little true. Perform, or suppress. Rarely anything in the middle.

"It's not helping me take you seriously." He set down his pen and stood, crossing the room to stand before me. Once again, I felt like I was being examined—like any minute he might start critiquing my posture.

I straightened my back, as if to lift myself up to his height. A losing game, of course—I wasn't short by any means, but he was very tall.

"But I promise you," I said, more seriously—making sure to inject a little of that shame, that fear, into my voice, "that my fear is real. I can be an asset to you on that battlefield, Commander. But I certainly can't do anything for you if the Arachessen kills me first."

He took me in, considering.

"You'll have no bodyguards," he said. "Every man and woman with me will be focused on their task and their own survival. I won't ask any of them to put your protection over that."

"I understand that."

"I'm not sure that you do."

I laughed. "You have no idea the things I've seen. The things I've done. I'm a killer too, Atrius. Don't underestimate me."

His eyes narrowed. Then he turned around and rummaged through a pile of packs in the corner. When he returned, my heart leapt—he was bearing my sword, which had been taken the night Erekkus had brought me from the inn.

He said nothing as he handed it to me, nor as I cradled it for a long moment.

And then, just as I was about to open my mouth to thank him, he drew his sword and swung it.

The strike was perfectly executed—so sudden and swift and glass-smooth it barely rippled the air, and it was aimed right at my throat.

He was good. Fast. But I was faster. I sensed the movement before he could execute it.

I drew my own weapon, letting the scabbard fall to the ground as I met his swing.

The clash of our weapons, steel against steel, reverberated through the tent. My weapon—sleeker than his, a rapier compared to his saber—strained under the weight of his strike.

But he didn't rely on his strength alone. He didn't let the contest hold for more than a few seconds before he pulled back and came at me again.

I couldn't let him draw blood. I knew he, like his men, surely wielded blood magic. One nick of my skin and I was done.

No, I wouldn't let him get that far.

I matched his speed, anticipating his movements. It was harder than I was used to. Most minds hinted at their next move before their muscles did, but not Atrius's. It was as if he fought completely in the moment, not thinking ahead but wholly reacting, relying on instinct.

Our steel met again, again, again. We circled around the room, dancing through the small space, the close quarters making each strike focused and efficient.

I didn't mind fighting. Didn't mind letting him toy with me. Actually, I relished the opportunity to observe him—even if every new piece of information seemed to only hint at a new mystery.

I stumbled as a particularly strong blow nearly flung me through the tent wall. A smile twisted his lips—just a hint of satisfaction, there and gone again.

That little smile changed everything. Enough playing. It was time to end this.

I let my breath steady, let the threads of my magic reach across the room. I drew one from myself to the other side of the tent, just behind Atrius.

Pulled it tight. Tight. Tight.

Stepped into it.

The world collapsed, shifted, rearranged in less than a second, and then I was standing behind him.

Atrius was tall, but not so tall I couldn't position my blade against his throat, my other arm wrapped around his body.

"I win," I said.

I tried not to sound smug.

Tried.

His body was pressed against mine. I felt his muscles tense with surprise, even if no part of his presence betrayed it. Felt the exhale as he realized what I'd just done.

He raised his hands.

"Impressed?" I asked, unable to help myself.

"Mm."

The sound was more of a grunt.

So he was a sore loser. Noted.

I lowered and sheathed my blade, and he did the same.

"I've heard the Arachessen know how to do that kind of thing," he said. "Never witnessed it."

"We can do much more than that," I said, and immediately cursed myself.

We. I hoped he'd dismiss that as a holdover habit from my years of service. But if he noticed my slip, he didn't show it. Instead, he turned and regarded me stonily.

"So?" I said. "Are you convinced now of my competence?"

He looked me up and down. A muscle in his jaw twitched, like whatever he was about to say physically pained him.

"Good enough," he muttered at last, turning back to his desk. "Fine. You can come. Now get out of my tent. I have actual work to do."

CHAPTER THIRTEEN

Maybe I should have considered further that I had deliberately chosen to sabotage Atrius's army before I'd insisted on marching with them.

On the optimistic side, at least if I was there in person, I'd get to confirm that my sabotage worked.

Atrius moved, as I'd instructed, on the night of the full moon.

It was cold that night, the fog thick and soupy. The moon, which Atrius had watched so closely, was now only visible in fractured glimpses through the clouds, which blotted out the stars and inky night. The mist smeared all light to murky sunspots, making Atrius's band of warriors look like a long trail of silver ghosts in the moonlight.

I rode near the front of the group, near Erekkus, who did little to hide how appalled he was that Atrius had allowed me to come.

"I've fought you before," he grumbled. "That's not the kind of skill that keeps you alive. Don't expect me to save you."

It bothered me more than it should have that Erekkus dismissed me so easily. *"You won because I let you win"* danced on the tip of my tongue—petty, childish competition that the Arachessen never quite managed to stomp out of me.

Still, it wasn't lost on me that, despite his complaining, Erekkus still remained close to me. I didn't need saving, and he'd see that soon enough, but it was still touching. Apparently he'd gotten a little protective over his ward.

Atrius's warriors were serious and disciplined. No one spoke on the long ride up to the heart of Alka.

There was no optimal way to approach the city. It was positioned high up in the mountains and spread over several stone islands connected by a network of unusual rock formations, which functioned as bridges between subsections. When the tide was very low, it revealed tunnels and paths that were normally hidden beneath the surf. Tonight, those paths were bare.

Atrius seemed pleased by this, at least as much as the man seemed pleased by anything. He took the extremely low tide as the gift given by my vision. He intended to use these tunnels and formations as additional entry points into the city, climbing up through them into the biggest of the city's secondary branches.

He broke his army up into many small groups, sending them to each corner of the city, surrounding it on all sides. Alka was difficult to approach not only because of the narrow, rocky paths and tunnels that were hard to scale and easy to defend, but also because it was so decentralized. The tunnels, combined with the other paths on the western land-locked side of the city, meant that he could surround Alka.

"Is he setting up a siege?" I asked Erekkus, as Atrius doled out his commands.

It would be what most would do to take out a city like this. Maybe the smartest path forward.

"We proposed it," Erekkus replied. "But no."

"Why not?"

"It takes too long and it kills a lot of locals."

The first part of that answer didn't surprise me. The second, though, made my brows rise.

"Why does Atrius care if he kills locals?"

Erekkus narrowed his eyes at me, as if I was asking a suspiciously foolish question, and got distracted by another captain's shouts before he could answer.

This thought nagged at me during the long approach to Alka, like a puzzle piece I couldn't quite figure out how to snap into place. I was here to assemble a diagram of Atrius's strengths and weaknesses that we could use to destroy him. He was a mysterious man, certainly, but until now I had felt that I was slowly peeling back the layers.

That little piece of information, though . . . it didn't fit with anything I thought I knew about him.

Atrius was silent as we climbed up the rocky paths. It was a difficult journey, the path so narrow that only two men could walk beside each other shoulder to shoulder. And this was the easiest part of the journey—from here, the incline dipped and then rose sharply to the central city, a rocky spire that towered high above us.

While our approach was quiet, no one was under any illusions that this was a sneak attack. Aaves surely knew that we were coming. It was just a matter of when, and how, he would choose to address it.

And now, when we reached the top of the path and the outer gates to Alka, high and locked up tight, my heart was in my throat, my body tense. The souls of Atrius's warriors stretched out around me, drowning me in a sea of their bloodthirsty anticipation. There was no feeling quite like that of a soldier about to go into battle. Excitement and terror, thrill and fear, all dancing right on the blade's edge between life and death.

Atrius's warriors were well-trained and battle-hardened. They were calm and professional. And yet, that feeling was the same. The same fear. Why did that surprise me, that these near-immortal creatures felt so close to death in these moments, too?

Atrius lifted a fist, and his warriors halted, the command silently understood all the way down the line. He paused at the gates, staring up at them. They were tall and thick, but just as ugly as Alka itself—great slabs of unfinished iron cobbled together with spiked chunks of metal and mismatched bars of half-rotted wood, still stained with the blood of the slaves forced to build it.

Far beyond the gates—so high above us that the spires were visible through the mist only as smears of orange light—was Aaves's castle. Our ultimate target. The head of the snake, to be sliced off.

Atrius took it all in—the hideous gates, the treacherous mountains, the distant gaudy castle—with a stony face. The faintest hint of disgust rolled from his presence, like a little wisp of smoke. He raised his hand, and four of his men took places on either side of him. Each pair held strange contraptions between them—the closest human comparison I'd seen to this were giant metal crossbows, but so large that each had to be supported by two men. At each tip was a little white-blue flame. One warrior from each machine strummed their fingers along the weapon's carved sides, little flecks of red light shivering at their touch.

Magic. The magic of Nyaxia, surely. The threads quivered in its presence, as if uneasy before something so unfamiliar.

Atrius kept his fist raised, his eyes regarding our target for a long moment, like a final challenge.

Then, so quietly that surely only I heard it, he murmured, "Knock knock."

He lowered his fist.

The four warriors braced themselves. Two flares of light blinded me.

Explosions of white fire blasted through the gates and kept going, all the way up to the night sky above the castle itself. The chaos was swift and immediate. I felt it in the air, in the threads, in the hundreds—thousands—of distant presences that just roared to life, lying in wait, now ready to hurl themselves at us.

With the gates in shambles and a wall of rock ahead of us, Atrius drew his sword and simply started walking.

AAVES'S WARRIORS CAME for us immediately. Battle was like a crashing wave—you feel the tension rising, rising, rising, feel the cold shadow of it over your face, and then suddenly it's everywhere, filling your lungs.

I was drowning.

So many sensations. So many minds screaming. The threads, typically laid out in calm serenity, grew tangled and confusing. And yet, with that chaos came an energy that I thrived on in some sick, shameful way.

Beyond the gates, we were thrust into a series of tunnels. Atrius's warriors needed to further split up in order to make it up the mountain as quickly as possible. On the other entry points, the other divisions of his army were making a similar trek. The tunnels of Alka were deliberately confusing—narrow, poorly lit, and twisting. We'd climbed up for miles to reach the gates, but the tunnels brought us back down, down, in damp, slippery paths.

The vampires, though, seemed undeterred. Darkness was their friend, after all. They were faster than humans, more sure-footed. And Atrius was right: his warriors were very good.

But no one was better than him.

"Stay close to me," he rasped when the first wave of Aaves's warriors descended upon us, and I obeyed.

Aaves's men were known for their brutality. They were drug-addled and sickened, but also frenzied and desperate, and those could be dangerous qualities. They came at us with axes, swords, machetes—weapons stolen from those they had raided, or cobbled together, as if they'd made a game of death. This was their home— they knew it well. Some of the vampires had to pause to make sense of the layout, unsure of how to fight such an unpredictable enemy. Even I, with the insight the threads gave me, still found myself surprised by the rare unexpected attack.

Not Atrius.

Atrius fought like it was what he was created to do.

What I had seen in our little sparring session was nothing. That was play. He did not hesitate. Did not stumble. Did not pause. Every strike of his sword found its mark, quickly, efficiently. He'd open wounds with quick sweeps and then use their blood as if it was another limb, pulling enemies to his blade or tossing them away.

He led the group as the tunnels grew narrower, taking the brunt of the waves of crazed Alkan warriors hurtling down at us. But it didn't matter if four men came after him at once, or six, or ten. He dismantled them, and all while his presence remained as smooth and untouched as a wall of ice.

I had never seen anything like it. There was no twitch, no hint of anticipation, not even when Aaves's men came flying at him from around corners. Every other fighter naturally revealed glimpses of their anticipation, and good ones were thinking several steps ahead of their opponent.

Not Atrius. It was as if he didn't anticipate anything at all—didn't even try. He simply responded. To do that while sparring with me was one thing. It was another to do it here, in battle.

It was incredible.

We fought through the tunnels, deeper and deeper. The walls grew tighter. We continued to split off into smaller and smaller groups as the paths deviated, rocks slipping beneath our feet. It was dark—an advantage for us, since vampires could see without light and I didn't need to see at all. My sword was bloody, the hilt slick with gore. I'd long ago lost track of how many I'd killed. Surely Atrius alone had taken down dozens.

Eventually, we reached an area of strange silence. We pushed forward, tensed, waiting for more attackers.

When several minutes of stillness passed, Atrius glanced back at me, asking a silent question. I'd already found the answer, reaching out with my magic to sense movement in the threads far above us. Too distant for me to make out individual presences, but something was there.

"There are people ahead," I said. "Lots of them."

Atrius nodded and readied himself. The sensation grew closer as the path dipped sharply, bringing us to the apex of three tunnels . . . and a morass of people. A wall of them—far more than the warriors Aaves had been throwing at us so far.

Many more than our dwindling group.

Behind me, Erekkus muttered what I could only imagine was an Obitraen curse.

"We fight through them," Atrius commanded, his sword raised in anticipation. "No hesitation."

But my steps slowed—because something here wasn't right.

The presences were now close enough to sense. And it was difficult to feel the emotions of such a large group, but these . . . they overwhelmingly reeked of fear. And these people were coming for us, yes, but it was a lurching, stumbling walk, like they were being packed into these hallways and forced down—

Just fear. Just—

I grabbed Atrius's arm just as the crowd of people was almost upon us.

"They aren't warriors," I choked out. "They're innocent. They're civilians."

Typical of these warlords. To use their starving, homeless populace as shields when he was starting to run out of warriors. Use them to flush us out.

Realization fell over Atrius's face in the same moment that the wall of bodies surrounded us.

He spat a curse. For a moment, I was absolutely certain I was about to ruin my cover—because Atrius, I was sure, was about to cut through all these innocent people, and I'd have to stop him.

But to my shock, Atrius lowered his sword just as the mass closed around us, shielding its sharp edge from the flesh jammed into every crevice of the hall.

He turned back and screamed a command in Obitraen. Then he lifted his sword above his head, high enough to avoid the bodies, reached back to grab my wrist, and pulled me forward, as if to keep me from getting swept away by the sea of people.

"Hold onto Erekkus," he told me—not that he had to, because Erekkus was already holding onto my other forearm, tethering us.

There wasn't enough air to speak. My head pounded, a nasty side effect of being surrounded by such an overwhelming quantity of people—and emotions—in such close quarters.

Neither Atrius nor his men killed a single person.

We just fought our way past the tides, pushing through the morass of sweaty, terrified flesh until it thinned, then disappeared.

Atrius and Erekkus released my arms, and I let out a shaky breath. My headache throbbed, but subsided. Sweat plastered my clothing to my body. Distantly, I sensed that mass of innocent people continuing down the tunnels to Weaver-knew-where, blind with terror, like a herd of panicking cattle.

Atrius muttered something in Obitraen to Erekkus, who nodded. It was harder than ever to sense Atrius's presence now, with my abilities so exhausted by the pack of people, but I glimpsed a faint whiff of disgust.

"Good to know that human kings have so much respect for life," Atrius muttered to me, and I couldn't help but let out a ragged laugh at that.

"I'm sure vampire kings are very kind to their subjects."

His lips thinned. "Maybe kings are the problem," he remarked. Then, before I could answer that, he lifted his chin down the hall. "How much farther?"

It was hard to tell how much closer, overall, we had come to the peak of Alka. The tunnels were disorienting, rising and plummeting in seemingly equal measure, twisting so frequently it was impossible to say which direction we were headed. Aaves's sea of humans hadn't helped that, either.

I paused, my breath coming heavy. "I need a moment," I said. My magic was exhausted, but I reached through the threads, letting my awareness ripple out in all directions.

Nothingness around us—not a soul. We hadn't climbed far. If anything, we were deeper than where we had started at the gates. I could sense the sea nearby, the salty brine scent stinging my nostrils.

I followed the threads up, up, up. Up to a cluster of auras far above us . . . to one in particular, far above them.

"He's far," I said.

"How far?"

My brow furrowed. The threads shivered and trembled.

I ran over them again, following them to the castle.

No, this wasn't right. I had to have missed something.

"There's no one for a long time," I said.

But that didn't make sense. Aaves had plenty of bodies to throw at us. And yet, the halls were empty.

I leaned against the wall. My palm touched wet stone.

The realization came too late.

There were many things that were very unique about Alka. The rocky terrain, its confusing tunneled construction, the many inter-connected formations that made up its body.

But perhaps the most dangerous was the tide.

It was an unusually low tide the night of a full moon, revealing paths that were usually underwater.

But the tides of Alka were vicious and swift and sudden, more so than anywhere else in Glaea or, perhaps, the world.

My vision had specified the crescent moon. I had taken us during the full. And Aaves had just driven us into the deepest tunnels of Alka. The ones that really belonged to the sea.

A sea that was ready now to take them back.

I whirled to Atrius. "We need to go back—" I said.

But the sudden wall of water swallowed my words.

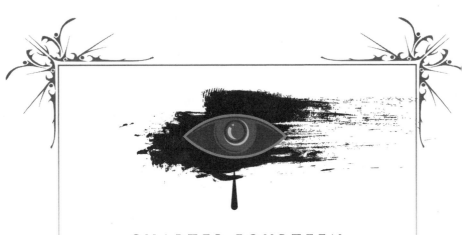

CHAPTER FOURTEEN

I'm six years old, and the water hurts so much as it fills my lungs. My mouth keeps opening and opening, like if I can get my jaw open wide enough I'll find air, but there's no air, there's just sour salt water and it just keeps filling me and filling me and filling me, and I know it will kill me.

I am six years old and I'm going to die.

The man's hands are firm at my throat, tangled in the back of my hair. I thrash against him but I can't fight his grip. His fingers are so tight around my neck, they hurt almost as much as the salt in my lungs.

Almost.

I'm six years old and I'm going to die.

WATER HAD FILLED my lungs by the time I was aware enough to realize what had happened. It poured into the tunnels with such force that it struck us like a giant open palm. My body hurt—something broke. I couldn't orient myself. We were moving fast, so fast I struggled to grab hold of the threads around me. The moment my consciousness returned, I clawed at the stone wall, breaking fingernails but failing to—

My body lurched as someone grabbed me—Atrius. I knew it was

him immediately. But the water was so strong, and he was being swept away in it, too. He held me for a moment and then I was pulled away from him again. My body crashed against what must have been Erekkus, who was forcing himself against the rock wall, trying to slow himself against the current.

Gods, what were we going to do? I reached for the threads, for something to root myself in. We were being swept through the tunnels, swept out to—

Atrius grabbed at me again, and once again he failed. This time, though, he opened up a gash in my forearm. I barely noticed the pain, but I wanted to snap at him for the distraction.

But then a moment later, a strange sensation bubbled up inside me, slow, warm, burning. My muscles tensed, tightening and moving without my permission.

What the hell was—

My body flew across the hall, fighting against the tide, and suddenly my head was above the water and a body was pressed to mine with a firm arm wrapped around my waist—

—And Atrius's very, very unhappy face was a few inches away from mine. One arm held onto me, and the other braced against a rocky enclave. Flecks of water showered against our faces, our heads barely above the rush. The tide was now ebbing and flowing, coming in bursts rather than constant force. I glanced behind me to see the flailing limbs of Atrius's warriors fighting to make it through the tide. Reverberations of their fear, high and sharp, plucked through the threads.

Even vampires feared death. And I knew that a death by drowning was among the worst.

"You said you'd be useful, Arachessen," Atrius spat, raising his voice over the roar of the water. "I saved your life. Now you save theirs."

His eyes were fierce and steadfast, like this demand was completely reasonable. And yet, perhaps I sensed a glimmer of fear from him now—only now, when his people were in danger.

"How do you expect me to do that?" I asked, the rush swallowing my voice.

He leaned close, the water from his lips brushing the crest of my ear.

"You're the witch," he said. "Don't your kind have their ways?"

Weaver damn him. I had no ways for this. Some of my Sisters were talented with water magic, but that was never my skill, and even then, I doubted any acolyte of Acaeja would have water magic powerful enough to stop this—maybe a follower of Zarux, the god of the sea, but that certainly wasn't my domain.

I looked around helplessly, reaching out to our surroundings. Stone. Water. Bodies. And fear—so much fear, growing more intense by the moment.

Terrible guilt, the weight of my responsibility in this mistake, swelled in my throat, burning. So many of these people were going to die.

Perhaps I should let them.

It was what a good saboteur would do. Let the conqueror's army whittle away. I had every excuse for not being able to help. How could I help, anyway? What could I do?

I'm six years old and the salt water hurts and I'm going to die.

I shook away the past, my own thread tangling with theirs.

I couldn't say why I made the decision, only that I was acting before it even consciously snapped into place. I reached above me, pressing my palm to the rough stone of the ceiling.

It was hard to focus on my magic with the water rushing around us. The bursts came harder now, sending Atrius and me under the water for seconds at a time, threatening to rip me from his grasp. But he held me tight, keeping my body pressed to his. I was grateful for that, an anchor, as I worked to find a connection strong enough to latch onto.

Against the tide, I kept my palm to the stone.

Stone was alive, in its way. Threads of life ran through it. It was stable and secure. Everything here was moving and changing. Not the stone. I could use that. There was space beyond this—more tunnels. We just needed to break through.

I'd never done something like this before. Weaver knew whether I was even capable of it. But it was my only idea. My only wild, stupid, ridiculous idea.

I drew a thread from myself to the stone, tightened it until it trembled between our souls. Another thread. Another. Three anchors, forcing my magic through it, and then half a dozen, and then more that I didn't bother to count.

How many would be enough?

"*Sylina,*" Atrius ground out, between clenched teeth.

He didn't need to say more. Time. We didn't have any. His men were barely managing to cling to the walls of the cave. Some had been swept away.

It had to be enough. I threw all my magic into that connection between me and the stone, yanked as hard on those threads as I would if I were flinging myself across the room—but instead of moving myself, I was moving the stone.

CRACK!

Before I knew what was happening, Atrius cupped the back of my head, yanking me against him. It was only seconds later that I realized why: to protect me as the crumbling rock came crashing down into the water. The two of us tumbled as the current, interrupted by the change in terrain, sputtered and crashed against the walls.

Above us, a hole revealed the tunnel above.

I didn't recognize the sound of my own laughter, frantic and manic, at first.

Weaver take me. My Sisters were never going to believe I'd just pulled that off.

For a moment, despite the circumstances, I was wildly proud of myself.

I glanced at Atrius, probably beaming, and something that almost resembled a smile flashed briefly across his face—and the sight of it sent a strange, satisfied thrill up my spine.

"Go," he said, releasing me and half pushing me up to the newly opened passage. Several others had managed to escape the current thanks to the partial dam of the rocks, and were already dragging themselves up, too, coughing up water along the way.

But my attention was being pulled to the others—those who had been swept back further by the tide and couldn't find their footing. Atrius's eyes found them, too—though he pushed me up to the opening, he was ready to fling himself back down the hall.

He was devoted to those that followed him. I would give him credit for that.

"No," I said. "I've got them." I put a firm hand on his chest, stopping him. Then I turned, drew a thread between me and the nearest vampire, and pulled it taut before I had the chance to second-guess myself.

"Wait—" Atrius started, but I was already gone.

The water was frigid. Despite the partial blockage of the stone I'd collapsed, the current was still strong here, flinging my body around like a rag doll. I grabbed Erekkus—a difficult feat, considering how much larger than me he was. I didn't give him time to react before I forced my head above the water, forced myself to steady just long enough to look at the gap in the rocks, at Atrius on his hands and knees looking back at me—

Draw the thread.

Step through.

I stumbled as my feet hit dry stone, staggering against Atrius and weighed down by Erekkus, who immediately went to his hands and knees and started hacking up water.

Atrius started to say something, but I snapped, "Get down there and be ready for them," and was gone again before he had time to respond.

The next two were difficult. The third, nearly impossible. As the bodies grew farther away from me, it grew more difficult for me to accurately reach them. I retrieved four more, all hoisted onto the rock landing panting and coughing, where Atrius dragged them up to safety. With each one, I was slower to return. Threadstepping took a significant amount of energy, and I was casting my net far. By the fourth trip, my heartbeat ached against the inside of my ribs.

Atrius caught my arm as I turned to go back for another.

"You're shaking."

My head was killing me. I had to sink all my energy into keeping my focus trained on the final presence I could still sense, though it was quickly drifting farther.

"I need to go."

"If you can't make it back—"

"I can save the last one," I snapped. "Do you want me to do it, or let them die?"

Atrius's grip tightened around my arm, echoing the tightness of his jaw, then he released me. "Go. Fast."

This one was hard. When the water hit me this time, it swallowed me whole. The warrior, a woman thankfully not much larger than I was, was unconscious. I grabbed her, but the rush of the water was unrelenting. For a moment, I was swallowed up in my own past, directions and senses erased.

I tried to turn to the shore. But I couldn't find it—was it that way? Or had I gotten turned around?

The slow tide of panic rose in my chest. An abrupt surge of water caught me off guard, sending my back smacking against the stone. The explosion of pain had me gagging on salt water.

I'm six years old and I'm going to—

No.

I was not going to drown. I was not going to die. I was watched by the Weaver, the Lady of Fate, and I was a master of the threads, not another puppet to be manipulated by them.

I needed to sense the landscape of the threads. But to do that, I'd need to focus. And that meant letting go of the current. That meant letting myself get swept away.

Damn it. Sometimes, I did hate this job.

I let myself go limp.

Reached to the threads.

They spread out around me, shimmery and translucent and difficult to see with a mind still half-distracted by incoming death.

I fell farther into the water. I barely felt it the next time the current sent me against the wall. I turned . . . reached . . . and . . .

There.

I felt him. Not just my target—not just the stone, but *him*. Atrius. A presence so unusual I felt it from even this far.

It was him I anchored myself to. I drew the thread tight, strong. I prayed it would hold enough to get us there.

And I stepped through it.

I collapsed against the damp stone. My sides and abdomen ached with violent coughs, lungful after lungful of briny water dripping to the rocks. Beside me, my rescuee did the same, and Erekkus helped her to her feet.

Someone touched me, and I jerked away.

"Stop," Atrius growled.

Pain, as my arm was lifted. I cursed as something was drawn tight around it, trying to yank my arm away.

"Stop fighting," he snapped. "You're wounded. I'm stopping the bleeding."

Bleeding.

My breaths slowed. My heart steadied. I felt my arm—the gash in it, now bandaged up tight.

Atrius regarded me like I was the subject of an assessment. "You can move?"

There was no concern in the question. Just pragmatism.

"Yes."

He extended a hand, and I still felt unsteady enough that I allowed myself to take it. His grip was rough and scarred. Hands that carried lifetimes.

I swayed a little on my feet when he let me go. I was sore, but my injuries were surface-level. More disorienting was the exhaustion of my magic. The threads seemed intangible and distant now, hard to grasp. Wonderful. That would make it fun to navigate these tunnels.

"We need to go," Atrius said. His gaze bored into me like a scalpel into flesh, trying to reveal what lay beneath.

"I'm ready," I said. I took my blade from him, let him hoist me up to the next level of the tunnels, and we were off again.

CHAPTER FIFTEEN

We'd gotten much closer to the surface by breaking through to the upper tunnels. Another wave of Aaves's warriors was upon us before long—fewer of them, thankfully, than last time, but enough to slow down our exhausted and much whittled-down group. If Atrius was feeling the strain of the journey, he didn't show it. The man was as ceaseless as the tides that had battered us, and just as immune, apparently, to the flaws of the body. Injuries, fatigue—none of it seemed to matter to him. He forged forward, taking kill after kill. It was hard to keep up with him, but I was determined. The paths were so narrow that we needed to spread out in a thin line—I worked hard to stay close to Atrius, the two of us finishing off each other's injured prey, covering each other's weak sides.

"Not much farther," I rasped out, as I yanked my sword from another body.

Atrius nodded tersely, already moving on.

We were in the midst of another lull in opposition when, at long last, we found ourselves approaching a starry sky ahead. "The end of the tunnel," Erekkus breathed, when we spotted it. "Thank the fucking Mother for that."

And I had to agree, it was nice to feel that sudden rush of fresh air. The castle was not far ahead now, looming over us forebodingly. It wasn't as big of a building as it appeared at a distance. Up close, one could tell that the way it blended into the jagged incline of the mountain bent reality in its favor. It was mismatched and gaudy, much like the gates we burst through to get into the city—like the entire thing was cobbled together in a stubborn rebellion of what a castle should look like. We were up very high now. The streets of Alka surrounded us—if they could be called such a thing, considering they were little more than streaks of packed-down dirt and rotted hanging bridges, which led to houses built precariously into the stone. The people of Alka were used to violence. They knew to stay in their homes and draw their curtains tight.

Still, vampire attackers—that was a whole different game than their usual squabbling warlords. The whole city vibrated with terror.

Atrius paused to take all this in. Then turned to look out over the sea, and the other islands of Alka, where stone bridges extended like crooked spider legs to the mainland. The relief rolling from his presence when he spotted his soldiers slowly making their way toward the inner city was perhaps the most palpable emotion I'd ever sensed from him.

He'd lost many. Surely he knew that, too. But right now, it seemed like enough of a victory that he didn't lose them all.

He turned to those in our little splinter of his group. He shouted a command in Obitraen, then turned ahead and set his gaze squarely on the castle: our final target.

He pointed his sword, and we marched.

Kinder rulers, perhaps, would not have wanted to fight in streets filled with civilians. Aaves and his ilk were not kind rulers. His people, as he'd proven over and over, were just pawns to be used to hold onto his power. His warriors yanked them from their homes as we approached, cluttering the already-difficult paths with terrified bodies who wanted nothing to do with any of this. They flung makeshift explosives, oil-soaked rags, from the windows of the lower levels of the castle, sending the rickety wooden homes up in smoke and burning the smallest of the bridges.

Even with my magic so exhausted, the fear—the pain—of those people was overwhelming.

I could not save them. I knew this. I didn't try—most of the civilians were dead by their king's own hand before we even reached them, more useful dead than alive to slow us down. Atrius's men didn't touch any of them, sheathing their blades as they pushed through the morass of human traps. Yet as we progressed through the city, cutting down the crazed warriors who flung themselves at us from the castle, the number of innocent corpses grew.

Accidental deaths. Inconsequential deaths, in the eyes of men like Aaves. Elderly, women, children. As we pushed through a section of the city that was on fire, I saw a little girl hanging out of a window, body limp, eyes wide and staring straight ahead sightlessly. There was no presence there. She was dead. Freshly dead—her newly-severed thread still trembled with fear.

I didn't realize I'd stopped there, next to her, until Atrius put his hand on my shoulder.

"You'll burn," he said gruffly. "The fire is close."

And yet maybe he saw all the signs of my anger—the fists clenched at my sides, the tremble of my jaw. Maybe he felt me shaking when he steered me away.

Atrius was not supposed to see any of those things—anything that was real. But I was too furious to even scold myself for it. And when he ducked close to my ear to mutter, "How many more before we can kill him?" I almost laughed out of sheer sadistic glee.

I pointed ahead to the gates of the castle. "We just fight our way through." I trailed my finger up—to the top of the spire.

Even depleted, it was easy to sense Aaves up there. Disgusting worm that he was.

Atrius glanced back. His pronged approach had worked well—his soldiers were now pouring into every facet of the city, taking over every segment simultaneously. But the downside was that each group dwindled as they needed to split off in more directions. I had been so lost in my bloodlust that, foolishly, I hadn't realized just how far ahead of the others Atrius and I had gone.

The others in our group still lingered behind, occupying the last of Aaves's men.

"You want to wait for them?" I asked.

He let out a low chuckle, like I'd just said something unintention-ally amusing. "I don't wait for anyone." Then, "How many in there?"

"The castle? Many."

"Too many?"

I paused, realizing what he was asking: *Too many for us?*

Yes, there were many warriors in that castle. Lots of people who would want to kill us.

But I thought of Atrius and the way he killed like breathing. Con-sidered my own training and the significant trail of bodies I'd left during my journey through this city.

I considered my own fury.

"No," I said at last. "Not too many."

Atrius smiled. This was what he wanted to hear.

CHAPTER SIXTEEN

The Arachessen were not supposed to feel extreme emotions —infatuation, elation, terror, hatred. These things clouded our minds. They made it impossible to be impartial. Arachessen were encouraged to be passionate, of course—passionate for our Weaver, our Sisters, and our pursuit of Rightness. But our passion was a steady love, deep and calm like the sea on a clear night. We were told that there was nothing more dangerous than a storm.

My darkest secret was that I had always struggled with this.

Atrius and I left the gates of the castle wide open behind us, forging the way forward for his men to follow. But we didn't wait. We fought our way through the castle. I would barely remember any of it later, because I was lost in the tumultuous seas I had so often been told to avoid—lost, and unashamed of how much I loved it.

The castle was garish and disgusting on the inside, cluttered and dirty, once-fine silks and furniture stained with blood and cum and wine. Aaves was only the most recent of a long string of warlords who ruled over this pile of shit—there were countless other men like him who fought among each other like dogs to sit on the prime seat.

I hated men like this.

I hated men who used their power to gorge themselves. Hated men who thought it was acceptable to murder their own people as long as it gave them one more chance at hanging onto their golden toys.

I hated the men who sent their own terrified people into a stampede to stop us.

Hated the men who burned a little girl alive.

I hated them all so much, and I loved that I felt that way.

The Arachessen taught me that my emotions should always be a calm sea.

But sometimes, those storms snuck up on me. And once the waves swallowed me, it was hard to find the surface.

I wasn't counting how many people I killed when Atrius and I tore through that castle. Maybe a dozen—maybe twice that, or three times, or four. It had been a long, long time since I had lost myself like this.

I'd forgotten how good it felt.

Now I understood why Atrius fought as he did—no anticipation, just perfect awareness of his current moment. In the waves, nothing exists but the next move, the next strike, the next wound, the next body you yank your sword from—every one of them a justice long overdue.

We fought our way up the first flight of stairs, then another. Atrius's men must have been following us by then, but I paid no attention to them if they were. Nothing existed to me, after all, but the man at the top of those stairs.

We found him, at last, on the top floor, in a small room full of grand things. The far wall was open, revealing the expansive view of the full moon hanging in the mist-soaked sky over the ocean. Aaves was a skinny, greasy man clad in ill-fitting silks. Even his presence was repulsive—full of desire and anger and pain and selfishness.

All of his bodyguards had already thrown themselves at us and died for it. There was no one left to save him.

The coward knew it, too. When we rounded the corner, he was kneeling on the ground, holding his dagger.

His head snapped up and his eyes went wide when he saw us approaching. For a moment he lifted the dagger with trembling hands, like he was considering using it as a weapon.

Fool.

I didn't realize I'd laughed until Atrius glanced at me, like the sound made him see something he'd missed before.

And perhaps it made Aaves realize how foolish he was, too, because he then turned the blade on himself, pressing it to his own throat.

"Vampire scum," he spat, though his voice wavered ever so slightly. "You don't get the satisfaction of my death."

I knew when the blade broke his skin, opening a trickle of blood down his wrinkled throat, what a mistake he'd just made.

Atrius scoffed. He raised his hand, his long stride unfaltering, and Aaves flung away the dagger as his limbs went rigid.

Behind us, Erekkus and the others had slowly filed into the room, exhausted and blood-drenched. They were all perfectly silent, their attention fixed on Atrius as he held Aaves in place.

I couldn't look away, either.

"You think your death is a satisfaction?" he sneered.

A flick of his fingers, and Aaves's body reeled toward Atrius as if dragged by an invisible grip. He was terrified, every muscle trembling, his mouth gaping but making no sound.

Atrius caught him at the entryway to the balcony, grabbing him by the neck and hoisting him to his feet. His eyes had turned *red*— deep, violent red, as if his soul was drowning in bloodlust.

"I've killed demigods," he snarled. "Your death means *nothing* to me."

And I didn't so much as breathe as Atrius's teeth closed around Aaves's throat, ripping it out in one brutal movement, the blood spraying like flower petals over the marble floor.

Aaves let out one final agonized gurgle. Atrius spat a chunk of bloody flesh over the balcony into the sea, grabbed the diadem from Aaves's head, and, in one more swift movement, pushed the body over the rail.

The room was full now with Atrius's warriors. They were stoic, as if witnessing something religious.

Atrius turned to them and raised the diadem. Perhaps one might have expected this to be met with wild applause or cheers. It wasn't. It wasn't a celebration or a gloat. It was a gesture of acknowledgement: *We have won.*

Atrius shouted a command, and just as silently as they had filed into the room, his warriors turned and began to leave it.

For a long moment, Atrius stayed like that, the diadem raised, breath coming hard, watching his warriors depart.

Then he let the crown fall to the floor with a clatter, unsheathed his sword, and pointed it at my throat.

CHAPTER SEVENTEEN

I raised my hands and backed up. I hadn't yet caught my own breath—the adrenaline of the battle still pounded in my veins. And yet, there was something about having a sword shoved in your face by the most efficient killer you've ever met that immediately sobered a person.

"What did I do to deserve this?" I said.

"You lied to me."

Atrius's presence was impossible to read even at the best of times. Now, with my magic thoroughly exhausted, it was no use to even try.

"You got your victory," I said.

"At a steep cost. This was not the right time to make this move."

Ah, shit.

I forced down a strange tightness in my chest—nervousness, yes, but also an unexpectedly strong wave of guilt.

"You made it clear to me that you understood seering to be unpredictable," I said. "Perhaps you avoided a greater bloodshed, or an all-out defeat, by acting when you did."

"Tell me," he said, "was the entire vision a fabrication, or just parts of it?"

"I risked my life to save your men. Would I do that if I was trying to sabotage you?"

He seemed unfazed. "If you were smart, then yes."

Weaver damn him.

"I have no interest in working for a man who doesn't understand the nature of seering," I scoffed. "To think I actually started to believe that you were more enlightened than the others. You're just another self-absorbed king who wants to be told what he wants to hear."

I had watched Atrius kill enough times by now to recognize the way he coiled, like a snake preparing to strike.

Weaver, I was going to die here if I didn't come up with something, and fast. But then, he also hadn't killed me yet. If he'd really been fully convinced of my dishonesty, he wouldn't have bothered to allow me to talk.

He needed me. He knew it. He wanted me to give him something that would make him believe me.

Desperate, I reached for the threads, the sudden push greeting me with a stab of pain to the back of my head. Atrius's presence was a wall, as always, but I followed the threads to him and pushed— pushed—

Give me something, Weaver. Anything.

With enough force, sometimes an Arachessen could snag bits and pieces from a person's past or future, like a difficult, highly abridged, even-less-useful version of seering. Usually, it provided nothing useful. But I was desperate.

I pushed against Atrius's presence and was greeted with a barrage of fragmented images and emotions.

Mountaintop night sky cold cold cold the prince isn't moving blood on a blade wipe it with cloth the prophecy was a lie a sea of ash a sky of mist and—

"The prophecy," I blurted out. "I know about the prophecy."

Atrius's shock actually showed in his face. Radiated from his presence. He lowered his sword a little in a way that seemed unintentional.

Then a sheet of cold rage fell over his gaze.

"What are you talking about?" he snarled.

I'd just made a huge mistake.

"You didn't let me complete my Threadwalk," I said, carefully. "You stopped me. Because you didn't like the . . . grounds upon which I tread."

"Don't seer about me."

I raised my palms a little more. "I know. But because you stopped me, you didn't get the full truth."

His throat bobbed. He looked genuinely torn as to whether to kill me or not.

"What did you see about the prophecy?"

I smiled sweetly at him. "I'll tell you if you promise not to kill me."

"I don't make those kinds of promises."

"I'll take a lowered sword." I wanted that thing out of my face. It was still covered with the guts of Aaves's goons. What an insulting way to die.

He ceded. Barely.

I leaned back against the wall.

"Tell me," he demanded. His shoulders were heaving in a way that I suspected had nothing to do with the exertion of the last several hours, which didn't seem to bother him until now.

I noted this carefully—this prophecy. The mountain. Nyaxia.

The prince.

All these things were very important to Atrius. The only times I had ever witnessed him upset were when they were mentioned.

That was useful.

"The truth?" I said, raising my palms in concession. "Maybe it's a mistake telling you this, but what I know is vague. Only that it exists. I sensed it in my Threadwalk. After I saw . . . you. If you won't take my head off for making that reference."

Atrius didn't take my head off, but he still looked like he was considering it.

"I know you have a greater mission," I said quietly. "I know this is about more than just conquering for you. Even if not, I can't offer you the specifics. Not without your cooperation."

Weaver, I was pushing it. And yet, somehow, even as the words flowed over my lips, something deep inside me thought . . . perhaps they were true. There *was* more to this than Atrius was showing me.

His face shifted, revealing so little and so much—all but confirming my suspicions.

"What benefit do I have in lying to you, Atrius?" I murmured.

"Either you kill me, or the Arachessen will. To be honest, I would prefer you do it." My toe nudged one of the bodies on the ground. "At least you're swift about it."

"Only sometimes," he said.

He was deep in thought, sword still hanging at his side—staring at me hard, like he was trying to take me apart.

I chanced taking a step closer. Tipped my chin, cocked my head. I had no big, beautiful eyes to bat at him, but I knew the body language—curious, innocent, submissive.

"If you want to know more about this—this prophecy, I could Threadwalk again and—"

"No."

Just as swiftly as he'd drawn his sword, he sheathed it. The tension broke. He turned away. It was as if he'd never considered killing me at all.

"Go find Erekkus," he said. "He'll give you orders. We have plenty of work to do."

ATRIUS DID NOT rest before cementing his hold on Alka. He ordered a sweep of the towers, eliminating the last of Aaves's men, who hid in the shadows, foolishly throwing themselves at Atrius's warriors while wielding frying pans or dinner knives. They were easy to root out.

I wasn't sure what I expected Atrius to do once that was done—strip the capital for resources, perhaps, or set up his men in the civilian homes—but it wasn't what he did.

I was with Erekkus, dragging away bodies from the first floor of the tower, when Atrius appeared on the balcony that overlooked the crumbling homes of Alka's people. Everyone stopped their work, necks craning. Erekkus was pulled away by another soldier who said something in Obitraen to him.

"What's going on?" I asked Erekkus, when he nodded and returned to our work.

"Atrius is addressing the people. They're going to get everyone out of their houses to listen."

Addressing the people? I couldn't quite name why this was unbelievable to me—maybe it was because the idea of Atrius making a speech seemed absurd, or maybe it was shocking to me that the vampires considered the citizens of Alka people worth addressing at all.

"They're going to terrify people. Everyone's going to think they're about to get rounded up and slaughtered."

Erekkus shrugged. "Maybe. But they're not."

"Why not?"

He chuckled. "You're not the first one to ask that question," he muttered.

"Atrius doesn't kill the civilians of the cities he conquers." I couldn't quite tell if there was a question mark at the end of that or not.

"No. He doesn't. Not one of them, if he can help it."

I thought about Raeth.

If he can help it.

We hoisted another body over the edge of the ravine, to be burned in the pit below. It made a series of very unpleasant cracking noises on the way down.

"You're surprised," Erekkus said.

"He didn't strike me as the forgiving type."

Erekkus laughed, like I'd said something legitimately hilarious, the sound punctuated with a grunt of exertion.

CRACK, as another one of the bodies fell against the rocks.

"Why is that funny?" I asked. Despite myself, I was panting. These bastards were heavy.

"Atrius has an interesting moral code."

"I'm just surprised, given—"

"Given that we eat humans. Last one?"

He pointed to one final body, a silk-drenched old man with a clearly broken neck, and we crossed the room to drag it over.

"Yes," I said.

"I'll be honest, Sister, a lot of us do think we should be eating a whole lot better on this trip than we are. But—" Another grunt, as we hauled the body over the edge. *CRACK.* "—everyone respects Atrius. And Atrius believes he can't rule this kingdom while also eating its subjects, which, I begrudgingly have to say, does make sense."

I stopped mid-movement. My brows rose without my permission. *"Rule,"* I repeated.

"Yes, *rule,*" he muttered. "There's more to go. Let's get down there."

Somehow, it had never occurred to me that Atrius's ultimate intention was to rule Glaea—as in, actually *govern* it, its people included. I didn't know why he wanted this kingdom, but it had never even crossed my mind that being a decent ruler to the humans that lived here was a possibility. I knew what life was like for humans in Obitraes—to say that humans were second-class was putting it kindly, despite some minimal protections. I imagined his intentions for the humans of Glaea were likely more of the same, at best. Anything otherwise was . . . confusing.

The citizens of Alka were, of course, as terrified as I'd predicted when Atrius's soldiers shepherded them out of their homes and into the streets. But Atrius didn't keep them long. His speech was brief and straightforward.

"People of Alka," he said, voice calm despite its booming volume over the Alkan skyline. "Your king is dead. I claim this city-state in the name of the House of Blood of Obitraes, in the name of our Dark Mother, Nyaxia."

I stiffened. It was the first time I'd heard Atrius mention Nyaxia directly. Yet he didn't dwell—his voice remained flat and matter-of-fact. He was no charismatic orator.

"You may be frightened for your lives and those of your families," he went on. "Do not be. We will not harm you. We are your protectors, not your enemies. We do not tolerate violence against us, but otherwise you will not be injured or punished. You will not be removed from your homes. You will not have your possessions taken from you. You have no need to be afraid."

The Alkans were, of course, very afraid. It didn't really do much good to be reassured by a blood-soaked vampire warrior with horns.

But Atrius seemed to think that his deed was done. He stepped away from the balcony after that—no grand finale, no inspiring words of wisdom, no great declaration of victory. It was almost funny how little fanfare there was.

That was that. Atrius returned to the castle, the soldiers ushered people back to their homes, and the night wore on.

DISCARDING THE BODIES of the warlords in the castle was easy. Finding those of all Atrius's lost warriors was much more difficult. When the tide went out again the next night, Atrius sent men through the tunnels in an attempt to drag out the bodies of those who had drowned during the invasion. The remains were laid just beyond the boundary of Alka's rocky inner city, where Atrius's army had set up their camps.

There were many of them. I watched the lines of bodies grow, though I found myself looking for every excuse to be away from the fields where they were being kept.

Later that night, nearing dawn, Atrius's men gathered along the rocky shore. We lined up along the cliffs before the bodies, each wrapped in scraps of fabric that had been dyed deep red in messy buckets of makeshift stain. Only Atrius stepped closer to them. He was silent. We were silent. No one breathed. No one spoke.

Atrius's presence was still—and yet, when I pressed closer to it, reaching for what lay beyond that wall, I felt such deep, mournful sadness.

I drew away fast after that, like a finger from a flame, surprised by the intensity of what I'd just felt.

Atrius showed none of it. He walked along the line of bodies. One pass, then two, then three. And finally, he turned around, and Erekkus handed him a torch. The wrappings had been drenched in accelerant—the bodies took to flame quickly as Atrius knelt before each one, offering them a sendoff in the fire. And then he stepped back and he watched them burn.

For a long time, we all watched.

An hour later, the soldiers began to disperse, solemnly turning away and returning to their duties. Then more and more trickled away, until Erekkus did, too, nudging me along with him. Dawn was near. They had to return to their tents.

Only Atrius remained.

He stood there alone before that wall of fire until dawn kissed the horizon, and only then, reluctantly, did he turn away.

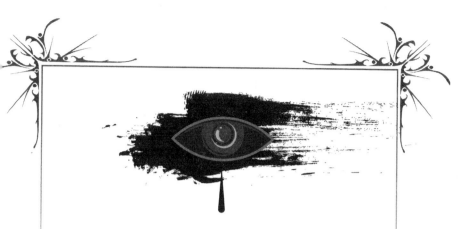

CHAPTER EIGHTEEN

H e wants you."

I woke up only moments before Erekkus stuck his head into my room. Atrius and some of his leadership had moved into the tower—now cleaned and devoid of dead warlords— and I, important as I was, was among the chosen few to accompany him. Apparently I'd missed a real bed, because all I wanted to do was sleep.

"Knock," I grumbled. "I have a door now."

Erekkus said, "He's in a fucking sour mood. Good luck."

"What does he want?" I pushed the covers back and rolled out of bed, not very gracefully.

"Hell if I can figure it out," he muttered.

A breeze rolled through the window, making me suddenly very aware of my clothing—a nightgown that was once owned by one of the warlord's concubines, and definitely looked the part. I'd just been *so happy* to see clean clothes. I didn't much consider that anyone might see me in it.

I crossed my arms over my chest.

"Tell him I'll be there after I get dressed."

Erekkus, noticing my dress, snickered a little.

"Don't be indecent," I huffed.

"I don't think *I'm* the indecent one here." Then, "I don't think you want to keep him waiting. He was very insistent you come now."

"But—"

"That little thing will probably put him in better spirits," Erekkus said breezily, turning away. "We can dream."

"WHAT THE HELL are you wearing?"

The first words out of Atrius's mouth when I walked through the door.

I gritted my teeth.

"I heard you were very eager to see me," I said sweetly. "I didn't want to keep you waiting as I changed."

"Close the door."

I did. Atrius had claimed the warlord's chambers, of course, though it was almost funny now to witness him among all this cheap finery. He was sprawled out in a velvet armchair near the fireplace, a gaudy purple thing marred by cigarillo burns and several very suspicious-looking stains. His limbs skewed out limply. He was shirtless, the fire playing over the lean furrows of his muscles.

It wasn't the first time I'd seen Atrius half-dressed. More than by his appearance, I was startled by his demeanor. Everything about him, from his stance to his expression to the few flashes of emotion he allowed to slip through his walls, reeked of utter discontentment.

He eyed me.

"You look ridiculous," he snapped.

"What, you don't like it?" I made a show of flouncing the little lace-lined silk skirt. "Shocking, since Aaves was clearly a man of great taste."

"Don't let any of the soldiers see you in that. Come here."

The words were cold and clipped. Erekkus wasn't joking. Atrius *waɩ* in a sour mood.

I did as he asked, crossing from cold marble tile to slightly dirty white bearskin.

Up close, I could sense something noxious pulsing in his aura—he tried to tamp it down, hide it behind that steel wall that usually shielded all his emotions, but it was too powerful to hide. I felt it like the throbbing heat of a fire on the other side of a door. It was just as painful, like a wound, but unfamiliar—I'd sensed many illnesses before, physical and emotional, and none felt quite like this.

I frowned. "What's wrong?"

He looked to the flames and didn't answer, his scowl deepening.

I kept reaching toward him with my magic, prodding gently, succumbing to my curiosity. I risked touching his hand, just to get a stronger sense—

He jerked it away.

"I hear that some of the Arachessen can use the power of Acaeja to heal," he said. "Can you?"

His tone was so sharp and aggressive that it sounded more like a rebuke than a question.

I fought the urge to grimace.

"Not well, unfortunately."

I had never been much of a healer. Some of my Sisters specialized in it—they were able to read the threads within a body and use them to manipulate wounds or illnesses, though it was a slow process and not as instantly helpful as a healer trained under the magic of gods more naturally attuned to medicine. Still, I'd seen them perform remarkable feats with it.

I had trained in the method, as all Arachessen did, but it had never been a strength.

"But you know something," he said.

"I can try."

I couldn't remember the last time I'd used those skills. Years, surely. Weaver, I hoped I remembered at least something. I was very conscious that Atrius's blade had been at my throat not all that long ago.

Atrius didn't seem comforted by this answer. He didn't so much as look at me, still scowling into the fire.

I knelt before him on the rug, the rough fur tickling my bare knees.

"What's wrong?" I asked. "Are you injured?"

He took a long time to answer, and still, he did not look at me.

"An old injury," he said.

"Sometimes the worst ones. I did something to my knee a decade ago, and I still feel it. Suppose it's an occupational hazard of our lifestyles, isn't it?"

My attempt at levity fell pathetically flat. I was starting to think that Atrius was simply immune to being charmed. Or maybe I just wasn't very good at being charming.

"So you can help?" he said gruffly.

"I can try." I gave him a gentle smile. "Where is the injury?"

"'Try' isn't good enough."

My smile withered. It was getting harder to pretend.

"Well, it's the best I can offer you."

His eyes snapped to me, the normally cold amber suddenly searing hot beneath the firelight, verging on the red I'd witnessed in battle.

"Dozens of my men are dead because of your mistakes. Maybe your abilities aren't good enough."

The words were hurled with perfect aim, direct and deadly sharp in their honesty. That didn't surprise me—I knew Atrius could be cruel. What did surprise me was that they hurt when they landed, bringing with them the memory of rows of red beneath the moonlight and a wave of nausea that I struggled to swallow back.

"Then maybe you should have kidnapped a better seer," I snapped, before I could stop myself. "It was never my choice to come help your band of monsters."

He went rigid.

"What a *sacrifice* you're making," he sneered. "Let's see how long it takes the Arachessen to take you away if I dump you at the gates. Days or hours? Do you think they'll leave me the pieces, or just feed them to the wolves?"

Another mark perfectly struck. Not just harsh words. No, they were accurate, yanking back the curtains on the things the Sisters often did not like to think about. The threads held us together, and the threads held our vows. A Sister who had broken her vows was in pieces. And so, that would often be her punishment for abandonment.

Sometimes I wished I could close my eyes against unwelcome images. Instead, I needed to let those memories pass through me, and then watch them go.

Sharp words lingered at the tip of my tongue, prodded loose by his. I had to take a breath to fight them back.

"I sense that you're suffering," I said. My voice was tighter than it should have been—I should have leaned into "comforting, healing presence," but instead landed somewhere closer to "frustrated schoolteacher."

"I may not have been the best healer in the Arachessen, but I studied it. They drilled it into me just like all the rest." I gave him a weak smile. "I can try."

His eyes flicked back to me. Lingered.

Then, at last, he pressed his palm to his chest. "Here."

I was confused. I didn't know what kind of injury he could be referring to. "Your . . . pectoral muscles or—?"

"It's more complicated," he snapped. "It's—" He looked away again and let out a huff. "Never mind. This is none of your concern. I'll be fine on my own."

Weaver help us all. I rubbed my temple. "If the choice is between trying to help you and suffering through your sulking for the foreseeable future, then for the sake of everyone who has to be around you, just let me try to help."

I wasn't prepared for it when, in one abrupt movement, he turned, grabbed my wrist, and pressed my hand to the center of his chest. The movement practically yanked me onto his lap, my forehead nearly bashing against his.

"Do you feel that?" he said—and there was a hint of hopelessness to his voice, something that almost sounded like a plea.

I was ready to snap at him, but the words died on my tongue.

Because I *did* feel it.

His skin was neither warm nor cool, instead exactly the same temperature as the air. His chest rose and fell heavily under my palm, and I could feel the pulse of his heartbeat—vampire hearts beat slower than humans', but his was quick right now, perhaps with anger or fear.

But what gave me pause was beneath all of that—something intertwined with his presence, his threads, into the very core of his being. It was so intense it drew a gasp from my lips. A withering decay that seemed *alive*, like it was trying to push further into him. I sensed, too, the strain of holding it off—the exhaustion.

My lips parted, but words escaped me. Our faces were so close, his breath warmed my mouth.

"So you see it now," he said.

"What is this?" I choked out. "I've never felt anything like this."

Once the initial shock faded, curiosity took over. Life as an Arachessen was not a boring one—I'd witnessed or inflicted every kind of injury, physical or magical. I'd seen curses before. Most of them felt like a cloud surrounding their target, something that slowly burrowed further. This . . . this was strange because it *started* so deep within him, like it was trying to eat its way out instead of in. It would have taken a very powerful sorcerer to plant it that deep.

I searched my mind for Obitraen history—for what I knew of the House of Blood.

"Is this your curse?" I asked. "The Bloodborn curse?"

A shiver of shame. My hand was still pressed to his chest—our bodies nearly entangled. In my surprise, I'd let my weight settle onto his knee, and his grip on my wrist had me practically curled onto his lap. Despite his impenetrable self-control, this close even he couldn't hide his truth from me.

I knew he didn't want to answer.

"No," he said. "It's something more than that."

"A curse, though. An . . . additional curse."

He was hesitant. "Yes."

"How did you—who—"

I pressed my hand harder against his chest, lost in my morbid fascination. It was probably some of the most advanced magic I'd ever seen. No, it *was*, without equal, *the* most advanced magic I'd ever seen.

"What—what *is* this?"

I couldn't help reaching deeper, pulling it apart with my magic. I was now fully in Atrius's lap, but no longer noticed the awkwardness of it.

He asked gruffly, "Can you help?"

Weaver, what kind of a question was that? I didn't even know how to answer it. My gut instinct was, *Absolutely not. No one can. Whatever this is, it's incurable.*

I chose my words more carefully.

"I—I don't know. I think it would take a very powerful healer to cure—"

He let out a growl of frustration. "Not *cure*. I'm not a fucking fool. Just—"

I had been so transfixed by this—this *thing* inside of him that I had barely been paying attention to Atrius himself. Not until now, when I felt something strangely vulnerable from within his presence. It was so innocent, so guarded, that it almost seemed wrong for me to sense it at all.

He let out a breath. "Time. I need *time*."

Desperation burrowed, carefully hidden, into all the little crevices of his soul. I swallowed a stab of sympathy—*sympathy*, for the conqueror of my home.

Weaver fucking help me.

And yet I wasn't sure if it was all an act when my voice softened in my answer.

"I'll try," I said, and beneath my palm I felt Atrius let out a long, slow exhale of relief.

I shifted awkwardly, suddenly conscious of my position on Atrius's lap. I needed to scoot farther onto him to stabilize myself—I'd lose awareness of my body when I did this, so I needed to make sure I wasn't about to just let myself slump onto the floor. I placed my other hand on his chest, next to the first.

"Don't let me fall," I muttered, and before I could think too hard about the way his hands gripped my hips, I threw myself into the threads.

I limited my awareness to him and this thing eating him alive within—reached deeper, and deeper, and deeper into the threads. Everything else fell away, reduced to distant gray fog. I was wildly exposed for someone in the presence of an enemy, but this demanded my full focus. It was so far within him that I had to push a little further with every breath, like trying to walk against the brutal winds of a storm, hands shielding my face.

With every step, I ventured further into darkness.

The curse was deep inside Atrius—near to his heart, his soul. It was a ravenous thing, devouring all the threads of his life force into a tangled, rotting mass, pulled tight like a clenched fist.

I could do nothing about the rot. That was magic far more advanced than mine. But the tangles . . .

I reached for his threads and grabbed hold of one.

An involuntary gasp, as a surge of terror cracked through me. It was raw and tender, like a child's fear. For a moment, I froze, staggering against it—against the way it reminded me of my own childlike fear belonging to a version of myself I left behind long ago.

Keep going.

I kept my hold and continued. Slowly, I worked at unraveling the threads. Some were irreparably gone, consumed by this thing inside him, but others could be extracted if I did so gently and cautiously.

With each one I freed, images flashed through my mind. Faces—so many dead faces, black blood seeping from their lips and pooling in eyeless sockets.

Cold. Muscles in legs screaming against the exertion of a long hike. You look up and the sky seems so close, closer than you ever thought it could be.

Another thread. I gently worked it free.

Nyaxia's eyes are the sky, a gradient of sunset that does not move with her face. Her beauty is staggering, breathtaking—painful, actually, like looking upon something you were never meant to see.

Pain pulsed at the back of my skull, in my magic, in my soul. My own threads were intertwined with Atrius's now, working this deep. It was harder for me to focus. Harder for me to keep my grip on the threads as I grew closer to the core of the curse.

Still, I worked.

Another thread.

You fall to your knees in the snow. You can't feel anything for the cold.

Another.

The head in your hands has his eyes still open, silvery amber, staring past you.

A sudden spike of pain, this one so intense it drowned out everything else. I froze, my body going rigid.

I lost my hold on the threads.

In a faraway world, my body fell.

I was only barely coming back to awareness when rough hands caught me, but clumsily, limbs tangling with mine. The next thing I knew, Atrius and I were on the floor together, both slumped over in the furs. I reached out and my hand instinctively found his chest again, right over his heart. His breath came heavily. The pain that radiated from his inner presence still throbbed in my own.

He was in such *unimaginable* pain. How could anyone exist like this? He had done so, I could tell, for a long time. This was old pain, etched deep into him, beyond walls he had constructed over the course of years to keep it in.

He started to push himself to his elbows and help me up, but before he could, I rolled onto my knees and pushed him back down.

"What are—" he started.

"Shh," I said, gently pushing him back to the furs, my palms against his chest again.

I reached for his threads. This time, I stroked them gently—I had worked whatever I could free from his curse, but this was something else.

No, like I'd told Atrius, I was no healer. But I knew how to sedate—though usually for far less benevolent purposes than this.

Atrius went rigid. His eyelids fluttered, though he yanked them back open every few seconds. He didn't have the strength to raise a mental wall against me, but he tried anyway.

I slid one hand down his arm, my thumb tracing a comforting circle.

"Don't fight it," I whispered.

"I don't have time—" he choked. "I have to—"

"Shh."

He was tired. So, so tired. When he gave up, he did it all at once.

His hand slid around mine, so his palm lay atop it. I could feel his eyes on me, holding on for as long as he could.

"Thank you," he rasped, finally.

And then he let himself fall.

I LAY THERE next to him for hours. The sun rose, leaving streaks of pinkish daylight seeping under the drawn velvet curtains, the castle growing quiet, and I remained.

Atrius slept heavily, but fitfully, despite the sedation. In the beginning, he stirred every hour, muscles twitching and deep lines of concern or anger or terror spasming over his forehead. In sleep, he had a much lighter hold on his presence—or perhaps my connection to him still lingered from earlier that night. I could feel that fear, just like that terrible cold, seeping out.

I didn't wake him. With every nightmare, I sent him another comforting wave of peace until he finally stilled.

With every one, I solidified the realization that this was likely the first time Atrius had slept for more than an hour or two in a very, very long time.

Eventually, the gaps between his nightmares grew longer. In the dead quiet of midday, my own exhaustion started to set in. It had taken so much of my energy to treat him. My magic and my body were spent.

I didn't remember drifting away—only that when sleep came for me, I accepted it with open arms.

CHAPTER NINETEEN

The caress on the bare skin of my shoulder almost tickled. Almost.

I was warm. Peaceful. Something gentle was stroking my skin, back and forth, in feather-light touches. My hair rustled as if by a distant breeze.

Such a nice sensation.

I had no thoughts yet, only nerve endings. Only a foreign, primal sense of safety and companionship and . . .

. . . Something else, something that whispered of things I only let myself feel alone at night.

The touch ran up my arm again.

This time I was aware enough to feel the goose bumps rise with the stroke of that fingernail. My skin shivered, the chills circling the most sensitive parts of my body—my breasts, my inner thighs—like a pleasant plea for more.

Mm. A nice dream.

I arched my back. Felt a thick hardness against my rear. Felt a firm wall of a body. A low groan reverberated through me as arms pulled me back against that warmth, and lips pressed against the shell of my ear.

I stiffened.

All at once, I was awake.

My dream was very much not a dream.

I was no longer sleepy at all. I jerked upright, sending Atrius rolling roughly onto his back, blinking blearily, obviously disoriented.

I cleared my throat. "Good—"

It wasn't really "good morning" for vampires, was it?

"—evening."

He blinked at me. The sedation would make him groggy. He seemed like he had to fight his way back from sleep.

Then a slow horror fell over him.

He practically leapt to his feet.

"I apologize," he said. "I was—I thought—"

I was grateful for the many years of training that allowed me to look utterly nonplussed, even if I didn't feel it. I held up a hand and gave him a small smile.

"It's nothing."

"I thought you were—" He cleared his throat. "I had . . . dreams."

Oh, he had dreams alright. As if I didn't notice the way his eyes lingered on how much skin I had showing now. Or the way his hands were folded over his lap.

I told myself that this was good. It was better for my task if he wanted to fuck me. The closer I could get to him, the better.

Weaver, he was actually *blushing*. That was so amusing it made it blissfully easy to ignore the little, uncomfortable truth—that it had felt good to be touched that way. I didn't want to think too much about how my own body had responded to his.

"It's fine," I said. "Really. Besides, I get the impression a good dream was probably a nice break for you."

I was being overly charming, worming my way into his affections. And yet . . . it was still the truth. The ache of his pain still throbbed under my skin, a distant echo. I knew how to withstand pain, but even I couldn't imagine living with that every day.

For a long moment, he didn't say anything. His hand wandered to his chest and pressed there, as if in wait.

"You are in a lot of pain," I said.

His eyes flicked back to me, a wordless rebuke, but I stood firm—confronting it, even if he wouldn't.

"I won't tell anyone," I said. "I know you aren't a man who likes to reveal your weaknesses."

His jaw tightened. He let his hand fall. "Good. I expect as much."

I stood. His stare lingered on my body. I was suddenly aware of exactly how much skin this stupid little scrap of silk didn't cover.

I only smiled.

"Enjoying the view?"

"Go change into real clothes," he muttered. "Before the others see you."

"Why? Are you jealous?"

Risky, to tease him like that when he was so obviously embarrassed. I wasn't sure why I did it, other than an inexplicable, compulsive need to make light of the uncomfortable sensation I couldn't shake.

He gave me a flat glare.

"No," he said. "They don't need any more distractions."

"I'm a distraction? That's very flattering. And here I thought you didn't notice."

A beat. An odd expression crossed his face. Almost a smile, maybe — albeit from someone who had never witnessed one before.

"I'm not the blind one," he said.

I was so caught off guard that a choked laugh escaped me without my permission, and maybe I imagined the glimmer of satisfaction that slipped from between the walls of Atrius's ever-guarded presence.

No, he wasn't the blind one.

I was, and yet I still was very conscious of his bare skin as he led me to the door.

"I NOTICED YOU didn't come back to your room yesterday."

It was a long, busy night. Atrius was preparing to march out again soon, leaving behind a skeleton force to keep control of Alka, which meant there was a lot to do here and not very much time to do it.

What I had done to help Atrius was outside of my usual abilities, and stretching myself like that had exhausted me thoroughly. My head ached for the rest of the day, and I was unusually clumsy because the threads around me were fuzzier and more difficult to grasp.

By the time I collapsed into the armchair in my bedchamber, I was more than ready to sleep. But at Erekkus's comment, my head snapped up. I arched my brows.

"You noticed?"

"It's my job to keep track of your comings and goings, actually." He narrowed his eyes at me as he slumped into the chair across from mine. "Was wondering all night why you're so tired."

"When Atrius told you to keep track of my comings and goings, I don't think he was telling you to keep track of that kind of coming."

Erekkus snorted, then leaned forward. "So there *was* coming."

Weaver help me. That's what I got for stupid jokes.

"No. There was not."

"I'm not sure I believe you."

"He's your friend. If you want to hear the tantalizing details of his sex life, go ask him. He'll tell you the same thing I did."

Erekkus let out a bark of a laugh. "Friend. Goddess, you think I'm Atrius's *friend*. As if Atrius has *friends*."

That snagged my interest. "You two seem to get along. He talks to you more than the others."

"Perhaps, but it's like . . ." He frowned, searching for the right word. "Do you have stray cats here?"

"Not many anymore, but I'm familiar."

One of the first animals to go in the famines. Anything in the cities with meat on its bones was captured and eaten by starving families. Domestic animals never made much of a return after that.

"Well," Erekkus said, "he's like a cat. He doesn't have friends. He just tolerates your presence."

I said, with exaggerated disbelief, "And *yours* is the one most tolerable to him?"

He scowled at me. "I could say the same about you, Sister. Apparently he managed to 'tolerate' you *all day long*."

"Nothing salacious. I swear." I raised my hands and barely managed to stop myself before I added *on the Weaver* to that statement. "He just needed my help with something."

"I'm sure he did. I imagine the dress helped. If one could call it a dress."

I scoffed. "Not like that."

"Told you," Erekkus grumbled. "Just his type. Beautiful trouble."

That was a little flattering.

I found myself wondering if whomever Atrius had been dreaming about had been beautiful trouble.

Erekkus rose with a series of grunts and groans. He made his way to the door and paused there.

"Well, whatever you did, thanks," he said. "He was in a much better mood tonight."

Then he left, closing the door behind him, and the room was silent. I crawled to my bed and fell into it. My body and soul were exhausted. I closed my eyes and waited for sleep to take me.

And then, in the secret silence, where no one could see me, I trailed my fingertips up my own arm. Just out of curiosity. Just to remember how it felt.

A meaningless touch.

Strange thing to crave.

A KNOCK JOLTED me awake.

I forced myself upright, awareness settling around me. Someone was at my door. Not Erekkus. Not Atrius, either.

I rose and opened it, revealing one of Atrius's errand boys.

"Apologies for waking you, seer," he said. "He requests you."

Nothing more needed to be said. I found Atrius near the fire again, slumped in that chair. This time, there was no talking. He gave me a mildly embarrassed look and opened his mouth, and I stopped him before the words made it out.

"It's alright," I said. "I know. You don't need to explain."

The compassion in my voice surprised me.

The progress I'd made last night had loosened the knot inside him, though the pain was bad again tonight. We didn't speak as I worked at it, freeing what little I could of his threads from the hold of the curse, then afterward ushering him into sleep. This time, I followed him there not long after.

He came for me the next night, too, and the next. And then finally, on the fifth night—the last night we would remain in Alka—I went to his door of my own accord when dawn approached.

When he opened the door and stared at me, I said, "I thought I would save us the time."

He was silent for a long moment, then nodded and let me in.

Helping him was hard work. It did not come naturally to me. It left me drained and depleted. So why was it that a small part of myself was relieved when he let me inside? Why did I find an uneasy comfort in the warmth of his soul next to mine? I had no nightmares of my own in his room. I didn't know what to make of that.

Maybe we're all just animals, I thought to myself, as I dozed off that night, my grip still loosening around Atrius's presence. *It's nice not to sleep alone.*

CHAPTER TWENTY

V asai?"

I choked on the word, like it went down my throat the wrong way. I took a sip of water to disguise it, letting my hair hide my face as I ducked my head with the movement.

The name should have meant nothing to me.

Fifteen years should have reduced it to nothing but a distant memory that I wasn't even supposed to have. Once one became an Arachessen, the time before was meaningless. That's why the Arachessen preferred to recruit very young children. Clean slates. But at ten years old, my slate had been very, very dirty, and I never forgot that. I kept trying to scrub it blank.

This involuntary reaction was a stray mark that never should have been allowed to remain.

I swallowed another gulp of water. Atrius stared at me. I couldn't rely on the darkness to hide my face.

"Yes," he said, his tone adding an unspoken, *Obviously.*

He sat cross-legged, straight-backed, on his bedroll, which was covered with open books and papers. His tent was mostly bare. We were moving fast these days. He didn't bother wasting his time or his men's setting up furniture. Actually, he seemed more comfortable this way—on the ground surrounded by a chaotic sea of plans. He barely appeared to pay attention to them, anyway. From what I saw, captains handed him papers and he glanced at them and then made some kind of deranged decision based on whatever direction the wind was blowing that night. It made the mission of trying to understand his strategy much more difficult—even from such intimate spaces as his tent.

I spent a lot of time in strangely . . . intimate situations with Atrius, now.

We had left Alka's capital weeks ago, and still, every night, I went to his tent. I helped him with his curse. I helped him sleep. I fell asleep beside him. The routine had grown rote, second nature. Now we barely spoke while we did it. When nightfall came again, we awoke without a word to each other, and I returned to my own tent. I never brought it up. I knew he didn't want to acknowledge it, and this was the time to build his trust in me.

I would wait, I decided, before I started to push. It would be better if he was the one to start talking first. For now, I knew that every night I went without asking questions he didn't want to answer, he'd trust me a little bit more.

Tonight, he'd started to talk. And now I scolded myself for having the reaction I did.

"Vasai is the only natural next target," he said. I could feel his stare—the curiosity in it. He was, I'd gathered, unexpectedly perceptive when he wanted to be. I wished he was a little less so.

He was right, of course. We'd traveled north at a quick pace. The Alkan territory was large—a substantial win for Atrius, as it provided an important corridor north, one that his army could use to travel for hundreds of miles. Over the last several weeks, Atrius had sent splinter groups of his army to secure some of the smaller cities in Alkan territory, but none of them would pose much of a threat with Aaves gone and Alka's capital under Bloodborn control.

But now, we were reaching the edges of the land that Alka could help us traverse uncontested. Atrius would need to continue farther north—continue to the Pythora King himself.

That meant crossing through Vasai.

"Of course." I took another sip of water in an attempt to clear the lump in my throat. It didn't work very well.

Vasai was only another city on a map. Nothing more.

"I expect it to be more of a challenge," Atrius went on. "I hear that its warlord is a formidable man."

"Tarkan."

I didn't mean to speak.

I rubbed my chest. It hurt fiercely. Maybe I'd eaten something too acidic at dinner. The vampires kept me well-fed, but since they didn't quite know what humans ate, it was often with hilariously mismatched collections of random food. Lately there had been a lot of oranges.

"You're familiar with him," Atrius said.

"He's a warlord. Everyone is familiar with him." I gave Atrius a weak smile that, I hoped, was charming. "This is why you're very lucky to have a local guide."

He looked unconvinced. "Hm." Then he rose. "Meet me two hours before dawn, later tonight. I need you to seer on this."

I rubbed my chest again. It burned fiercely. Those damned oranges.

"Alright," I choked out, standing.

He eyed me. "What's wrong with you?"

"Nothing."

"You're acting strange." He paused, then added, "Stranger than usual."

Weaver fucking damn him.

"Tell your men to stop feeding me buckets of oranges," I snapped, striding to the door. "It's bad for digestion. Maybe protein! Protein would be nice!"

I left him standing there and huffed my way over to my own tent before he could stop me.

Later that night, I was brought a beautifully roasted quail.

"He wants to see you after you're done eating," Erekkus told me.

The quail was delicious, but for some reason, every bite tasted like ash.

ATRIUS AND I walked in silence beyond the boundaries of camp, hiking through sandy plains until we reached a little pond. We didn't talk, save for Atrius asking, "Was the quail better than the oranges?" to which I replied, too shortly, "Yes."

My chest was still burning though. Gods help me.

He didn't say anything else after that. We drew the sigils together in silence. I caught the rabbit and did the bloodletting. I whispered prayers to the Weaver, and he leaned against a dead tree trunk and watched.

"Vasai," he said, as I settled cross-legged in the sand. "I intend to move soon. Any information is—"

"I know."

My voice was tight. I regretted my tone the minute the words left my lips. I didn't know what was wrong with me tonight. Showing all kinds of things I shouldn't.

The night was damp and foggy. The mist clung to my skin, indistinguishable from the faint sheen of sweat. The heat of the fire licked at the tip of my nose.

With eyesight, the flames would have been too bright to allow me to see the corpse of the rabbit, flesh melting, lick by lick, in the flames. But the threads allowed me to see it perfectly. The rabbit's open eyes ran down its cheeks like cracked eggs.

"Your heartbeat is fast," Atrius said.

I gritted my teeth. Suddenly, I understood acutely why he had been so short with me the first night I helped him. It was unpleasant for someone to see things about you without your permission.

"I'm focusing," I muttered.

Normally, starting a Threadwalk was like walking into a lake, step by step, allowing the water to accept you with each one.

Tonight, it was like my toes touched the water and froze.

The tension pulled tighter in my muscles. My heartbeat quickened another beat.

Weaver damn this.

I gritted my teeth. I did not walk into this Threadwalk smoothly.

I leapt into it like hurling myself off a cliff, crashing into the water below.

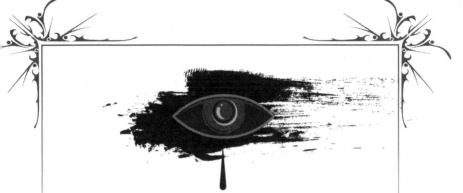

CHAPTER TWENTY-ONE

The water was blood.

I was drowning in it. I drew in a gasp, and it pooled in my lungs, burned in my chest. The impact of my body hitting the liquid hurt, the force of stone against flesh. The threads blurred past me.

I was falling.

Falling past them.

Falling into this sea of blood.

Move, Sylina. Move move move.

I thrust my hands out just in time.

Pain ripped through my palms—but I'd caught a thread, barely, against what felt like an avalanche of pressure pushing me down. It took all my strength to pull myself up as the thread ate into my palms.

My head broke through the blood. I drew in a choked gasp of air and wiped it from my face—or tried to, while my palms bled, sliced open from the razor-sharp thread.

Center yourself.

But it was difficult to do that here, with the world swirling in chaos. An overwhelming sensation of . . . *nothing*, smallness, helplessness weighed down on my shoulders. I managed to get my feet positioned on the thread, but my entire body reviled the idea of taking a single step.

Enough. My inner voice sounded so much like the Sightmother's, a single harsh command.

I walked.

Every step was labored, difficult, as if fighting against harsh wind. The mist grew thicker. The blood around my feet rose with the slow inevitability of an incoming tide. The dread in my heart rose, too, beat by beat, step by step.

Show me something, Weaver, I whispered.

Her words were distant, intangible, like a collection of sounds of the wind.

Perhaps you do not wish to see.

I do, I insisted.

The Weaver did not believe me. I did not believe myself.

But the mist thinned, revealing silhouettes of strange, broken shapes; first as distant flat gray, and then—

Bodies.

All of them were bodies. Bodies twisted and broken beyond recognition. Bodies impaled on stakes or smashed between ruined buildings. Bodies burnt like the rabbit I had sacrificed for my Threadwalk, eyes running, skin peeled.

I wavered on the thread, nearly falling. The fear beat in my veins like a drum.

Something nudged my foot. My eyes—I had eyes here, I had never known anything else—fell to my feet. They were small, bare, dirty. My sister lay there, blue eyes staring at me wide and unseeing through tendrils of blond hair, clutching at her stomach, blood bubbling between her fingers.

It's all going to be alright, she whispered.

I snapped my head up.

Not my sister. Just some person another version of me knew a long time ago.

I need the future, I told the Weaver—told myself. *Not the past.*

The threads intersect, the voice whispered, a teasing caress at the crest of my ear. *This is the nature of life.*

No. I didn't accept that. I was a daughter of only the Weaver. I was a Sister of only the Arachessen. I had a task to complete.

I kept walking, chin up.

Show me more.

The silhouettes around me, limp like abandoned puppets, sprang back to life, floundering as if traveling backward in time. Waves of vampire warriors surrounded me, moving in skips and lurches, fragments of many different moments in time.

The battle was vicious. The vampires were more skilled, obvious even in these shattered flashes—but the Vasaians were numerous, throwing themselves at their aggressors like lemmings over a cliff.

The blood around my ankles rose and rose. More red than black.

My heart pounded rapidly. I kept walking, step by steady step, but at this point, I wasn't choosing to, nor could I have stopped myself.

Death was everywhere.

The mist rolled in and out. A violent crack of silent lightning, and it all went dark.

When the light returned, it revealed the same broken bodies as before. Broken bodies. Broken homes. Broken souls.

Please, a woman begged, crawling over the wreckage, dead-eyed. Her palms were raw and bloody as she stretched them toward me, but she didn't react when the wounds were touched. She was lost in a Pythoraseed haze. *Please,* she begged.

No, I said. *No. I can't. I don't—*

Someone was speaking at the same time as me, our voices layering over each other. The little girl was small and dirty, with messy dark waves.

Someone grabbed her wrist and pulled her forward.

Familiarity clenched in my chest, a sudden reprieve from the fear that choked me.

I knew that figure. The two of them walked ahead of me. The boy was only a handful of years older than the girl, perhaps thirteen to her nine. He was skinny and lanky with a head of messy copper-chestnut hair.

Don't look at them, he told the girl.

Alright, I thought, and didn't.

I just walked. I was still very afraid. But I felt a little less so now, following him.

Distantly, someone was calling me, but I couldn't make out the words.

Just look straight ahead, the boy said to the little girl. *Alright? Just look straight ahead and don't look anywhere else unless I tell you.*

Alright, I thought. *I can do that.*

I kept walking. I kept looking straight ahead.

Suddenly, the girl stopped short. She turned around and stared right at me. Her eyes were bright blue. Striking, actually, surrounded by her dark hair and all the blood and dirt on her face.

The boy stopped, too, glancing at the girl, confused.

Then he turned around.

I let out a horrible choking sound—a scream that didn't have enough air.

Suddenly the boy was not a boy. Suddenly he was an adult, still lanky, still skinny, still with the same blue eyes and messy hair.

His throat was open, his abdomen torn apart, revealing glimpses of pulsing gore.

His eyes widened.

Vivi, he choked. His voice was warped, drowning with blood. He reached out. Stumbled toward me.

I couldn't move. Fear paralyzed me. I couldn't look away. Couldn't look anywhere but straight ahead, just like he had told me.

Vivi! he begged again, coming closer.

I tried to move, but threads tangled around my ankles—so many threads, past and present and future, intertwined and tightening and—

He grabbed me—

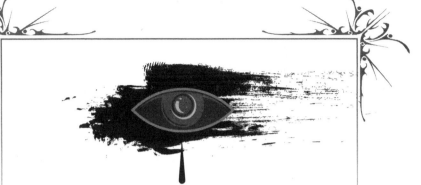

CHAPTER TWENTY-TWO

I couldn't breathe. My lungs frantically tried to pull in air and failed. I was drowning in blood. I was dying. I was—

"Sylina."

The voice was a blade, cutting through my panic.

Someone was holding onto my shoulders, gripping me tight. I wasn't falling.

I wasn't falling.

I couldn't see. The threads were chaotic, my grip on them slippery. Pulling the world into focus seemed impossible.

"Drink," the voice commanded, shoving a canteen into my bloody hands. "Now."

Atrius.

The name was the first tangible thing that came to me.

I did as he told me, taking a gulp of water. I immediately choked on it, then had to thrust the canteen back to him as I flung myself to my hands and knees and retched into the sand as he held my hair back.

When I was done, he pulled me upright again.

"More," he said, pushing the canteen back into my grasp.

I did. This time I didn't choke. I took one gulp, then another, and then I was throwing my head back and drinking the whole thing while water ran down my chin.

By the time I finished, the world had fallen back into place, though my heart still felt like it was about to fracture my ribs.

Atrius still held onto my shoulders, watching me with a thorough, assessing gaze. I nearly jumped when his hands fell to mine, gently closing around them—noting the wounds.

"You're shaking," he said.

I didn't want him to feel that. I extracted my hands from his grip and folded them in my lap.

"I'm fine."

He stared at me. I wondered if he was waiting for me to scold him for pulling me out of a Threadwalk—*again*. I should have. It was dangerous.

But I couldn't bring myself to. Not when I was secretly grateful he had done it.

"What did you see?" he asked. His voice was low and heavy, like he knew the significance of what he was asking.

The truth still pulsed through my veins, too powerful to acknowledge. I couldn't give him all of that. Too vulnerable. Too close to parts of myself that were supposed to be gone.

"It's going to be bloody." I stood and immediately regretted it. I just wanted to put more space between Atrius and me, so he would stop looking at me that way.

I leaned against a broken tree trunk more heavily than I hoped was visible.

"There will be steep losses if you attack Vasai," I went on. "Lots of blood will be spilled."

"Whose blood?" he asked. "My soldiers' blood?"

This question, reasonable as it was, speared me with a sudden bolt of rage.

"Bloody for everyone," I snapped.

"So you saw our defeat."

My jaw clenched.

I couldn't risk lying to Atrius again. If it was my own decision, I might take the risk. But the Sightmother had given me a direct command. I was not to sabotage him further.

Yet I couldn't bring myself to answer his question.

The nonanswer, it seemed, was answer enough. Atrius exhaled. "I see," he said.

He sounded a little relieved, and in this moment, I utterly despised him for that.

"The Pythora King's warlords are not above using civilians as their shields," I said. "You saw that in Alka."

His eyes hardened. A faint echo of disgust shivered through his presence.

"I did."

"You thought Aaves was bad? Aaves was a lazy nobody who stumbled onto his throne through corrupt incompetence. Tarkan is far, far worse."

Atrius's eyes narrowed. "You believe he needs to be treated as more of a threat."

He sounded skeptical. Atrius, I had learned, was somewhat arrogant when it came to the skill of his military force.

I knew, logically, I couldn't fault him for looking at all of this through that lens. Yet I resented him for it.

Atrius rose too, pacing along the edge of the sigils in the sand, scattering the impeccably drawn lines. "He has a large army," he said, as if to himself. "Larger than most of the warlords. But from what I've seen, they're unskilled. My warriors could handle them easily."

My jaw tightened. I whirled around.

"Who do you think makes up Tarkan's famous *army*?" I spat the word like it was a mockery, because it was. "It's not an army. It's a slave pit. You're right, they're unskilled. They're unskilled because a third of them are children."

I was showing too much. Letting my mask slip. That was a mistake.

I wasn't sure what I wanted from Atrius, but what I got was . . . nothing. Just a flat stare.

Weaver help me. What did I expect? I knew what kind of atrocities went on in Obitraes. Such a thing probably didn't seem so egregious to him.

I drew in a breath and let it out, collecting myself.

"You asked me to Threadwalk, and I did," I said. "And what I saw is that it is a bad idea to attack Vasai with pure brute force. That's all I can tell you."

"Is it?"

Atrius approached me, one measured step after another.

"Yes," I said.

"Did your vision show," he said, slowly, as if every word was its own command, "that we wouldn't win?"

He knew the answer, of course. Knew why I couldn't bring myself to say it.

I bit my cheek for a long moment. Too long.

"We *would* win." He answered his own question. "The bloodshed would be his."

He sounded downright smug about it.

My fingernails cut half-moon marks in my palms. I wouldn't beg a vampire for anything. Let alone a conqueror. I should let it go. Let him act. Let him win. Follow my orders, and earn his loyalty.

I just—*couldn't.*

"You don't want to rule over a dead kingdom," I said. "I respect you for that."

I paused, reconsidering. What did my respect mean to him?

"*Your soldiers* respect you for that," I corrected. "I've seen that since the moment I arrived here. You can win by your strength alone. But, please, it's—"

I bit my tongue. *Please.* Begging.

"It isn't the wise way," I said, at last.

He didn't speak. I resisted the urge to shift beneath his stare, so steady it felt like he was peeling back layers of my skin.

"I intend to avoid meaningless bloodshed, but I don't know what gave you the impression that I came here to avoid all of it," he said finally. "I'm here to win. To take what your king doesn't deserve. He took it by force, just as centuries of conquerors have before him. We evolve, but war is the same. It isn't up to me to redefine that."

I knew this. Knew it was a downright laughable idea that a Blood-born conqueror, of all people, would be the one to take some kind of moral high ground.

And yet . . . why did some part of me think he would?

Why did some part of me think it *would* matter to him?

I didn't say anything, letting the silence stretch on—letting Atrius fall into his obvious contemplation. After a long moment, a scowl flitted over his mouth, as if in reaction to a silent argument he'd been having with me in his head.

"You actually think I care at all about the fates of some useless human ingrates?" he spat.

It was a challenge.

And . . . a real question.

"I do," I said, and to my shock, it was the truth. "I don't know why. But I think, maybe, you do."

He scoffed. Paced. Turned. And then, finally, turned back to me.

"Suppose I listen to your foolish advice, for some ridiculous reason I still can't make sense of. What alternative is there? How do you expect me to take down a city-state with no army?"

It was, I had to admit, a very valid question.

I considered this. Then I straightened. Suddenly, I no longer felt unsteady on my feet.

"You might recall," I said, "that I was an assassin for fifteen years."

Atrius stared blankly at me. Seconds passed.

Then the bastard burst into laughter.

CHAPTER TWENTY-THREE

The Arachessen taught that the desire for vengeance existed only in the weak. There was no such thing as justice—not mortal justice, anyway, only that of the gods and the Weaver's threads of fate. Something far too complex for us to understand. A desire to seek it was not only pitiful, but stupid—one who truly trusted the Weaver knew that a human assessment of right and wrong was flawed and inconsequential.

I knew these teachings well. I recited them to the students I taught. In general, I believed them.

But maybe I did still succumb to those marks on my soul the Arachessen had not been able to wash away, sometimes. Because the thought of killing Tarkan—the thought of killing him with my own hands—was downright intoxicating. I did not acknowledge that perhaps I had some reasons for doing this beyond the desire to avoid bloodshed in Vasai.

Then again, the more I talked, the more I genuinely believed it was the better of the two courses.

Yes, Tarkan had a large army, but it was scattered and poorly trained. The vast majority of his soldiers were only loyal because of their crippling addictions to a steady stream of Pythoraseed—a stream controlled by Tarkan alone. He was a distrustful man. He promoted few, and truly trusted fewer. He had clung ruthlessly to his own power, but as a result, he created a machine with a single, critical weakness: him.

If Tarkan himself were dead, his army would be useless. It didn't matter how big it was then.

We didn't have to slaughter his army. We only had to kill him.

Atrius listened as I told him all of this, his expression blank.

"And you intend to do that yourself," he had said, not bothering to hide his skepticism.

"Do you know how many assassinations I carried out as a member of the Arachessen?" I paused at that—I actually wasn't sure of the number. I settled on, "Many. And most of them were very powerful."

Though none were Tarkan—even if, every assignment, I hoped they would be. I knew better than to suggest him as a target, even though he was important to the Pythora King's reign, which made him a perfectly viable one. The Sightmother would have her suspicions about why I wanted him. I wasn't willing to risk damaging her opinion of me.

"I'd be a fool if I let my only seer run into the enemy's grip alone," Atrius said. "Someone else will do it."

I arched my brows. "Who among your warriors can be an assassin? They aren't exactly subtle."

"I'll do it myself."

I laughed before I could stop myself, which made Atrius's scowl deepen.

"I've killed things you've only dreamed of," he said.

My laugh faded. I had no doubt that was true.

I've slaughtered demigods, he'd snarled at Aaves.

Demigods. I wanted that story sometime.

"I've seen you fight," I said. "You're good. But you aren't subtle, either. One glance at you and everyone will know you're a threat."

That was a light way of putting it. Atrius outright reeked of "predator."

"And you?" he said coldly, gesturing to me—gesturing, I knew, to my blindfold. "You're better at being subtle?"

I smiled. "Perhaps my appearance is unusual. But don't worry about me. I know how to kill quietly."

At that, a flicker of a smirk. He leaned closer, and to my shock, his fingertips brushed the soft underside of my chin.

"Hm," he said. "To think I let such a dangerous creature sleep beside me every night."

I froze momentarily, caught off guard. Was he teasing me? Was it a joke? Atrius either had no sense of humor or the strangest one I'd ever encountered—which was saying something, coming from the Arachessen.

Or was he flirting with me? That thought seemed even more incomprehensible than the joke.

But, I reminded myself, it was good for my mission if he wanted me. Another avenue to his trust.

If I were a better Arachessen, I would have seized the moment. Instead, I awkwardly pulled away, startled by the strange double beat in my chest but showing him no sign of it.

"Nor should you forget it," I said, which earned another one of those peculiar almost-smiles.

He leaned back in his chair, crossing his arms.

"Fine," he said. "Tell me, formidable assassin, how this plan of yours would work."

TARKAN WAS AN eccentric individual—a Pythora broker who had managed to climb the ranks of the Pythora King's regime until he became one of his most trusted and most vicious mentees. He had carefully cultivated an image of himself as a god-chosen oracle. It was, of course, all bullshit—the peculiarities that he claimed were ancient customs were actually grossly twisted or misinterpreted, and most were complete fabrications based on nothing but his power-hungry whims.

One of them was that he liked the faces of his concubines, both men and women, covered as they entered his palace—to feel as if he owned their very visages, to be looked upon by no one but him and those he chose to share them with.

Revolting.

But useful, given my appearance.

Before leaving for Vasai, I veiled myself. My clothing was the weakest part of my act—Atrius had sent back to Alka for more of the clothing from Aaves's prostitutes, and while those dresses were certainly fine, they were . . . of a very different style than what Tarkan liked his to wear.

I was not especially crafty, but I was resourceful. I'd managed to assemble something halfway appropriate from one of the long gowns and a series of silk and chiffon scarves that I arranged over it in sweeping drapes—including one over my head and face.

When Atrius saw me in this, he outright snorted. Like an amused horse.

"What?" I'd said. "Not appealing to you?"

"Humans are so strange," he muttered.

I couldn't bring myself to argue with that.

But I hoped that Tarkan or those of his inner circle wouldn't laugh, too, when they saw me. It had been years since I'd seen one of Tarkan's concubines in person. My attempt at recreation might not be accurate—or be easily exposed as a disguise. I knew if I had to, I could slip away and kill my way through the castle—though I'd prefer not to have to.

Once my costume was intact, I took my path into the city. The route was just as I remembered it: a little gap in the walls that led to the dense streets of the inner city, not far from the steps of the Thorn Palace.

Right away, the sounds and smells of Vasai assaulted me. I was grateful I could let my little stumble be a part of my role—the concubines usually could not see more than vague shapes through their shrouds, so they often clung to the arm of a handler as they moved through the city. I was alone, and sagged against a dirty brick wall instead.

A sudden, intense wave of anger pulsed through me—anger with myself and at my past. Fifteen years of training, fifteen years of meticulous study and devotion. I was just as good as my Sisters, just as hardworking, just as committed.

And yet.

One whiff of that salty, sweat-thick air, one moment of those city sounds that had not changed in twenty years, and the past yanked me back to its side as if by a collar around my throat: *You thought you escaped, but you will always be mine. Look at all these marks you cannot wash away.*

Places had souls. The threads that connected us to locations were just as alive as those that ran through living beings. And the soul of Vasai was rotten. Sick and tangled and festering with the broken dreams of the people who lived here.

It was every bit as bad as it had been all those years ago. For every shouting voice of a marketplace vendor or jovial joke of a drunken gambler, there was a slurred moan from someone slowly dying of Pythoraseed use—or withdrawal. For every scent of a food stall or blacksmith, there was the sour-sweet, nostril-scalding aroma of decaying Pythora burned and re-burned too many times by desperate addicts.

This entire place smelled like death. Like a corpse—a fresh one, one that still held some tragic trace of the life ebbing away.

Those memories did not belong to Sylina, I reminded myself. That rot did not belong to me. I could leave it on the skin of another little girl I left behind a long time ago.

I swallowed the bile rising in my throat, straightened my back, and continued through the city, stumbling across the congested cobblestones.

The headache set in fast this time—crowded places like this would always do it, but this one got to me quicker than usual. I remained close to the walls, leaning against them like some poorsighted woman too wrapped in silks to see a thing, mumbling timid apologies to those I tripped over.

It didn't take long to make it to the Thorn Palace. Tarkan had coined the name when he took over Vasai. Some twenty years ago, it had been called the Mansion of Roses. I was far too young to remember what it had looked like then, but I could imagine it—probably gleaming and polished. Then Tarkan came and renamed it as a mockery of the regime that came before his—a reference to the many spears, swords, and bolts that jutted from the outer walls as a result of the brutal on-slaught that had earned him his throne. He didn't take the weapons down after the exchange of power. Instead, he added to them, turning a symbol of nauseatingly elegant beauty into a grotesque monument to death. Sometimes, a notable criminal's execution would entail hanging them on one of the palace's "thorns" until the birds picked the carcass clean.

Places had souls. The Thorn Palace's was ugly and covered in death. A place where thousands of threads were severed.

The stairs to the entrance of the palace were poorly maintained marble, littered at the bottom with trash and limp, barely conscious bodies. I staggered up the stairs slowly, step by step. I could sense the awareness of the guards at the top, two men who watched me with vague, amused curiosity and made no move to help.

"Your business?" one of the guards grunted, once I finally reached the top.

I panted behind my veil and smoothed my skirts around me—the act of a disgruntled concubine who was frustrated and trying not to show it.

"Is it not obvious?" I crooned, motioning to myself.

"Where is your handler?"

"He was ill. Had terrible runs." I twisted my lip in disgust and let them hear it in my voice. "Nothing fit for the presence of his excellency, of course, but he summoned me today and it was important to me to be here as he commanded."

The guards stared at me for too long. One of them chewed on some Pythora leaves he seemed like he had been working on for quite some time. They were high out of their minds, of course, though they held it far better than the townspeople crumpled at the base of the stairs did.

Tarkan's men were unskilled and replaceable. The ones I really had to worry about would be farther into the castle, guarding Tarkan himself. But these two would be easy to fool. I doubted either of them had held this post for longer than a few months.

They exchanged a glance.

"Fine," the chewing one grunted. "I'll take you in."

He extended his arm to me, and I took it as if I was very grateful to finally have someone who could actually see to lead me around.

The guard escorted me into the palace. It was warm and stuffy inside, the air damp. Someone desperately needed to open some windows. Still, it was far cleaner than Aaves's pit of depravity—Tarkan, at least, had a more sophisticated idea of power than Aaves's indiscriminate obsession with furs, silks, and drugs. Tarkan, like the Pythora King himself, controlled his followers with their addictions, but never partook himself. Smart men knew better.

There were a lot of people on the first floor of the palace, mostly the chosen few of Tarkan's followers who were allowed to enter. Primarily men. A few women. Many were teenagers or younger, hands at crude weapons hung by their hips that they seemed overly eager to use. They'd probably be dead the day they did.

I didn't make small talk with the guard as he led me up the grand staircase, and he didn't try. Instead, I stretched out my awareness, feeling the threads around me.

Only clusters of presences down here—blurry, out of focus, their own awareness dulled by the drugs. I reached up, to the floor above. A few more of those types, faceless guards with unsharp minds, but not many.

I stretched further as we reached the top of the stairs. It was far to sense, most auras distant and difficult to read. But Tarkan's . . . he was easy. A shard of glass in a pile of feathers.

The guard led me down the hall, the presences of the others growing more distant. Tarkan kept his inner circle small—he'd allow his followers to the ground floor, but few of them any higher. Even the grand staircase wouldn't lead up directly to his suite. Hence why I was being taken down a deserted hallway, to a smaller stairwell. A set of windows ahead, at the end of the hall, overlooked Vasai's sparse eastern slums and the rocky plains beyond them, all bathed in the silver light of the moon.

The guard started to turn the corner to lead me up the stairwell.

I made my move.

He was easy to kill. Yes, he was bigger than me, but he wasn't expecting to fight right now—least of all against a concubine, and least of all in the halls of his own master's palace. The downside of this ridiculous outfit was that it made it hard to move. The upside was that it provided lots of places to hide a blade.

My dagger was out and across his throat in seconds. My other hand clamped over his mouth before he could let out his gurgling grunt of shock. I positioned myself to break his fall before his body hit the ground.

There was a lot of blood. I'd intentionally chosen red for my dress. By the time anyone noticed, it wouldn't matter.

I dragged the body—still twitching—into a nearby room and shut the door behind him. Then I went to the window and unlatched it.

A welcome gust of cool air hit my face, drying the sweat on my cheeks and flecks of blood on my veil. I lifted my chin to enjoy it for a moment, while a large figure hoisted himself up to the windowsill.

I grabbed Atrius's hand and helped him in. He hit the ground with impressive silence. Erekkus was right. He was like a cat.

He'd climbed up hundreds of feet. Clung there for Weaver knew how long, and without being spotted.

I was glad my face couldn't show it, but I was impressed he'd pulled it off.

He rolled his shoulders and smoothed his hair, which was messy and windswept.

"Do you know how hard it was to follow you?" he muttered.

"You didn't have to come."

He let out a grunt that somehow managed to say, *I did have to come, and you're insulting both of our intelligence by saying otherwise.*

It was almost impressive how much he could communicate with those things.

I would never admit this aloud—I didn't even want to admit it to myself—but a small part of me admired the fact that Atrius had insisted on doing this personally. If *I* was considered too important to risk, I'd told him, what did that make him?

But Atrius was firm. He would go. That was that.

No one could say he didn't get his hands dirty. I couldn't imagine Tarkan, even during the height of the wars, clinging to the side of a building by himself for hours on end.

"We don't have much time," I whispered, then pointed to the stairwell. Atrius glanced at the pool of blood slowly spreading from behind the door I'd stuffed the guard into and nodded.

The minute I'd killed, the hourglass had turned. Now the real game started.

We crept up the staircase, me leading with Atrius a step behind. I kept my awareness attuned to our immediate surroundings, but also peered ahead, to those on the floor above. Tarkan was easy to spot, but it was more difficult to keep track of the exact locations of the others.

We emerged in a narrow hallway. This was clearly a back path, originally intended for servants and others too unfit to be seen by nobility. But paranoia drives one to inventive measures. Tarkan had decided that this was the only way his followers would be able to reach him.

The first hall was empty. I could sense Tarkan's general proximity, but it was harder for me to understand the specifics of the castle layout. People and nature were easy, their threads bright and clear. Architecture . . . that was more difficult.

I paused at the juncture of two hallways, reaching—

Atrius's sword was already out, body coiled. Something came over his presence when he was getting ready to kill—a certain determined ruthlessness, a singular focus, like he was preparing to do what he had been born for. "Which way is he?"

"That way, I think." I motioned, still preoccupied with the threads. "But—"

The answer was more than enough for Atrius. He started to move.

A moment too late, I felt them.

I grabbed his arm and wrenched him back with all my strength.

Atrius realized what I had a split-second later. Perhaps he smelled them—perhaps his superior vampire hearing helped. One moment I was grabbing him, and the next, I was pressed between the wall and him as he flattened his body over mine into a shallow enclave.

Seconds later, the voices drifted down the hallway.

One of Atrius's hands pressed to the wall above my shoulder. The other held his sword, while I gripped his wrist—both of us battling for that arm. Every muscle of Atrius's body was tight, ready to strike.

All that taut energy surrounded me, raw power contained only by my grasp.

His breath rustled the silk fabric of my veil.

I shook my head slowly. I felt his eyes burrowing through that silk, like hands pulling back layers.

The guards around the corner, oblivious, wandered closer.

"—doesn't have a chance against him," one of them was saying. "Have you seen him fight? Dunno why he's trying."

The other one let out a slurred scoff. "It's not just about strength, idiot. He's *scrappy*. You've never seen 'im in action."

"I've seen enough not to throw my money away. You just wish it was you in front of all those people."

Tournaments. Sporting events. Mindless small talk.

I decided not to remember that I knew someone who used to talk about sports that way once.

Atrius's eyes slipped to me. Then to the hallway, where the voices grew closer. To me again.

We couldn't speak. But I knew what he was saying.

My fingers tightened around his wrist. I shook my head.

No. Wait.

A slight narrowing of his eyes.

Another shake of my head, harder this time.

No.

The boys wandered closer. They were high, or drunk, or both. One of them kept laughing at his own jokes.

This close, I could feel all Atrius's strength, the warmth of his body enveloping me. It was distracting—especially because I kept thinking about what that body was capable of doing to those boys around the corner. His muscles still trembled, straining against my hold, but he didn't pull away.

His chin dipped. The tips of our noses touched through the veil, and despite the fabric, I still felt the urge to twitch back at the touch. Not that there was anywhere to go.

He mouthed, *Why?*

No sound. But I saw the word on his lips. Weaver, I felt it on my own.

I just shook my head again.

What I hoped he'd understand: *If you go out there and kill those boys now, then it starts the battle early. You'd better be ready to fight through the rest of them with me.*

We'd have to do that later, of course—and I didn't know what to make of my oddly strong certainty that however many there were, he and I alone could take them. But I hoped to put it off as long as I could.

In the hallway, the voices stalled. The boys had moved on to discussing who they were betting on for the next horse race.

Atrius stared at me, brows low over his silver-and-gold eyes. Then his fingertip rose and flicked the edge of the veil, making the silken fabric ripple.

And he mouthed, *I hate this thing.*

Beneath the silk, my lips thinned. Then, despite myself, curled into a smile.

I could've sworn that maybe the twitch of Atrius's lips was almost a smile, too.

"What time is it?" one of the boys asked.

A pause, then the other muttered, "Shit. We're late."

The footsteps, quicker this time, moved back down the hall. Away from us.

I cocked my head in a way that I hoped said to Atrius, *See? I was right.*

He narrowed his eyes in a way that said, *This time.*

I finally released his wrist. My grip had been so tight that my knuckles were sore. He glanced down at his arm as the voices finally disappeared around the far corner, raising his brows at the red marks.

I shrugged and motioned down the hall—a wide-open passage for us now, bringing us that much closer to Tarkan. We moved unobstructed through one hall, and then another. At last, I peered around the next corner to find a set of majestic double doors, two guards standing before them.

I quickly ducked back behind the corner and nodded to Atrius.

He leaned close, so close I could hear him while he was barely speaking.

"How many?" he murmured, lips brushing my ear.

I couldn't count. Not exactly. "Many."

His mouth curled. "Too many?"

Ah. This was our game now.

Despite myself, I found myself returning the smirk. I shook my head.

"No," I whispered.

This, once again, was the answer Atrius was looking for.

He raised his hood, covering his horns and his hair, casting a harsh shadow over his face. I took his arm, donned my best teetering stumble once again, and the two of us emerged around the corner.

We stopped before the double doors and the guards. I inclined my head. Atrius kept his tipped down, hiding his face beneath the hood.

"I am here at his behest," I said.

There was no need to use names or titles. There was only one "him."

Hidden beneath my scarves, my hand crept to my dagger.

The guards glanced at each other. Then at each of us—skeptical when they looked at me, and even more so at Atrius.

"We had no word of anyone coming today," the guard said. "Let alone at this time of night."

I had been able to fool the guards at the front door. Those were expendable. These, though, were Tarkan's personal guards. Carefully chosen. Well-trained.

"Are you sure?" I said, letting my uncertain pout slip into my voice. "I—I'm very late, but I don't want to disappoint him. He wanted me here *tonight*."

The guards exchanged another glance—

And then blood painted the space between us.

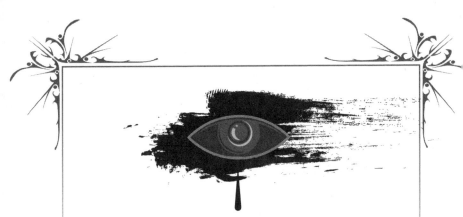

CHAPTER TWENTY-FOUR

A trius and I moved the moment the guards' eyes left us. He took the one on the left, stabbing him through with his sword and snapping his body aside with a flick of his blood magic. I took the one on the right, driving my dagger through his throat. We tossed the bodies to either side of the doors like sacks of flour.

Within the chambers, commotion stirred immediately. The threads trembled, like the reverberations after a sudden discordant strum of an instrument, as those inside responded.

We didn't give them time to prepare.

We burst through the doors. Tarkan's wing was large, much more an apartment than a bedchamber. He kept his most trusted warriors close, even in the dead of night, though apparently still did not respect them enough to give them beds to sleep on—most of the men who jerked awake from their drug-laden sleep now had been sprawled out on sofas and armchairs, and a few even on the fur rug. I wondered if Tarkan had increased the number of people within his chambers in light of Atrius's movements across Glaea.

Several of the guards inside had been awake, stationed to watch for an attack. They were ready.

But so were we.

We dismantled them. Then continued to carve our way through

the men who threw themselves at us. We naturally fell into position, back-to-back, covering the areas that the other couldn't reach. I stretched threads between our opponents and slipped between them, disappearing and reappearing at their throats before they had time to register the movement.

So quickly—so disconcertingly easily—Atrius and I fell into a rhythm. Smoother, even, than what we had done in Alka. I struck, stunned, maimed. He finished.

Through the carnage, as we cut through the first wave, Atrius rasped at me, "Where?"

Where is Tarkan?

That was the only thought in my mind, too. I could feel him there, like a splinter wedged into my fingertip.

I pointed my blade to the bedchamber. "There."

There were other guards there, too—just a few. I sensed them rushing into Tarkan's bedchamber from the opposite wing of the apartment. Arming him, perhaps, or maybe attempting to help him escape.

They wouldn't get the chance for that.

The two of us stepped over the freshest bodies toward the bed-chamber door.

But Tarkan wasn't Aaves. He wouldn't meet his death cowering at the foot of his bed. Tarkan had gotten where he was today because he was a warrior.

The door swung open.

After so many years without eyesight, one starts to forget what it feels like to see something in that form. Yet there were some images that remained seared into my mind as I had once seen them—some that I didn't want to remember, and some that I wished I could remember more. I was not supposed to hold any of those memories, whether in love or hatred. I was supposed to wipe them all away like the Arachessen taught me.

But the memory of Tarkan's face remained with me, another mark that still stubbornly remained on my slate.

I experienced him differently now, of course. But the image of him as I'd seen him nearly twenty years ago still struck me when he opened that door. He was a tall man, hair neat and slicked back—even in sleep, apparently—and beard well-groomed. I could sense the age in him now, the way it hollowed his cheeks and weighed down the fragile skin around his dark eyes. And yet, so much was the same. The hard angles to his appearance, brutal and selfish. The way he looked at the world like it belonged to him.

Strange, how the past didn't feel so strong until all at once it surrounded you again, like the tides swallowing the tunnels of Alka.

Tarkan didn't say a word to us. He just nodded, and the two guards with him lunged at us.

Atrius disposed of the first one easily. The second came at me. He was wielding an axe—the brutal tool of someone trained by a warlord, but a fine one, perhaps given to him by Tarkan himself. He was a decent fighter, but nothing special. The frenetic choppiness to his movements, too-quick and too-abrupt, hinted that he was under the influence of Pythoraseed—good quality stuff, if it helped him move faster rather than slowing him down.

Maybe that was why I didn't recognize him at first.

Not until I blocked one of his strikes, and the proximity of him sparked something in the back of my mind, something I just couldn't place—

I hesitated too long. He swung.

Across the room, Tarkan lunged, wielding a jewel-encrusted saber. Atrius's hood had fallen back. The two of them faced each other down with the vicious focus of wolves preparing to tear each other apart.

The edge of my opponent's axe caught my veil as I pulled away, tearing it partially from my face. Frustrated by the fluttering fabric, I ripped it away, and swung back to counter—

But my attacker's eyes went wide. His axe clattered to the ground. His shock rippled all the threads in the room.

"Vivi?" he breathed.

Naro.

All at once, the familiarity hit me. The sound of his voice brought it back.

At the last second, I diverted my strike. I nicked his ear and sent myself stumbling against the sofa.

I whirled around.

The blood drained from my face. Weaver, it felt like it drained from my entire body. My hands were numb. I needed to fight, but couldn't make myself move.

His presence was so different than it had been then. Blurry with years of drug use, older, harder, and scarred.

And yet—how could I not have recognized him?

How could I not have recognized my *brother*?

You have no brother, the Sightmother reminded me. *Sylina has no brother.*

"Vivi," he breathed. "It's you—even with that thing on your face, I—"

He staggered toward me, and I pulled back.

Hurt reverberated through his presence. Confusion.

He lurched forward again, and I took another step away.

"What the fuck are you doing here?" he said.

I couldn't think.

I couldn't think about any of this now—

Behind me, Atrius let out a wordless hiss of pain as Tarkan managed to get a shot in, wounding his shoulder. He recoiled, then turned back to his assailant, crimson murder in his eyes.

Tarkan.

I was here for Tarkan. Tarkan was the goal.

That was all that mattered now.

I let that little ball of fire in my stomach grow, let it burn away my confusion and fuel my focus.

I drew a thread between Tarkan and I and stepped into it easily, reappearing behind him.

But he was fast. He'd seen his guards fall to my Arachessen tricks. As soon as I reappeared, he flung his elbow back.

Pain stabbed through my ribs.

I wavered, but held my stance.

He whirled to me just as I swung my sword.

When I was a child, I thought Tarkan stood twenty feet tall. He seemed that way from the tops of his parade carts, from the statues of him hoisted in the town squares.

He was not twenty feet tall. He was six feet, maybe, if that. And yet when he loomed over me, for a moment, I felt that way again. Like he could crush me.

But I wasn't a child anymore. I wasn't powerless.

I let out a roar and blocked his strike before he could land it. Countered before he could move. I opened a gash in his side, earning a curse and a snarl. To his credit, he didn't waste his breath on taunts.

He lunged at me, then fell abruptly backward, like a puppet yanked by its strings. Beads of crimson hung suspended in the air. His threads warped, as if manipulated by an outside force.

Atrius.

The two of them tangled again. Tarkan was off-balance, startled. The next strike had him reeling.

Atrius could have finished him then. I saw the opening. I knew he did, too.

But yet, Atrius held him for a moment. Shot me a glance over Tarkan's shoulder.

And he nodded at me.

The understanding snapped into place. He was presenting Tarkan to me. He was *giving* me this. I didn't know why. I didn't have time to question it.

I swung, aiming right for Tarkan's exposed back—

—And someone knocked me away.

My back struck the wood of the sofa, forcing the breath from my lungs, pain shooting through my spine.

Naro pinned me down, his chestnut hair falling over his face.

I snarled, "Get off me!"

"I can't." He shook his head, his face hardening, despite the wrinkle of confusion over his brow. "You can't. You—"

I do not have a brother.

Sylina does not have a brother.

I told myself this before whacking Naro across the face with the butt of my sword, sending him sprawling off the couch.

I leapt to my feet. Atrius had Tarkan against the wall now. It was the end.

Tarkan's face was a mask of hatred—his presence vibrated with it. He knew death was coming for him.

"Fine," he snarled. "See how my city—"

But Atrius was not in the business of allowing final words to those who didn't deserve them.

He now had Naro's discarded axe in his free hand. With a single clean strike, he carved it straight through Tarkan's throat. Blood spewed, painting graceful arcs across Atrius's face, the carpet, the furniture. Some of it landed on me.

I swallowed a thick wave of envy.

Naro let out a ragged, wordless cry, charging for Atrius. I grabbed him and held him back, but he slipped my grip.

Atrius turned. His face was cold and unmoving.

He raised the axe as my brother—my stupid, foolish brother—ran straight for him.

You do not have a brother, a voice reminded me.

And yet, I screamed, *"No!"*

I threw myself in front of Naro. Atrius barely stopped himself before taking off my head. Naro tried to run right through me—whether to Atrius or to the mangled body of his dead master, I didn't know. His presence was erratic, lurching in so many directions at once.

And yet . . .

It was him. *Him.* I didn't know how to make sense of that. I didn't know if I wanted to.

Out of sheer desperation, I braced myself against him and put my hands on either side of his head. I reached deep into his threads. They were tangled and broken, many of them consumed by the haze of drugs and pain.

I did the only thing I could: I sedated him. And after a few seconds, the tremors subsided. He slumped to the ground, unconscious.

I stood there, hands still raised, breath shaking.

I had thought this would be a triumphant moment. And yet here I was, in the same room as Tarkan's body, and I had barely even looked at it.

I felt Atrius's eyes on me. The quiet was suddenly deafening.

I turned. He stared at me with a hard, questioning gaze, the gore-covered axe still poised in his grip.

What could I say? I didn't want to show Atrius the truth. I couldn't even admit it to myself. I was supposed to be hiding myself from Atrius—not showing him things that no one was supposed to see.

I reached for a lie and came up with nothing.

And yet, I got the impression that he already saw some piece of the truth.

I choked out, "Please."

"He's one of Tarkan's guards."

"*Please.*"

Begging. Pathetic. All I could think to do.

You have no brother, the voice reminded me, again. *If his death is the Weaver's will, it is the Weaver's will.*

And yet I—I couldn't. I *couldn't.*

I hated when Atrius looked at me like that. That unrelenting steel stare, right through my gut. He did not ask who this person was. He did not ask why I wanted to spare him.

Something in his aura softened.

He didn't say a word. He simply turned to Tarkan's body, grabbed his hair, and hacked his head off with several wet *THWACKS* of the axe.

He turned to me. "You were right," he said. "This way was cleaner."

Then he strode to the balcony, head in hand, to go claim his new city.

CHAPTER TWENTY-FIVE

Yes, I had been right. Under other circumstances, maybe I would have been preening more that Atrius recognized it.

Tarkan's city fell apart without him. The crumble was near-instantaneous. Atrius's warriors were ready to sweep the city as soon as Tarkan was dead. They did so efficiently and, for the most part, bloodlessly. Few of Tarkan's warriors were willing to fight for anyone but him, and if their survival wasn't threatened, they were no threat to anyone else.

Within days, Vasai was firmly secured under Atrius's rule.

I didn't even feel anything when Atrius conceded this to me, or at Erekkus's impressed whistles. I went through my tasks with rote mindlessness, and when I was free, I went to Naro's side.

Atrius didn't kill him. I didn't know how to think about the fact that he spared him for my benefit. I knew Atrius was not a man made for mercy.

I put that question off for another day.

Instead, I sat beside Naro and waited.

My sedation should have worn off quickly, but he remained unconscious for days. Only the beginning of it was my magic. The rest, likely the after-effects of the drugs. He trembled and gasped in his sleep, sweat slicking the scar-dotted landscape of his forehead. I dabbed the sweat away with a cloth and dripped water down his throat.

I had never so strongly simultaneously hoped for opposite things: that he would wake up, and that he wouldn't.

Near dawn on the first night, Erekkus came to the room and paused in the doorway. I turned, then hurriedly rose.

Atrius. I'd completely forgotten.

"I apologize," I said. "I'm late to go to—"

But Erekkus shook his head. "No. He sent me here to say he doesn't need you tonight." His gaze lingered on me, then on Naro, listless in the bed.

"You've found a pet," he said.

"He's not—" I bit down my objection. What could I say? I didn't even know what the real answer was.

"I'm just watching over him," I said.

Erekkus never did much to disguise his expression. He didn't hide how confusing he found this situation.

"The others are celebrating," he said. "Probably not a good idea for you to join. Not that you'd want to. But if you want anything special—"

I turned back to Naro. "No. I'm fine."

"I have some food here for—"

"I'm not hungry."

A beat. Then he said, "I'm supposed to make sure you eat. If you don't, I'll be the one in trouble for it."

My hand went to my chest, pressed over the strange twinge there. I turned around again. Erekkus held out a bowl of rice and meat. "Just take it," he said. "Goddess knows he doesn't want it back."

I took the bowl from him. It was still hot—very fresh.

Atrius.

I swallowed past the lump in my throat. "Thank you."

"I'm not the one to thank." He glanced at Naro again. Then back to me. His expression softened a little, like he saw something unwillingly revealed in my face.

"I know we're . . . different. Vampires. Humans. But there isn't one of us that doesn't know what this feels like."

"This?"

I shouldn't have opened the door. I regretted it the moment the word left my lips.

Erekkus gave me a sad smile. "We're used to saying goodbye to our own," he said. "More than most vampires."

My chest ached with a sudden, powerful clench of anger. Anger because I didn't want to reveal that Naro was "my own" at all. Anger because, even if he was, I wasn't saying goodbye to him.

"Thanks for the food," I said, tightly, and shut the door.

NARO'S EYELIDS FLUTTERED open the next day, as the sun was lowering in the sky over Vasai.

The vampires were all tucked away at that point, save for those who guarded the Thorn Palace and the other key buildings of Vasai, so I'd opened the curtains. I rarely did that now, even on my own. The sun held little appeal to me, experiencing the world as I did. But Naro—he, perhaps, might appreciate some sunshine once he woke up. He had loved the sun, back in those days, even though he didn't have the complexion for it. He'd spend the summertime sprawled out on warm rocks beyond the outskirts of the city, baking in the heat like a lizard, then peel himself off and return home bright pink and cursing at every accidental touch.

Sure enough, when his lashes fluttered, the first thing he did was tilt his face toward the warm rays of light.

Then his eyes opened more, and he turned to me.

I wished I could see him as I did then—see him with eyes, not threads. And yet, a cowardly part of myself was grateful for it. I knew if I could see him the way I had as a child, the marks of life and time would be so stark. I sensed them written all over his threads.

He'd had a hard, hard life.

His threads, beneath the twisting trembles of his Pythoraseed cravings, shivered with sadness, too.

I wondered if perhaps he saw the same thing when he looked at me. For the first time since I had begged the Arachessen to take me

in, I had to swallow a wave of shame in response to the way an outsider looked at me—for what, I couldn't describe.

"Vivi," he whispered.

I should have corrected him—*Vivi doesn't exist anymore, my name is
Sylina*—but the words stuck in my throat. Being here, next to my big
brother, made me Vivi again.

His hand, trembling violently, reached for my blindfold.

"What is . . ."

I caught his wrist, setting his hand down. But he still stared at
that blindfold. His face hardened.

"You joined them."

Hurt struck me. Then indignation.

You joined them, he said, with such judgment. What right did he
have to say that to me?

He joined *them*. I had given my life to a goddess and a Sisterhood
and a greater power he couldn't even begin to understand.

He had given his life over to a damned warlord.

"You joined *them*," I said, my voice a little harder, quicker, than I
intended. Then I loosened a breath and softened.

It wasn't his fault. Wasn't his choice. He was a child, too. Just
trying to survive.

"I looked for you, Vivi," he whispered. "I looked for you for so long."

One of the downsides of having no eyes was that there was nothing to distract you when images of the past returned. I had carefully
erected a wall between Sylina and Vivi. Sitting here, next to Naro,
destroyed it.

He and I had made it so far together. We survived the deaths of
our parents, our sister. We protected each other from every danger—
him saving me from the furious shopkeeper who tried to drown me
for stealing, me saving him from the city guard who was ready to
beat him to death. No matter what, it was him and me. Together.

I tried not to remember the night that Tarkan's soldiers rolled
through the city, the fighting reaching a crescendo, the fire and explosives lighting up the night as bright as midday.

"You were gone," I whispered.

I was alone.

Naro wasn't home. He was nowhere to be found. The explosives tore up most of the city. I waited for so long. I stood at the window and watched as more and more blocks went up in plumes of acrid smoke.

I waited even as our neighbors all fled. I waited even when the last one to go, an elderly woman with a crooked leg, stopped to bang on my door.

"We must leave, you foolish child," she'd told me, trying to drag me away. "We must go right now."

"My brother—"

"He's already dead," she snapped. At the time, I'd hated her for saying that. Now, I understood the fear beneath her harsh words. She had likely watched the deaths of so many children. She didn't want to see another one.

But I'd been furious with her. I hit her, yanked my arm away, and ran back into the house.

I would not go without Naro.

"I waited for such a long time," I whispered.

"I was trying," Naro said. "I tried to get back. But I got stuck in the western quarter. I was injured."

I'd waited.

And then the explosion hit our little house, too.

I remembered little of it—only the loud noise, and then the silence afterward, unnatural silence. I was lucky. If the old woman hadn't come, I would've died. I only survived because I was in the back of the shack, not out in the street.

I'd opened my eyes to see the night sky, and nothing else. No house. No streets. No old woman.

"I came back as soon as I could," Naro said, voice cracking. "And I found the house—"

At the same time, we both choked out, "I thought you were dead."

And then we both laughed, our voices a little too high and manic, and for far too long.

I thought my brother was dead, and he wasn't. He was alive and he was right here in front of me.

Those simple facts left me dizzy and lightheaded.

I wasn't sure when, but we'd started holding hands, his clutched around mine like he wasn't sure I was real. He'd always had uncommonly long fingers, though now they seemed more bonelike than they were before, the knuckles swollen and the pale skin nicked with scars.

I was never going to let go of him ever again.

But then his gleeful grin faded. He reached for my blindfold again. "But you did that," he murmured. "Y-you—"

I had never before allowed myself to feel anything but gratefulness when I thought of my decision to join the Arachessen. Now, for the first time, I felt embarrassed by it.

Then, just as quickly, angry for even feeling that way.

I pushed his hand away again.

"The Arachessen is my family," I said.

I wished I couldn't feel the hurt in Naro's presence at that. Nor the disgusted pity.

"Family that take your eyes?"

I clenched my jaw, letting out air between my teeth.

"And what about the vampires?" Naro spat. "Are they *family*, too?"

Weaver. Talking to Naro had pulled me from between my three roles. Suddenly it hit me just how much I had revealed to my brother, even in this short conversation. Already, I had said far too much of the truth—especially considering that vampires slept mere rooms away.

"They're—" I lowered my voice. "It's complicated, Naro."

But Naro's anger rose and rose. His threads quaked erratically.

"It isn't *complicated*," he said, pushing himself upright. "You—you broke into the Thorn King's palace to murder him. Y-y-you—"

The Thorn King.

The words skewered me through the chest, driven by the intensity of Naro's fury. That wasn't false. Influenced by his withdrawal symptoms, yes, but not false.

"*The Thorn King*," I hissed. "What the hell are you doing, calling him that, after what he did to our home?"

But Naro's threads were unraveling now, his composure collapsing. His body trembled violently, and he fought to push himself out of bed and kept failing.

"You killed him," he snarled. "Y-you k-killed him. You and the vampire, Vivi—you *killed* him!"

"Yes," I snapped. "Tarkan is dead and you're free now. I know you had to do what you had to for survival. I don't—" I stumbled over the words, involuntarily. "I don't blame you for that. It isn't your fault—"

"*You killed him!*" Naro roared, and tried to fling himself out of the bed, only to go crashing to the floor.

Weaver, no.

My heart was beating fast, my throat tight. I no longer felt the sensation of tears, but my nose and throat prickled.

Footsteps approached, probably alerted by the noise. I knelt beside my brother and, with shaky hands, pressed my fingers to his temple, sending him the strongest sedation I could.

He thrashed for a few seconds longer, then went limp.

Atrius stood in the doorway. I felt him there, but I ignored him. I didn't want him to see me like this. I couldn't open my mouth to speak, anyway. It wouldn't be words that came out.

Naro was larger than me, but skinny. It was awkward, not diffi-cult, to lift him back into the bed.

Still, Atrius took a few steps forward, moving to help while avoid-ing the rays of sunshine.

"I've got it," I choked out.

Naro settled back into bed. I pulled the covers up around him. Even asleep, the tremors racked his hands and arms, even the small muscles of his face.

Pythoraseed. A horrible drug. It was worse to see the way it had consumed and destroyed his threads than it was to see it in his body alone.

Seconds ticked by as I stood beside him. Atrius watched silently.

Then, he said, "Come."

"I'll stay here."

"Staring at him won't do anything."

There was something in his voice, something tender and a little painful, that made Erekkus's words float through my mind:

We know what this feels like.

"I'd like to talk to you," he said. "Business."

I swallowed thickly. Turned. "Fine."

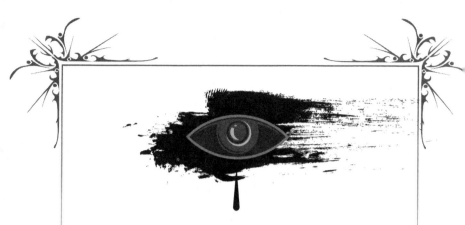

CHAPTER TWENTY-SIX

Atrius led me to his bedchamber. Unlike in Alka, he didn't take the warlord's room this time—mostly because Tarkan's was covered in blood and guts. Instead, he'd chosen a more private, smaller apartment on the top floor of the castle. It was separate from the rooms of his closest advisors and guards. A good example of his arrogance—he was totally unconcerned by potential threats.

When I first met him, I would've seen this as a weakness, nothing more than hubris. Now . . . I had to admit, it seemed like it would take a truly incredible assassin to end Atrius.

This thought floated through my mind before I remembered that *I* was supposed to be this assassin.

The heavy curtains were drawn in Atrius's room, leaving the chamber dim, lit only by a fire and several lanterns.

After Naro's explosively emotional presence, Atrius's wall seemed even thicker than ever.

"You need healing," I said. "I'm sorry, I—"

But Atrius just shook his head. He gestured to one of the armchairs by the fire, and I sat.

He went to the table and retrieved a ceramic cup. He held it out to me, and when I just stared at it, he took my wrist, lifted it, and pressed the warm mug into my hands.

"Tea," he said. "Apparently expensive. Tarkan liked it."

He didn't let go of the cup, his hands over mine.

"You're shaking," he said.

"I'm tired."

He did not believe me. But he let me go and took a seat on the other armchair, anyway.

For a very long, very awkward moment, neither of us spoke.

"Drink it," he said. "You've barely eaten or drank in two days."

I laughed flatly. "You're keeping track."

"It's impossible not to notice everything, with you."

I wasn't sure what I expected from him. But it was not that.

I took a sip of the tea because I didn't know what else to do. It was a little bitter and a little sweet, and just the right amount of hot.

It was, I had to admit, nice.

"A brother," Atrius said. "Yes?"

Weaver, how did he know?

"He looks like you," he said, answering my unasked question. "And he called you that name. Vivi."

The corner of my mouth twitched with a sad smile. Odd to hear Atrius say it, his accent rolling over those two sharp syllables.

"That was my name before the Arachessen," I said. "Long time ago."

"It suits you."

"I didn't—I didn't know he was alive."

The words slipped out without my permission. Maybe I meant them more for myself than for Atrius.

It's not your fault he ended up this way.

You didn't know he was alive.

Atrius picked up another mug, but he didn't drink from it, just held it in his lap. "I've heard," he said, "that the Arachessen take their recruits as young children."

"I was . . . older than most. They almost didn't take me because of it. Ten."

"That is still very young for humans," he murmured. "Isn't it?"

I swallowed. "Yes."

The last day—days? Had it been days?—had been a blur. For the first time since the attack—since finding Naro—I allowed myself to think back to it. Funny how two days ago, the idea of seeing Tarkan dead was so exhilarating. In reality, I'd barely glanced at his body. And I'd paid no attention at all to the rest of Atrius's takeover. Totally abandoned the role I was supposed to play.

"I'm sorry I haven't been present—"

Atrius just raised his hand.

"You knew Tarkan," he said.

It wasn't a question. Atrius, I'd come to realize, did not ask questions. He made demands or statements. In between, he'd quietly gather information.

Sometimes too much of it.

I hesitated with the tea halfway to my lips. Then took a sip.

The more I showed him, the more he would trust me. I told myself this and ignored the tiny part of myself that found an odd comfort in sharing these things with him.

"I grew up in Vasai," I said. "I never met Tarkan personally. But . . . I was a child during the Pythora Wars. I saw him make his takeover."

I thought back to our attack. To the moment Atrius had Tarkan's throat, and he still hesitated, giving me that shot.

"You were going to let me be the one to kill him," I said. "Why?"

His eyes slipped to the fire. "I could see that you wanted it. And you deserved it."

He said it simply, like it was fact. And I hated that this flooded me with—with—what, affection? Gratefulness?

It shouldn't have. Yes, he was right, I desired revenge. But that was a vice. It was no great kindness that he had offered me.

Still . . . it meant something, even if I wished it didn't.

Atrius set the cup aside and leaned forward, his forearms on his knees.

"You may have gathered by now," he said, "that my people have had a . . . fraught history."

"You mean the House of Blood's curse."

Perhaps he flinched at that. Perhaps it was a trick of the firelight.

He hesitated before saying, "That was the start. Nyaxia's spiteful curse, two thousand years ago. But . . . my people have endured far more than my kingdom's suffering." His face hardened briefly, then his gaze fell back to me. "Humans may believe that vampires don't understand what powerlessness feels like. And for many, maybe that's true. But those that follow me do. We understand loss. And we know that it is the worst kind of powerlessness."

The words were stilted. But the meaning behind them was softer than I knew what to do with.

I cleared my throat.

"You said you wanted to talk business," I said. "How long do you intend to stay in Vasai?"

Atrius blinked, as if caught off guard by the change of subject.

"Not long," he replied. "A week or two. Then we will move on to Karisine."

It stood to reason that Atrius would want to move quickly. We were getting closer now to the Pythora King—his ultimate goal. And Karisine was the next major city-state standing between us and the north.

My brow furrowed at that. I was grateful to have something to think about other than Naro or the past I wasn't supposed to remember. Battle strategies and espionage were comparatively so simple.

Karisine was a well-fortified city, especially considering that Atrius was losing numbers with every city-state he needed to maintain control of. The idea of taking it by brute force seemed outrageous, and unlike Tarkan, its ruler had not set herself up for such easy assassination. Furthermore, Vasai and Karisine were closely connected by a number of communication routes, far more than Alka had. They'd be prepared for Atrius's arrival.

I was supposed to be learning how to understand Atrius by now, but I couldn't fathom how he intended to pull that off.

"It's going to be . . . challenging," I said, choosing my words carefully.

A suppressed smile tugged at the corners of Atrius's mouth. Like he was a cat secretly hiding a canary in its teeth.

My brow twitched. "You have a plan."

"I always have a plan."

I wasn't sure that was true. He always managed to make it work, I would give him that. But part of what made Atrius so difficult to understand—what made him such a formidable enemy—was that his plans didn't make sense to anyone else but him. Sometimes I thought he conducted warfare like he fought in battle: entirely in the moment, responding to every change in circumstances in real time, impossible to anticipate.

"So?" I said. "Prove it. Enlighten me."

He seemed to debate whether he wanted to or not.

"Are you familiar," he said, "with the island of Veratas?"

"Yes, but—barely. It's . . . a nothing island, isn't it?"

Tiny. Uninhabited. Close to the eastern coast of Glaea.

"It was," Atrius said. "Easiest conquering I've ever done."

My brows rose now. "Conquering."

Again, he was silent for a long moment, his eyes far away, a gentler smile playing at his lips. It was a strange expression on him, all those hard lines softened, even under the harsh light of the fire.

"There's a settlement," he said.

He spoke so quietly I almost didn't hear him—like he was bestowing a precious secret to me, delicate as butterfly wings.

"They've lived there for a few months now," he went on. "The husbands and wives and children."

My lips parted in shock. His civilians? The families of his soldiers were . . . right over there, in Veratas?

"I—I'd assumed they were in the House of Blood. In Obitraes."

Atrius shook his head. "No."

I knew he wouldn't answer. But I had to ask anyway.

"Why?"

His threads shivered slightly, as if beneath an unpleasant cold breeze.

"My people," he said, "are not welcome back home."

My people.

All this time I thought he'd meant the House of Blood. No. He meant *his* people—the ones who had followed him all this way.

His eyes lowered to the carpet, the fire reflecting flecks of gold in them.

"So," he said, "I've had to find a new one for them. Or find a way to let them return to theirs."

The wall over his presence, normally so impenetrable, suddenly disappeared, letting forth a wave of deep sadness. Not my brother's wild grief. This was quiet and constant, like something that had just been accepted into one's bones.

I felt an echoing ache in mine—something that, perhaps, had always been there but I tried not to look at too closely.

"Why?" I murmured. "Why can't you go home?"

Atrius's eyes at last flicked back to mine, steel-stark against the firelight.

For a moment, the vulnerability in them shocked me.

And then the wall returned, and his back straightened, and his face hardened again. He cleared his throat, as if to force away the remnants of his honesty.

"My cousin, one of my generals, will be launching another offensive from the island," he said. "Her men will roll in to support us from the sea, under the cover of the mists."

He was trying to make this discussion businesslike again. It didn't work. We had exposed too much to each other.

All at once, the realities of my role crashed down on me. In one day, three versions of myself who were not supposed to coexist—Sylina the seer, Sylina the Arachessen, and Vivi the lost little girl—had collided in the most confusing ways. The pieces of myself didn't fit together. They were ugly contradictions.

A lump in my throat, I rose and crossed the room, each step closer to Atrius shivering up my spine.

What are you doing, Sylina?

He said nothing. But his eyes didn't leave me, the way a predator's tracked their prey. And yet, it wasn't quite a predator's hunger that shivered in him.

I lowered myself onto the arm of his chair, my legs touching his, practically in an embrace.

He didn't move, but I sensed his heartbeat quicken.

I pressed my palm to his chest. His skin was warm, almost hot, like he was fighting back a fever. Beneath his flesh, I felt his curse eating at his threads, a gaping, starving mouth of necrosis.

"You're in pain today," I said softly.

"It's fine."

"You didn't call for me."

"You were busy."

"I'm surprised that mattered to you."

His head tilted slightly—so, so slightly, like it wasn't even intentional—as if to resist the urge to bury it in my hair.

He didn't answer for so long that I thought perhaps he wouldn't. And maybe I was grateful for that, because no matter how much I told myself that I was getting close to him because it was my task, I knew whatever he would say would cut too deep.

I was right.

"It matters," he murmured.

Two words that could mean nothing—should mean nothing.

It felt like they meant everything.

"Your brother will be safe here," he went on, "for as long as he needs."

My chest clenched. I was grateful for the hair curtaining my face. But then gentle fingers pulled it back, placing it carefully behind my ear, the brush of his fingernails against my cheek striking me breathless.

"Thank you," I choked out.

I wasn't acting.

Others would tell me that Naro would die of his addiction or its withdrawal. Others would imprison or execute him as a war criminal. I couldn't blame anyone for either of those things—certainly not Atrius, the monster, the cursed vampire, the conqueror.

And yet. Here I was, being presented with this gift. Compassion. "Why?" I asked. "Why are you helping him?"

An aching pulse, like the throb of an old wound. "Because we lose the past so fast. We should cling to those who made us who we are. And because, if the one I considered my brother was alive, I would want someone to do the same for him."

Brother.

I thought of a body in the snow at the feet of a furious goddess, a wave of grief, and a hole that would never be filled again.

So many things about Atrius almost made so much sense. Almost. Like I was missing a critical puzzle piece.

I whispered, before I could stop myself, "Why do you want to conquer Glaea?"

A beat. Then, "Because I'm an evil, power-starved monster."

He said it so flatly, like it was an actual answer. Not long ago, I thought that was the truth, and would have told him as much.

But now . . .

Atrius could be monstrous, perhaps. But he was not Tarkan. He was not Aaves. He certainly was not the Pythora King.

Now it was my turn to expose him, to force him to let me see what he would prefer to hide. I touched his chin and tilted it toward me. When his eyes flicked to me, they remained there—like he could see right through my blindfold, to the broken eyes beneath it.

I murmured, "I don't believe you. I want the truth."

This was what I had been sent here for. Truth.

I told myself all of this, far in the back of my mind, as if there was not a part of me that wanted his truth for more complicated reasons.

He flinched, the faintest twitch of muscles across his face.

"I can't give you that."

"Because your people need a new home."

A pained hint of a smile. "If only it was that simple."

My palm was still pressed to his chest, over the loose cotton fabric of his shirt. Slowly, I slid my hand up, inside his shirt—finding bare skin.

He stiffened, but didn't stop me. Nor did he move. He barely breathed.

Deep inside him, the curse burned and ached.

"The past is devouring you."

He let out an almost-laugh. "So bold of you, to talk to me that way." Rough, scarred fingertips touched my face, the contrast between his skin and the touch so stark it made my heart stutter. His gaze lowered, lingering on my mouth.

"Do you think I don't see," he said, voice low, "that the past is devouring you, too?"

I knew that a wounded soul craved another to mirror theirs.

That was all this was.

But my soul was hurting, too. And perhaps I, too, craved someone who understood that.

I didn't move my hand from Atrius's bare chest. Nor did I move when his hand slowly flattened against my cheek, fingers tangling in my hair, cradling my face.

And when he came closer, closer, until his breath mingled with mine, I let him.

Even when the space between us disappeared entirely.

His mouth was soft. Almost shy, at first. And when my lips parted against his, a little ragged breath escaping, he took the opportunity to deepen the kiss, his tongue, soft and damp, sliding against mine, releasing his own shuddering exhale.

Gods.

He was alive, and broken, and familiar, and mysterious, and dangerous, and safe. And for one terrible moment, I *wanted* so fiercely, I forgot everything else. My hand slid against the topography of muscles in his bare chest, running down over his abdomen and settling at his side. His grip tightened in my hair, pulling me, and gods, I let him—let him urge me closer, let his tongue roll deeper into my mouth, let myself open up to him. My other hand found his cheek, his hair, running through the smooth tendrils and resisting the overpowering urge to grab it and pull him closer.

He broke the kiss but I chased it, tilting my head for another angle. Every time we came together again it was fiercer, like waves crashing in a storm. Our bodies were now entwined, my breasts against his chest.

And I could no longer pretend this kiss was his alone.

Because Weaver, I wanted more of him. Wanted to embrace the darker, forbidden sides of the desire that sleeping beside him every night had stirred. The kind of desire I was only allowed to explore by myself at night, my hands between my legs, or occasionally with another Arachessen willing to bend the rules with me up to wherever we decided the line of our vows had been drawn.

He wanted me. I knew it now, by the rigid length of him pressing through his pants. I had known it for weeks, every time we lay down together and woke up in an embrace.

My palm against his bare skin kept moving, sliding along the muscles of his torso—sliding down. When the tip of my little finger brushed against the waistband of his trousers, he abruptly jerked away.

That was enough to make me snap back to awareness.

My face was hot. My heart pounded wildly. For a moment, Atrius and I just stared at each other, his eyes wide.

What had I just done?

The realization of what more I almost did—what more I *wanted* to do—hit me like a bucket of cold water.

His nostrils flared, and I realized that he was taken aback by his own desires, too—perhaps even more than I was.

He rasped out clumsily, "Not tonight."

I slipped my hand from his shirt and extracted myself from his lap as gracefully as I could manage. I was determined not to show that I was shaken. Yet I was so aware of the way his throat bobbed when his gaze ran up my body, and the way he tensed when I stepped away from him.

Not tonight. I wasn't sure what that meant. Did that mean, *Another night?*

I had taken a chastity vow. Yes, I had seduced men—and women— many times in the course of my missions. It never made it as far as sex. But for some Sisters, I knew it had. Everyone knew. Even the Sightmother. Even, of course, Acaeja. We accepted it as a sacrifice for the greater good and looked the other way.

I couldn't think about that.

I gave him a smile that tried to be charming, but probably looked weaker than I intended. "You're right," I said. "It's gotten late—"

I started to turn away, but Atrius caught my wrist.

A long moment of silence stretched out between us. He stared at me with those eyes that seemed to skewer right through me.

And just when I thought he didn't have anything to say at all, he spoke. Four words in Obitraen.

"What did that mean?" I asked.

He just shook his head and let me go. "Take care of your brother," he murmured, and turned to the fire.

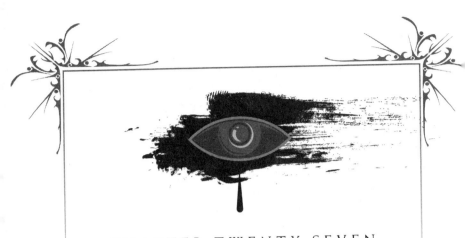

CHAPTER TWENTY-SEVEN

Naro did not improve over the next several days. Instead, his condition deteriorated. This went far beyond injuries from the battle. Pythoraseed addiction was a greedy beast. Withdrawal set in fast, and once it had you, it would keep devouring until there was nothing left but a shell. It was almost always deadly.

Soon, Naro was delirious. He was rarely awake. When he was, he was unaware of the world, spitting out slurred collections of words that didn't qualify as sentences. I remained by his side, and no one bothered me, even though there was plenty of work to be done before the army moved north again.

I knew that Atrius had ordered that I was not to be disturbed. But I tried not to think too much about Atrius—about the kiss—when I was at Naro's side.

I had hoped that Naro might be one of the lucky ones who would be able to get through withdrawal. I didn't know why I bothered dreaming of this. I wasn't one to let myself drown in silly, baseless hopes. And it *was* silly—even those early in their addiction usually died in withdrawal, and I had no reason to think that Naro, someone who had apparently been at the Thorn King's side for a decade now, had any chance at all.

Before long, Naro was never conscious and struggled to breathe, constantly drenched in sweat, his skin clammy and gray-tinged. His fingertips had grown dark, mottled red. His body no longer knew how to function without Pythoraseed.

I hated myself for the decision I made then. In the middle of the day—one of our last days in Vasai—I rose from Naro's bedside and wandered through the palace halls. The place had been gutted, Atrius's men having spent the last weeks rummaging through all the rooms, stripping them of supplies and weapons stores.

Tarkan had controlled his entire army through Pythoraseed. I knew there had to be some here. Probably a lot. Yet as I raided room after room, my frustration grew. Threads were superior to eyesight in almost every way—but in this situation, my lack of eyesight didn't help me. Drugs have no soul. No threads. The only way I could find them would be by searching like anyone else. And so I searched, and searched, and searched. Hours passed. I found nothing. When I reached the final door on the second floor and opened it to an empty room, I let out a frustrated sigh that ended in a sob.

Naro was going to die. He was going to die, and I couldn't help him.

I felt Atrius's presence behind me before I saw him. And yet, despite feeling him so acutely, he still was better at sneaking up on me than anyone.

I froze. He stared. Neither of us said anything for too long.

I had finally started to gain Atrius's trust. Maybe more than that. And then I had pulled away. That had jeopardized everything I was here to do.

I started, "I was just—"

Atrius held out his hand. A small velvet pouch sat in his palm.

My mouth closed. I didn't need to open it to know what this was.

"Take it," he said. "This is what you're looking for."

It was pointedly not a question. He knew exactly what I was doing, and the depths of my shame swallowed me up.

But I wasn't so ashamed that I didn't take it.

I closed my hand around the pouch. In turn, Atrius's closed around mine, stopping me from pulling away.

"I'm destroying most of it," he said. "All but the smallest amounts we can keep on hand for the people who will die without it. But even they likely won't live long."

I swallowed the lump in my throat, tight with grief and anger.

No. That was the greatest cruelty of Pythoraseed. Warlords liked it because it made their soldiers sharper and easier to control. Soldiers liked it because it made a short, terrible life more tolerable. But in either event, it was a death knell. Withdrawal would kill you. But so would the drug itself, slowly eating you alive from the inside.

Naro would die if he did not have Pythora.

He would die if he did, too. Maybe just a little slower.

As if reading my face, Atrius said, "It is a cruel substance."

"Yes," I agreed.

He let go of my hand. I tucked the pouch into my pocket.

"Give him only what he needs," he said. "Parse it out."

I nodded, and we didn't say another word to each other.

Later, I went into Naro's room and emptied the pouch into my palm. The seeds were so tiny, each one donning a little fungal sprout. Most preferred to grind it up and snort it, or smoke it, but ingestion would be enough to keep Naro alive.

I took a single seed and pressed it into Naro's mouth, until his teeth parted. I dripped some water between his lips to make sure he swallowed.

He still didn't wake—I had given him the bare minimum to keep him alive, not enough to make him functional again. But I held his hand for the rest of the night, so grateful for the way his tremors subsided that I couldn't even feel guilty.

{SYLINA.}

I had fallen asleep by Naro's bed. At first, I thought the Threadwhisper was a dream.

I lifted my head. It was heavy. Naro was fast asleep, peacefully for the first time in a week.

{Sylina.}

I snapped upright. It had been months since I'd Threadwhispered. The sensation was strange now.

Asha. I recognized her voice, even distant—she was far, probably beyond the bounds of the Thorn Palace. But that still meant she was here, in Vasai.

[I'm coming, Sister,] I told her, grabbed my boots and my cloak, and quickly hurried to meet her.

It was late afternoon. The sun was low in the sky, tinted dusky orange by the thick cloud cover. I found Asha waiting beyond the bounds of the city limits, where buildings gave way to the harsh, rocky plains. I hadn't spent time out here since I'd arrived in Vasai. For a moment, the memories of the time Naro and I would spend out here as children, scavenging for discarded trash or small animals we could kill and eat, overtook me.

But those thoughts quickly disappeared when I found Asha.

Because she was not alone.

The Sightmother was beside her.

I almost stopped short. The Sightmother never came to check up on missions personally. A part of me was grateful to see her, like a child relieved to be reunited with the safety of their mother. Another part of me balked, my palms starting to sweat. Suddenly all I could taste was Atrius's kiss on my mouth. Suddenly all I could feel was the Pythoraseed in my palm.

But when I drew closer, and the Sightmother's comforting presence, strong and stable, surrounded me, those insecurities withered away.

"It is so good to see you, Sylina," the Sightmother said, giving me a warm smile and reaching out to grasp my hands.

Weaver, I missed them. My Sightmother, my Sisters. It was like I'd drifted away over the last few months and now had been reminded of home. I'd worked long missions before, but never this long, and never alone. I had forgotten how effortless communication could be with those who understood me so implicitly.

Asha greeted me, too, then excused herself to act as lookout, leaving me alone with the Sightmother.

"I'm happy to see you," I said. "I didn't expect you to come yourself."

"This is important." I felt her threads reaching for mine, like hands cradling a face to examine it. "How are you, Sylina? It has been a long time."

How I wanted to lean into that comfort. I had forgotten how good it felt to be near something certain.

"I'm well, Sightmother."

"I was surprised to find you back in Vasai."

She didn't say more. Didn't reference Vasai's significance to my past. Neither of us had to.

"I go where the Weaver sends me," I said.

A beat of silence. Her presence curled around mine like an embrace. And yet, I couldn't help but stiffen a little, knowing that the Sightmother saw so much more than even the most talented Sisters did—knowing that my presence might betray things I would rather she not see. Like the burn on my lips and my hands.

"We don't have much time," the Sightmother said. "I've come because you must have an update for me by now. I see that the conqueror has made considerable progress in his task."

"He . . . yes."

Work. My task. Once, that was blissfully straightforward. Now I found myself choosing each word gingerly, like steps across a fragile bridge.

With her prompting, I went on to tell her about my time with Atrius—carefully, using only facts. What he asked me to seer about. How we took Alka. How we took Vasai. Then I told her of his future plans—that he intended to move on Karisine next, to open a pathway to kill the Pythora King.

And here, I hesitated.

It was relevant for me to tell the Sightmother about his plans for his cousin to support his attack, and in doing so, tell her about the civilians living on the island of Veratas.

Yet, I remembered the careful, tentative tone of voice Atrius had used when he told me about them—like I was being entrusted with something precious and delicate.

I had split seconds to make the decision.

Civilians, I decided, were not relevant. It didn't matter.

It didn't matter, I told myself, as I ended my brief without mentioning Veratas, and as I listened to the Sightmother's long, thoughtful silence.

"Hm," she said, finally. Her fingers played at her chin.

"It's been months," I said. "I've remained very close to him. You asked me to understand his ultimate goals, and I have. After all I've learned, I have a recommendation."

The Sightmother's brows rose, shifting above the teal blue of her blindfold. "By all means, tell me."

"With every battle I've seen and plan I've witnessed, he has attempted to minimize the risk to human citizens. It doesn't always work, but that doesn't change the fact that he tries. And that's because he intends to rule this kingdom. He sees the humans as his people, as much as the vampires are."

The Sightmother did not hide the skepticism on her face nor in her presence.

"I didn't believe it either at first, but I've seen it proven time and time again," I said. "He has more respect for the lives of the humans here than the Pythora King does. And perhaps—"

No—no *perhaps,* no *maybes.* I was stronger than this. I had a recommendation. I would make it.

"The Pythora King has killed tens of thousands of innocent people. More. And we have been fighting against him for decades. For what? What have we achieved?"

The Sightmother said nothing, her presence unreadable.

"The Bloodborn conqueror may not be our enemy," I said. "Perhaps Atrius would make a much better ally."

The silence of the Sightmother's presence now seemed ominous. Still, she said nothing, and so, neither did I. I let the statement stand, even though some desperate part of me was frantic to walk it back.

"Atrius," the Sightmother said at last, voice flat. "How familiar you've gotten."

My stomach twisted. The Sightmother's disapproval was always a cold blade.

Atrius's kiss burned unbearably on my lips.

"You told me to grow familiar," I said. "Just as you asked me for my recommendation."

"And that recommendation is what, exactly? You haven't fully said it."

Too late to back away now.

"Abandon our mission to kill him," I said. "Ally with him instead. Help him overthrow the Pythora King."

"And crown a vampire king instead?"

I wasn't ready to promise the Sightmother that Atrius would be a perfect king to this country. But I had seen the way Atrius cared for those who served under him. That was worth something. It was a rare quality in a ruler.

"He trusts me," I said. Was that the truth? I didn't know if I could make that promise, either—though the memory of his face in the firelight, just him and me, floated through my mind. "He could be guided. He respects the Arachessen's power. We could help him. He could become—"

"I told you that Acaeja disapproves of him and his mission."

I struggled to fathom this. My entire life, I witnessed the worst of what the Pythora King was capable of. I knew it better than anyone—better than the Sisters who had been too young when they became Arachessen to remember life outside the Salt Keep. "Atrius is a vampire," I said, "but the Pythora King is a monster. How can the Weaver possibly—"

"Are you questioning her will, Sylina?"

The Sightmother did not raise her voice. She did not need to.

I closed my mouth. No matter how many years passed, her rebuke stung just as it had when I was a child.

"No," I said. "No. I am not."

The Sightmother's stare and her grip on my presence didn't let up.

"There is something else you want to tell me," she said.

I resisted the urge to flinch. I had gotten spoiled having my thoughts to myself lately, and grown lax about guarding them. With the Sightmother's disappointment still simmering in my chest, I wasn't especially eager to humiliate myself even further. I was only going to prove to her that I was what the other Sisters whispered about me.

And yet. I had to ask. Not just because the Sightmother already saw the shape of my secret, but because my brother's life was worth my humiliation.

"When we marched on Vasai," I said, "I met someone from my former life. Naro."

The Sightmother had no reaction.

"He's . . . he's very ill. He was taken advantage of by Tarkan for decades. He has been addicted to Pythoraseed for years, and it has ravaged him. If the withdrawal doesn't kill him, the drug will. But—"

Until now, I had been successful at keeping my voice calm and measured. Here, a little crack slipped through before I could stop it.

"But Arachessen healers might be able to help him. They might—"

"You're asking to allow an outsider into the Salt Keep?"

The Sightmother's voice was kind, as if comforting a child. But the harsh phrasing of the question hurt to hear, because I knew how it sounded.

The Sightmother stepped closer. Her aura wrapped around mine. What had been overbearing before now turned into an embrace.

I no longer cried after the damage to my eyes. But sometimes, I felt the symptoms of it—the prickling behind my eyes, the choked sensation in my throat.

"I could take him somewhere else," I said. "And they could come to him—"

The Sightmother took my hand. Her thumb rubbed it, back and forth, back and forth, the steady cadence of a heartbeat. She had done this since I was a child. At the time, I was so grateful to have such affection. I thought I would never feel a loving touch again. And in the Sightmother's, I thought, *This is it. I'm finally safe.*

Now, for one horrible moment, I resented it. I resented it so fiercely I almost yanked my hand away.

"Sylina does not have a brother," she murmured. "You know this. I know I do not need to tell you this."

She was right. I'd taken vows. I'd given up my former life. I'd cut out every influence. And back then I was so grateful for it. There was nothing about my old life that I wanted to keep. Nothing but death and loss and fear and hurt that I never wanted to experience again.

I'd been so quick to throw away Vivi.

But I hadn't known then that I was throwing away Naro, too. I thought Naro was already gone.

Never once had I questioned my vows to the Arachessen.

Not until now.

And immediately, I hated myself for it. I thrust that shameful thought away, far into the back of my mind, and slammed the door.

"I know, Sightmother. I only . . ."

Her thumb moved back and forth, back and forth, across my hand.

"You have had a more difficult thread to walk than your Sisters," she murmured, voice soft. "You have a burden to bear for the rest of your life. I understand that. The Weaver understands that."

And yet, her words made me feel so deeply ashamed.

She placed her hands on my cheeks and tilted my head toward her, kissing my forehead.

"We will always help you walk the path back home."

This should have been comforting. After all, what was a family but those who helped you find your way back to what was Right?

But today, it did not feel comforting.

The Sightmother withdrew, her attention slipping away. Her head cocked, and I suspected that she was being whispered to by Asha.

"I need to go," she said. "The night is coming soon, anyway. You should be going."

I nodded. I kept careful hold on my presence, pulling myself back to the image of stoic professionalism.

The Sightmother reached into the bag at her side and withdrew a sheathed dagger. She handed it to me without ceremony, like she was passing off a piece of bread at dinner. But when my hands closed around it, they went a little numb.

"It's blessed," she said. "One strike with that, close to the heart as you can get, and he'll be dead."

Dead.

I fought so, so hard to keep both my face and my presence calm.

"We've learned enough," she said. "Let him get through Karisine and kill him whenever you can do so safely. Then return to the Salt Keep."

She didn't give me time to respond. She simply turned around and disappeared, stepping into the threads and leaving me there holding my blessed, cursed dagger, the order so much heavier than the blade.

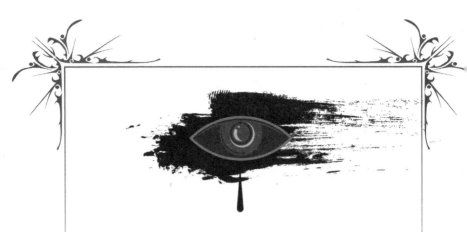

CHAPTER TWENTY-EIGHT

I took the long walk back to the Thorn Palace, treasuring the lull of the dusky hours. When I returned, Atrius was waiting for me in my room.

I stopped short. He was standing by the window, peering through a slit in the curtains at the view beyond, where the sun was just disappearing beneath the rocky horizon.

The weight of the dagger at my hip felt like it doubled.

"I'm glad you let yourself in," I said, flat with sarcasm.

Our usual banter. Nothing was different.

"It's all my castle now." He turned around to face me and said, "Your brother is awake."

My heart skipped a beat. I had to stop myself from turning around and running to Naro's side immediately.

"I've been thinking," Atrius went on. "Of course, you will be traveling with us to Karisine. And if you wanted him to, I would allow him to come."

My brows rose a little at that. Of course, Naro couldn't travel— nor would I want him to. Coming with Atrius's army was probably the most dangerous place he could be, no matter how much I might selfishly want to keep my brother close.

As if following the same thought process, Atrius went on, "But we both know that would be difficult in his current state. So. I've made arrangements."

A tiny part of myself didn't even want to hear this, because I knew it was going to be hard. And yet, I was also shamefully desperate for Atrius's help.

I stepped closer.

"Arrangements?"

"Vampires don't have experience with Pythora addiction. But we have drugs of our own that are just as powerful. It . . . has been a problem in the past. Among soldiers." His hands were clasped behind his back. He crossed the room in slow, wandering steps, like he didn't even intend to move. "Some Bloodborn healers have learned some treatment methods. They aren't perfect. They might not work on humans. But—"

"Thank you." The words pushed up my throat with the burst of wild hope in my chest. "That's—just . . . thank you."

He looked as uncomfortable being thanked as I was thanking him. We were close now, both in the center of the room. His eyes traced my face.

"I can't make promises," he murmured.

He said it like an apology.

"Even if you could," I replied, "I wouldn't believe them."

I was grateful for his honesty. For his imperfect effort. No one who had survived the lives we had could deny the value of that. Most never try at all.

The dagger strapped to my thigh now felt like a vice, slowly tightening.

"My people have learned to fight for the impossible," he said. "We wouldn't survive otherwise."

The words resonated more than I wished they did.

"Thank you," I said again, and Atrius left me alone without another word.

ATRIUS WAS RIGHT. Naro was awake. He looked like a living corpse, but he was awake.

Still, he didn't seem that interested in talking. He gazed out the window as I sat beside his bed, barely responding to my greeting or questions: *How are you? Are you feeling better? Do you need anything?*

Nothing.

Until at last, my frustration rising, I asked, "Do you want to look at me when I'm trying to save your life?"

At that, he let out a little half laugh—the sound hurt because it so resembled the one he'd made as a teenager, responding to some joke or ribbing by another street kid.

"Do I want to look at you? Do I *want* to?" At last, he turned his head. "No, Vi. I don't. Why would I want to look at you and see what you've done to yourself because I wasn't there to protect you?"

My jaw shut tight. The pain came first. Then the anger.

"Because you thought I was dead for sixteen gods-damned years."

He scoffed again, this one so violent it sent spittle flying across the bedspread, and I jerked to my feet.

"What about you? I'm not here refusing to look at you, even though every time I do, all I see is the decaying corpse of a person that you've become."

"See," he spat. "You don't *see* anything."

"I see *far too fucking much,*" I shot back. "I see more than eyes ever gave me. And right now, I fucking hate it. I hate that I have to see everything that Tarkan rotted inside you. Everything that you rotted inside yourself."

I could be cruel when I was hurt or angry. The Sightmother had reminded me of this many times. Such emotions were not welcome in the Salt Keep, and if they managed to worm their way in, they certainly should never be bowed to.

Fuck it. In this moment, I was too upset to care.

"How *dare* you judge me," I snarled. "I'm not the one killing myself over some Weaver-damned Pythoraseed. I'm ashamed of you."

Naro's presence was explosively loud, every emotion bold. The hurt was so piercing it almost made me stagger backward. He lurched halfway upright in his bed, as if to lunge at me, but the shine in his eyes betrayed the hint of tears.

"I served my king," he ground out. "I—I gave everything for him because he gave me everything. I had nothing. Do you fucking understand? I had nothing. He saved me. Not you. Not your fucking cult. *Him*. There's fucking honor in that, you spoiled little girl. *Honor*."

I was so angry that my blood buzzed in my ears. So angry that I couldn't even think. I was grateful for it, because if I had been better at thinking, I might've noticed the echo in those words—*I gave everything for him because he gave me everything.*

How many times had I thought those words about the Arachessen? How many times had I been told them, about Acaeja?

"Right now, *I'm* the one saving you," I spat. "*Me*."

I straightened my back. Drew in a deep breath. Let it out slowly.

Calm yourself. Center yourself. You are just one small piece of a great tapestry.

The mantra didn't help.

Naro glared at me. Then his gaze turned back to the window, his knuckles white against the bedsheets.

I swallowed a pang of regret for my harsh words.

My voice was calmer when I said, "I need to leave tonight. You will stay. Healers are coming to treat you and—"

"Vampire healers?"

My jaw tightened against the urge to snap back, *Any kind of healers who will take you, and you'll feel damned lucky for them.*

Weaver, a few days with Naro and suddenly even my language was back to my old street rat days.

"They are knowledgeable about recovery from drugs," I said evenly. "They may be able to help you. So let them."

Naro didn't say anything. Didn't look at me.

Fine.

I went to the door. Though my back was to him, his presence was still so unsettled, a ball of anger and hurt. Despite the anger and hurt of my own, it made my chest ache.

I turned back one last time.

"Naro."

His eyes slipped to me.

I love you. I wanted to say it. I should. Even if my petty spite clawed the words back. We used to say them to each other all the time as children, casual affection, when our love for each other was the only constant in a life of uncertainty.

Instead, I said, "Please. Let them help you."

I love you.

His face softened. His presence, too. And after a few seconds, he nodded.

"I will," he said.

I love you, too.

I'd take that.

CHAPTER TWENTY-NINE

We rode out that night. Once again, the process repeated—Atrius left a force in Vasai to hold things down, gathered his increasingly smaller army, and we left for Karisine.

It would be a significant journey, traveling through the deserted rocky plains of northern Vasai until we approached the Karisine border. There, we'd move to the coast and wait for word of Atrius's cousin and her army.

The journey, at least, was uneventful. Tarkan's army was headless without him. No one followed us into the plains, and no one came to fight us back from the north.

"It's odd, isn't it?" Erekkus remarked on our first day of travel. "If an Obitraen kingdom were being invaded like this, I can promise you the kings of any of the three Houses wouldn't be letting you take a single step forward."

At this, Atrius had grunted a *hm* of a response, eyes trained to the horizon, which I knew meant agreement.

I agreed, too. I wasn't sure what to make of it. The Pythora King gave significant power to his warlords—that was key to how he had managed to take control of the kingdom twenty years ago—and warlords were often self-serving in how they chose to exercise it. In the beginning, I thought that the lack of a direct move from the Pythora

King was because of poor relationships with distant warlords and an unwillingness of others to sacrifice their men for each other's benefit.

Now? Now Atrius was making significant headway. It seemed downright strange that the Pythora King wasn't shifting onto the offensive by now, instead sitting back and letting Atrius pick off city-state after city-state.

Why?

This question was on all our minds as we traveled. Erekkus said it aloud, frequently. Atrius never said it aloud, but I knew it was just as present in his mind.

Still, mine was in other places, too. Atrius gave me a seal that allowed me to send letters by magic back to Vasai, which I was deeply grateful for. The minute we stopped for our first daybreak on the road, I spread out a sheet of parchment in my tent to write to Naro. My pen had hovered over the page for a long time. I was so certain that I needed to write him, and yet, with the paper in front of me, I had no idea what to say.

I settled on a few clipped sentences and a single question: *How are you?*

It wasn't enough, and it was too much. Eventually, frustrated, I folded it up, stamped Atrius's wax seal on the back, and waited until the letter dissolved into nothingness.

WHEN DAYBREAK APPROACHED, for reasons I didn't quite understand, I went to Atrius's tent.

I announced myself and didn't wait for him to answer before I let myself in. He was sitting on his bedroll, papers spread out before him. He was shirtless, and wearing loose linen pants that fell low around his hips. I could feel the warmth of his flesh from across the room. The removal of even a single layer between us was so noticeable, I found it distracting.

"I didn't call for you," he said.

"I know."

I closed the tent flap behind me, then crossed to him. He didn't move. I was so aware of the way his attention tracked my every movement. I wore my nightgown—very thin white cotton. It would be mostly transparent against the backlighting of the lanterns.

I'd debated changing before I came here. I could hear the Sight-mother whispering in my ear, *It's good if he wants you. It's good if he trusts you.*

In the end, I kept the nightgown—and left behind the dagger that would have been far too visible beneath it.

I knelt before Atrius. His presence rolled over me, stable and strong. I wondered if he had intentionally started letting his guard down around me, or if I had simply learned how to read his threads over these last few months. Now it seemed impossible to think that I had ever felt nothing from him. He had one of the most complex souls I'd ever felt—so many contradictions, all kept under such delicate control.

I pressed my hand against his chest. His walls parted for me. His pain was excruciating, even though he tried to hide it.

"It's been a week," I said. "You're hurting."

He lay his hand over mine. My skin tingled where his palm, rough and calloused, engulfed it in warmth.

"It's not an order," he said softly.

A twinge of complicated compassion, as I realized how much he really wanted me to know that.

"I know," I murmured. "I want to."

Another twinge, as the words didn't feel as forced as I thought they would.

Atrius let me work, undoing as much of the damage of his curse from the last week as I could. And then, together, we drifted to sleep. I kept my hand to his chest. And this time, I let him pull me into an embrace, our bodies curled around each other, his aura and his body enveloping me like a cocoon.

I had to keep his trust, I told myself. It was important to maintain that, for when the time came.

But I was not thinking about plans or daggers or wars when I fell asleep in Atrius's arms.

I was thinking only of the words I'd said to him, but felt in my own heart:

It's been a week. You're hurting.

It had been. I was.

But now, for the first time in eight days, I finally slept.

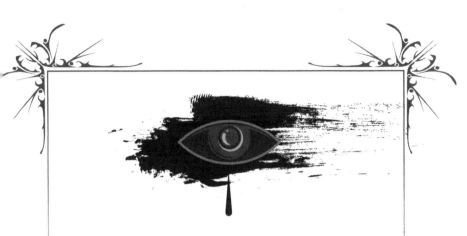

CHAPTER THIRTY

Atrius was uneasy.

The long trek across the plains had been slow and laborious as the terrain grew rougher, but remained uneventful. We made it to the northern border of Vasai, moved to the coast, and waited.

And waited.

And waited.

Days passed. Atrius's cousin did not appear.

Atrius and I slept together every night. By our third day on the coast, despite my magic and my sedation, he was waking up every few hours, staring at the ceiling of the tent.

I could always tell if he was awake, even when he didn't move or speak. His body and his presence betrayed him in all the wordless ways.

I rolled over and propped my chin up on my hand.

"You're concerned about your cousin," I said.

Atrius didn't confirm it. He didn't have to.

My brow furrowed. An uneasy feeling knotted in my stomach.

Three days was not a long time when it came to the movement of armies. Yet, I sensed something uneasy in the air, too, and I wasn't in the business of feeding Atrius meaningless platitudes. Neither of us had the time or energy for that.

"I'll Threadwalk on it," I said. "When the sun goes down."

He nodded, stared at the ceiling for a few minutes longer, then got up, abandoning the prospect of sleep.

AS SOON AS the sun set, Atrius and I went to a deserted stretch of coastline. I hadn't realized just how much I had missed the ocean these last weeks until a gust of wind hit us and brought with it the scent of salty brine. The beach here was especially pungent, full of vegetation and seaweed, unlike the beaches farther north where the Salt Keep stood, where there was nothing to rot in the water but stone. This area was damp and foggy, often warmer than the surrounding regions. The mists that Atrius had been relying on to hide his cousin's fleet were thick and soupy—I could feel the moisture hanging in the air like a blanket.

Atrius stared out into those mists, silent, jaw set. I did, too, the hair prickling on the back of my neck.

Neither of us had to acknowledge it aloud. The foreboding.

I pulled myself away from it, gathering materials and drawing sigils in the sand. Eventually, Atrius joined me, and together we caught a lizard scampering in the rocks and killed it, dripping its blood over the sigils and then tossing it into the fire.

Then I sat down at the edge of the waterline so the cold, salty water lapped at my dress, facing the fire.

Atrius had seen me do this several times now. We both knew the routine. But just before I was about to let myself fall into the vision, he abruptly stepped forward.

"Be careful," he murmured, close enough that his lips brushed my ear, and his breath made goose bumps rise over my flesh.

"I know what I'm doing," I said. A ghost of a smile flitted over his lips. And he stepped away, as I let myself fall into the threads—back, and back, and back.

I WAS FALLING. I was falling so fast I couldn't grab onto anything. It was almost as bad as it was the last time I Threadwalked—almost— but at least now, I was expecting it.

Threads flew by, smears of silver. I managed to grab one of them, hurling myself onto it so awkwardly that it hit my stomach and knocked the wind out of me. Then I hauled myself to my feet.

Everything stilled. The other threads faded into the background, millions of possibilities yet to be explored. The sky was a velvet night, calm and star-speckled.

I focused on the thought of Atrius's fleet, bending the thread before me toward it.

Show it to me, I whispered into the night, and began walking along the thread.

The mists rolled in thick. The stars disappeared beneath the fog. I was disoriented, the thread wobbly beneath me, but I just kept walking.

And walking.

And walking.

My brow furrowed. I should have felt something by now.

But nothing. Nothing but mists.

Perhaps seering on the fleet wasn't enough. Perhaps I needed to go farther.

Veratas. Show me Veratas.

The mists grew suddenly, brutally cold. Goose bumps rose over my skin. Shivers racked my body. I braced, but kept walking.

A figure appeared in the mist, far ahead of me.

Atrius's cousin, maybe?

My steps quickened. The figure was walking, too, though much slower than I was. When I got within a few paces, close enough to make out their presence, I stopped short.

"Sightmother?"

Her back was to me, and the mist obscured her. But even in this intangible dream world, I would recognize the Sightmother anywhere. I briefly considered the possibility that she was actually *in* this Threadwalk with me—shared Threadwalks were possible, though rare and very difficult. But this version of her . . . she was silent, ephemeral, like a ghost.

A knot twisted in my stomach, disconcerted by her presence here, even if I didn't know why.

In a few long strides, I caught up to her. She walked beside my thread in steady, even paces. She wore her red blindfold, the ribbon unusually long, fluttering behind her—a lone shock of color in a world of misty gray, except for—

My attention fell to her bare feet, and the crimson, bloody footprints they left behind her.

The sense of looming dread rose.

What could this mean? That the Sightmother was in danger?

But before I could push the vision deeper, her head snapped toward me.

She didn't speak. But her hands reached out, cupped together as if to pass something to me. I opened mine—

—And gasped in pain.

Scalding liquid burned my skin. I tried to jerk my hands away, but the Sightmother grabbed them and forced my palms up—forced them open to receive the fresh, bubbling-hot blood.

And then, she was gone.

With a strangled cry, I lowered my hands to let the blood fall away, flecks of it splashing onto my feet. Weaver, it *hurt*, like even the remnants ate through my skin second by second.

A path through the mist opened before me. There were no intersections in the threads now. Only one path forward. Inevitability.

There was nothing more frightening than inevitability.

Stop, something inside me screamed. *You don't want to see.*

But I had a task. I continued. The thread cut into the bottom of my feet. *Drip, drip, drip*, as the blood from my feet and the blood from my hands fell to the glass abyss below.

The mist faded.

The smell of salt filled my nostrils. The breeze was warm and pleasant. Somewhere distant, the wind rustled the leaves of vegetation. The ocean sang its rhythmic song against the shore.

Pleasant.

Foreboding.

I kept walking. Faster now.

The beach surrounded me. It was beautiful—the kind of place I would dream of as a child, when I thought the ocean was a mythical thing far away. It was nighttime, the sand bathed in silver. Dwellings dotted the shore, some wood with thatched roofs, some well-constructed tents. The tents were familiar. They were the same style as those I slept in every day, alongside Atrius's army.

All were empty. No footprints in the sand, save for my own.

Hello? I called out.

No one answered.

Show me the settlement, I pushed the vision, even though every nerve in my body screamed, *Get out of here, turn back, go away. This is wrong.*

Now each step was a compulsion. My hands were in agony, the skin bubbling, the *dripdripdrip* of the blood faster than ever.

I broke into a run without meaning to, past more empty houses and empty tents, tall trees closing in around me.

And then I tripped.

Something hard jutting up from the ground sent me to my knees.

I pushed myself up and craned my neck to look behind me.

There, sticking up from the dirt, was a—was that a rock? It was black and textured, partially buried.

It's a rock, I told myself.

You know it is not a rock, another voice whispered.

I crawled to it, head spinning.

You know this looks familiar, the voice jeered.

No.

I started digging. My hands were so bloody they slipped against the sand. My fingernails snapped. I kept going, clawing at handful after handful of dirt, praying to my god—praying to his god—that I was wrong.

I was so frantic that my fingernails, or what was left of them, had torn Atrius's face by the time I revealed it, marring those too-hard, beautiful features with deep rivulets of red-black vampire blood.

No.

I couldn't breathe. Couldn't think. This was no longer a Threadwalk. No longer a dream. Everything about this was real.

I grabbed Atrius's exposed horn to pull him from the sand.

But his eyes remained wide open and sightless. Blood smeared his skin, red from my hands and black from the wounds I'd accidentally gouged.

"Atrius," I choked out.

I dug more, pulled more, trying to get him out—

And then he came free.

Not all of him.

His head.

His throat had been severed, the cut messy and dripping. His hair was matted with blood. I let out a choked sound of horror, but I couldn't let him go. Couldn't look away.

Look, the voice whispered.

And I lifted my head. Forced myself to take in something other than Atrius's head.

And then I realized it—that the town was not empty.

No, I had missed the many, many rocks, one every few feet, in the sand of the beach, in the gritty dirt of the trees, in the vegetation.

Rocks that were not rocks at all. Rocks that were actually pieces of shoulders, or heads, or hands, or legs.

Hundreds of corpses.

In a panic, I leapt to my feet. I didn't drop Atrius's head—instead I clutched it to my chest, as if to protect him.

The clouds rolled in. Thunder roared. The first drops hit my head, hot and fast.

Of course it was blood.

This is a vision, I told myself. *I can leave. I can stop this.*

But no matter how many times I said it, I couldn't bring myself to fully believe it. Nor could I bring myself to drop Atrius. I clutched him tight, in a gruesome embrace, and threw myself from the thread.

And together, we fell.

And fell.

And fell.

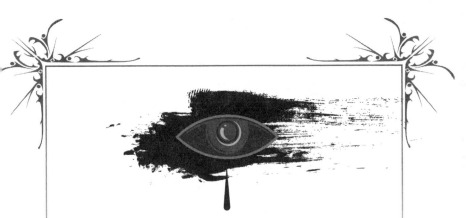

CHAPTER THIRTY-ONE

I was on my hands and knees, coughing violently, when my consciousness returned to my body. My chest burned. My stomach lurched. I gagged up a mouthful of stomach-sour salt water.

Atrius knelt beside me, his hand on my forearm. My clothes were soaking wet. I shivered violently.

"—tide is coming in," Atrius was saying, as he dragged me across the beach. "I don't want you to drown."

Atrius.

It took a moment for me to come back to myself—to feel his presence, strong and forceful and very much alive.

He let go of me on a drier stretch of sand, and I had to resist the sudden, overpowering urge to throw myself against him.

"Here." A heavy cloak fell around my shoulders. Atrius's hands stayed there, on my arms, for a few seconds longer than they needed to. "Stay near the fire."

I struggled to orient myself. "How l-long was I g-gone?"

I couldn't keep my teeth from chattering. The moon seemed higher in the sky. I must have been Walking for quite some time, especially if the tide came in enough to reach me while I was under.

"More than an hour."

Atrius settled beside me, watching me. He didn't need to ask. The question was in his stare.

I should have been thinking about how to lie to Atrius. I had been commanded to kill him. Yet the thought didn't even cross my mind. The truth poured out of me immediately.

"Something is wrong," I choked out. "On the island. Something is wrong."

Atrius's aura went cold.

"Wrong how?"

"I don't know." Visions were difficult to decode. Rarely literal. What I had seen could mean many things. But I was so utterly certain that, at its core, it meant *danger*.

"But something is wrong, Atrius," I said. "I'm sure of that."

He didn't question me. He knew better by now.

He rose abruptly, and I did, too, holding onto his arm to steady myself. Together, we set back off toward camp.

ATRIUS DIDN'T WANT to wait for the Bloodborn ships to make it up the coast. He ordered ships be sent from the coastal regions of Vasai—the closest he had available. What arrived were little more than fishing boats, certainly not the warship fleet that he'd arrived on, but if Atrius cared he didn't show it. He'd throw wooden planks on the water and paddle his way to Veratas if he had to.

There was no sleeping in the two days it took for him to arrange for the boats. Not for him, and not for me. I didn't want to sleep when I knew what dreams would be waiting for me—and lately, the dreams I had alone were never welcome. Instead, I threw myself into helping with the preparations.

While Atrius didn't share the reasons for his change of plans, the warriors knew that something was wrong. The mood over the camp was tense and uneasy. Among the most frantic was Erekkus, who pulled me aside the first free moment we had among Atrius's flurry of orders.

"Is this because of your seering?" he asked me, his grip on my arm white-knuckled. "What did you see? What does Veratas have to do with this?"

Erekkus's presence shocked me. The fear was so intense that his touch alone was painful.

"It's a precaution." The platitude tasted so disgustingly false on my tongue.

"Bullshit."

I didn't want to lie to Erekkus. I didn't want to tell him the truth, either, especially when Atrius had decided not to.

"It was Atrius's decision—"

"I have a child on that island!" Erekkus barked, his fingernails digging into my arm. "Fucking *tell me*, Sylina. *Please*."

My mouth tasted like ash.

A child. The thought left me reeling. Atrius had told me the island was full of his warriors' families. The realization that Erekkus had a child—that the child was among those civilians—

The image of that village with bodies protruding from the sand seared itself into my mind, stubbornly.

I laid my hand atop Erekkus's. His soul was frantic, barely kept under control by a fraying tether of self-control. I reached for his threads and, so subtly he wouldn't recognize it, I sent him calm.

"If I could tell you anything I knew definitively," I said softly, "I would. I promise you that, Erekkus."

His expression crumbled for a moment, like stone collapsing, before he straightened his back and turned away.

"Let's get those boxes to the shore," he said. "He wants them all ready to go as soon as the boats get here."

And just like that, we slipped back into work—our only distraction, and all of us were grateful for it.

The boats came quickly. The supplies were ready once they did. We loaded them up immediately. Only a small force of soldiers would be going on the journey, the rest remaining at camp.

Once it was time to board, Atrius turned to me. "You should stay—" he started.

But I snapped, "Do you really think that's going to work?"

Apparently not, because he didn't argue. Maybe I even sensed that just a tiny part of him was relieved to have me there.

I only had time to pack a sparse bag. It wouldn't take long to get to the island—it was only a few days away, secluded not by distance but by the thick mists that surrounded it. I threw together some clothing and food. Weapons, of course. My sword went to my hip, as usual. My dagger would go to my thigh.

But before I strapped it down, I hesitated. Alone in my tent, beneath the flickering lantern light, I unsheathed it.

The dagger the Sightmother had given me didn't look remarkable. It was simple and plain, no ornamentation, no ethereal glow— nothing to indicate that it had been blessed. And yet, the magic of it pulsed beneath my fingertips, warming the threads with the foreboding breath of death.

I shook away a chill, sheathed the dagger, and grabbed my pack, leaving all the rest behind.

THE MISTS WERE so thick that Atrius had to navigate based on maps and the compass, not sight. My abilities were useful, so I stood with him at the bow, helping to guide.

No one spoke. Atrius had been cagey about the information he dispensed. But these men had been fighting at his side for a very, very long time. They knew when something was wrong.

Eventually, the island's silhouette emerged through the soupy white. For its small size, it was majestic, the center rising into cliffs that disappeared into the thickening clouds. Forests and greenery clustered around the mountain's base, stretching out in all directions. Atrius steered our small makeshift fleet around the island, to its far eastern side, and docked us on a stretch of sandy beach.

The boats ground onto the shore. Atrius climbed from the boat first, when we'd barely stopped moving, and I was right behind him.

I shivered. It wasn't cold, but I couldn't calm the goose bumps on my arms. The beach appeared exactly as it had in my vision, right down to the narrow, trampled path leading into the trees.

Right down to the terrible emptiness.

Atrius surveyed the tree line as his warriors departed the ships. Then he turned back and looked at me. His face was set and grim—his presence even more so.

He didn't need to ask the question aloud.

I shook my head. I sensed no one. Not a soul.

"How far is the settlement?" I asked.

"A mile, maybe. Sheltered by the trees. Not too close to the shore."

A mile. Far enough that I wouldn't be able to feel them from here, anyway. Still, I felt little relief.

Atrius drew his sword before we continued, then nudged my arm and gestured to mine, prompting me to follow suit. Behind us, I heard a symphony of steel against leather as the soldiers did the same.

We journeyed deep into the forest. The farther we got from the shore, the warmer it grew, the air thick and humid.

In the threads, I felt something stirring, so weak at first I couldn't quite identify it.

"I sense something," I murmured to Atrius.

"What?"

"I'm not sure. We're too far."

His steps quickened. "We're almost there. Tell me if anything changes."

Ahead, a clearing parted before us, the moonlight pouring silver through an opening in the tree cover.

Exactly like my vision. Many tents. A few wood-and-thatched shacks.

The strange sensation in the threads grew stronger. Weaver, it was *odd*—so faint, and yet so constant and all-consuming, like a distant sound coming from all directions at once. It made my head throb. I'd never felt anything like it before.

"There's something here," I told Atrius, voice low. "I just . . . I can't tell what. Or who."

People? Were those vampire souls? They often felt different than humans did, but never quite like this—so weak and so loud at once.

The moonlight fell over Atrius's face. The cottages and tents were silent. A faint breeze blew through the trees.

Atrius turned back to his soldiers, lifted a single finger to his lips, and then nodded to the huts in a silent command—*search*.

I started to go, but Atrius grabbed my arm.

"With me," he said, low in my ear.

Together we peered into the first cottage, only to find it empty—not just empty, but looking as if whoever had lived there had simply disappeared. A glass was knocked over, broken into two jagged shards on a makeshift wooden table. A bedroll in the corner was half-rolled. A book was left open on the table, spilled ink beside it.

In every tent, every cottage, we found the same thing.

I still sensed no presences—or at least, I thought I didn't. It was getting so hard to tell, that strange buzzing growing louder and louder in my head, all the threads vibrating with it. I found myself nearly staggering into a doorframe because the interference made it so difficult to make out where I was going.

At that, Atrius's hand came to my shoulder, and didn't let go, as if to steady me.

"Where is it coming from?" he asked.

"I don't—I can't—"

Weaver, my head *hurt*.

Atrius's brow furrowed. His head dipped closer. His voice lowered.

"What is it?" he murmured.

I tried to cut through the noise. Tried to distill it into something I could make sense of.

I staggered from the hut and out into the clearing—farther still, where the tree cover canopied above us again. I tripped several times, not paying attention to where I was going, only to the threads. By the end, I was crawling on my hands and knees, pressing my palms to the earth, as if to drag my way along them.

And then my body stopped.

Every muscle tensed.

Dread fell over me, icy and razor-toothed, tearing me open.

I wanted to be wrong.

I wanted to be wrong so much that I reached out through the threads, past them, out to the goddess Acaeja herself—the goddess I had given my eyes and my finger and my entire life to—and begged her: *Please. Please don't let this happen.*

The goddess was silent.

The world was silent.

Save for a drop of something warm and thick and black-red on my hand.

I did not need to look up. But I heard it when Atrius did, because he let out this horrible, choked sound, strangled, like the air was dying in his throat.

Erekkus saw it next, and he wasn't nearly as quiet.

"Fucking goddess," he gasped. "Get them down! Get them fucking down!"

And then he kept screaming it, over and over again, in Obitraen, faster and faster, as he tried to claw his way up the trees.

Tried to claw his way up to the countless vampire bodies staked there, high in the branches above us, not quite dead and not quite alive. Dozens of them. Hundreds.

Drip. Drip. Drip.

And then I felt it—felt what the half-alive agony of the countless vampires had been drowning out in the threads. Movement. Lots of it. Out in the woods.

I leapt to my feet and whirled to Atrius, who screamed orders.

I threw myself against him without thinking, tackling him to the ground.

"Get back!" I screamed.

But the words didn't make it out of my mouth before the explosives hit.

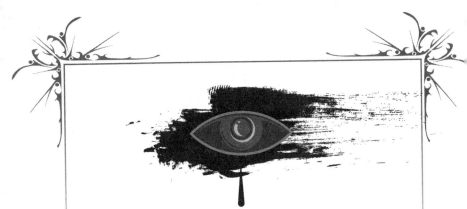

CHAPTER THIRTY-TWO

I'm nine years old and crawling from the wreckage of my home. I'm nine years old and I can't find my brother and—

"SYLINA."

I couldn't orient myself. There was too much activity, the threads tangled and impossible to read. I flailed my hands out, finding something warm and solid.

Atrius.

His presence was the first firm thing I could grab onto, strong and unique. The only thing that seemed tangible when everything else was moving around us—screaming, fighting.

"Say something if you want to let me know you're conscious," he grunted. "I can't see your eyes."

I almost choked a laugh at that, and I started a snarky response, but—

"Behind you," I choked out.

Just before the masked soldier came flying from the smoke, sword aimed right for Atrius's head.

He whirled around just in time, swords clashing. I tried to push myself up to my hands and knees, though that was difficult, with the threads so erratic. My own sword, which had been in my hands when the explosives hit, had to be here in the rubble somewhere. I felt around, my hands hitting hard rubble, frayed grass—wet, motionless skin of a body fallen from the trees—

Metal.

My dagger. Good enough. I grabbed it and managed to get to my feet. Atrius was already yanking his sword from the throat of his attacker. He turned to me for a moment, then his eyes widened as he grabbed me and skillfully drove his blade through another soldier's gut, seconds before they would have been on me.

Weaver, I didn't even sense it. How did I not sense that?

"Stay with me," Atrius ground out. "Right here."

A command. Firm and inarguable.

I couldn't even take issue with his tone. I was mostly blind. Staying with Atrius was my only chance of making it out of this alive.

I could barely make out what was happening around us, but I knew that it was chaos. Soldiers—the Pythora King's?—poured from the forest, mingling with Atrius's in a chaotic, bloody mess. Atrius's men were outnumbered, and I had no way of knowing how many of them might have been injured or killed with the initial round of explosives.

They were everywhere. Everywhere at once.

Atrius fought like an animal, like a force of nature. I couldn't track his movements. Couldn't even track my own.

And yet, when I finally managed to grasp onto a thread, it was that of a Pythora soldier—a soldier lunging for Atrius's back.

I acted before I thought. Something I had been scolded for countless times in the Arachessen—an impulse I'd thought I'd ground out of myself.

Apparently not. Because when I saw that blade coming for Atrius, I simply moved.

It was clumsy. A bad shot. I could barely grasp my surroundings.

My dagger made contact with our attacker's flesh somewhere—I couldn't even tell where—but seconds later, nothing existed but pain.

It's a strange feeling, when your body suddenly stops obeying you. Mine was a tool I'd learned to wield to perfection.

Until, all at once, it wasn't.

Distantly, as if in another world, I heard Atrius shout something—my name?

My palms were pressed to the dirt. I tried to get up. Failed. My hand went to my abdomen and felt warm blood bubbling between my fingers.

Shit.

I crawled over the sand, groping for my weapon. I couldn't feel the threads. Couldn't orient myself.

When I managed to grasp them, I sensed—

Sensed—

Atrius, standing over my attacker, hacking into him brutally, strike after unforgiving strike, long after flesh was beaten down into formless gore.

All around us, there was death. Death everywhere.

And yet when Atrius abandoned his very, very dead target and whirled around, he wasn't looking at any of that—not his own warriors or the people he had lost.

Only me.

His presence was an anchor. I held onto it tight, like a raft in a stormy sea.

But I was slipping.

Atrius fell to his knees beside me. When he pressed his hands to my wound, it took me a moment to realize the keening whimper I was hearing was mine.

He let out a wordless sound through his teeth.

My brow furrowed.

Surely I was hallucinating, to think that Atrius's presence, forever unbreakable, forever solid, forever silent, was now screaming—screaming in utter terror.

Over me.

Ridiculous.

I had the strange urge to tell him this, the way I always wanted to tell my brother amusing or outlandish things as a child, but when I opened my mouth, I felt as if liquid was flowing into my lungs.

Warmth surrounded me. It took me several long seconds of half consciousness to realize Atrius had lifted me. The sound of the battle fell into a distant, fuzzy din.

"Sylina," Atrius was saying to me. "Stay right here. Stay right here."

And then, closer to my ear, "*Vivi*. Stay right here."

Stop shouting at me, I'm trying, I wanted to tell him.

But I was falling further and further from the threads.

The last thing I heard was Atrius's voice, screaming so loud it cracked, hurling three words of Obitraen to his men over the sound of the battlefield.

It was in Obitraen, and yet somehow I knew exactly what he was saying:

Kill them all.

My fingers tightened around Atrius's shirt fabric. A sudden wave of anger rolled over me.

In my fading consciousness, I thought of another explosion barely survived by a nine-year-old girl.

I thought of civilians thrust into tunnels and used as human shields for a cowardly warlord.

I thought of my brother, once a teenager, now a man, sentenced to a slow, inevitable death.

I thought of innocent vampire children hanging from trees.

I thought of the fucking Pythora King.

And I thought, *Yes. Kill them all.*

And I did not think of the Arachessen, or the Sightmother, or the blessed dagger—or Acaeja at all.

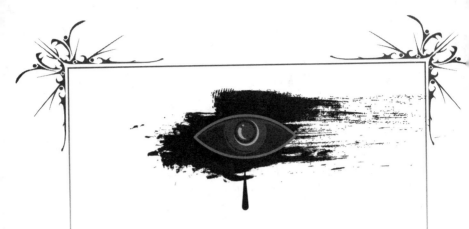

CHAPTER THIRTY-THREE

I jerked upright with a gasp.

Pain. Sharp, agonizing pain that cut me in two.

Where was I?

Someone was touching me. I lashed out at them before I was able to stop myself.

"Control her," an older female voice barked, and another set of hands grabbed my shoulders, pushing me firmly back to the bedroll.

The threads evaded me. But those hands—those were familiar.

"Don't kill the healer," Atrius growled, though I couldn't be sure if I imagined that he sounded relieved.

Healer.

I reached for my abdomen, and someone smacked my fingers away.

"Don't touch," the healer snapped. "The stitches are fresh. And my medicines only go so far on a human."

I steadied my breath, following the threads fanning out around me. They came into focus slowly, and brought with them a blindingly powerful headache, but I was just relieved to grasp my surroundings again. For a few terrifying moments back there, it had felt like I'd been cut away from the only thing that tethered me to the world.

I was back at camp, in a tent—mine? Atrius's? It was still so hard to grasp. The healer, a vampire woman, knelt beside me. Her presence radiated sadness and exhaustion.

I turned my head, which was slightly elevated, and realized that I lay against Atrius's lap.

When the memories from before I was injured filtered back, the first was Atrius's voice as I faded.

And then the explosions, and the bodies, and—

The bodies.

I bit my tongue hard, right over that old scar tissue. I still nearly drew blood. It didn't help.

If I had been lucky, the wave of rage I'd felt in my final moments of consciousness would have been a symptom of my delirious state. If I had been lucky, I would have woken up the steadfast, calm Arachessen I had been trained to be.

I was not lucky.

The healer stood and said something to Atrius in Obitraen, to which he responded with a nod and a few curt words. She left the tent, leaving the two of us alone.

It was Atrius's tent, I realized now. He'd brought me back to his.

I sat up again—slowly this time.

"She said to be careful," Atrius snapped.

"I am being careful."

I turned to face him. His weariness seeped from him like a stubborn scent. His walls were heavier than usual—they felt more forced, and like it was taking him more effort to hold them up.

But I could still sense what lay behind them.

I gingerly touched my wound. No, the vampire healer had not been able to help me the way an Arachessen healer could have, but she still did a damned good job. The wound hurt, and it would still bleed if I pulled the stitches, but it was far from life-threatening. Interesting that Nyaxia's magic could be used to heal humans, too, albeit imperfectly.

"How many?" I choked out.

The terrible, ironic echo in those words didn't hit me until they left my lips. But Atrius heard it immediately, and his face fell.

"Too many," he murmured. "Too many."

His answer twisted in my heart, right into the secret wound that had bled there for twenty years.

I knew it was coming. I knew that those people hanging in the trees were already dead, whether their hearts still pumped weak amounts of blood or not. But that did nothing to lessen the shards of anger inside me at Atrius's answer.

Outside the tent, voices collected. The amount of rage and grief in the presences around us left me dizzy.

"How long have—"

"We killed all of the Pythora King's men." Atrius's lip twitched into a sneer, weakly, as if this bloodshed was barely enough to bring him satisfaction. "Not a single human soldier made it off that island alive. We ensured that. Even if we had to pay heavily for it."

A small victory. It didn't feel like much. The Pythora King would have only sent a small group to the island, knowing they would be sacrifices. Those lives were a small consolation for the number they had taken.

"We took back all the wounded we could," Atrius went on. "Including you. But there are many more."

A strange flicker over his face—something I couldn't quite decipher. He stood.

"You rest. I need to—"

But I started to stand, too.

He caught my arm when I was halfway up. "What are you doing?"

"I'm no great healer," I said, "but I'm not useless—"

"No."

"I'm not going to argue with you."

I stood up and was greeted with a wave of dizziness. Atrius didn't loosen his hold on my arm.

The threads were alight with activity outside. Pulling him along with me, I staggered to the tent flap and thrust it open.

Weaver help me.

Atrius's army had been destroyed.

To one side, dozens of bodies lay lined up, wrapped up in white fabric. An entire swath of tents to the east had been destroyed. Everywhere around us, warriors hurried to help their injured comrades.

A ragged breath left my lips.

"This isn't just from the island."

Too many injured here. Far more than Atrius had brought to Veratas.

"No." His voice was low. Thick with anger.

Slowly, I pieced the truth together.

The Pythora King had somehow learned of the island. Attacked it. Used it as bait.

And then, when the most capable of Atrius's forces were gone, he had struck—the island, *and* the camp.

At least here, Atrius's men appeared to have been able to hold their position—if only barely. But the Pythora King's goal probably had not been to destroy them. What was the fun in that? No, his goal was to break them, because that's how he had won his country, too. By breaking the people within it.

I yanked my arm away from Atrius and started forward. He reached to stop me, but I snapped, "Would you want to sit in there and do nothing?"

His mouth closed. Understanding flickered across his face—as if recognizing something familiar in me.

He let his hand fall to his side.

"Know your limits," he said. "Be careful."

I nodded, and he straightened his back, and the two of us threw ourselves into the fight against the inevitable.

CHAPTER THIRTY-FOUR

The hours wore on fast. I could move, albeit slowly and a bit painfully. My headache was far worse than my wounds. I followed the direction of the healer, attending to those she couldn't get to quickly enough. My healing magic was weak, especially for vampires, but I could ease pain until she arrived.

I did not stop working. When the sun rose, we moved to tents and continued our work. When the sun set again, we moved outside once more.

With every body I leaned over, every soldier who, in the throes of delirium, asked about their wife or husband or child, with every suffering person who knew their death was near, with every one who slipped away despite our best efforts, the steady beat of rage beneath my skin grew louder.

Eventually, after countless hours—Weaver, countless days—I turned to the healer and asked, "Who's next?"

She wiped the blood from her hands. "No one."

At first, I didn't understand what she meant.

"No one is left," she said. "We've done all that we can do. Now we wait." She went to the tent flap and opened it. "Sleep. That's what I'm going to do."

I did go back to my tent, because where else would I go? But immediately, I knew I couldn't stay there, no matter how exhausted I was. The idea of sitting alone with the pained echoes in the threads was sickening.

So I stripped off my blood-and-sweat-drenched clothes, and threw on a fresh dress. I didn't even consider my bedroll before I went outside.

It was very late—nearly dawn. The air was damp with humidity, though cold. The mists seeped into the sky, tinged rosy with the faintest hint of distant, oncoming dawn. It was unnaturally, eerily still. Like nature itself was holding its breath. The smoke from the last of the funereal pyres had risen into the sky, melding with the mists, the scent fading into the salty smell of the ocean. By tomorrow, both would be gone. The only traces of those who had died would be the ashes, which Atrius's men would cast into the sea.

But the people who remained behind would be marked by that grief forever.

I didn't realize fully how much the way I looked at the vampires had changed until this moment—until I realized how they bore the scars of loss just as strongly as humans did.

I stood at the entrance to my tent for a long time. Then I began walking.

I wasn't sure how I knew Atrius was not in his tent, even long before I was close enough to feel his presence. Nor why I wasn't surprised when I reached the beach to find him standing by the shore, staring out to the horizon.

For a moment, a sharp stab of mournful regret rang out in my chest—regret that I no longer could see what it must have looked like in sight alone, with all its intangible imperfections. I could imagine it, though—his silhouette dark against the silver waves, his hair like a waterfall of moonlight. Maybe, if I could see him that way, I would have felt the overpowering urge to draw him, the way I had once felt the urge to draw the sea.

When you see the moon rise, he had said to me once, *some might say there's something more to it than coordinates in the sky.*

I'd thought he was just mocking me then. But right here, I understood it.

I took my shoes off once I hit the sand, leaving them abandoned behind me. There was something grounding about feeling the damp sand against my toes. Atrius didn't move as I approached. Didn't look away from the sea.

A breeze blew, stealing strands of my hair and Atrius's toward the sea. His nostrils flared. I took a step closer, which made his gaze snap to me.

"You shouldn't be here."

In his presence, a twinge of hunger rang out—subtle, and yet, I knew that whatever he was allowing me to sense was only a fraction of what he truly felt.

Atrius, I knew, was starving in a way that went far beyond physical hunger. I could feel that in him, vicious and yearning, making the hairs stand up on the back of my neck.

But I only said, "It's where I want to be."

I didn't realize until the words left my mouth exactly how true they were.

His jaw tightened.

"You shouldn't be near me."

True, a voice whispered in the back of my head. But the danger wasn't him. The danger was myself—or maybe something even bigger, the natural tension of oil and fire inching closer.

I didn't dignify that with an answer this time. Instead, I took another step.

It was answer enough.

We stood there beside each other for a long, silent moment, acutely aware of each other's presence and saying nothing. And yet, saying everything—because just standing here, next to each other, our shoulders inches away, felt thick with meaning.

"It was stupid of you to put yourself, bleeding, next to a bunch of injured vampires," he said at last.

"You have a funny way of saying thank you."

A beat. A glance. And then, more quietly, "Thank you. For helping them."

"Thank you for saving my life."

"I wasn't sure if I had, at first." The statement came with a strange chill, gone before I could feel it too closely.

Then he added, beneath his breath, "Too many, I couldn't."

His voice made me think of Erekkus's screams. The kind of sound that followed a person for the rest of their life.

I said, "I looked, but I couldn't find Erekkus."

"He's gone."

"Gone?"

"He needed to be alone. I'm in no position to stop him."

"How old was his little one?"

"Ten."

An ache in my chest.

"Young."

"And yet what kind of life did she have for those ten years? All of it spent . . ."

Atrius's voice trailed off.

Then he whirled to me, eyes bright, mouth twisted into a sneer.

"You shouldn't be here," he said again.

But I just stepped closer again. Pressed my hand to the center of his chest, over his sweat-stained cotton shirt. Far beneath my touch, his curse writhed.

I didn't want to give him sympathy. I barely even considered it. When Naro and I clawed our way to survival through the worst of the Pythora Wars, we lost so much. In the beginning, when our parents were killed, people used to say, *I'm sorry*. And then the years passed, and the bodies piled higher, and no one said they were sorry anymore. The loss was just another unfair part of life. No one needed platitudes. When my sister died, people gave us bread instead. It was much more useful.

I felt so alone then. Now, as an adult, I knew that the reason why people were distant was not because they didn't feel our loss, but because they felt it too much. They had no room for more. I thought perhaps one day, I'd stop feeling it, too. Perhaps one day, it would fade. The Arachessen promised me it would.

It never did.

Maybe the Sightmother had lied to me. Maybe I was just never good enough to be an Arachessen. But the truth was the truth. Fifteen years had passed, and now here I was, as angry as ever. Angrier. And tonight, I felt Atrius's loss just as strongly as my own.

And I just couldn't anymore.

I. Just. Couldn't.

"Why?" I said. "Do you think I'm afraid of this? Afraid of you? As if I don't feel the darkest parts of you every night. As if I don't recognize—"

"You recognize it because you feel it just as much." His words were hard. All sharp-edged accusation. Strange, though, that such cruel words held such tender affection beneath them. Like he was challenging me to meet him at this most difficult terrain, somewhere that hurt, somewhere that was just as angry and broken as we were.

It was wrong of me.

But I wanted it, too.

His hand touched my chest, too, mirroring mine on his, my heartbeat strong and fast beneath his skin.

"In the beginning I doubted you," he breathed, his words close to my face. "I doubted why the Arachessen would let you leave. But now I see why they didn't want you. Because you're just like us. Just as cursed by the past. And that curse just keeps fucking taking, doesn't it?"

"You're right." My mouth twisted into a sneer without my permission—my teeth gritted against my words. I thought I'd feel shame to admit it to myself. I didn't. I felt so blissfully free. "I understand you. I'm just as broken. Just as angry. I hate them just as much. Nothing will make that alright. Nothing. Once I thought a goddess could. But I was wrong."

I fought the urge to take the words back as soon as they left my lips. But that was out of guilt. Not because I didn't feel they were true.

Beneath my palm, the curse inside him pulsed, as if struck.

"But I think you know that, too," I murmured. "All about goddesses and broken promises. Don't you?"

He laughed, vicious as torn flesh. "You want to see the truth, Sylina? Do you have room in your heart for another dark story?"

He was taunting me. Like his jeering tone could chase me away. He was wrong.

I thought of the fragments of his vision, still burning in my memory and throbbing in his chest. The snow. The cold. A young vampire man's head in his hands. And Nyaxia, cold and cruel and drenched in hate.

"I live in dark stories. And I've been living in yours for nearly four months. If you're going to invite me in, invite me." I pushed against his chest, hard. "I already see you, Atrius. I'm not afraid."

So quick I wouldn't even sense the movement, his other hand clutched my hair, tilting my head back toward his. I could feel his words over my lips when he spoke again, low like shifting gravel.

"You want my confessions, seer? Fine. Once, a long time ago, just like you, I thought my goddess would save us. And I gave her everything. Everything."

The walls, all at once, shattered. And the wave of pain, of rage, of darkness and fear that rolled over me threatened to sweep me away. I had been reaching deep into Atrius's presence—now, his emotions, such perfect mirrors of my own, surrounded me.

Far in the threads, I sensed an old memory—a city of white and red, powerful spires and moonlit crimson glass windows, framed against mountainous peaks.

"Do you see that?" His mouth came to my ear, breath hard and ragged. "That was my home once. A long time ago. My cursed, damned home. The House of Blood. When I was young, I met a man who was an idealist. A prince. My prince. And some wretched seer's prophecy said that he would save the House of Blood from itself, and I believed in him."

His voice sounded like glass breaking, all pain and anger. It poured through my threads, mingling with my own.

"So I followed. I built his army. I led his warriors. People who trusted me. And together, we journeyed to places no mortal, human or vampire, should go."

The images melted, reformed. I couldn't even make sense of the next fractured memories—buildings floating in the night sky, shadowy figures walking on misty nothingness, bodiless faces peering through the darkness. All of them too distant, too quick, to capture.

"We were to earn back the love of Nyaxia. We would prove to her that the House of Blood was worthy of her. The things we did—"

A ragged breath. His threads pulsed like a quickening heartbeat, as if horrified and terrified by the memories, even now, even all these years later. Goose bumps rose on my arms.

"No mortals," he breathed, "should do what we did. We committed acts worthy of fucking gods. Great things. Terrible things. All in Nyaxia's name. All to prove our love to our goddess. For *decades*."

His jaw tightened there, shook against the silence. Every part of his presence railed against this exposure. He was trying to reassemble his defenses, reel in what had broken free.

But I whispered, "And?"

One word. A beckoning hand. An open door.

Why? Why did I want to know, even if it hurt? Even if it made it harder—perhaps impossible—to rebuild my own walls?

He let out a shaky breath. He was trembling, every muscle taut.

"And we went back to her," he whispered, slowly, between clenched teeth. "My prince and I. We gave her every head she asked for. Every artifact. Every slain monster. *Everything*. And then we went to our knees to ask for our salvation." A single, enraged tear slid down his cheek. "And I will never forget the sound of her *laugh*."

And as if I had been there with him, I could hear it, too, floating through the past to the present, as beautiful and terrible as funeral hymns.

"She said we were fools," he spat, "to think that our ancestors' disrespect could ever be forgiven. She left me with two gifts that night, and two commands. The first gift was the head of my prince, and the first command was to carry it back to the House of Blood to present to the king and queen. The second gift . . ."

His throat bobbed. His hand fell over mine, over his chest, where the curse pulsed.

He didn't need to speak. I knew.

"And the second command?" I whispered.

A long pause. Like he couldn't bring himself to say it.

"She wanted a new kingdom conquered in her name," he said. "I offered that to her, with my own life as collateral."

And suddenly, it all clicked together.

"My people would not be allowed back home after being scorned by Nyaxia. The king and queen saw us—all of us—as complicit in their son's death. They still wanted to believe a prophecy existed. Still wanted to believe that their goddess could save us." His face hardened, like cut stone. "They had followed me to the ends of time. They had nowhere left to go. I was desperate to save them, even if I couldn't save myself. So I made a deal with the very goddess who had forsaken us."

I swallowed past the lump in my throat. His pain surrounded us both, scalding, and I knew it had been burning for years, decades, centuries.

I understood it so painfully well. The desire to believe that something larger than you could save you, even after it struck you down again and again.

"And now here we are," he ground out, lip curling. "The innocents I was trying to protect, slaughtered. The warriors I was trying to save, now dying at the hand of a human tyrant. All for a goddess who spited us already. All in the name of *blind fucking hope*."

Another tear glided down his cheek, the silver damp pooling in all those stone-cut lines of utter fury.

His fingers tightened in my hair.

"Tell me I'm a fool."

He was shaking with rage, so thick I could taste it in his exhale against my lips.

I shook my head. "No."

He let out a choked breath, his forehead leaning against mine.

"Tell me to stop."

Four words that could mean so much. *Tell me to stop*—stop this war, stop the search for redemption, stop the quest for vengeance, stop *this*, whatever dangerous thing was about to happen in this moment, inching toward inevitability.

I didn't want him to stop any of it.

I wanted Atrius to destroy the Pythora King. I wanted him to do it slowly, painfully, relishing revenge. I wanted him to let me help. I wanted him to save his people. I wanted him to earn Nyaxia's respect.

I wanted to burn it all down with him.

I murmured, "No."

Another wordless sound, a choked groan. "You shouldn't be here."

This time he spoke against my mouth—not quite a kiss, but the promise of one.

I whispered, "Why?"

"Because you make me ravenous."

You make me ravenous.

Those words buried in my soul. I felt the truth of them. Felt, somewhere innately, that he had said them to me once before—in Obitraen, the night he kissed me.

And I understood it. The hunger for revenge, for salvation, for blood, for sex, for death, for life, for all the things we'd been denied.

I felt it all.

"Good," I whispered.

And the word was swallowed up between us as his mouth crashed against mine.

CHAPTER THIRTY-FIVE

The kiss was a seamless continuation of what we'd ended weeks ago, in his room. This was not the quiet, confusing safety of the nights we spent curled up in each other's arms. This was not the stoic respect we'd built for each other over these last months.

This was a drawn blade, a battle, a fire. This was deadly.

I loved it.

My mouth opened against his immediately, accepting his breath, his tongue, his lips, and offering him my own. My hand slid from his chest to loop around his neck—his down my side, gripping tight where my waist met my hip.

My body arched against his, helpless with the desire to feel as much of him against me as I could. The threads caught fire the closer we were, the deeper I could fold myself into his presence. The sensations of him intoxicated me—his mouth, tongue sliding against mine in a way that felt like both an offering and a promise, his fingers clutching at me like he wanted to absorb me into himself.

We were warned of this, as young Arachessen. That sensations, physical connection, would be unusually powerful for us given the way we navigated the world. Like most things based in emotion, this was treated as a danger, a weakness to be culled.

My only clear thought in this moment now was, *Horseshit.*

Yes, it was a danger. But how did I not realize then that was the appeal? I wanted to hurl myself off this cliff.

I was ravenous.

We staggered backward in a tangle of limbs and wet clothing and frantic kisses and sickening lust. Atrius was leading me—I didn't know where until my back pressed to a wall of stone. The ocean was cold around our ankles, swelling with the tide. He'd dragged us behind a cluster of large rocks jutting from the sand.

Privacy. Because we were just out here, on the beach. And I didn't even care.

He broke our kiss, pushing me forcefully back against the rock. But I seized the moment to tear at his shirt, the buttons pulling apart with blissful ease.

And immediately, like a thirst-starved creature to water, my hands were all over his skin.

I hadn't wanted to admit it then, but I knew the first time I touched him, something had changed forever—a door cracked open in forbidden parts of myself. I could ignore it. For a time.

But never forget it.

Because touching Atrius was like immersing myself in every forbidden pleasure at once. His aura was so unbearably strong, unrestrained lust and hunger and anger and grief and—and all the things I tried to control in myself.

My fingers trailed down his torso, starting at his chest, then tracing the swell of his pectorals. Down, over the lean, defined muscle of his abdomen, marked with scars that each strummed a different vibration in the threads.

He let out a wordless, sound against my lips and pushed me hard against the rock. His fingers played at the strap of my nightdress, perilously thin.

"Yes," I breathed, and he let out a low groan as he ripped the straps at once, letting the cotton fall into the salty water around my ankles.

It wasn't as if the nightgown was doing much to protect me from the elements, but in its absence, my body reacted immediately to its exposure. Goose bumps rose over my skin. My breasts, already aching with desire, hardened and peaked against the misty air.

I wanted him against me immediately, skin against skin. But he hesitated. His awareness was such a physical force. I could feel his eyes lingering on my body, not just my breasts and the apex of my thighs, but the rest of me, too—every muscle, every curve.

And then his lust crested in a sudden wave, washing us both away, and he was everywhere.

His kiss was vicious, like a predator chasing down prey, and I met it with equal force. The sensation of his bare flesh against mine was overwhelming.

I couldn't breathe. Couldn't think.

Only feel.

His hands ran over my body, down my hips, lingering at my backside. I tangled my hands in his hair. I barely realized I was moaning against him, pathetic whimpers against his kisses.

I freed one hand to slide it down his body. I was bolder than I had been that night in his room. This time, I slid right into his trousers, running my grip down the length of his cock.

Oh, Weaver. Gods.

He hissed into my mouth and closed his teeth around my lower lip, making me gasp at the spark of pain.

I barely noticed it.

How could I pay attention to anything but this? But him, and the way his whole presence rearranged around that single touch?

His kiss stopped, movements slowing. He was breathing heavily, his heart thrumming hard—so hard I felt the beat of it in my own skin.

He pulled back, just enough to look at me, a stare that rippled through my entire body.

And then he dropped to his knees.

"Open your thighs for me," he commanded, and didn't even let me obey before he positioned one of my legs over his shoulder, his mouth finding my center.

Holy fucking gods—

He wasn't patient. Neither of us had that in us tonight. The first lick, demanding and starving, sent me a wave of pleasure that swept away everything else. I had to bite my tongue hard, so hard, right over that scar ridge, against my scream of pleasure, and still released a mangled moan.

He buried himself deeper between my legs, tongue unleashing a surge of impossible sensation. At my whimper, he let out a pleased growl that made me shiver.

I'd felt pleasure before. But this—I couldn't—

"Wider," he growled, urging my thighs apart. There was no playfulness in this, no flirtation. Only command.

I obeyed, challenging as it was when my legs were trembling. One of his hands slid up my body, flattening just shy of my breasts—holding me firmly against the stone, as if to make sure I remained upright.

"Mm," he murmured. "Better."

This time, with the better access he had, I couldn't choke back my scream. My back arched against the rock in a violent spasm as his tongue worked at me—licking the length of my slit, pausing to tease at my bud, returning to my entrance.

With each movement of his mouth, I unraveled more.

My heart was pounding, like a trapped rabbit. My skin burned. Weaver, what was he doing to me? I wanted more of it. All of it.

Pain, faintly, as his sharp fingernails dug into the tender skin of my thigh, as he pushed it open further—so he could plunge his tongue into me.

Fractured curses imbued my garbled moans, as he returned to my clit.

Then he smiled against me, and I could feel something hard—something sharp—against that sensitive flesh, that flesh that begged for everything from him—

And I felt his hunger. His lust.

All of it matched by mine.

"Yes," I choked out. "Do it."

I didn't question my own irrational willingness. I wanted it.

The reaction of his presence was swift and immediate, like the twitch of his cock in my hands.

The hand on my stomach, now the only thing keeping me upright, trailed fingers back and forth along my skin.

I understood what that movement was saying: *I will not hurt you.*

His mouth moved to my inner thigh. His teeth bit quick, a strike that made me gasp—more pleasure than pain, and whatever little pain there was disappeared when he drank.

Weaver help me. Weaver kill me.

I had heard that vampire venom could have a . . . pleasurable effect on human prey. But this was beyond my wildest expectations. Every nerve was aflame, pulsing from that wound. My hips bucked against him, chasing more, chasing friction, chasing penetration—fruitlessly, because he held me firmly still against the wall, at his mercy.

"Gods. *Atrius*—Weaver—I—"

The words were unintentional, jumbled, slurred.

His satisfaction rolled through me, the threads drawn so taut between us that we were like one being. With a satisfied moan, his lips left my wound. When they returned to my slit, his mouth was warm and wet—with my blood and my desire.

And when he feasted upon me this time, licking the blood clean with thorough care, he slid two fingers inside of me.

This time, I had to bite down on my hand to dampen my scream. My knuckles tightened around his hair. My body writhed in his grasp.

I fell into utter oblivion.

And when I became aware of my body again, Atrius's presence was all around me once more, his body pressed to me, his mouth against mine, leaving the taste of blood and sweat and my own desire on my lips, sweet and salty. My thighs had parted around his hips, his hands and the pressure against the rocks keeping me up.

Already, my hips were moving against the hardness of his cock, my hands sliding down his trousers until the hot flesh sprang free.

My body knew what it wanted. Knew what it needed.

He needed it, too. Our hunger, our lust, pulsed between us. Now I understood why the Arachessen banned sex. It was too much. Too powerful.

Though then again, it had never felt like this with any of my other dalliances.

I couldn't think about that now.

I couldn't think of anything.

My heat aligned with his cock. When the tip pressed against me, we both let out mangled exhales into each other's mouths.

But he broke away, breath heaving.

"You've never done this before."

Always a statement, never a question. He knew. How did he know?

"I've done enough," I said. Though even as I said it, it seemed foolish to relate whatever those were—tasks of seduction or curious experimentation—to whatever this would be.

Our bodies shifted against each other in minute, involuntary movements. His length twitched against my folds, slick, and though we both bit back our moans, I felt the shiver of our barely constrained lust through the threads.

Animals against bars.

Bars that were breaking.

"I'll start slow," he ground out. "But it may be difficult for me to—if I start to lose control—"

His words were clumsy and awkward. But I didn't need words to understand him. *Ravenous*, he had said.

Atrius was a man terrified of losing control. And I was asking him to balance on the knife's edge.

I kissed him deeply, our tongues mingling as his cock strained at my entrance once again. He was shaking. Weaver, *I* was shaking.

"I don't need you to be gentle with me," I whispered.

No. I wanted all of it.

His teeth closed around my lip, his nostrils flaring.

His mouth trailed to my ear, suckling at my lobe for a moment, before whispering, firmly, "Tell me to stop, and I stop."

And then he pushed.

Weaver fucking save me.

My thighs spread wider. I clutched him, my fingers clawing at his shoulders, as he impaled me, inch by inch. My body was begging for this, begging for him to be inside me—and yet the pain was there, too, undeniable, acute and burning as I stretched around him. When I thought there couldn't possibly be more of him, my awareness moved down to find several inches of thick, glistening flesh between us.

And Weaver, yes. He was taking his time. Being gentle. One hand braced under my backside to hold me up against the rocks. The other stroked my hair. His muscles were tense, trembling.

He'd work himself into me slowly, if that's what I needed. What I wanted.

It wasn't what I wanted.

I stilled, drawing in a breath. He stilled, too, face turning against my hair. Listening. Waiting.

But instead of giving him the words he was looking for, I tightened my legs around his waist in one abrupt movement, pulling him into me in a single thrust.

He hadn't been expecting that. He let out a groan, fingers tightening around my body, while I sank my teeth into his shoulder—hard enough that I tasted blood. A whimper escaped my throat. The sudden burst of pleasure-pain consumed me, so intense my body tightened against it.

For several long seconds, we stayed like that, locked together in every way. Even our threads had been tied, intertwined, like strands in a braid. I felt his desire as clearly as my own—and with it, too, his concern, as he cradled my head against his shoulder.

Strange, how our breathing synced up of its own accord, our chests rising and falling at the same rapid rate.

I had never felt so close to another soul before.

It terrified me.

It intoxicated me.

Heartbeats passed. The pain, initially sharp, faded to a distant throb. I felt as if I had been split open, full in a way I never had been before.

"Good?" Atrius murmured into my hair, at last.

In response, I shifted my hips, testing the way it felt to move with him inside me and—

Weaver.

I threw my head back and let out a low, long moan. My entire body shuddered with the movement, rolling against him.

The pleasure was worth the pain. Gods, it was better for the pain.

He stiffened, nails tightening around me, fighting the primal desire to move with me against the desire to be gentle with me.

But I had already told him I didn't want gentle.

I used my thighs to urge him to withdraw, and a slow, predatory smirk spread over his lips as he understood what I was doing. What I was giving him permission to do.

Another stroke, harder this time. I urged him back into me fiercely. The balance of sensations now skewed pleasure, hunger, desire for more.

I was louder this time, my moan a strangled gasp, which earned a wordless, approving sound from him.

Weaver, I wanted to bottle that sound and keep it. That pleasure imbued his entire body, his threads, vibrating in mine.

This time he ground against me, hips circling as if to make sure his cock branded every part of me, as deep as he could go.

Oh gods—*gods*—

He hit something there, something deep, making me claw at him and let out a fully involuntary cry.

I yanked him closer, a rough movement with my legs, harsh and demanding.

A challenge.

The bars of the cage snapped.

He kissed me hard, his tongue invading my mouth with the force of his next thrust, which left me whimpering against him. Suddenly, his hands were at my wrists, roughly pinning them above my head, forcing my body to stretch against the stone—exposing it all to him.

His next thrust wasn't gentle.

It was exactly what he had warned me of. His presence, a force of pure lust and impulse and raw, uncontainable power surrounded me, and I let it take me over, let my own soul meld with it, our threads now so tangled that neither of us would be able to tell where one stopped and the other began.

I relished it. Relished the control and the relinquishment in every stroke, every thrust, every time his cock bottomed out within me, grinding against me. Pleasure built there, where we were connected, the entire universe disappearing except for him and me and our bodies and everything that I still wanted from him. Weaver, *needed* from him.

Gods, what a fool I was for thinking his tongue was the pinnacle of what pleasure could be. That was nothing. Nothing compared to feeling him surge into me, again and again, before I could catch my breath.

With one particularly powerful thrust, my entire body arched against the rock, the sound escaping my lips wild and wordless and too-loud. My body rocked against it, matching the force, chasing the pinnacle of pleasure that rapidly rushed toward me—rushed toward both of us, I knew, because I could feel it in his aura, maddening and close, fraying our final threads of control.

I needed him to sever it with me.

My head nearly slammed back into the stone with the force of our passion, but one of his hands slid between my hair and the rock, the other still holding my wrists firmly above my head.

He held himself there, deep, both of us trembling around it. The sudden lack of friction was torturous, even if the depth hit me exactly where I needed him.

I tilted my head to kiss him, but he inched back, so our lips were only barely brushing.

"You don't come yet," he growled.

Weaver damn him.

I moved defiantly against him, making both of us let out hitched moans.

"I feel how much you want it, too."

As if in agreement, I felt his length twitch inside me, like he had to physically hold himself back from fucking me with those final few strokes.

There was nothing sweet in his smile, sharp with hunger.

"I dreamed about this," he murmured. "What you might look like, unraveled and desperate, in the seconds before I let you go. I want to savor it."

Our words were harsh, playing into the game we'd started—that this was about hunger and desire and lust and nothing more. But I felt something else stir deep in his presence then, right around the word *savor*. Something I felt echoed in mine.

It was almost enough to break through the feral desire with just a hint of fear.

Almost.

"Ravenous," I ground out. "That's what you said. Ravenous people don't savor. We take." I jerked my hips against him, and his entire body went taut in response. "So take me, Atrius. Take me."

I meant for it to be a command, just as harsh as his. At first it was. But those last words, that last *"take me,"* turned into a plea.

I felt it in Atrius's whole self the moment his self-control snapped.

There was no snarky retort, no flirtatious response. Just a sudden, dark wave of his determination—

—And then movement.

He withdrew slowly, agonizingly, and then thrust back into me.

Again, faster. Again. Again.

If he was vicious before, this was downright brutal, fierce and unrelenting. Moans and sobs and curses and prayers tore, mangled, from my lips—not that I could hear them. Not that I could hear anything.

Nothing except Atrius's voice, rough in my ear:

"Now you come for me, Vivi."

A commander's order.

I had no choice but to follow it.

My climax hit me with the force of a tidal wave, an explosion, something that ripped me apart and left me in pieces. Desperately, I clung to Atrius, my muscles contracting around him—my magic, too, reached for him in those final moments, letting his pleasure meld with mine, reaching deep into his threads and immersing myself within him.

He came as I did, his lips grunting my name as he buried his face against my throat. He clutched me tight, muscles trembling, and that embrace was the only piece of the physical world that remained constant as everything else fell away.

Aftershocks of pleasure surged through us in clenched muscles and shaky breaths.

And then, peace.

Atrius's head sagged against my shoulder. His arms now encircled my body to hold me up rather than restrain my wrists.

The nature of the embrace shifted, from something primal to something . . . else.

Slowly, my awareness came back to the world. It was silent, save for the sound of our heavy breaths and the sea, lapping around our ankles. The mist was warming with sunrise—

Sunrise.

"Atrius," I said, panicked. "The sun—"

But Atrius simply lifted his head and kissed me.

It wasn't frantic or lustful. Not angry. Not hurt.

It was sweet, tender, his lips soft against mine and tongue gently caressing my mouth.

Then he stepped back, finally withdrawing from me, leaving me feeling oddly empty. The water was a shock of cold against my feet.

Without a word, he pulled his trousers back up, retrieved his discarded shirt from the rocks, and slid it over my shoulders.

And then he scooped me up, cradled my head against his chest, and carried me back to his tent—leaving my nightgown crumpled in the water, discarded there with my broken vows.

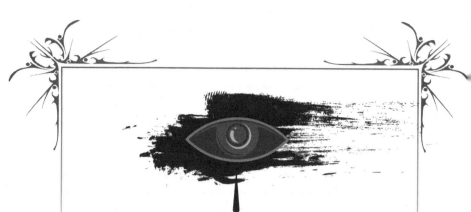

CHAPTER THIRTY-SIX

Atrius and I both slept easily. We crawled over his bedroll, curled up in each other's arms, and tumbled immediately into a river of exhausted slumber.

I dreamed that night of a little girl standing before a stone keep in the mountains, and her amazement at seeing the ocean for the first time. But even in my dreams, I could not remember what it had looked like then, to those eyes. And even in my dream, that upset me—I just kept staring at the sea and weeping, even though I didn't know why.

The Sightmother pulled me away, cradled my face, and wiped my tears away.

"The Weaver demands sacrifices of her chosen few," she said. "Isn't it a small thing to give up, to earn the love of a goddess? To earn the love of a family?"

In my dream, I watched that little girl. I had no body. I could not speak.

But I wanted to shout at her, *You don't understand! You already have a family. And you aren't just giving up your eyes. You're giving up the sea.*

But I could not shout with no voice. The Sightmother took my young self by the hand and led her into the Salt Keep. I could not call for her. I could not follow. I had given the Weaver my body, and my voice, and now I had nothing left.

THE FIRST THING I became aware of when I awoke was Atrius's breath, deep and steady. His scent and his presence surrounded me—the latter quieter, softer, than usual. I still wore his shirt, stained with the scent of him and the sea. His body curled around mine, arms loosely encircling me, face pressed to my hair.

It took several long seconds for what had happened last night to sink in. The memories, each more intimate than the last, hit me piece by piece—the kiss, my ripped nightgown . . . Weaver, his *mouth* . . .

A flush found my skin. As if to check whether it had all been real, my fingers slipped down to my bare legs—pausing at the two small wounds on my inner thigh, now scabbing over.

And if there was any doubt of the rest of it . . . well, the soreness between my legs put that to rest.

A smile flitted over my lips.

And then, just as quickly, it faded.

I had fucked him. The man I had been tasked to kill.

I had broken my vows to the Arachessen. Broken my vows to Acaeja herself.

I thought I had been making that decision clearheaded last night. But now, all at once, a violent burst of guilt twisted in my stomach. Not rational guilt, not logical guilt—this was the delirious guilt of a child, terrified of a parent's wrath.

I extracted myself from Atrius's embrace, careful not to wake him. My pack from the trip to the island was here, tucked away in the corner with Atrius's things. The sight of it there, so easily accommodated into his life, made a lump rise in my throat.

I was sure the island had been scattered with the belongings of the people who had lived there or the warriors who had been attacked there. All had likely been gathered and sorted by Atrius's soldiers.

But not mine.

Atrius carried mine himself, just as he had carried me, even when his people were dying.

It wasn't until this exact moment that I realized: as far as Atrius was concerned, I was one of his people.

I pulled the bag free and opened it. The clothes inside were wrinkled and reeking of sea salt. They, and the canvas of the bag itself, were dotted with browning spatters of blood. Mine, of course—too red to be vampire blood.

The dagger was right on top.

I unsheathed it. It was now sunset, light seeping through the canvas of the tent. Pangs of it glistened on the cold steel. Still unremarkable in appearance, of course, but just holding the weapon in my hands, I could feel the magic forged into it. Powerful.

My awareness fell behind me, to Atrius's sleeping form. In my absence, he had curled up a bit more, his face pressed to the pillow. His presence was soft like this, the hard edges of his pain and determination sanded away. He seemed almost childlike.

If the Sightmother were here now, she would command me to kill him.

I couldn't pretend that wasn't the case. That this was exactly what she had imagined when she gave the order. And if I did it, I would be welcomed back to the Salt Keep with open arms. No one would ask about my virginity, and even if they knew, they would pretend they didn't. Many Arachessen slept with their targets. Hell, even if I hadn't, many would assume that I did.

In the scheme of the greater will of the Weaver, there wasn't a soul who wouldn't look away, as long as they thought I did what I did solely out of devotion to my mission.

A version of myself from four months ago would have seen this as such a clear-cut decision: *This is the moment. Take it.*

I saw it as a clear-cut decision now, too.

Because there was no part of me, not even the part steeped in guilt, not even the little girl who thought she owed her entire life to Acaeja and to the Arachessen, that even considered killing Atrius in this moment.

I could not do it.

I would not do it.

I sheathed the dagger.

Atrius's eyes opened. He never woke up slowly or groggily. He was always simply *awake*, immediately. Today was no exception, and when those eyes snapped open, they fell to me as instantly as if it were nothing less than instinct.

My heart twisted, a sensation that was one part pleasant, one part painful.

He didn't say anything, but reached out his hand—a silent beckoning.

Another twinge in my chest.

I crawled back to the bedroll and sat cross-legged beside it. His hand fell to my thigh, fingers brushing the wound he'd left. He lingered there for a moment, like he, too, was reliving the night before.

"You look better."

Atrius's way of asking, *How are you feeling?*

"I feel better."

His hand didn't move. I was so conscious of that touch that it was almost distracting—and yet, strangely comforting. I hadn't been prepared for how intense skin-to-skin contact with Atrius was. Not the first time I touched him, not last night, and not now.

A flare of desire in his presence as his eyes ran over me told me he was thinking the same thing. And Weaver, it was tempting—the idea of crawling back into bed with him and disappearing into carnal bliss.

But Atrius was not one to find it easy to distract himself, sex or no. And sadly, as much as I sometimes wished otherwise, neither was I.

"Sun is falling," I said.

We both knew what that meant. Night began, and the work began.

Solemnness rolled over Atrius's face. "Yes. I need to find out how many we lost in the day."

A pang of his hurt mingled with my own. It didn't matter that they were vampires. The scenes I witnessed these last few days were far too familiar—too reminiscent of every death I'd seen at the hands of the Pythora King. It didn't matter what their teeth or blood looked like. That suffering was the same.

In the wake of the worst events we'd seen, the Sightmother would always remind us that death is nothing to be mourned, simply the will of the Weaver. The others seemed to find comfort in this. But I never could.

For most of my life that had been something shameful.

Not today. Today, I was glad to feel it—the anger at all those countless deaths.

"The Pythora King will pay for it," I said quietly. "Soon enough. You'll avenge all those lives."

Atrius's gaze and his attention slipped far away, a shiver of mournfulness tingeing the air between us.

I felt his unspoken question.

My brow furrowed. "What?"

He let out a light scoff, a wry smile twisting one side of his mouth. "You see too much, seer."

"I see just enough, conqueror."

The smile lingered, then faded. Finally, he said, "I don't know if this is the right thing."

The words came slow, like such a blatant admission of uncertainty stuck in his throat.

I'd thought Atrius couldn't shock me anymore. But this—this shocked me. "Why?"

"These men and women have been with me for decades. I took them away from their homes. They followed me into nightmares. And never, not once, did they question me." His eyes lowered to the bedroll, his jaw tight. "And where have I led them, to thank them for their loyalty?"

"You led them here."

"A human kingdom that isn't their home. Because they can't go back to their homes, due to my actions."

My hand fell over his before I could stop myself, clutching tight. "You led them to a second chance."

"This place doesn't deserve their bones. This place doesn't deserve the bones of their children."

"It doesn't deserve our bones, either. And gods, how many we've given it." My lip curled into a sneer, my fingers trembling around Atrius's hand. "You say you don't belong here. But neither do the

Pythora King or his warlords. And they've stripped and abused and destroyed this kingdom. The suffering they've inflicted on the people here—" I choked on the words, and the images they conjured. "It's unforgivable. And we let it happen for too long. No more. Someone needs to make him pay for it. And if you won't, I'll find a way to."

The last sentence took me by surprise. I wasn't planning to say it. But Weaver, I *meant* it.

Maybe I had broken my vow to the Arachessen. But this—this was a vow I would keep.

I had sworn myself to the Arachessen, and for so many years I had helped them fight against the Pythora King. But I was tired of fighting. I was ready to win.

Atrius was quiet.

Finally, he said, "We can't take Karisine like this."

My heart fell, shattering against the harsh realities of our situation.

No, we couldn't. His numbers were smaller than ever. Even before, he'd been relying on his cousin's help to take Karisine. Now? Conquering it by brute force was out of the question, let alone taking the city-state that lay beyond it. And after that, we'd still have to cross treacherous cliffs to make it to the Pythora King's isolated palace at the northern shore.

Even if we did have the manpower to make those moves, it would be slow, and it would guarantee many more losses we couldn't afford.

My fingers tightened, nails biting my palm.

"We don't have time to chip away at this," I said. "If he was as easy as Tarkan—"

Atrius's seriousness broke for a moment, a smirk twitching at the corner of his mouth. "You look murderous."

I scoffed. I *felt* murderous. "It's a shame that all problems can't be solved by cutting off a head."

Atrius went very still.

My brows furrowed. "What?"

"Mm."

That little nonanswer, absentminded, his eyes distant, told me it was not nothing. And then, slowly, that smirk returned, this time clinging stubbornly to the corner of his mouth. A now-familiar smug sensation rolled from his presence.

I sat up straighter.

"What an ominous silence," I said.

"Mm," Atrius replied, unhelpfully.

"You have an idea."

I didn't mean for the hint of admiration—Weaver help me, maybe even excitement—to creep into my voice.

"It's not an idea yet."

Yet.

I arched my brows, silently commanding, *Tell me.*

"Maybe you've inspired me," he said. "You taught me the value of severing the snake."

"And this snake is the Pythora King's head?"

"If it was, would it work?"

I paused, considering this.

The warlords were installed by the Pythora King, but they were self-serving and weak on their own. I doubted the handful that remained in power would be able to put up much of a fight if the Pythora King was gone, nor especially inclined to sacrifice themselves for a king too dead to impress.

"Yes," I said. "But how would we do that?"

The Pythora King wasn't like Tarkan, residing in a castle in the center of a bustling city. He was incredibly isolated, his palace surrounded by mountains.

Atrius reached into a pile of papers in a box and withdrew a beaten-up roll of parchment, which he unrolled over the ground—a map of Glaea.

"You're the local guide," he said. "You tell me. Give me a way to reach the Pythora King without fighting my way through three more warlords."

He said it so simply. Like it was just a given that such a thing existed. Like it was a given that I had the answer. And his threads were steady—no doubt, no question.

A bittersweet sensation tightened in my chest, as it hit me just how much Atrius genuinely believed in me.

I leaned over the map, running my fingers over the lines of raised ink. Seeing through the threads sometimes made it slow to interpret ink on paper, but I knew the layout of my homeland so well, I barely needed the map anyway. My fingertips traced our location, running north—first by the western path, through Karisine and Ralan. Then they drifted west—to the bumpy, violent slashes of ink that represented the Zadra Cliffs, an expansive maze of rocky mountains that ran all the way up to the northern shore. On the far eastern side of them, hidden well within the treacherous cliffs, the Salt Keep stood.

The Pythora King had chosen to build his castle just beyond the Zadra Cliffs because they were the ultimate protection. No soul could get through them. What paths did run between them were narrow and treacherous, and overrun with slyviks—giant reptilian beasts, the kinds of creatures children invented in nightmares. Worse, those roads were impossible to navigate, both because of their directionless winding and because heavy mists destroyed all visibility.

Yet, my finger lingered there over those mountains.

I could feel Atrius's aura growing more smug.

"The paths there could take us to the Pythora King," he said.

Always statements, never questions.

"Maybe. But they're impassable."

But even as the words left my lips, I wasn't sure that was true. History was full of stories of armies that had attempted to cross the cliffs and failed, damning themselves.

Human armies.

"You don't believe that," Atrius said.

I straightened, taking him in. The smirk now permanently curled his mouth, the pleasure echoed in his soul. Despite everything against us now, I had to admit to myself I did enjoy witnessing him this way.

"Vampires are hardier than humans," I said. "It will be a difficult journey, but your warriors can endure it far better than humans. The hard part will be navigating."

That was the real killer. Theoretically, one could get through the pass in a few weeks or less, if moving fast. The problem was that no one was ever moving fast, because it was impossible to tell where you were going.

Atrius's eyes glinted.

"But we have the help of a good seer," he said, voicing what I didn't yet say. "Someone who doesn't rely on visibility at all."

It was stupid. It was brilliant.

It was the best idea we had.

And Atrius and I were both grinning—grinning at this ridiculous glimmer of hope. Neither of us had to confirm aloud that we would do it. Of course we would. It was insane, and it was our only chance.

Atrius's hand fell over mine, and the touch sobered me. Suddenly, the harsh realities of what I was about to do struck me, dizzyingly.

My smile faded.

Atrius took me in for a long moment. I heard the echo of his words—*you see too much*—because suddenly, I felt that he did, too.

"I have been thinking a lot, these last few months," he said, "about what ruling this kingdom would look like."

His hand flipped, palm up, so he was holding mine.

"I never intended to take this country away from its people," he went on. "I had a pact to fulfill, yes, but I actually wanted to rule it. And rule it well. But no matter what my intentions are, I'm a foreigner. A vampire. I would need someone else beside me. Someone who represents the people I rule far more than I do."

My lips parted.

For a minute I thought he was implying—but he couldn't be saying—

I managed to choke out, "Are you asking me—"

"I'm not asking anything. I'm telling you that I would like that person to be you, Sylina. And you can do with that information what you will."

I opened my mouth again. Closed it.

Weaver help me.

"I didn't know you were so old-fashioned," I said. "One fuck and suddenly you're proposing marriage and crowns and—"

"Not marriage." He blurted that out fast, then winced. "Not that I—what I meant was—"

It would have been more amusing to see Atrius flustered if I wasn't also just as flustered.

He let out a breath. "This arrangement isn't about me. It's not about us. It's a title that you deserve because you are a good leader. You are intelligent. You are compassionate. You know what the people of Glaea want and need. You have lived the lives of many here. And I know that if you were to be tasked with their well-being, you would advocate for the lives of these people until your dying breath. That makes you worthy of power, Vivi." A wry twist of his lips. "And so damned few are."

He said it so matter-of-factly, as if he were listing the contents of an inventory, and yet I could feel in his presence how deeply he *believed* them.

And when he used my old name—my real name—it was like an arrow right between my ribs, guilt flooding me like hot blood.

I wasn't sure what I had done to make him think so highly of me. And I so desperately wanted to be the woman he thought I was.

I couldn't speak. Weaver, I could barely even breathe. When I said nothing, he straightened and cleared his throat.

"You don't have to decide anything now," he said.

But I had decided.

In this moment, I decided all of it.

Atrius was our answer. Our path to finally overthrowing the Pythora King and making this damned kingdom what it was meant to be. He would be a good ruler. He would accept guidance from his people, human or not. I believed this.

I refused to let another soul wither under the Pythora King's rule. And I refused to kill Atrius.

I was no fool. I knew what this meant. When a Sister betrayed the Arachessen, she was carved into pieces and left throughout Glaea— damned to never be whole again, physically or spiritually.

I had only one bloodless path forward, and that was to try one last time to convince the Sightmother that Atrius could be a worthy ally.

And if that failed . . .

Well. Atrius had been prepared to sacrifice his life to his goddess to save his people.

I would be willing to make the same sacrifice.

Atrius was looking at me strangely, his brow furrowed. His thumb swept over my hand and I realized it was shaking.

"Vivi," he said softly. That was it. Just my name, and in it, the question he didn't ask.

For one powerful moment, I wanted to tell him all of it. The truth. That was a selfish desire.

Because if I told Atrius the truth of why I had been sent here, that made me a traitor. And a wartime leader, when confronted with a traitor, only would have one choice. He would need to execute me. Even if he decided I was too important to sacrifice, he wouldn't trust me, and he *needed* to trust me if he and his people were going to make it through the Zadra Pass alive.

Or.

Or, even worse, he would try to save me.

And Atrius could not do that. The Pythora King was his enemy. The Pythora King needed to remain his only focus. Not the Arachessen. He couldn't save me *and* kill the Pythora King. Trying to might destroy him.

Somehow *this* was the possibility, not my execution, that left me breathless with terror. Strange, because it never would happen that way. Atrius was a ruthless leader. He'd kill a traitor.

I told myself this, over and over, as he gazed at me with such concern, thumb rubbing the back of my hand.

I gave him a weak smile. "I just . . . I can't think about any of that until that bastard is dead. That's all."

He nodded, like this made perfect sense to him.

"Of course," he murmured.

It was now dark. The sun had set. Atrius stretched, then started to stand. "I'll let you get dressed. Then we have work to do."

But I caught his arm and pulled him back down. And before I knew what I was doing, my hands were on either side of his face, my mouth against his in a deep kiss.

After a moment of confusion, his stance softened, pulling me closer.

I kissed him for a long, long time.

CHAPTER THIRTY-SEVEN

The moment the sun went down, the night was bright with activity. Soldiers and healers crawled from their tents immediately, ready to tend to the wounded or to keep gathering supplies. Vampire healing had done wonders—my own wound was now little more than an afterthought.

I took the long way back to my own tent, walking along the coastline. In the distance, the moonlight caressed the rocks by the shore. I couldn't help but think about what had happened there last night. Weaver, I wondered if I'd left claw marks on those rocks.

Then I abruptly stopped.

A distant presence caught my attention—a familiar presence. The pain in it left me breathless.

I climbed down to the shore and approached another cluster of jagged stones. The figure was curled up between them, sitting in the damp sand, knees pulled up to his chest. He had a blade that he twirled skillfully in one hand, driving it hard into the damp sand over and over again. *THWACK.*

"Erekkus," I said softly.

He heard me. He didn't look at me.

He yanked the blade from the sand, twirled it, drove it back in. *THWACK.*

I approached him and sat beside him. Up close, his aura vibrated with such agony, it tore through me like broken glass. His expression was drawn and exhausted. One side of his face was burned—his flesh purple and slightly blistering. He had not bothered to avoid the sun.

"I don't need platitudes." He sounded hoarse, like he hadn't spoken in days.

"I didn't bring any."

THWACK, as he stabbed the blade into the sand again.

"I don't want to talk," he said.

My heart broke for him. I knew that feeling so well. His soul screamed for his daughter—sitting this close, I could practically see the girl's face.

I had read in my studies that many vampire societies, especially in nobility, resented their children—that they often killed or mutilated their offspring, viewing them as competition for their power. In the beginning, I had assumed that Atrius's people were the same as all the others. Now, I was ashamed of that assumption.

Of course they weren't the same. Atrius's people had fought every injustice. They had nowhere to go. They banded together and found comfort in each other instead. Just as I had, long ago.

And now, they grieved just as I did.

"I'm not asking you to talk," I said.

THWACK. Erekkus whirled to me, teeth exposed in a pained snarl.

"Then what the hell do you want?"

I laid my hand over his—around the hilt of his blade.

"I'm asking you to act, Erekkus."

Beneath my touch, his knuckles trembled.

"I'm asking you," I murmured, "to help us kill the bastard who took your daughter away."

His jaw shook. His throat bobbed.

"Can you do that?" I whispered.

For a long moment, Erekkus didn't move.

And then he stood, yanking his weapon from the sand.

"Yes," he said.

THE DAWN WAS damp and humid. I was exhausted. The last two nights had been spent aggressively preparing for our imminent movement into the Zadra Pass. I'd been so weak I hadn't even had a moment to steal away, even during the daytime, when Atrius would pull me away into his tent to discuss strategy with me. By the time he was sleeping, usually I was, too.

But today, I knew I couldn't put it off any longer. I'd slipped out after Atrius had finally fallen asleep, creeping from the tent as silently as I could manage. I left him a note in case he woke before I returned: *Gone for a walk. Be back soon.*

It felt almost deceptively mundane for the situation we were in, even if it had been true.

I walked far beyond the bounds of camp, out where the terrain grew so rocky it was difficult to navigate. The mists were thick today, and the air hot. By the time I made it to a calm patch of water—a little pool left behind when the tide went out—sweat plastered my clothing to my skin.

I knelt beside the tide pool, my hands hovering above the water, laying flat against the surface. The threads of the water bloomed to life beneath my touch. I drew in a deep breath and let myself feel them—them, and myself, and the connection we had to each other.

It was, in the midst of everything else . . . oddly calming. It had been a long time now since I had meditated in practice.

I reached through the water, and its threads, and its connections, deeper and deeper and deeper—all the way to the Salt Keep. Its presence was always so recognizable even over great distances. For fifteen years, it had been the north on my compass, the one stable thing in an ever-changing world.

I had one more chance to mend that gap. One chance to convince the Sightmother that Atrius could be an ally. Or if not, one chance to make sure she believed in my loyalty, at least long enough for us to get through the Zadra Pass.

The seconds passed, and then minutes, and no one responded. Not the Sightmother, not Asha, and not the other Sisters.

That was . . . unusual.

I reached for it again, this time through a different combination of threads. Perhaps they didn't sense me.

Again, nothing.

I tried again, and again, before finally leaning back on my heels.

My heartbeat was a little too fast. Nausea simmered in my stomach.

It didn't have to mean anything. Sometimes, reaching the Salt Keep didn't work. The Sisters were busy, and the Sightmother was busier. It wasn't unheard of that Sisters weren't able to make contact just because no one happened to be waiting around at the Salt Keep for them.

But I had come too far to lie to myself. I had a bad feeling about this.

I touched the dagger at my side—the dagger that had not come anywhere near Atrius's heart.

Tomorrow we marched for the Pythora King.

I just needed to get through that. Afterward, the Arachessen were welcome to kill me for my disloyalty.

I stood and walked away, leaving the untouched pool behind me.

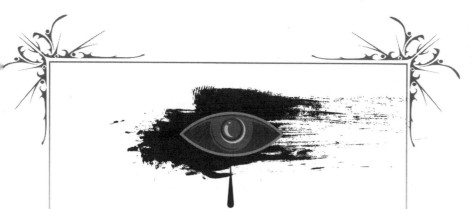

CHAPTER THIRTY-EIGHT

The pass reeked of danger. Everything about it felt like a place inhospitable to all life. The stones were foreboding and jagged, leaving barely enough room between them to cut through, even for the most surefooted travelers. The fog was so thick here that it blotted out the sun completely—so thick that I could feel it in each breath, and in the threads themselves, like all senses were coated in a thick, blurred layer. The slyviks weren't visible, not with eyes nor even with the threads, but I could sense them distantly, like flitting, deadly shadows, impossible to pinpoint.

I could understand why this place had claimed so many lives. The journey through the pass could take a human fourteen days, if they were very, very quick. But no one was quick, because attempting to navigate the maze of the pass with eyes alone was a foolish, losing proposition.

Atrius, arrogant as he was, figured we could make the trip in seven days.

In theory, maybe he was right. Vampires were hardier than humans. Their eyesight was far better in the dark. They healed faster, didn't need as much food to survive. And, Atrius pointed out smugly, they had me—our key to making it through the pass without getting lost.

I wanted to believe him. Needed to believe him. Time loomed over me like the shadows of the slyviks I knew were waiting for us ahead. How long would it take for the Arachessen to kill me?

Not long. They were very efficient.

Seven days, I figured, could work.

Atrius and I stood at the front of his army. Not many of his warriors would make the journey with us—he had lost so many, and more still needed to stay behind to care for the wounded. It seemed laughable to think that this army of one hundred men could be the downfall of the Pythora King.

But then again, these weren't men.

Still, as I stood beside Atrius at the narrow gap between these jagged rocks, feeling my own mortality's breath at the back of my neck, I found myself with a strange sensation: raw, genuine fear.

Time, Atrius had told me once, the first time I healed him. *I just need time.*

I understood that now.

That morning, before we left, I had sat down to compose what I knew would likely be my final letter to Naro. All of them had been stilted and awkward, more full of the things I didn't say than the things I did. Mundane questions that didn't matter: *How are you feeling? How are they treating you? How is the weather in Vasai?*

He never responded, of course.

This morning, I sat before that blank paper for a long time without writing. It seemed disingenuous to give him my usual forced small talk, even if it was the most comfortable option.

I had given up the comfortable option.

I would likely die soon. He would likely die soon. Both of us were being slowly strangled by those who had taken all our faith. We had no one to blame but ourselves.

What the hell were we pretending for, anymore?

So this time, I wrote what I really meant.

Naro—
I love you.
I'm sorry for the ways I failed you.
I forgive you for the ways you failed me.

Maybe in the next life, it can be different. But if not, what I feel in this one remains the same.

I love you.
Vivi

It was a short letter. Just a few sentences. And yet, what else was there to say but that? What else could I offer him?

Now, at the entrance to the pass, my death looming over me, I thought of that question again. It was all I had, but it still didn't feel like enough.

I could feel Atrius staring at me. He was as nervous as I was, but his presence still comforted me. I swallowed past a thick lump in my throat, heavy with fear and guilt.

"What's wrong?" he asked.

His voice was abrupt, and yet gentle.

He saw too much.

"Nothing," I said, and started to walk forward, but he caught my arm.

"What is it?"

I paused, fighting that same sensation I'd felt when I wrote Naro's letter earlier today—like Atrius's question was another blank page in front of me.

I turned back to him.

"I need you to promise me something," I said.

A ripple of concern. His brow furrowed.

"Promise me that you keep going," I said. "Even if you lose me. Promise me that your only goal remains the Pythora King."

Silence. His concern grew stronger.

I reversed his grip, so I was now holding his hand, pulling him closer.

"Death is what happens when you stand still," I said. "Don't stand still. Not for anything."

Finally, he lowered his chin in a nod.

A wave of relief fell over me. I turned back to the pass before us.

It felt, I supposed, exactly like what a path to the underworld should feel like.

"Are you ready?" I asked.

He wasn't. I could sense that. But he still said, without a hint of uncertainty, "Yes," because Atrius worked only in absolutes. I appreciated that about him, even though I knew it would be the very quality that would end me.

"Good," I replied.

I was the one to take the first step, leading us into the mist.

I HATED FOLLOWING the threads through rocks. They were so much more opaque than soil or water, with so little life running through them to cling to. These ones were among the worst—endless expanses of serrated death.

The gaps between them were so narrow that no more than two of us could walk shoulder-to-shoulder, and even that was tight. I led the group, the navigator pointing our way. Though the vampires had far better eyesight in the darkness than humans did, the dark wasn't the problem here—the mist was. A human would be functionally blind here. The vampires could see what lay directly before them, but little more. Certainly not enough to work their way through the maze of stone alone.

That was my job.

I clung to the cliff walls, pressing my hands to the damp stone, threading my awareness through them. It took all my focus—I kept stumbling over the uneven terrain because I couldn't keep track of our larger path while also seeing what lay directly in front of me. Atrius remained by my side, one hand keeping his sword at the ready, the other holding onto my arm, as if he was terrified of losing me.

We walked for hours. The one benefit of the pass's brutal environment was that it shielded us so well from the sun that we didn't need to stop to take shelter from it. There was little difference between night and day. As a result, time blurred. The vampires had far better stamina than humans. They didn't need to rest as often.

But eventually, I was suffering. My head pounded. The ache of my injuries from the recent attack, still not fully healed, nagged at me, and the constant focus was exhausting.

"You need to rest," Atrius said after a while.

I didn't even dignify that with an answer. I just kept pushing forward.

There wasn't enough time.

Atrius did, eventually, command that everyone rest, though I'd long lost track of the hours by then. I couldn't even sense the fall or rise of the sun through the mists. By now, even the vampires were exhausted, gratefully sliding to the ground at the order, reaching for their canteens of deer blood.

I couldn't make myself move from the rock, my fingers still curled against the stone.

After a moment, Atrius gently took my hand. The moment he pulled me away from the stability of the wall, my knees buckled.

He caught me and the two of us sank to the ground together. My head was spinning. I felt, for the second time in my life, truly blind—my exhaustion so deep that, in this dead place, I couldn't grip any of the threads around me.

Except for Atrius's. His presence, solid and unshakable, was a single stable harbor.

He didn't say anything, but his worry radiated through me like a trembling string.

"Drink," he muttered, pressing a canteen to my mouth—tilting my chin up when I struggled to hold it myself. The liquid inside was sweet and thicker than water. Whatever it was, my body screamed for more of it from the first drop.

"A tonic," he said. "It's better for you."

He'd prepared for me. Gotten human-specific tonics to help me make the journey. I knew him well enough by now that I shouldn't have been surprised by this, and yet . . . my heart clenched a little.

He pulled away the canteen, and my head sagged against his shoulder. I wouldn't admit it aloud, but I needed this, to be cradled against his body. His aura grounded me after so many hours throwing myself far away in the threads.

"I need to stay awake." My voice slurred. "There could be slyviks—"

"You need to rest," he snapped. "Here."

Something touched my lips—a little piece of jerky. I took it and chewed, or did my best to.

"I'll watch," he said.

I swallowed the jerky, with significant effort.

"But you won't be able to see—"

"Enough." His hand reached out to caress my cheek. Something about the harshness of the word combined with the softness of the touch made all further protests fade.

He laid his sword beside him, and I settled deeper into his hold, my head sliding down into his lap.

The last thing I remembered before sleep took me was my hand curling around his—a mindless impulse, like a compass drifting north.

I SLEPT SO deeply that when the warm liquid spattered over my face, it took me several long seconds to realize that it was blood.

But once I did, I knew it was Atrius's immediately.

His pain was a sharp twang to the threads, loud enough to snap me back to awareness. At first I couldn't grip anything else, jerking upright only to fall against the uneven rocks, the mists and darkness and all-consuming lifelessness of the pass surrounding me.

The sound that cut through the air was a high-pitched scream, not unlike a child's terrified wail, starting bone-chillingly high and then falling into a guttural chatter.

My grip on my surroundings snapped into place. I jumped to my feet.

A slyvik.

A slyvik that had Atrius.

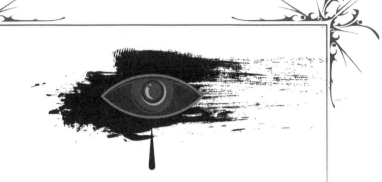

CHAPTER THIRTY-NINE

veryone had heard stories about the slyviks—they were, after all, the sort of creatures that lent themselves particularly well to childhood ghost stories and nightmares. But not even the wildest of those tales could match the reality of witnessing one in front of you. It wasn't their appearance that made them terrifying—it was their entire presence. Legend said that they were no natural beasts, that they had been created by Sagtra, the god of animals, to be the ultimate hunting opponents. Gods, I could believe that.

The slyvik moved in fits and starts, its slender, scaled body contorting eerily around the craggy stone. Its arms—webbed—allowed it to glide, hurling itself from wall to wall so quickly that neither vampire eyes nor my magic could fully track it. It had a long, serpentine neck and a face that seemed shaped specifically to accommodate its massive jaws.

Jaws that were currently closed around Atrius's arm, as he slashed and fought fiercely.

I took this in just in time for the slyvik to drag him up like a rag doll, spread its wings, and leap into the mists.

I bit down on his name, a scream that bubbled up in a burst of panic.

Behind me, the other warriors had jumped to their feet, a ripple effect of awareness spreading down the line as they realized what happened. Erekkus pushed past me, starting to shout, when I said, "Shh!"

If there were more of them, the last thing we wanted was to bring the others down on us—or down on Atrius. I leaned against the stone, my heart beating wildly.

"We have to go after him," Erekkus hissed, doing a poor job of keeping his voice down.

"I am going after him," I shot back. "Let me concentrate."

Weaver, I couldn't orient myself. I had never seen a creature with such a slippery presence. The slyvik seemed to leap from thread to thread, the movement in between impossible to track, almost like—like it was Threadwalking—

Another screech reverberated through the fog, this one an even higher-pitched wail. A spark of pain in the threads.

I prayed it was the slyvik's.

I felt it jerking wildly. Felt it venturing closer and then—

"Sylina," Erekkus said, "no more waiting."

I pushed him back, my jaw clenched, arm trembling against the wall.

There.

It wasn't the slyvik's presence I latched onto. It was Atrius's. I grabbed my sword, held onto that thread, and flung myself into the darkness, while Erekkus's shout of my name echoed behind me.

I TIMED MYSELF well. My blade struck flesh. The slyvik screamed. Something whiplike and cold snapped against my face, making my ears ring with the impact, but I fought through the shock to grab onto the beast—not that I knew what I was grabbing onto, just whatever my arms could reach. I dug my blade deep into its flesh, giving me something to hold as I tried to make sense of what I'd grabbed—

A tail? Was this its tail?

I was whipped ferociously before I could brace myself. *SNAP*, as the reptilian flesh smacked against the stone. Sheer luck that I wasn't sandwiched there.

I got my bearings just in time to reorient myself—just in time to sense Atrius, still dangling from the creature's jaws—

"Vivi," he gasped, like he didn't mean to speak aloud.

"Move!" I ground out.

A shift in his resolve, as he realized what I'd just done: bought him a critical moment of distraction.

He seized it.

I couldn't tell where his blade struck, only that it struck deep, judging by the vicious spasm through the threads. The slyvik screeched, a sound that turned my skin inside out. A burst of air threw my hair back from my face as it dropped Atrius from its jaws, spread its wings—

—and *leapt*.

Time slowed. When my stomach dropped out beneath me with the sudden jerk of weightlessness, I was utterly terrified. And as Atrius fell to the ground, one hand outstretched to reach for me, that terror was shared between us.

I wondered if he was thinking of the promise he'd made me. I was.

But there was no time to be afraid. I wanted to live long enough to see the Pythora King's death.

Or at least the death of this fucking lizard.

Rigid determination fell over Atrius's presence. His hand opened. I recognized what he was getting ready to do.

I'd move when he did.

The world shook as the slyvik careened against a wall, turned so fast my neck felt like it was about to snap, then leapt again, leaving me clinging to it in another stomach-churning free fall.

I prayed to the gods that this thing was a male, as I jammed my dagger as hard as I could beneath its tail.

And at the same time, a fine mist of salty, acrid blood filtered into the air, as Atrius's magic seized control.

A spasm rocked the slyvik's body. I couldn't let go yet, not with it this far into the air. I clung to its tail as it whipped from stone to stone, clawing deep gauges into the granite as it writhed in pain. Still, it slid down with each leap.

Another disorienting jolt.

From the ground, Atrius's focus was entirely on us. I could feel his magic attempting to manipulate the creature's blood, albeit with limited success—slyviks, it seemed, were as resistant to blood magic as they were to most other weapons.

My shoulder was killing me. My left arm was struggling more and more to cling to the slyvik's tail, now slippery with blood. I'd slipped a little—the hilt of my blade was now just out of reach, lodged in the beast's flesh.

In the rare seconds of stillness, I reached for it. My blood-slicked fingertips barely managed to brush the hilt.

Weaver fucking damn it.

I managed to push myself a couple of inches farther up its tail when—

My stomach lurched as we fell—three terrifying seconds of utter weightlessness.

My breath jerked from my lungs.

I'm going to die, I thought, matter-of-factly, and then used the momentum from that fall to throw myself forward.

It was a miracle I didn't topple to my death. A greater one still that my hand actually wrapped around the hilt of my weapon.

Below me, I felt Atrius's presence, strong as a heartbeat—shaking with the effort of the magic he was using to pull the beast down. Erekkus was at his side now, bow drawn—ready to make the shot. Not close enough yet. Not quite.

With the last of my strength, I hoisted myself onto the slyvik's back—just for a moment, just long enough to throw myself off it.

Just long enough to aim my blade at its wing, thin and membranous and spread wide for me in this critical second.

I lunged. My blade tore open the delicate skin as I fell.

I hit the ground hard. Everything went distant and fuzzy. The sound of the slyvik's scream of pain sounded as if it was underwater.

"Shoot!" Atrius commanded.

Three arrows lodged into scaly skin. The slyvik's agony rang clear and vivid in the threads—oddly mournful. It fought death the whole way, thrashing with increasing weakness. But finally, the creature slumped to the rocks.

I pushed myself up just as it fell, its final breaths labored, before slowly fading.

The air was, once again, unnaturally quiet.

I approached the dead slyvik. It had fallen awkwardly into a narrow part of the cliffs, so its body was suspended above us. One broken, shredded wing dangled to the ground, its twisted neck wedged against the stone.

When it was moving, it was difficult even for me to get a full sense of the scale of the creature. Now, I felt a little dizzy that I'd just thrown myself at that thing. It was perhaps the length of four grown men, nose to tail.

I touched the wing, and a darker realization settled over me as I sensed the remnants of its aura.

"This is a juvenile," I said.

Erekkus muttered an Obitraen curse.

"What were you thinking?" Atrius's voice snatched my attention away. He approached me, palpably furious. But my attention immediately fell to his shoulder, which was soaked in blood, and his right arm, which hung uselessly at his side.

"You're welcome," I said.

Erekkus eyed the corpse. "A *juvenile,*" he repeated.

His tone of voice said it all.

"I don't think they get much larger than this," I said, "but they do get stronger. And cleverer. They usually don't venture this far south."

"Or wander away from the pack," Atrius said.

No surprise that he'd done his research.

Erekkus's eyes went wide. *"Pack?"* he yelped, grabbing his bow again.

"There aren't others here," I said quickly. I pressed my hand to the stone again, making sure I hadn't just made myself a liar—but I felt no other living creatures but us, save for the distant reverberations of what must have been other slyviks far ahead.

"This is a young male," I went on. "They're often driven away from the pack when they reach maturity."

"And this one wandered far from home."

Atrius touched the corpse's tail, and I wondered if I imagined the brief pang of sadness in his voice, at something that maybe seemed a bit too familiar.

My attention fell again to his shoulder. And his arm. He still hadn't moved it at all.

I cursed myself for not being a more useful healer.

Atrius must have read the look on my face. "It's fine," he muttered. "You're right-handed."

A brief pause, like it struck him I had noticed. Then, he said breezily, "I'm just as good with both hands."

Arrogant man.

"We'll patch it up," I said. "And then we need to get moving. We've wasted too much time already."

Erekkus was already rummaging through his pack, withdrawing a roll of bandages and a bottle of medicine. He started to approach Atrius, then, when Atrius scowled at him, he handed them to me instead.

"Tell the others to be ready to move," Atrius told him, wincing as I poured the medicine over the wound. Up close, I could feel the heat of the broken flesh—the teeth had cut deep and torn, and the saliva posed risk for infection. Nasty stuff. I prayed that his vampire hardiness would fight it off better than a human could.

"That wouldn't have happened if I was awake," I muttered, as I lifted his arm to wrap the bandage over his shoulder.

His other hand caught my chin, tipping it toward him. "You did an incredibly foolish thing," he snapped.

Weaver, I was sick of being told how stupid I was.

"You—"

But then he said, "Thank you." And his kiss was so soft and quick that I barely felt it before it was just his breath cooling on my lips.

I paused, startled more than I'd like, before resuming my bandaging.

"You'd do it for me," I said quietly. It was the only thing I could think to say, and I wasn't even sure why—until I realized that it was undeniably true.

Atrius and I didn't say anything else as I finished his bandage. I secured it, and then we were off into the mists once again, one step after another.

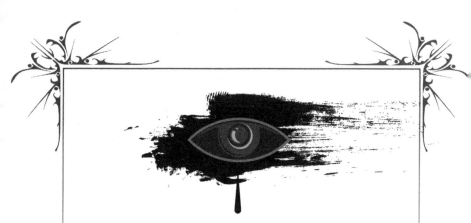

CHAPTER FORTY

The next days came and went in a blur. Walking until exhaustion. Eating until sleep. Sleeping in shifts, in the sparse, fractured hours. Waking and walking. Repeat. There was no sun or moon to track the passing of time. The terrain grew rougher, my shins and ankles sore and bruised, and often scraped because I couldn't focus on navigating for the group while also navigating for myself. I leaned on Atrius more and more heavily, and in turn, he leaned more on me—because as the stone grew rougher, so did our path forward. Now, the path branched very frequently, forcing me to stretch my awareness through the stone far ahead to cut off dead-ends and find the safest route forward.

Sometimes, even the paths that went nowhere stretched on for miles, making it almost impossible to truly tell which was the right way. At some of these branches, I sagged against the rocks, my cheek pressed to the stone, sweat beading on my forehead as I reached through the threads for many long, agonizing minutes to make a decision.

I was forever conscious that the stakes of these choices were high. The farther we went, the more frequently we came across the remnants of travelers who were far less lucky than us. Some were ancient bones, clad in dented, cracked armor rusted away with time. Others were fresher—fresh enough that one could make out the teeth and claw marks from the slyviks who'd picked their body clean. The freshest we came across were a pair—an adult and a child.

Erekkus had paused at that one, a brief, powerful stab of sadness in his threads.

"Why would someone bring a child—" he'd started, and then shut his mouth abruptly, as if halfway through the question he'd understood exactly what the answer was.

Of course he did. We all did. Desperation. Perhaps the same desperation that would make a man bring his child to wander the world to strange foreign countries, searching for a new home.

Atrius laid his hand on Erekkus's shoulder, gently nudged him forward, and we didn't look at that tiny little corpse again.

As we drew farther north, I began to sense the slyviks more frequently. With every branch in our route, I was now checking not only for dead ends that would have us walking in circles to our deaths, but also for the beasts. This far north, they tended to congregate in groups, which made them slightly easier to avoid but also much more dangerous to encounter. Sometimes, I took us on dangerously convoluted detours in order to avoid clusters of them that I sensed nearby. Though it slowed us down, I couldn't bring myself to regret the decision when we'd hear those not-distant-enough screeches.

Atrius kept track of the days with marks in a little bloodstained notebook he carried in his pocket, though I was skeptical of how accurate his sense of time was. I was convinced that none of us, him included, were really sure how much time had passed.

The cycle was endless. Walk. Sleep. Walk. Hold our breaths. Change course. Walk.

Atrius's totally unreliable estimation was that seven days had passed when I felt it.

We had come to yet another fork in our path. The elevation had started to ramp up, and the space between the rocks had gotten even narrower, so our two-by-two path of soldiers had become a long, winding single-file line. I'd turned my ankle some miles back the day before, and I wasn't the only one who had injured myself on the terrain. We were moving slowly.

Worse, we were running out of food.

A terrible question had started to nag at the back of my mind: *What if I had brought us the wrong way?*

Those doubts were whispering loudly in my ear at this particular fork in the road, when I leaned against the stone and felt for the threads . . . followed them . . .

I jerked upright, nearly sending myself toppling backward into Atrius's chest.

"What?" he asked, alarmed.

"Shh," I hissed.

I pressed myself to the cliffs again.

I was terrified I had imagined it. Terrified I'd just made a mistake. But no.

No, I hadn't imagined any of it.

I turned my face against the cold, dusty rock and let out a shaky breath that sounded more like a sob than I meant for it to. I wasn't sure whether to laugh or cry. I ended up doing a little of both.

Weaver damn us.

Atrius gripped my shoulder and leaned close. "Vivi, what?"

I shouldn't like it when he called me that. But I did. Life was too short to lie to yourself. Very short now.

I straightened and turned to him.

"We're less than a few miles from the end of the pass," I said.

Gods, I had never seen Atrius grin like that. I thought he was going to weep with joy.

"But there's an entire nest of slyviks between us and the end," I said.

Atrius's face fell.

"Right," I said.

The slyviks liked the colder air. Most of their nests were near the northern border of the cliffs. We'd gotten lucky and stumbled upon a whole damned mess of them. I couldn't count exactly how many I sensed, but I knew it was a lot. The best I could give Atrius was, "More than fifteen."

His expression didn't change at all, but I could tell just how hard he was working for that stoicism. "And less than?"

I didn't answer for a long moment. And then guessed, "Fifty?"

Atrius hissed a curse, and Erekkus threw back his head and laughed and laughed.

I couldn't blame him. I wanted to laugh, too.

So how could an exhausted, half-starving, injured group of soldiers, forced into narrow, slow lines, defeat as many as fifty of some of the greatest predators nature or gods had ever produced?

We stood together, silent, for a long time, all mulling over that question.

"We're overdue for rest," Atrius said at last, which I knew was his way of saying, *I have no idea what to do and I need time to think about it.*

No one had any better ideas.

AFTER THINKING IT over for a few more hours, the main conclusion we came to was that we were screwed.

We couldn't fight our way through the slyviks—a single juvenile had nearly killed Atrius and me. Even prepared, there was no way we could handle dozens of them, especially with no space to maneuver. They were aggressive creatures. They wouldn't just let us pass.

Erekkus, Atrius, and I talked in circles, trying to find a solution. Which really meant that Erekkus and I talked, and Atrius sat there stonily, staring off into the middle distance, looking furious, and occasionally chiming in with some idea we all knew wouldn't work, including him.

Eventually, in a fit of frustration, I went back to the stone and felt it, reaching through the threads again.

"What are you doing?' Erekkus snapped. "You said there was no other way."

He was getting very, very testy.

I shushed him and leaned against the wall.

Yes, I'd already confirmed—multiple times—that there was no way to circumvent the nest, at least not without running a very high risk of sending us all off to our deaths.

"So what are you looking for?" he asked, irritated, and I shushed him again, louder.

"Let her work!" another of the soldiers barked, and Erekkus whirled to him, fists clenched, obviously desperate for an outlet for his frustrations.

Weaver save us. Men.

I tried to ignore the squabbling in the background and focus. Honestly, I couldn't have answered Erekkus's question if I'd wanted to—I didn't know what I was looking for, other than some piece of information I'd missed, something critical that would save us. A miracle, I supposed.

The slyviks hadn't dispersed, and they hadn't gotten any less active. Actually, perhaps there were even more of them than before, though it was impossible to tell for sure. There was a lot of interference in the threads from this far away, partly because slyviks' movements were especially difficult to track, and partly because there were so many other nests nearby in other branches of the paths. All those movements blurred together from so far away.

It was strange, I thought sleepily, that such territorial creatures—

Something hard jostled against my back, knocking me away from the wall. I let out an *oof* as a stray elbow clipped my ribs.

I came back to awareness to Atrius shouting at Erekkus and the other soldier in clipped, harsh Obitraen, the two men hissing curses at each other as they reluctantly separated.

Atrius returned to my side and stared after them disapprovingly.

"Childish," he grumbled. "They need to be thinking about more than their egos."

I shrugged. It was almost a little comforting that men fighting for dominance over things that didn't matter was universal, human or—

I stopped breathing. My hand flung out to Atrius's shoulder. When I let out a weak laugh, he gave me a look that questioned my sanity.

He was about to question it even more.

"I have it," I said. "I know how we get past."

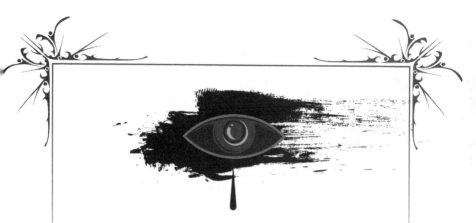

CHAPTER FORTY-ONE

I t was probably when the slyviks roared, all together, that I thought maybe this was not the best of ideas.

One slyvik's scream was a bone-chilling sound—dozens of them, layered on top of each other, echoed like an orchestra of death. We were so close to them now that their smell stung the air, a scent of decay and blood. I no longer had to sense them through the threads—I could feel their movements through the vibrations in the rock as their powerful bodies hurled from wall to wall.

I stopped around a corner. Atrius nearly stumbled into me. The visibility was especially poor here. Even vampire eyesight was mostly useless.

I whispered, very, very softly, "They're over there."

A muscle feathered in Atrius's jaw. His presence exuded resolute focus. If I'd had time to think about anything other than the blood-thirsty beasts mere feet away from us, I might have stopped to appreciate exactly how fearless Atrius was. I wondered if Nyaxia had appreciated what she'd had in him—probably the only man alive who'd throw himself into any inconceivable task a goddess might toss his way without a second of hesitation.

And yet, when his gaze slipped to me, that resolve flickered. Just a little, so quick I almost missed it.

He'd wanted to come up with a way that I didn't have to do this. I knew that, even though he didn't express it aloud. But we both knew that I was critical to this plan. *He* didn't have to be, though—that, we'd argued about. It didn't make sense to put the most important person here in this position. Let it be Erekkus, I'd said. Let it be any of his men.

He wouldn't hear of it.

So here we were. About to do perhaps the most dangerous, stupidest thing I'd ever done, and if we got ourselves killed, everything would be over.

The stakes were, if nothing else, exciting.

"Are you ready?" I whispered to him.

He looked at me like this was a stupid question.

Of course. He was always ready.

He stepped in front of me, slow and silent. In his arms were three canteens, which sloshed with blood.

One more reason this had to work: because if it didn't, the vampires would starve to death.

Atrius uncorked the canteens, one after the other.

The first, he tossed slightly down the path, the blood spurting out and trailing over the rocks below. Then, after pausing a moment, he took the second and hurled it as far as he could into the darkness of the mists.

Immediately, I felt the stirring interest in the slyviks. First one, then the others. Clicks and purrs, then growls, echoed from down the tunnel.

I grabbed Atrius's wrist. "Now," I hissed.

We'd gotten their attention. The blood gave us a head start. Now it was time to run like hell.

Or stumble like hell.

It was the best I could do in the darkness. I clung to the walls, one arm extended behind me to grip Atrius's, and felt our way forward as we ran. Behind me, I heard the steady sound of blood dripping onto the rocks as Atrius dumped the final canteen behind us, leaving a crimson trail. When it was empty, he dropped the container.

And then we heard them coming, stirred by the scent.

My steps quickened. Atrius's strides lengthened, our gaits shifting.

I thought it would be impossible to truly run over these rocks. I was wrong. When you hear a herd of slyvik screams behind you, you *run*.

"Which way?" Atrius barked. The air itself shivered with the beat of countless wings. We stumbled as the earth shook with the weight of their bodies against the rocks, growing frenzied.

The moment they saw us, the shrieks pierced the air. I could've sworn they were of delight.

The hair stood up on the back of my neck.

"That way," I ground out, and dragged Atrius left, to a smaller path between the cliffs. Now only my fingertips brushed the walls, maintaining just enough of a connection to the stone to sense the path back.

I'd tried to memorize the route before we started. I prayed I remembered right.

Another shriek curdled my blood. Atrius broke into a sprint, dragging me with him.

Weaver help me. Gods, I'd better remember that path.

"There!" I choked out, just in time, and the two of us rounded a corner sharply, nearly slamming into a wall.

The slyviks were great hunters. They didn't lose their prey. Seconds later, we heard them behind us. They were gaining.

Soon they would be on us.

Neither of us could speak—no time for that—but I could feel the pressure building in Atrius's presence, like a thread growing taut. Could feel his hand creeping toward his belt, just in case.

We were close.

We had to be.

I reached into the threads, checking our path—

Pain shot through my shin as it struck a sharp rock.

I stumbled, my knees nearly hitting the ground. Warm blood spurted down my leg. Atrius grabbed me roughly and yanked me upright again, dragging me along, and not seconds too soon because that time, I felt the slyvik's breath on my back.

We were going too slow.

I could feel the same realization settle over Atrius.

A little farther.

The turn was up ahead, just a little more—

I grabbed Atrius and we took the next corner, gravel sliding beneath our feet, and I could feel movement in the threads above even if I didn't have the time to focus on it, and we were going to make it—

SNAP.

I was yanked backward with enough force to knock the breath from my lungs.

The slyvik's roar surrounded me, shaking my bones. A burst of damp, hot air engulfed me.

My shirt. It had grabbed my shirt—

Before I could move, Atrius sprang into action. It was beautiful, the way he moved, with such sudden viciousness—like nothing ever caught him by surprise. His sword was out, and by the time I realized what was happening, his strike had already landed—right into the slyvik's eye.

A screech of pain rattled the earth. The ground hit me hard, my legs collapsing under me. Atrius fell back, too, rolling and falling back into a clumsy crouch behind me. Before us, the slyvik reared back, blood dripping from its face, wings spreading wall-to-wall. Behind it, other snakelike bodies slithered through the mists as its nest-mates caught up to us, heads of teeth and starving eyes curling through the gaps in the stone to corner us.

This time, I couldn't keep the fear down.

Atrius froze, too, his hands gripping my shoulders, like he was ready to go down fighting for both of us if he had to.

My fingers curled around my weapon.

We'd both go down fighting.

The slyvik before us prepared to strike—

And then a cacophony of animalistic shrieks pierced the air.

Not from in front of us. From behind us.

The flood of relief left my body momentarily limp.

Because we had made it. We had made it.

The slyviks' heads snapped up, peering into the mists, far beyond us. Their bodies coiled, readying for a fight. The roars lowered to glottal hisses and clicks. Stone screeched with the bite of claws.

Behind us, the same sounds echoed back, as the other nest of sly-viks prepared for a fight.

Territorial men—human or vampire or slyvik. The one thing you could always count on.

We were never going to get past the slyviks with our strength or our stealth. The only chance we had was to distract them with something far more interesting than some prey.

And a rival nest? Well. That *was* interesting.

I'd never felt anything quite like the sensation of those short, end-less seconds—like the electricity hanging in the air before a lightning strike, or the quiet in the sea before a tidal wave crests. We were in between two deadly forces of nature about to destroy each other.

It was, in a strange way, beautiful.

Then Atrius's fingers tightened around my arm, and he whispered in my ear, "Run."

We dove out of the way just as the slyviks lunged at each other.

The wave crashed. The lightning struck. This fight, of creatures utterly oblivious to any goal other than ripping each other to pieces, was just as powerful.

They collided in an explosion of teeth and wings and scales, and we bolted.

The air was thick with the screams of slyviks, sounds of such range and pitch that I never imagined an animal could make them. We couldn't speak to each other even if we'd tried. I couldn't stop to navigate our way through the stone—surely the vampires couldn't see much of anything, either, through the mist and the writhing bod-ies of the slyviks. But they knew the plan. They knew the signal. When they heard the commotion break out, they knew there was only one thing to do: run for their damned lives.

It was a straight run out, I'd told them. I'd been careful to sound very confident about it, even though, in reality, I wasn't completely sure—it was so hard to sense the specifics of the rock formations this far away, and through the disruptive presences of the slyviks.

If there were turns or another split in the path . . . we were done.

We ran, dodging stray claws and flying tails. I felt the soldiers, too, following behind us, moving as fast as they could.

Weaver, there were so many of these things—my upper estimation of fifty had to have been right, even if I couldn't stop to count. The claws and teeth and scaly bodies seemed to go on forever, the wails growing louder as the clash between the two nests escalated, more and more of them rising to the front of the pack for their attempt at asserting dominance.

My sword slashed wildly at whatever got in our path, without any time to look or judge. Blood spattered my face—my own or slyvik, I couldn't stop to tell.

When I sensed a change in the threads ahead, at first I thought I was imagining it.

But after several more stumbling steps, dodging a stray talon that nearly claimed the left side of my face, the truth of it dawned:

The end of the pass.

Not far ahead at all.

"Atrius," I choked out, and he knew without me saying anything else exactly what I meant. He lifted his sword above his head and let out a roar—a warrior's roar, a predator's roar, a sound that seemed fit to match the screams of the slyviks around us.

And with that roar, one juvenile too far away from the rest of the fight figured he'd take his chances here instead, and leapt down at us. Atrius was already responding before my warning shout had left my lips.

The beast came at him with its mouth open, razor teeth bared, and Atrius didn't hesitate as he brought his sword down on its throat, decapitating it in a single smooth stroke.

I choked out a shocked laugh, but didn't stop running—none of us did, not until the ground beneath us leveled and the walls opened up and the soul-deep darkness of the cliffs fell away.

I just kept running, and running, and running, until Atrius grabbed me and forced me to slow. The moment I stopped moving, my legs folded beneath me. I sank to the ground—actual *ground*, not rocks. My breath ached in my ribs.

Atrius sank down with me, his hands on my shoulders. A slow smile rolled over his face. Then he turned back—to see the rest of his warriors, now finished pouring through the opening in the cliff face, bleeding and bruised and exhausted, but very much alive.

My cheeks ached with my grin, which probably looked slightly manic. "I didn't know if we were going to make it."

"I did," Atrius said, matter-of-factly, and I found it so amusing I decided not to tell him that I had been there, and I knew for a fact he had some doubts.

Beside us, Erekkus flopped over on the ground, laughing and muttering a string of curses to himself.

I was still swaying a bit with the shock of what we'd just done.

"You *decapitated* one of them," I said. "One strike."

A smirk he was trying and failing to suppress twitched at the corners of his mouth. "I did," he said.

He just sounded so smug.

I couldn't help it. I laughed. Let him get a little full of himself. That was worthy of some admiration.

He laughed, too, softly, and he let his forehead fall against mine, and for a few breaths we both just reveled in the fact that we had survived.

Then, as if in unspoken agreement, we straightened.

We weren't done. Actually, the slyviks were nothing compared to what we were about to face.

Together, we stood.

The end of the pass was abrupt, spilling us out into an expanse of sandy plain. It was cold here, and the mist nearly as thick as it had been in the cliffs, only just thinning enough that I could sense the moon above—a perfect crescent.

The quiet felt like a warning.

Because there, looming over us to the north, emerging from the sparse trees on a cliff that overlooked the churning, angry sea, was the Pythora King's castle.

A strange calm fell over me. What did it say, that I had been afraid when picking a fight with the slyviks, but wasn't afraid to go kill the Pythora King?

Maybe it just meant that anger was the antidote to fear. I hated the Pythora King so much that I had little to be afraid of. I would die either way. Let me die with my blade in his throat.

Atrius was staring at the castle, too, and I could sense the same calm resolve in him. We moved at the same time—our bloody, sweaty hands clasping together.

"Is that his?"

Erekkus's voice was quiet with rage. Gone was his comical glee at having survived the pass.

Our silence was enough of an answer.

Finally, Atrius turned to him. "We don't have time to rest. Get them ready—"

But the words didn't make it out of Atrius's mouth before a wave of soldiers poured from the forest.

CHAPTER FORTY-TWO

They were shockingly well-prepared for us. It was as if he knew we were coming.

The Pythora King was known to be isolated and para-noid, keeping his castle closed to all but very few select followers. He relied on the cliffs and his neighboring city-states to shield him from invaders, and didn't keep a heavy force of warriors at the castle itself. But something must have changed recently, or maybe he had been bracing for Atrius's potential retaliation, because there was an entire damned army here. A small army, yes, but it was enough to catch us off guard coming straight from the cliffs, and they were charging at us before we had even caught our breath.

How they'd known we were here that quickly, I couldn't fathom.

I didn't have time to think about it.

At the approaching battle cries, Atrius's warriors were on their feet immediately, rallying as if they weren't already starving and in-jured and exhausted. Atrius roared a command in Obitraen, and we charged, meeting the Pythora King's men with blades out and teeth bared.

Immediately, the field devolved into chaos.

Atrius's men were outnumbered, but they were also far more skilled than these Pythora-afflicted soldiers. Blades clashed, blood spurted, voices roared as steel met steel, Atrius's men forced to fight three-to-one. They were everywhere—pouring from the forest, from the barracks to the east and west, from every direction but the Pythora King's palace itself.

"Go!" Erekkus screamed, single-handedly holding off four soldiers, yanking his sword from one of their throats as he whirled to us. "We'll hold them."

He jerked his chin up to the cliff ahead—to the steep upward steps, and the castle perched atop them. His presence reeked of fury, mouth twisted into a bloodthirsty snarl.

Atrius's lips thinned. We were preoccupied, too, fighting through body after body. Though they were cumbersome, they weren't threatening. Still, I could sense his hesitation—torn between seizing this moment and leaving his men behind.

Tearing his blade from another body, Erekkus edged closer, teeth bared.

"Go make him fucking pay, Atrius," he said. "We have this."

Resolve sat heavy in my heart at that, echoing his.

Yes. We'd make him pay.

Atrius's will hardened, too. His jaw tightened. He gave Erekkus a firm nod, and a quick clap on the shoulder that might as well have been a tear-soaked promise.

Then he turned to me. He nodded to the castle.

"How many?"

I couldn't tell. Not this far away, and certainly not surrounded by this many souls.

"I don't know," I said, honestly.

"Too many?"

The smirk had already started at the corner of his lip.

I felt it at the corner of mine, too.

It didn't matter that we were exhausted, injured, weak. We were this close to the Pythora King's throat.

"Never," I said.

Atrius casually took down another charging soldier, then grabbed my hand.

"Good," he said, and I held him tight, drew a thread tight between us and the stairs, and together, we slipped through it, ready to face whatever lay on the other side.

Up HERE, IT was too quiet. Too still.

Atrius and I had to fight our way across the fields between my thread steps, swiftly distributing death as we cut through the hordes. Between our efficient fighting and my use of the threads, we made it past the onslaught quickly, disappearing into the trees beyond and re-emerging on the steps that led up the palace.

The contrast between here and the world below was chilling. We were barely steps away, and yet here it was so quiet, the only sound the echoes of the battle we had left behind. We were ready, blades still poised, waiting for someone to chase us—waiting for someone to fling themselves from the doors of the castle.

It didn't happen. I didn't sense a soul.

The Pythora King kept his guards at arm's length, yes. But . . . no one?

It was too easy. So easy it felt dangerous.

We made our way up the winding steps of the cliff, to the castle at its peak.

"Castle," actually, was a generous word for it. It was a relatively small building, albeit beautiful, carved from a single piece of stone. Every face of it was covered in intricate carvings, each telling stories of the gods of the White Pantheon.

As we ventured farther up the steps, the columns on either side of the pathway held these stories, too. The outstretched hands of Vitarus, the god of abundance and famine, one coaxing forth crops and the other distributing plague. Ix, the goddess of sex and fertility, placing a rosebud in the womb of a weeping woman—granting her a child. Each column was a tribute to another god, their importance in the hierarchy of the White Pantheon rising as we traveled higher. I couldn't help but pause at Acaeja's column, halfway up the steps—she stood upright, blindfolded, a web of threads tangling from her outstretched hands, faceless silhouettes caught within it like flies in a spider's net. All of us at the mercy of fate—the mercy of the unknown. I touched my blindfold, swallowed back an uncomfortable pang of guilt, and kept walking.

There was no column for Nyaxia, of course. There would be none for a goddess shunned and exiled by the White Pantheon. Atrius barely glanced at the carvings. Maybe by now he was used to the way humans worshipped our gods. Maybe, after all he'd been through, gods now meant nothing to him at all.

We didn't speak until we neared the top of the stairs—the empty stairs—and Atrius leaned down to whisper in my ear, "Anything?"

The threads were so silent, so devoid of life, that it was almost uncomfortable. It felt . . . unnatural, like the threads were being manipulated in some way, not unlike how I felt on Veratas. Except, while the soul of the island had been so overwhelming I had been effectively blinded, this was the opposite—a blanket of silence that choked out everything.

Still, somewhere deep inside the walls of the castle, I could sense . . . something. I wasn't sure what. The Pythora King? A single soul alone, far within a house of stone, might feel that way. From this distance, it was hard to tell.

"He's in there," I said, with more confidence than I felt.

"No one else?"

Atrius did not hide his apprehension. Rightfully. All of this seemed wrong.

I shook my head. Neither of us were comforted by that answer.

We reached the top. The two columns that guarded the entrance honored the leader of the White Pantheon—Atroxus, the god of the sun. Ironic, for a place so steeped in fog it likely never saw any.

It seemed far too simple to just open the front door and walk through. Simpler still for that door to be unlocked. When Atrius put his hands on either side of the double doors and pushed, I was legitimately shocked when they ground open.

Before us, a streak of cool, misty light spilled into a vast, grand room, our silhouettes stretched across the tile floor. Torches and lanterns lined the walls, as if this place had been occupied moments ago but had suddenly emptied. Like at any second, a slew of wealthy lords and ladies could come spilling out of all these darkened doorways, lounging on the various velvet couches with their expensive wines perched in their hands.

Before us, at the end of the long carpet, across the massive room, was a large, arched doorway, and steps beyond it that led up.

There were few records of the layout of the Pythora King's palace. The building was ancient, among the oldest in all of Glaea. When the king took control twenty years ago, he had been careful to destroy as many descriptions of the place as he could. He was, after all, very paranoid, and the less anyone knew about the layout of his home, the better.

But no one could wipe all mentions of a thousand-year-old monument away, and no one was better at collecting information than the Arachessen archivists. I'd pored over every scrap of paper I could find, every mundane letter from the courts of previous kings, to piece together what I would face when, one day, I would be able to slay the Pythora King.

I knew what lay up those steps.

"The throne room," I whispered. The words stuck in my throat. My pulse raced, my hands sweaty around my blade.

Atrius's eyes burned into the side of my face as his steps matched mine.

We crossed the room, leaving behind the cold darkness of the misty plains for the warm darkness of the castle, which smelled strongly of Pythora blossoms and faintly of mold. That intangible presence I had sensed outside grew stronger, albeit still . . . strange in a way I couldn't pinpoint.

We passed beneath the archway, ascending the stairs. Step by step, the throne room unfolded before us—first the elegant arched ceiling, painted with chipped frescos of the gods' wrath, then the gold molding and the arms built into it to hold stained-glass lanterns.

We reached the top of the stairs. The throne room was just as grand as ancient visitors had said it was centuries ago. Probably even grander, to those viewing it with eyes, but its beauty was so aggressive, so ornate, that I still felt it through the threads.

At the end of the long, long room stood a single throne, high upon the dais.

And slumped in that chair, lounging to one side, was the Pythora King.

For a moment, Atrius and I both tensed—waiting for a shout, a command, an acknowledgment.

None came.

My brow furrowed. Atrius's jaw tightened.

I couldn't shake the strange numbness in the threads, the unnatural silence that felt like cotton stuffed into my ears, but I still followed when Atrius crossed the throne room, his steps firm and long, sword ready.

The Pythora King did not move or speak.

And we were several strides away from him when I realized why.

"Atrius," I choked out, just as he lifted his sword and drove it into the king's chest, piercing through layers of purple silk and hair-mottled skin.

The king slumped a little. His eyes, which stared blankly into the middle distance, fluttered.

Atrius stood there for a long moment, gripping his sword, eyes narrowing first in confusion, then realization. Perhaps he, too, was noticing all the other marks on the king's body—a slash or three at his throat, tears in his chest, a brutal mark, perhaps from an arrow, right over his heart.

The steady—unnaturally steady—rise and fall of the Pythora King's shoulders said he was not dead.

But he was certainly not alive, either.

He was a breathing corpse, and we weren't even the first people to kill him.

Atrius stumbled back, yanking his sword free. The thick, purplish substance that stained his sword and globbed at the open wound only vaguely resembled blood.

"What in the—" he muttered.

A familiar presence fell over me like a long shadow.

Suddenly everything felt very cold.

Suddenly I was very, very afraid.

In a single abrupt movement, I stepped in front of Atrius, pushed him back, and bowed my head.

"Sightmother," I breathed. "It's such a relief to see you."

I tried to make myself believe it—make every single one of my threads vibrate with my love for her, my gratefulness.

"I wish I could say the same," the Sightmother said, emerging from the darkness to stand beside the Pythora King, a single casual hand on his shoulder.

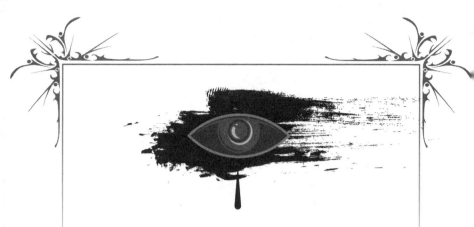

CHAPTER FORTY-THREE

I wished I could communicate with Atrius wordlessly. I wished I
could tell him to put that damned sword down, *right now*. Because
I knew he was confused, too, but all he knew was that I was
a runaway Arachessen and this was the Sightmother, and he had
promised to protect me.

If he tried to protect me, he would die.

I held my hand out behind me, a single splayed palm that I prayed
told him clearly, *Stop*.

And what did it say that a childish part of me, the part of me
who had been raised by this woman, couldn't stand to see Atrius kill
her—or the other way around?

What was she doing here?

I hadn't asked for backup. They certainly hadn't indicated they
would give me any. But perhaps I had been wrong when I'd inter-
preted my unanswered call to the Keep as a sign that the Arachessen
had discovered my betrayal.

Perhaps she had changed her mind.

Perhaps she had come here, knowing we were coming for the
Pythora King and . . . and killed him before we could.

It didn't make sense. But it was the only scenario I could string
together.

I was normally good with words, good with playing different

roles while thinking fast. But my confusion slipped to the surface now, despite myself.

"I don't—did you do this, Sightmother?" I gestured to the king—the corpse, more like it. "After all this time, have we finally—"

The Sightmother approached me, step by step, and cupped my cheek. She smiled. Her touch was overwhelming—she let all her emotions pour through it. Intense motherly love, fifteen years' worth of it. The pride of a commanding officer.

And sheer, bloody, cold-as-steel anger. Anger that only cut deeper for all the warmth she felt, burying into my gut and twisting.

Her smile soured as her lip curled.

"What," she asked calmly, "are you doing here?"

I had experienced fear before. But never fear like this.

There was a right answer to this question. There had to be. I frantically told myself this, forced myself to believe it.

I could give her that perfect answer. I should try.

Instead, I asked, just as calmly, "What are *you* doing here?"

"I came to meet you, of course."

This answer was not comforting. Instead, it chilled me down to my bones.

I stuffed that fear as far down as I could, hidden beneath decades' worth of genuine love for the Sightmother.

"I'm so happy to see you," I said. "But why is the Pythora King—"

"The Pythora King is more than a man."

I didn't understand. I didn't even know how to frame the question on my lips.

"The Pythora King has not been a man," the Sightmother said, "for a very long time."

A terrible feeling rose in my throat. A buzzing in my ears, like the breath of a monster behind me, a realization that I didn't want to turn around and face.

I said, quietly, "Sightmother, I don't understand."

Her smile flickered. She laughed softly. "Come, Sylina. You're so intelligent. How can you tell me you never suspected?"

Never suspected what? I wanted to say. But I didn't want to open my mouth to let her hear my voice. Didn't want to betray my own confusion.

"There is power in suffering," she said. "There is power in having something to fight against. We taught you that. And you know it better than most."

My ears were ringing.

I didn't want to believe what she was saying. Couldn't believe it. Because if I was putting these pieces together right, it meant I had just spent my life fighting against a king that didn't exist, in service to a Sisterhood that had lied to me. Lied, in the name of the very evil that I was so determined to wipe off the face of this kingdom.

Something inside me simply collapsed. Just came apart. I opened my mouth but found no words. I choked them back, because whatever would come out would just betray my devastation.

Think, Sylina. Focus.

"You were never supposed to know," the Sightmother said. "If you had obeyed, you still wouldn't."

Her face hardened. I felt the shift in her presence, something deadly, like a sword being drawn—except the magic of the Sightmother was more deadly than any piece of steel.

"And why didn't you obey, Sylina?"

She stepped closer, and that little movement was enough to make Atrius's thread of self-control, already tenuous, snap.

He pushed past me, his still-bloodied sword out. "Get away from her," he ground out, and the four words were all command, a way I had never once heard another person speak to the Sightmother. But what struck me more was the protectiveness that permeated his presence with those words, primal and unguarded in a way that Atrius rarely was.

I cringed, because if I felt it, the Sightmother certainly did, too.

Her brows rose.

And with a flick of her hand and a powerful burst of magic through the threads, Atrius was on his knees, straining against a body that would no longer cooperate with him, his threads bound by the Sightmother's spell.

Her head tilted to me. "Perhaps now I'm starting to understand some things."

I did not give myself time to question the words that flew from my lips next. Didn't allow myself to think about their consequences.

"You told me to gain his trust, Sightmother," I said. "I have. All you're seeing is evidence of my commitment."

Weaver, how my chest ached, when I felt the shock in Atrius's soul. The hint of betrayal, still now just a suspicion of something he didn't yet want to believe.

"I see evidence of your disobedience," the Sightmother snapped.

"I tried to consult you," I said. "I couldn't reach the Keep. I did this for the will of the Weaver—"

"The Weaver commanded you to kill him."

The Sightmother's voice boomed through the ancient halls, obliterating the silence along with my secret.

It took every shred of discipline not to show that I'd stopped breathing.

Atrius's presence went cold. He could no longer avoid the realization.

I had been expecting his anger. I could have been prepared for that. Instead, what I got was his hurt. Pure, raw hurt—the hurt of that vulnerable version of him I saw when we were alone every night, soft and unguarded in sleep. A child's hurt.

When I was only ten years old, the Arachessen tested my ability to withstand pain. I had hardened myself to it, told myself that if I could endure disfigured eyes or broken bones or missing fingers, I could endure anything.

And yet now, even as I bit down hard on my tongue, right over that ridge of scar tissue, I thought this pain might break me.

But I wouldn't let it break him.

"Now," she said. "Where is that dagger?"

I didn't even have time to refuse it before she held out her hand— and suddenly, the knife was in it, weight missing from my hip.

I had only seen the Sightmother fight a handful of times. It was never a fight so much as a slaughter.

I didn't even sense her moving until the blade was hurtling toward Atrius's heart.

I screamed, *"He is god-touched!"*

The blade stopped, hovering in midair. The Sightmother's head tilted, cocked like a bird's. It was rare that I felt anything at all from her presence, given how skilled she was at hiding her emotions—but at this, I sensed a little glimmer of interest.

"Forgive me," I choked out. "I was . . . just taken aback. I should have explained sooner. I tried to reach the Keep. No one answered me."

"God-touched."

She pulled the weapon back to her hand. A harsh command in those two words: *Go on.*

"He was touched by the goddess Nyaxia herself," I said. *"Nyaxia,* Sightmother. Imagine what an offering that would be to Acaeja."

There were few things most of the gods of the White Pantheon valued more than a sacrifice of another's acolyte in their name— especially an acolyte of a rival god, and most of all one hated as much as Nyaxia. Yes, Acaeja was the most tolerant god of Nyaxia, but tolerance was not alliance. A gift this great would hold significant weight.

The Sightmother went still, the dagger still raised. I couldn't read either her face or her presence. Then she reached out with her free hand and grabbed Atrius's chin, roughly forcing his face up to hers as he strained against her binding.

She withdrew her hand just as abruptly.

"Cursed," she said. "Cursed by Nyaxia."

"But she made a bargain with him, too. He acts on her behalf. Taking land from Acaeja in the name of his heretic goddess. Surely, the Weaver would appreciate that gift."

The Sightmother considered this.

I bowed my head, hands open before me in a show of piety and obedience.

"Forgive me, Sightmother. I—I acted too rashly. As you've warned me against many times. And if the punishment for that is death, I—"

"Enough."

In two long steps, she crossed the dais, and then her hands were on my face. My body's reaction to her touch was visceral—part of me wanting so desperately to lean into it, as I had for the last fifteen years, and another part wanting just as fiercely to pull away.

"I have raised you, Sylina," she murmured, a slight crack in her voice. "I am well aware of your flaws. I spent two decades trying to protect you from them. You always had such potential—" She cut herself off, her palm sliding to my cheek, and for a long moment she stood there, unmoving.

It was hard for me to gather my own courage, stifle my own anger, to peer through the gap in the door that had opened before me.

"I want to give Acaeja this," I murmured. And because I knew that the Sightmother could feel my threads, I made sure the words were as close to the truth as possible. How sickeningly easy it was—to let her see how much I still loved my goddess and my Sisterhood, even as I reeled from their betrayal. "Let me redeem myself, Sightmother. *Please.*"

The plea rolled so convincingly from my lips. Maybe that made me every bit the hypocrite I accused the Sightmother of being.

I could feel Atrius's eyes burning into my back like the heat of the sun. I could not let myself feel it. Could not acknowledge his presence.

The Sightmother regarded me for a long, long time. I could have sworn I felt something so foreign in her presence—uncertainty. *Conflict.* Until this moment, it had never occurred to me that the Sightmother could experience such things. I'd always thought that once you reached a certain level of power, a certain level of faith, it was like Acaeja wiped all those thoughts away. Why would an acolyte of the unknown feel any uncertainty? Doubt any decision?

Funny, the clarity that comes in the most terrible moments. I never realized before that this was why I had chosen Acaeja as my fixation, out of all the gods of the White Pantheon.

She was the only one who promised comfort in the unknown.

But even that had been a lie, because now I saw that the Sightmother felt just as uncertain in this moment as any other fallible human.

She leaned her head close to me, our foreheads nearly touching.

"Fine. You have earned your second chance, Sylina," she said, each word weighted, like a heavy gift.

My relief flooded me. I smiled with a shaky breath. "Thank you—"

I didn't even feel her magic—her sedation—until it was too late, and the ground was rising up to meet me.

The last thing I sensed wasn't her loving stare, grateful as I was for it.

No, it was Atrius's—cold and unblinking, seeping with the blood of my betrayal.

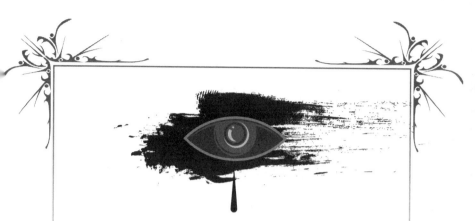

CHAPTER FORTY-FOUR

I dreamed of Naro. We were children. I was nine years old, him thirteen. We were out in the deserts past the borders of Vasai, sitting on a rock that was hot with the remnants of the sun. It was late in the day. I had a chipped cup of pineapple juice in my hands, which Naro had stolen for me on our way out of town. Our lives were hard and sad, but in these moments, we were content.

I giggled at some over-exuberant story he was telling me, his gangly limbs flailing and freckled face contorted. He finished his imitation of the shopkeeper who'd run after us, a grand finale featuring a stumbling caricature of the man's clumsy run, which had me rolling with laughter.

"Careful!"

Naro snatched the cup from my hands.

"We suffered for that, Vi. Don't spill it."

My laughter faded. Naro sipped the juice, staring off into the sunset. He was starting to look a bit like a man in the right light, his jaw harsher and dotted with the beginnings of stubble.

"One day," he said, "It won't matter. Everything will be different."

I knew that he was talking about a future in which we didn't have to worry about spilled juice or what we would eat tonight, or where we would sleep, or whether tomorrow might finally be the day that one of Tarkan's guards got us. But for some reason, the truth of that statement made a nauseous feeling coil in my stomach.

I shivered, suddenly cold.

"Yes," I said. "That'll be good. I can't wait."

Naro turned around and looked at me. His smile faded. His stare lingered for a long time, like he'd forgotten what he was about to say.

Then he replaced his lopsided grin and handed me the cup again. "But not now, alright?" he said. "And when it happens, you can't forget this. None of it will matter if you forget this."

I took a gulp of pineapple juice, relishing the sweet sting of it on my tongue. "This?"

"Who we are right now." He rustled my hair, and I scowled and pushed his hand away. "Remember that, Vivi, alright?"

I didn't like Naro talking to me like this. It was too sentimental of him. It made me feel like something bad was about to happen.

I stuck my toes in the sand and wiggled them around.

"Alright?" he said.

"Alright," I said.

And it wasn't until I agreed that the uncomfortable feeling came over me—the feeling that I had just lied to the most important person in the world to me. That not only would I not remember these times, I would one day crawl over rocks and sacrifice my body and give up my name all *to make sure that I forgot,* to erase this version of myself from existence.

A sudden panic fell over me. I should have said more to him—I should have given him the promise he really wanted. But when I turned to him, frantic, Naro was gone. The skyline of Vasai was in tatters. And the cup of pineapple juice was now full of rancid black blood.

I AWOKE IN the Salt Keep.

The familiarity of the place hurt now. All the smells and sensations. My body recoiled from it.

The memory of what had happened in the Pythora King's castle came back to me immediately.

The Pythora King.

The Sightmother.

I barely made it to the washroom before I emptied my guts, not that there was much to hack up.

I let myself stay there, leaning against the basin with shaky arms, for exactly ten seconds. Ten seconds to feel the panic and despair and fear.

That was all I could afford here, in the Salt Keep, where not even emotions were private.

That was all I could afford when there was work to do.

I straightened and washed out my mouth. Then I stripped off my clothes—still the dirty ones from my journey to the Pythora King— and left them in a pile on the floor.

I needed to think.

The Sightmother wouldn't leave me alone long. Did the other Sisters know what had happened? The insecure part of me feared they did—what if everyone had always known, and I was the only one who never guessed it?—but my logical mind knew the answer had to be no. Information in the Arachessen was carefully controlled and even more carefully doled out. It was rare for anyone to know much of anything about other Sisters' missions.

The sickening implications of this made my stomach lurch again, and I had to pause to swallow down another wave of vomit.

A knock sounded at the door.

I knew it was the Sightmother.

This was not the time to keep her waiting. And nakedness didn't mean much to Sisters anyway, all things considered. Still, I was very conscious of how exposed I was when I went to the door and opened it.

The Sightmother took me in. I wondered if she sensed my unease, even though I was careful to hide it.

I thought instead of the Sightmother as the person I had so ad- mired for the last fifteen years. I thought of the possibility of losing her, and my Sisterhood, forever. I let myself feel that unease, instead. An acceptable emotion to let her see.

"Yes, Sightmother?" I asked.

"Get dressed," she said. "Your gown. Then come join me in my dining room."

My dining room. She was inviting me to her private wing, in the upper levels of the Keep. I'd only been there once, and briefly. Few were allowed.

I wasn't sure how to ask this question.

"Are the others—"

"No. Just us."

I couldn't decide if I was grateful for that or not.

The Sightmother gave me a soft smile. Maybe I was looking too somber. "You are going to meet a goddess today, Sylina," she said. "This is a gift most never get."

Weaver, I felt sick.

But I returned her smile.

"I'm honored," I said, and made myself believe it to be true.

She nodded back into my room. "Get ready. Be in the dining room soon. We don't have much time."

Every Arachessen had a single gown that was many times finer than anything else she'd ever worn. Usually, it was gifted to us on our eighteenth birthday, and then sat untouched in our closets for years after that. The gown was intended for one purpose alone: to be worn in the presence of our Lady of Fate, Acaeja.

Most never got the opportunity to wear their dresses. Actually, as far as I knew, none of my Sisters ever had.

Mine was red as blood.

The bodice was made of beaded lace, and the skirt of flowing silk chiffon. The hem where the bodice met the skirt was decorated with a series of tear-shaped beads, which were intended to resemble flower buds but now just seemed like drops of blood. The neckline wrapped around my throat, exposing my shoulders, with chiffon sleeves that dangled down my arms.

I could sense all these factual aspects of the dress, just as I could sense that it was incredibly well-made, certainly worth the large amount of money that had been spent on it. I couldn't quite know how I looked in it, or if it was as lovely in that intangible way as it seemed like it would be.

As I brushed my hair and put on a fresh blindfold—red that perfectly matched my dress—I wondered if I looked beautiful. There was a certain appeal to leaving behind a pretty corpse.

Whatever the Sightmother was able to sense of my appearance, she must have been pleased, because her smile was one of genuine pleasure when I joined her in the dining room. She wore her gown as well, teal blue, just as ornate as mine. The room was large, the ceilings high and made of glass, revealing the red dusk of the sky above. But the table at its center was small, designed to sit no more than five people. Today, it was only set for two.

She gestured to the place setting across from her, and I sat down.

The food smelled incredible. I didn't realize until now exactly how long it had been since I'd eaten fresh cooking.

The Sightmother sipped her wineglass. "Eat," she said. She'd already started on her own meal, her steak half-gone. "You'll need your energy tonight."

I had no appetite. I daintily cut the meat and took a bite anyway. It was perfectly made, but tasted like ash.

"Thank you," I said. "It's very good."

A waste of words. I had so many questions to ask. Some, I might be able to. Others were far too dangerous.

"It's alright," the Sightmother said softly.

My knife stopped moving.

"What, Sightmother?"

"I sense your fear, Sylina. There's no shame in fear. I was terrified the first time I met Acaeja."

I felt no lie in her words. Nothing but kind compassion.

I had still been partly convinced that she was going to kill me. But perhaps I could chance the questions I most desperately wanted answers to, if I asked them carefully.

I set down my silverware.

"I do have a question," I said.

The Sightmother's brow twitched over the ebony silk of her blindfold. "I'm sure you have many."

"Why are you allowing me to do this when I disobeyed your orders?"

Her smile faded.

"Many people asked me, years ago, why I allowed you to stay at the Salt Keep," she said. "Considering your age."

Normally, every time someone mentioned the way I came to be here, I'd bristle with shame, like it was a terrible flaw being pointed out. Something unpleasant and bitter lingered on my tongue now, but it wasn't shame. It was a different kind of anger, directed not at myself but at the Sightmother.

"The truth was that I saw such potential in you," she said. "I saw . . . parts of myself, perhaps, in you. Even all those years ago. There can be beauty in what makes us unique. I sensed that what made you so could be a great benefit to the Arachessen."

My hands shook slightly around my knife. I couldn't believe what I was hearing.

It was what I had wanted to hear my entire life. That validation.

"It was always made very clear to me that my ten years before the Arachessen were a detriment to my position here," I said, keeping my voice carefully level.

"In some ways. Yes."

"But you never believed that."

Another calm smile. "It isn't so simple, Sylina. Something can be both a detriment and a strength. Suffering makes us strong. You, Sylina, have suffered so greatly. And you have grown so, so strong because of it—and because you had so much to prove. Complacency does not make anyone strong."

I had to focus on keeping my breathing level. Needed to speak past the painful lump at the base of my throat.

Puzzle pieces, slowly, were clicking together, even though I hated the picture they revealed.

"Then you've done me a great service," I said. "Just as you've done Glaea a great service."

For a moment I thought I'd pushed too hard, mentioning Glaea, my implication clear. But I kept my presence still, all those feelings of love and loyalty and gratefulness at the front of my mind. And at last, the Sightmother inclined her chin.

"Complacency does not create strength," she said again. "Not in you. Not in Glaea, either. You have fire, Sylina. Think of a version of yourself who was not forged in those flames. Think of how soft you would be." She shook her head. "That is not what's Right for this country."

Right. As if this is what Acaeja wanted for us.

I put my hands under the table, folded over my lap, terrified they would betray me. I could control my presence, but, apparently, not those damned shaking hands.

"It's . . . a shock," I said. "The truth of the king."

"I know. It will take time to come to terms with it."

"How long . . . ?"

The rest of the question faded into too many others: *How long has the Pythora King been dead? How long have you been ruling over a never-ending war? How many deaths are on your hands?*

My sister's? My mother's?

"Does it matter?" she asked.

Yes, I wanted to say. *It matters more than anything.* But instead I lowered my chin, as if to concede. "No. I suppose it doesn't."

"A long time," she said. She took another sip of her wine. The smell of it was too pungent—it was a ceremonial drink, I was sure, likely loosening her lips and her inhibitions in preparation for the ceremony she'd soon have to perform.

"Who else knows?"

I dreaded the answer to this question. Because despite everything, they *were* my Sisters.

"The Sightmother who came before me," she said. "Two of my highest advisors. And now, you. It's . . . a truth most aren't ready to understand. I've gone through great lengths to protect it."

I thought of the various Sisters who had been shunned from the Arachessen, punished with death and dismemberment for crimes never disclosed to us. I wondered whether any of them had simply been removed for knowing too much.

"Yet you're letting me live," I said.

"I told you, child, that we would need your fire for what's ahead." The smile she gave me was so warm, so loving—so sickeningly genuine. I could even feel her pride and affection in her presence. "Do you know what your name means, Sylina? It means *bringer of rebirth*, in the tongue of the gods. I saw your greatness when I meditated on you, that day I brought you here and found that name for you. Fate is ever-changing. I wasn't sure if you would come to fulfill those expectations. But now, I believe that you can. The offering you've brought us has convinced me of that. That's why I want you here to meet Acaeja with me. Because you are the future of the Arachessen. The flame in which we forge the next version of ourselves. I saw that fifteen years ago, and I see it even more clearly today."

My eyes stung. The lump in my throat had grown unbearable. If I opened my mouth, I'd sob.

The Sightmother put her hand over mine. Her thumb rubbed comforting circles over my skin.

"You have won, Sylina," she murmured, her voice cracking. "Now come with me, and help me forge this new world."

She swallowed the last of her wine in a single gulp, then rose.

When she held out her hand for me again, I took it.

CHAPTER FORTY-FIVE

I t's a tricky business to get the attention of a god—a matter of luck
and fate. Some gods were busybodies, often meddling in the affairs
of their human followers, likely to notice even minor slights. Others
were aloof, disinterested in the land of mortals altogether. Most var-
ied between the two, depending on your favor and their moods. Some
humans were gifted summoners, able to draw upon the gods at will,
but that was a rare, rare power. For most of us, summoning a god demanded complicated rituals and powerful magic, and even then, you
might not manage it.

If you did, you'd better have something interesting enough to
show them. Gods did not like having their time wasted.

The Sightmother did not plan on wasting Acaeja's time.

She led me to the roof of the Salt Keep, over the west wing, an
area in which I had never been allowed. I had only seen this platform once before, and only from a distance. It was carved directly
into the obsidian stone of the Keep—a large, circular base, two steps
around it.

It was a calm night, the sky clear, revealing the full moon. The
sound of the distant waves crashing against the rocks, far below us,
was a constant, steady heartbeat.

I could recognize all those things. And yet, the old image of
the scraps of color floating in the winds came to me now, and I so

desperately wished I could see it all from up here. A sight that my ten-year-old self no doubt would have found incredible.

It would have been a nice final thing to see.

I had time to think this only for a moment, because then my attention turned to the presences on the platform—one above them all, too strong to ignore.

Atrius.

Erekkus was there, too, bound and restrained, as well as five other vampire warriors—had they been captured from the battlefield? I didn't let myself wonder, or else risked feeling things I wasn't supposed to feel. Two shrouded, elderly Arachessen stood along the outskirts of the circle, presumably the advisors that the Sightmother mentioned at dinner. The vampires were all heavily sedated. Still, I sensed their anger thrashing wildly—unsuccessfully—against the haze of their half consciousness.

None of them fought as hard as Atrius, though.

They had to have used more powerful magic on him than the others, I could tell immediately, and even then, it had barely been enough. His aura held none of the frantic, directionless fight. Instead, his fury was steady and constant.

He was in the middle, shirtless, his body sagging against a stone pillar. His hair was unbound and messy over his shoulders and chest, which was covered with still-bleeding wounds from our battle. His lashes fluttered as he strained to keep them open.

When I stepped onto the platform, his head struggled to lift. I sensed, agonizingly clearly, the sudden burst of emotions that ran through him at the sight of me—all of them contradictory. Affection. Protectiveness. Hurt. Anger.

All of them there and gone in an instant, hidden behind that steel wall.

Weaver, I envied him, because it was so much harder for me to choke down everything I felt. I couldn't even let myself acknowledge it, because if I did, I wouldn't be able to shove any of it back into its box.

In the presence of the Sightmother, I had to feel nothing but gratefulness. Loyalty.

I forced those things to the front of my mind, forced them to drown out everything else. I was an Arachessen. I was a daughter of the Lady of Fate. I was an acolyte of Acaeja. That was all I ever had been. All I ever would be. All I ever wanted to be.

The Sightmother led me across the narrow, silver-railed pathway to the altar, her lush, cerulean-blue skirts rustling with each movement. Her steps had grown a little shaky, her hands clutching the silver rail. I was sure that if her eyes had been visible, her pupils would have been massive. The cocktail of herbs and drugs in her wine, designed to open the passage between her and the world of the gods, worked quickly.

By the time she made it to the altar, she was barely standing up straight. I had to offer her my arm so she could make it up the steps.

The Sightmother sagged over the altar, her palms pressed to the stone, head bowed, catching her breath.

"I can already sense it," she said. "The path to the gods."

Even her voice sounded distant.

"All of my strength will be needed to call the attention of Acaeja," she went on. "To keep the way open. It will be up to you to make the offering."

With a shaky hand, she reached into her silk robes. Then she withdrew a dagger, the fine blade gleaming silver in the moonlight.

The dagger. *My* dagger.

"You'll know when," she said. "You'll feel it. Give her his head first. And then the blood of the others." She laughed a little, a weak exhale. "The head of a vampire touched by Nyaxia. What an offering. We'll have earned quite a favor tonight, Sylina."

"Yes," I agreed. My hand closed around the hilt of the blade, so cold it almost made me flinch. My voice sounded like it belonged to a stranger.

Atrius's stare, steady and hard despite his near-unconsciousness, pierced my back inch-by-inch, his attention dripping down my spine like blood.

Anticipation hung thick in the air.

At last, the Sightmother lifted her head. Straightened her back. Every muscle moved with such uncanny grace, an unnerving shift from her drug-hindered movements seconds ago. She lifted her chin, face tilted to the sky, palms open at her sides, as if to offer as much of herself to the heavens as possible.

"It's time," she murmured. "Light the fire. Let's begin."

CHAPTER FORTY-SIX

If there was any doubt that magic was thick in the night here, the
way the blaze went up—like it was ready to consume the entire
world—put it to rest. I had to leap away from the fire pit, my hands
shielding my face, the moment I dropped the match. My Threadwalking ritual fires were laughable compared to this. This was a
spire of light that pierced all the way through the sky, like the flames
were trying to reach for the gods themselves.

And the gods, in turn, reached back.

A powerful crack of magic split the sky, the earth. There was no
sound, no movement, and yet we all reacted to it as if it had been the
force of an earthquake. The hairs on my arms stood upright. Every
inhale burned, like the air itself had turned into something not meant
for human lungs.

The Sightmother's head snapped backward, her face lifted to the
night, light pouring from her palms, her mouth, the eyes beneath her
blindfold. That light pooled in the sky like cream poured into black
tea, swirling slowly, cracks of lightning collecting in its center.

To open a passage to the gods required incredibly powerful magic.
Only a handful of people in the world were capable of it. A part of
me expected the process to be long, drawn out, like one of our many
archaic rituals.

Now, that seemed naive of me.

Of course calling upon a god wasn't a pretty, ceremonial act. It was a sledgehammer against a door. A ram against a gate. It was a scream so loud that no creature, mortal or god, could ignore it.

And the gods, indeed, took notice.

Maybe it was the way the light shifted, the sky turning mottled purple against the blaze of the Sightmother's spell. Maybe it was the way sound dulled and heightened at once, my ears ringing. Maybe it was the way all the threads reoriented, as if disrupted by a much greater force, leaving me swaying. My physical body felt very far away, and my hair lifted around me, as if I were floating underwater.

Shadows, distant silhouettes, collected within the growing pool of light above us.

And just as I could sense the presences of the mortals around us, I could sense *them,* too—the gods. A presence more powerful than I had ever experienced. It made me want to collapse in supplication, like my soul itself had been stripped from within my skin.

The Sightmother couldn't move. She couldn't so much as speak. But through her focus, she managed to shout through the threads, *{Now!}*

I had fallen to my knees, though I didn't remember doing so. I forced myself upright—difficult, on such violently shaking limbs.

I turned to Atrius.

And somehow, his presence made all the rest of it seem tolerable. A steadiness tethering me to shore.

His hair floated around him too, tendrils of silver suspended in weightlessness. He'd somehow managed to keep himself on his feet, though the other vampires and even the Arachessen acolytes were on their knees. His face tilted to the sky, watching the shadows peer down at us.

He looked at the gods like they were a challenge.

But when I approached him, one labored step after another, his gaze fell to me.

I touched his face, my fingertips caressing the solidness of his cheekbone, the softness of his lips, the scar along his jaw.

Even with my senses obliterated like this, he smelled of snow. Fresh and cool and new.

His eyes traced my face, and I could feel that stare like he could feel my fingertips—mimicking my movements on him, forehead and lips and chin.

Here, before him, I was more exposed than I was before the gods.

I had managed to hide my true self from the Sightmother, a woman who could see the depths of my inner presence. And yet, I could not hide myself from Atrius. He saw all of me. Whether I liked it or not.

Good. Because I needed him to see me now. See the truth.

We had one chance.

My free hand fell down his arm—gripped his wrists, as if in comforting reassurance or heartfelt apology. The leather of his restraints was smooth against my palms.

My other hand held the dagger up between us.

"There is no greater offering to a god than the acolyte of another," I said.

I raised the blade.

And then, so fast I prayed no one else would have time to react while so blinded by magic, I sliced Atrius's bindings, and shoved the hilt into his hands.

"Don't stand still," I whispered.

Knowing he would understand.

Knowing he would know what I was telling him to do, right now, in this moment, with the gods steps away and the Sightmother consumed by her spell.

His eyes widened. The shock in his presence reverberated once, for half a breath, before it settled into resolve.

Already, the acolytes' heads were beginning to turn to us. But Atrius and I had fought together so many times. I knew he didn't need much time to kill.

And indeed, this strike took him only seconds:

Seconds to lunge across the altar at the Sightmother.

Seconds to draw the blade across her throat, violent and quick, not even giving her time to scream, her voice fading to a wet gargle.

Seconds for him to hold her back by her hair, letting all that blood pour over the altar, and lift his chin to the sky.

"Goddess Nyaxia," he screamed. "I give you this gift. An acolyte of Acaeja. The blood of a tyrant queen, and the crown of a White Pantheon kingdom. I spill this blood and claim this kingdom for you, my Mother of the Ravenous Dark, Nyaxia."

His voice cracked. Bathed in such intense light, no one else could see the single tear slide down his cheek. No one but me.

He choked out, "My pact with you has been fulfilled."

Yes, it was difficult to get the attention of a god.

But this? This was enough.

In fact, it was enough to get the attention of two.

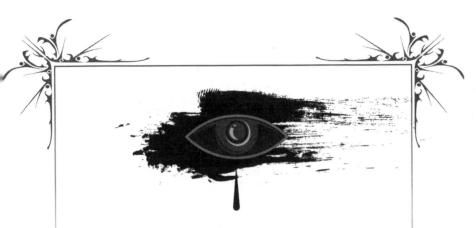

CHAPTER FORTY-SEVEN

I had thought my vision of Nyaxia had been debilitating. I had been wrong. It was nothing compared to what she was in person—a force so great that you had no choice but to bow, a beauty so intense you had no choice but to avert your gaze, a presence so strong that the threads themselves couldn't define her.

All at once, she was here, and all at once, the world rearranged to suit her.

She was as she had appeared in the vision—the tendrils of long black hair, floating like freestanding night, the pale skin, the blood-drenched mouth, the eyes of nebulas and galaxies. And yet, she still was so much more.

The terror that fell over me had me on my hands and knees against the stone.

And yet, through that fear, my attention fell to Atrius—Atrius, who now hacked off the Sightmother's head, presenting it to his goddess.

He didn't show it, but I could feel his fear, too. He was drowning in it.

He bowed to Nyaxia and held out the head to her.

"My lady," he said. "A gift for you."

Nyaxia chuckled. The sound felt like a fingernail up my spine—a promise of something either very pleasurable or very dangerous.

She reached down and took the head, examining it.

"My," she purred, "and what a gift it is."

"I promised you a kingdom of the White Pantheon conquered in your name," Atrius said. "I do not make promises I don't keep."

"And yet I didn't expect the head of my cousin's devoted acolyte." A slow smile widened over Nyaxia's mouth, another drop of blood trickling down her ice-pale skin. "A kingdom is one thing. But this . . . what a delightful surprise. For too long my cousins have thought my children are free for them to hunt. How nice to see the roles reversed."

The earth itself shivered with her pleasure. I'd never been in the presence of such wicked delight. I knew that gods, petty as they were, loved to be offered sacrifices that spat in the face of their rivals. But this . . . Nyaxia seemed to love the spite of it more than the gift of the kingdom she had sent Atrius on an impossible mission for.

She lowered the head and ran one blood-soaked hand over Atrius's cheek, a mother's caress. He stiffened beneath her touch.

"You," she purred, "have exceeded my expectations, Atrius of the House of Blood."

Just then, the universe shifted again. All the air ripped from my body, leaving me heaving on the ground.

It wasn't enough to say the threads rearranged. They changed. Suddenly they were more alive than they ever had been, every one of them bound to a new source—their only true master.

Only the Weaver herself could shift the threads of life itself like that.

"You always were far too quick to make your decisions, cousin," a low, melodic voice said—a voice that sounded like every age layered on top of the other, child and elder and everything in between, evermoving, like the unknown itself.

I forced myself to lift my head. Forced my senses to reach out for her—my goddess, my Weaver, Acaeja.

The entire world bent to her. No, flowed through her—like every sense and element and tiny speck of time was held in the palm of her hand. While Nyaxia emanated breathtaking, dangerous beauty, Acaeja's was constant, stable, like the powerful grace of the horizon where the stone met the sea. She had rich, deep skin, her features strong as stone, her large eyes pure white and clouded with mist that shifted and changed with every passing second. She had six wings, three on each side, each one offering a glimpse into another cryptic version of the future or past or present—snowy skies or churning seas or flames of a fallen kingdom. She wore a long, simple white gown that trailed over her feet, fluttering in the breeze. Her hands, which had ten fingers each, were fanned out in front of her. Each finger was tattooed with symbols that indicated a different fate— and from those fingers spilled threads of light. Threads of fate itself, surrounding her like the moon circling the earth.

A slow smile spread over Nyaxia's face—a wicked smile. "Acaeja. It's been so long."

"A shame for us to meet with my acolyte's head in your hands."

Nyaxia's smile withered. "I seem to recall once we met with my husband's head in yours."

The air grew suddenly cold, the stars shifting to storm clouds overhead.

Acaeja's presence soured. The fates in her wings darkened, all cold nights and smoldering ashes.

"We have discussed this many times, cousin," she said.

"And perhaps now you'll tell me that we'll discuss it many more," Nyaxia snapped.

Acaeja didn't answer. But a small, knowing smile curled her lips. "Yes," she said. "I expect we will."

"Maybe it isn't so bad for you to know what it feels like to mourn something," Nyaxia spat, sneering down at the Sightmother's head. "What do you feel for this witch, anyway? You have thousands more. I had only Alarus. Only him."

Her voice cracked over those final two words, and it struck me just how childish she sounded—how lost.

I had been so ashamed of my inability to shed my grief from fifteen years ago. And yet here was a goddess, one of the most powerful beings ever to exist, and her grief was still just as raw, two thousand years later.

The pain in the air hardened, sharpening to anger. Nyaxia's

flawless face twisted into a hateful sneer. "And all of you have exiled my people. You've hunted them. You kill them. I have defended Obitraes through force alone."

Acaeja regarded her steadily. "I loved Alarus as a brother," she said. "I have never had any quarrel with your people. And I have defended you, Nyaxia, from others who judge you in ways you do not deserve. I will not excuse the actions of the White Pantheon. But this—"

Nyaxia cut in, snidely, "This is what I have earned—"

"*This*, Nyaxia, is a new sin." Acaeja's voice did not raise. She didn't need it to. The power in it alone cut through all other sounds. "Your follower has murdered one of my most devoted acolytes. You intend to take a kingdom from the grasp of the White Pantheon. You have been wronged, cousin, I will give you that. But someone must pay for the blood that's been spilled here."

Her gaze fell to Atrius—Atrius, who was still drenched in the Sightmother's blood.

The terror that spiked through me at that, just her attention going to him, paralyzed me.

And before I could stop myself, I leapt to my feet.

"I am responsible."

The words flew from my lips before I gave myself time to reconsider them.

A bolt of raw fear speared Atrius's presence—even though he hadn't so much as flinched when it was himself under Acaeja's scrutiny.

I couldn't let myself pay attention to that, though, as both goddesses' eyes turned to me. The force of their attention alone nearly made my knees buckle, like my body could not withstand the power of their gazes.

"I'm responsible," I said again. "And it would be an honor to sacrifice my life to you, my goddess, in payment."

I couldn't acknowledge Atrius. I would break if I did. I had the attention of two goddesses on me—two of the most powerful beings to ever exist across time itself—and yet I felt his stare just as strongly as theirs.

Nyaxia laughed. "See, Acaeja? If you want to take a life in exchange for a life, here's a pretty, young one ripe for your plucking. But you will not touch my acolyte."

Nyaxia, it seemed, was suddenly very protective when it came to her rival gods. Perhaps more about competition than it was about benevolence, but I was grateful for it on Atrius's behalf either way.

I told myself that I had never been afraid of death. And yet, I couldn't stop the shaking when Acaeja turned to me, her ice-white eyes staring through me. She approached, feet gliding without movement over the tile floor.

She leaned down before me, our faces level. All the threads, every one of them, bent toward her, as if begging to return to their natural origin. Each layer of my soul peeled back for her, leaving me terrifyingly exposed, like at any moment she could reach into my rib cage and pluck my bleeding heart.

The past, the present, the future blended. I felt uprooted in time, a million versions of myself over a million moments now standing in this spot, on trial under her judgment.

"Tell me, child," she said, "why would you offer yourself up to me so willingly?"

One of her many fingers, this one marked with a thorned circle—the symbol of the heart—reached out and trailed down my cheek.

"Because I did betray my Sightmother." Despite my best efforts, my voice wavered. "And because I have offered you my entire life, and it would be a greater honor than I deserve to offer you my death, too."

She regarded me, face stone, the light of her eyes peering through even my most deeply hidden threads.

"It is useless to offer me false truths, Vivi," she said.

My heart leapt to my throat. "I swear it, my goddess, I—"

"Just as it is useless to offer them to yourself." That single finger slid down, over the angle of my chin, lifting it. "So very terrified of that beating thing within your chest. That is the wrong enemy, child."

My mouth closed. Acaeja straightened, drawing herself up to her full height. The light of her eyes flared, and the threads at her fingers shivered and rearranged, as if mapping the path to a new web.

"Your offering is very noble," she said, "but I do not want it. Your death is of no value to me. But your life . . . I see that something of great usefulness may come of that."

I released a shuddering breath.

But that brief, powerful wave of relief crashed down hard when Acaeja turned back to Nyaxia and Atrius. For a split second, I thought that perhaps I was about to witness Atrius's death—or a battle between the goddesses that would destroy all of us.

Yet Acaeja's voice was calm when she spoke again.

"I have great sympathy for your pain and your grief, cousin. So, I will let you keep these victories. Let you keep the head of my acolyte. Let you keep this kingdom. *But.*" Her face darkened, the light in her eyes shifting to blue. The sky above us grew unnaturally purple, soundless cracks of lightning dancing over the stars. "Know this, Nyaxia. You have crossed a line here today. Done what cannot be undone. I have fought too long and too hard on your behalf to be disrespected like this. And you know that if it were any other but me standing before you now, the punishment would not be nearly so light."

Nyaxia smiled sweetly. It reminded me chillingly of the smile I had seen in Atrius's vision—the smile that doubled as a death promise.

"I long ago tired of the White Pantheon's petty threats, Acaeja," she said. "If Atroxus or his ilk want to come for me, let them come. I will fight harder than my husband did. I have none of his compassion."

Acaeja stared at Nyaxia for a long moment. The threads on her fingers danced and wove, fanning out behind her wings as if running through a thousand possibilities of a thousand futures.

"I tried, cousin," she said, softly. "You will not remember it. But let the fates show that I tried."

And then, in a blaze of clouds and smoke and wings, Acaeja tipped her head to the heavens, and she was gone.

Nyaxia barely glanced after her.

"Such catastrophizing," she muttered, pushing a sheet of star-dotted hair over her bare shoulder. Then she turned to Atrius, and that slow, night-hewn smile spread over her beautiful mouth again.

"Atrius of the Bloodborn," she crooned. "You have served me well. You have exceeded my expectations. In return, I lift the curse I placed upon you, just as I promised."

She leaned down and touched Atrius's chest.

With that touch, a sudden burst of darkness overtook the world.

A soundless scream rang in my ears. My knees hit the stone ground before I knew what was happening, my body curling in on itself. The vampires restrained on the pillars slumped, barely conscious, against their restraints.

Atrius had doubled over, clutching his chest, his pain ringing out even through the chaos.

Nyaxia offered no further parting words. In that maelstrom of night, she was gone. And when it faded, my senses slowly slipping back to me, I pushed myself to my hands and knees only to immediately sense Atrius lying on the ground before me, lifeless.

I choked out his name and crawled to him. My head swam, and my limbs were wobbly beneath me. Darkness clawed at the edges of my senses, ready to pull me away at any moment.

But I still managed to make it to Atrius's side, my hands sliding over his bare chest.

Fragments of his memories flashed through me—memories of the way Nyaxia had cruelly killed the Bloodborn prince even after he had fulfilled her greatest demands. For one terrible moment, I thought that she had done the same thing to Atrius.

If she had, I would—I would—

I couldn't let myself finish the thought. I used the last of the energy I did not have to reach into Atrius's aura, as deep as my exhausted magic could take me, right down to the core of his heart.

And there, I felt his soul. Weak. But alive.

And there was no rot here. Nothing consuming him.

I let out a shaky breath and sagged against him. With the rush of adrenaline leaving me, so did the rest of my sparse energy.

Atrius shifted weakly. He lifted his head, grunted a wordless sound. One hand found its way to my arm—rested there for a moment, as if he wasn't sure what he was feeling.

His eyes opened, awareness returning to him just as mine slipped away.

His fingers tightened, and with that pressure, the reality of our relationship crashed down around me.

I had betrayed him. He would kill me for it. Any king would do the same.

These truths took root in my heart.

Perhaps I hallucinated the way he said my name.

I opened my mouth to speak as Atrius sat up, but darkness took me before the words could come. They'd be useless, anyway.

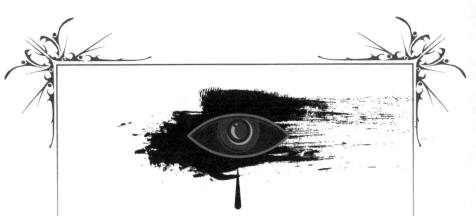

CHAPTER FORTY-EIGHT

I awoke in my room once again.

I recognized the location immediately. While before I had known it by its innate familiarity, now I knew it by an indescribable difference—every one of those familiar smells and sensations just a little changed, like the light had shifted in some inexplicable way.

I lay there, not moving. At first, I thought that the last day—had it been only a day? How long had it been?—had been a dream. Surely I had dreamed of betrayals and confessions and broken curses and goddesses—*goddesses*—standing right before me.

But my hand lifted and touched my cheek, my finger tracing the path a goddess had touched. The skin felt so deceptively normal. And yet . . . not normal at all.

The threads were tangled, my grip on them awkward. I sat up, reestablishing my hold—

—And came face-to-face with the conqueror.

He was lounging in the armchair in the corner, one heel propped up on the coffee table, a mirror of his pose the first time I had woken up in his presence, months and a lifetime ago. In his hands was a dagger.

The dagger.

"I was starting to think," he said, "that you wouldn't ever wake up."

He looked at the blade, casually twirling it from one hand to the other, not at me.

He would execute me with it. I was sure of it.

"I'm a bit surprised I did," I said, and if Atrius understood the implication of that sentence, he didn't react to it at all.

He didn't say anything at first, still examining the dagger, eyes lowered. I could not help but drink him in—the presence of him that had grown so intimately familiar to me. How could the man who was about to kill me feel so comforting? Why did I want to press his threads to my soul, deep enough I'd take their memory with me when I went?

I traced my awareness over the planes of his lowered, serious face, the tendrils of his hair—the ridged darkness of his horns, on perfect display with the angle.

"You still have those," I said. "Even though the curse is gone."

The corner of his mouth twitched. "She couldn't be too kind, apparently."

No, no one could say that Nyaxia was too kind. But then, no one could say it of any of the gods, I supposed. I had the distinct feeling that the only reason Acaeja had declined to take my head as repayment for the Sightmother's was, somehow, entirely selfish, even if I didn't understand why.

Useful, she had called me.

He turned the blade slowly between his fingertips. "So. This was the weapon that was intended to kill me."

My jaw tightened.

I was prepared for this, I told myself.

I inclined my chin. "Yes."

I wouldn't lie. Not anymore.

"I recognize it. You traveled with it for hundreds of miles."

"Yes."

"It's nothing special to look at. But when I wielded it, I could tell that it was magically enhanced." He flipped it in one smooth movement, grabbing it by the hilt. "Well made. Deadly. Which was fortunate."

Deadly enough to take off the Sightmother's head with just a few strokes. Fortunate indeed.

"The Arachessen take their jobs seriously," I said. "It had to be good enough to kill quickly."

"Kill a vampire warrior quickly."

I was prepared for this, I told myself.

I knew it was going to hurt.

I blinked behind my blindfold, ignoring the faint prickling. "Yes." I wouldn't defend myself. Wouldn't explain. What could I say to him? He had already seen the truth.

From the moment I had disobeyed the Sightmother's orders, I was ready to die for it. I preferred that it would be by his hand.

He stood up, and I did the same, bracing against a wave of dizziness that greeted me with the movement.

His brow rose, looking me up and down, and I answered his unasked question with, "I prefer to meet death standing up."

Another flippant echo of our first meeting. But this time, I had to say it past a lump in my throat.

He scoffed, "You think I'm going to kill you."

"Yes," I murmured. "I do."

"Do you know how long you've been asleep?"

I shook my head.

"Two days. Two very busy days. And yet, as I was clearing the Salt Keep and claiming the palace and solidifying my hold over this kingdom, do you know what I was thinking about?" He paused, like he expected me to answer. When I didn't, he said, "I was thinking about *you*. Your lies. Your betrayal." His gaze lowered to the blade. "I was thinking about this dagger."

Then those eyes speared me right through the chest, deadlier than any blessed weapon.

"And I thought about how you had used it," he said. "To protect your people and mine. To save my life. To slay your kingdom's tyrant." He dropped the knife to his side, knuckles white around the hilt. His words were rougher now, like they bubbled up from somewhere deep inside himself. "I thought about killing you for the crime of carrying a dagger you did not use. And I decided I couldn't. I told myself a million reasons why, but the truth is one I didn't want to admit."

My throat was so tight, I felt like I couldn't breathe. My heartbeat hammered against the inside of my ribs as he stepped closer, his stare fire.

"I cannot kill you because I know you, Vivi. I know every moment you lied to me, because I know every moment you told the truth. I know your truth. I can't ignore it. Even though it would be far easier if I could."

Weaver, I was prepared for death. *Wanted* death, over this— over feeling every one of his words pierce the most vulnerable parts of my heart.

I felt all of them deep inside myself. So terrifyingly true that every instinct told me to run.

I said, voice raw, "There is nothing I can say to erase what I did."

"I don't need your words."

He was so close now I felt his breath on my face. Felt that truth on my skin.

"So show me," he murmured. A command. A plea. Somehow both giving and taking, in equal measure. "Show me I'm right."

It went against everything I had always been. I wanted to cower from it. Wanted to hide.

Instead, when Atrius's hand rose to my face, I reached to the back of my head and untied my blindfold.

The little strip of silk fluttered to the ground.

I opened my eyes.

Arachessen were never without their blindfolds, not even in sleep. The air was cold and foreign against my eyes. My eyesight had been destroyed long ago. I had never even tried to examine the scraps of whatever remained.

But I could see Atrius.

Barely—just a little. I could make out the shape of his form, blurry and silhouetted, and the dim suggestion of his pale skin and silver hair.

Almost nothing. And yet, it was the most beautiful thing I'd ever witnessed. Beautiful in an intangible way that made me think of scraps of paint flying out over the sea.

It is the sea.

I opened my mouth to say something—wasn't even sure what—but what came out was only a garbled sob.

Atrius nodded, as if he still understood exactly what I meant, and he cradled my face between both hands. I closed my eyes, and he kissed one, then the other, catching the beginnings of tears on his lips.

His presence surrounded me, warm and stable and firm, such a perfect mirror of my own, scars and all.

I choked out, "I'm not afraid of death."

But I am afraid of this.

Atrius, of course, already knew.

"Me too," he murmured, the words warm against my lips, and I wasn't sure who moved first, only that our kiss was long and fierce and brutally honest with all that we didn't say.

My arms wrapped around him, and his around me. Our bodies intertwined. All lies withered in the space between us.

I kissed him and wept and kissed him some more, and I was so happy, I couldn't even be terrified.

CHAPTER FORTY-NINE

I stood in the gathering room alone for a long time before the Sisters were brought in.

First I walked through it without my blindfold, reminding myself of the differences between the version of myself now and the one who had last sat at this table. Not that I could see much of anything with my eyes in a room this dark, not even shadows. Still, there was something about feeling the air here on my open eyes that brought me clarity.

I had been dreading this meeting.

Atrius had first suggested it a week ago, and though he was the first one to voice it, I had been turning the idea around in my mind from the day I woke up in this new, infant version of my kingdom's new life. With the Sightmother dead, the Arachessen was a scattered and headless organization. The Sightmother's two oldest advisors, the only holders of her secret, had been killed when they foolishly attempted to recapture Atrius after the gods departed. But the rest of the Sisters remained here, in the Salt Keep. Atrius's men had captured most of them during his initial takeover, though some who had been away on missions hadn't been heard from since. They'd been treated well, though guarded very carefully, since then, while Atrius and I dealt with the immediate pressing needs that went along with taking over a kingdom.

But I knew I would have to come back, and sooner rather than later.

Every time I had sat at this table, I had felt so exposed—deeply connected to my Sisters and ashamed of what that connection might unwillingly reveal. I loved my Sisters, or at least I thought I did. Now, I pitied that version of myself, for whom love meant hiding so many different aspects of herself.

Yet maybe some of that girl still lived in me, because I broke out in a cold sweat at the thought of sitting at this table again, irrationally afraid of what the others might see in me.

Atrius, of course, had sensed my anxiety last night, as I tossed and turned in bed. He'd pulled me against him, curling his body around mine, and grumbled into my hair, "They'll listen to you. If they don't, we'll just kill them all."

I'd been grateful for something to laugh at, even though I wasn't actually sure that he was joking.

I felt the pressure of this meeting. That much was indisputable. But now that I was standing here in this room, the pressure was just the same pressure I felt before any of the many diplomatic meetings I'd had in the last few weeks. I had expected that this room would feel magical in some way. Blessed. Like it saw too much of me.

But I had already witnessed that—when I stared into the face of Acaeja herself.

I witnessed it every time I was in the presence of Atrius.

This? This was just a room.

Still, there was some power in ritual. I set out the chairs myself, placing them evenly around the circular table. I spread the salt. No, none of it was magic. None of it was godly. But it helped us all feel a little less alone in this world—and that counted for something.

When I sensed the Sisters approaching, escorted by Erekkus and his men, I tied my blindfold on once again in a show of respect to them and to our shared history. I was seated at the center of the table, in the chair the Sightmother once occupied, my fingertips pressed to the salt. The Sisters were ushered in and sat down in their seats. They all were healthy and clean. Still, I sensed their fear, wary and palpable.

Some held their hands to the salt immediately, grateful for something familiar. Others hesitated for a few uneasy moments before acquiescing.

Asha was the last one to act. Her presence was the coldest.

"You don't have to," I said, "if you don't want to. I just wanted you all to see my truth as I see yours."

Asha didn't acknowledge me and kept her hands on her lap. That was fine.

I turned my head, feeling all the familiar souls around me. I smiled. "It's good to see you all together again. I've missed you."

The truth. I didn't intend to speak anything but the truth tonight.

"I hope you've all been comfortable . . . even though I know the circumstances haven't been ideal these last few weeks. And I'm sorry for that. A lot has been changing."

"You killed the Sightmother," Asha spat.

A ripple of fear, grief, anger spread around the table. Erekkus took half a step closer, as if preparing to restrain Asha, but I held up a hand.

"I didn't," I said, "but I'll take responsibility for her death."

Her lip twitched with a sneer. "You were always so lost in your worldly wants. None of us are surprised that you murdered the Sightmother and fucked a vampire to make yourself a queen. And you expect us to follow you?"

Once, her words would have hurt.

Now, I felt nothing for her but pity. This was fear. That's all.

"No," I said. "I don't expect anything from you. I'm just trying to give you something. You can take it if you want, or not."

"And what is that?" she sneered.

"Something that was kept from all of us. The truth."

I pressed my hands against the grains of salt. I exhaled my nervousness.

I had never before been honest at this table.

"All I ask of you," I said, softly, "is for you to listen."

But tonight, I opened my soul, exposed the threads I had always been so desperate to hide, and I gave them all of it.

I gave them the truth.

I WAS BRACED for their response. What I had revealed to them was an affront to everything they had known about the Arachessen. We had all been raised to have complete, unquestioning faith in our Sightmother and our goddess. What I was telling them now . . . it was such a gutting betrayal that it would be easier for them to deny it.

Some of them grew angry as I talked, interjecting with vitriolic accusations. Others were withdrawn and silent. I answered all their questions. I gave them all the scant proof I could. I offered to take them to see the body of the Pythora King, in its clearly manipulated state.

For hours, we talked. I was honest about all of it—the things I knew, and the things I didn't. So many questions I still couldn't answer, no matter how much I wished I could.

And when I felt their heartbreak, I experienced mine all over again.

For better or for worse, we had built something beautiful in our unshakable faith in each other. I grieved it as it shattered. I was here to create something new with them, but that didn't change the tragedy of what had been destroyed.

Eventually, hours later, we had exhausted ourselves. Everything that could be said had been. We leaned over that unbroken chain of salt, simmering in each other's grief.

Only then did I lift my head and turn to all of them, reaching my presence out to theirs.

"I know that what I have told you is difficult to hear, and even harder to understand," I said. "I know that I'll be spending much of my life trying to understand it, too. I wish I could give you all the answers you're looking for. I—I wish I could find them for myself." My voice cracked slightly—I cleared it, swallowing down the emotion. "But while we can't control our reckoning with the past, we can control our future. The Pythora King, in whatever form he existed, is gone. Now we're left with a broken kingdom that needs us, and a world of opportunity of what can be done with the pieces." I drew in a breath and let it out. "How long, Sisters, has it been since Glaea belonged to its people?"

"The vampire is not one of Glaea's people," Naya pointed out.

"No," I agreed. "And he'll be the first to admit that, too. But I am, and I stand beside him. He isn't Glaean, but he knows what it is to be lost and betrayed by those who were supposed to protect you. He knows this kingdom deserves more, just as we do. And our voices are just as powerful as his. I know this is a big question, and I've given you a lot to consider. But that's all I'm asking of you. Consideration."

The words hung in the air for a long moment. I found myself holding my breath along with them.

Little Yylene, Weaver bless her, was the first to stand.

"Yes," she said, her small voice barely filling the room. "Yes. I'll help."

I couldn't suppress my grin. Not only at my first ally, but that it was her—the young girl who, like me, had always so struggled with her emotions.

Soon after her, another Sister stood, and another. They didn't say anything. There was nothing more to say. But I felt their solidarity all the same.

In the end, half the table stood that night, offering me their support—more than I ever thought I would get. The rest didn't offer their allegiance outright, but didn't deny it either, saying they needed more time to think. That, I understood. I'd give them as much as they needed.

When the meeting ended and the Sisters filed from the room, only Asha remained, her hands still on her lap, her face stone. A wall surrounded her inner threads—a wall so rigid that I knew whatever wounds bled within were deep.

Erekkus cast me a glance as the rest of the Arachessen left, silently asking if I needed help, but I shook my head and waved him away.

Then I shifted to the seat next to Asha and touched her shoulder. "Sister."

She lurched away from me, the rage in her aura lashing out in a sudden wave.

"You're not my Sister," she spat. "You don't deserve that title."

"Asha—"

"You're lying. You're lying about all of it. Do you think I don't see that?"

I said softly, "I am not lying."

"You were never one of us. You hated the Sightmother because she saw that—"

"I *loved* the Sightmother," I bit out. "She was everything I wanted to be."

She whirled to me, mouth twisted and teeth bared. "I gave my life to her. My *life*. Longer than you've been alive. And you expect me to believe that she had lied to us that way and no one ever found out but who—*you*?"

She spat the word, spittle flying across the table.

I was silent.

I knew, in this moment, that nothing I could ever say would make her believe me. She would live the rest of her life believing I was a liar, because the alternative was too difficult to stomach.

So I didn't try to argue with her. I didn't stop her as she lurched to her feet, tipping over her chair with a violent clatter, and left the room, leaving me alone with a table covered in smeared salt.

I had half my Sisters. Maybe more, when all was said and done.

I would take that.

CHAPTER FIFTY

The next night, Erekkus and I used the pools to travel to Vasai. After much discussion, Atrius and I had decided to make Vasai the new capital of the country. It had been the capital, once, long ago—but the Pythora King had been so isolated and so fearful for his own safety, he had taken to his castle, far to the north and separated from the rest of the kingdom he supposedly ruled. The Pythora King's castle would make a terrible capital for rulers who wanted to rule, not hide from, their people. Vasai, a bustling city that was centrally located in Glaea, was a perfect candidate.

The thought of returning to my old home didn't frighten me this time. Instead, it seemed oddly fitting for a new beginning to happen there.

Atrius was waiting for me when I stepped out of the pool just outside the northern end of Vasai. As always, he showed his affection in the way he helped me from the water, firm and protective, in the watchful way he examined me afterward, in the way he listened as I told him about the meeting—in the casual hand on my lower back, such a light touch, but one that gave me the stability to lean on.

When I was done, he updated me on what he'd been working on in Vasai in the days I had been away. Always, there was so much to do, but I loved it. He did, too, I knew. I secretly found it breathtaking, the way he lit up with enthusiasm when presented with a problem to solve. For centuries, he had just been helping his people survive. Helping them thrive suited him.

I was so engrossed in our conversation that I didn't notice at first that he'd taken a wrong turn on our way back to the castle.

I stopped short. "You're going to have to learn your own city better than that, conqueror," I said, pointing over my shoulder. "The castle is that way."

"I know," he said, and kept on walking.

I didn't move, immediately suspicious. "Where are we going?"

He didn't answer. Just kept walking. I had to awkwardly half run to catch up to him again.

"Atrius," I said, "where are we going?"

"Nowhere," he said, then stopped at the door of a little townhouse and knocked.

My brows rose, thinking to myself, *He's about to give some poor shopkeeper the fright of his life.*

But it wasn't a shopkeeper who opened the door.

It was Naro.

Naro, standing. Naro, with color in his freckled cheeks and meat on his bones. Naro, with that big stupid grin plastered over his face, just like it was when he used to look at me when he was fourteen years old.

Naro. Alive. Healthy.

"I thought you'd accept this detour," Atrius said.

"Well," Naro drawled, "looks like a queen deigned to visit."

I barely heard him. I just managed to choke out, "I'm not really a queen," and then I was flinging myself into the doorway and into the wild embrace I wish I had given Naro the first time we reunited, an embrace long enough and tight enough to communicate fifteen years of missing and regret, shared between us.

"You look—look—" I choked out.

"Yeah," he said. "I'm doing better."

I squeezed my eyes shut against the tears and hugged him tighter. Weaver, I would never let him go again.

Finally, he released me, looking from me to Atrius, who stood stoic and somewhat awkwardly beside me in the door.

"Come in," he said. "Let me show you the new place. Ah—" He frowned at Atrius. "Do vampires drink pineapple juice?"

WE COULDN'T STAY at Naro's for long, but even that brief visit was enough. I marveled at his improvement from the last time I'd seen him—the vampire healers, he said, had helped him immensely. Apparently, he even liked them enough that his distrust of vampires had lessened, though I still sensed some wary unease from him around Atrius.

That was alright. All of this, I understood now, was a journey. Naro would have to fight for his health and his sobriety for the rest of his life. Glaea would have to fight for a better version of itself. Vampires and humans would have to fight to figure out how to coexist. Atrius would have to fight for the trust of his human people. And I would have to fight my battles, too, step by step.

None of it would be easy. None of it would be simple.

But that night, watching my brother talk, looking so much like the boy I had thought I lost so long ago, I thought, *It's worth it.*

The fight will always be worth it.

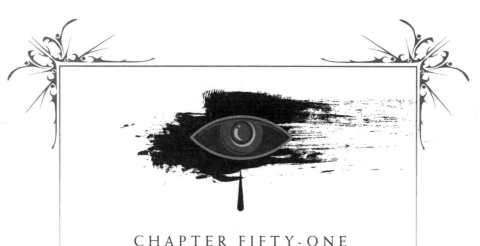

CHAPTER FIFTY-ONE

It was near dawn by the time Atrius and I finished our work for the day and stumbled, exhausted, back to the castle. The Thorn Palace—not that it was called that anymore—made for a beautiful place once it was cleaned up and stripped of its more brutal aspects.

Atrius led me to his bedchamber and kissed me, long and hard, against the door. I wasn't expecting the kiss, or at least not the intensity of it, his tongue slipping between my lips, his teeth nipping at one, then the other. The scent of steel and snow and the solid wall of his presence surrounded me, and the surprised sound that escaped my throat quickly fell into a moan.

His hands gripped my hips as he deepened the kiss, tipped my head back, pinning me against the wall. I could feel the stiff length of his desire pressing against me, and Weaver, my own desire matched it, coiling low in my stomach.

I didn't care if it made me pathetic. It had been too many nights away from him. I needed him.

My hand reached behind me and found the door handle. It was, of course, locked.

I groaned. "Get this open," I murmured against his mouth.

He grunted in agreement and I heard the jangling of silver and the rustling of his coat. When the door swung open, I nearly toppled backward.

Atrius caught me, then pushed the door closed.

I was already reaching for him, ready to tear off his shirt—silk be damned. I expected he would do the same to me. That was how we fucked—frantically, like we were still racing against time or gods or curses.

But Atrius broke my kiss. "Do you like it?" he said.

"Hm?" I was chasing his mouth again, but he lifted his chin, gesturing to the room.

"Do you like it?"

I hadn't even paused to take in the chamber.

The room was large and circular, tall windows on the western side revealing the horizon and a star-scattered sky. The furniture was finely carved—a massive bed in the center of the room, a set of living room furniture around the fireplace to the right, a glimpse of a beautiful washroom through a door to the left. A large bookcase, only half-full, stood floor-to-ceiling beside the fireplace.

"It was empty before," Atrius said, noting my attention to the bookcase. Then added, flatly, "Not a surprise, considering the previous occupant."

True. Tarkan didn't seem like the reading type.

But I couldn't even recognize this room as the place that tyrant had lived, cold and impersonal and full of suffering. This felt . . . comfortable.

"It's beautiful," I said, and meant it.

Atrius still held me against him, though the embrace now seemed less primal and more . . . affectionate. His fingers absentmindedly intertwined with mine. The gesture reminded me of the way he had stroked his horse's mane back when we rode to Alka—instinctive affection. Then, I'd been so confused by his gentleness. Now, I wanted to sink into it.

"I've spent decades living in tents and outposts," he said. "It's . . . been a long time since I had to make a home I would live in for a long time." His gaze slipped to me. "Or that someone else would."

I blinked. I wasn't sure if he was saying what I thought he was saying.

"This is your chamber," I said.

His throat bobbed. He stared at me for a long moment, like he was grappling with something he didn't know how to say, then turned me around and led me to the windows.

From the doorway, I had missed it. The little chair. The easel. The carefully arranged line of paint jars.

"It could be yours, too," he said, somewhat awkwardly. "If you wanted."

I couldn't speak. I touched the easel—touched each of the jars. I could sense their colors, but what delighted me even more was that, without my blindfold, I could see them if I held them very close to my face—just barely, just a tinge to the shadow.

So much more than paper.

Thank you seemed woefully inadequate. So instead, I turned around, wound my arms around his neck, and kissed him.

This kiss wasn't like our others. It wasn't desperate. Wasn't rushed. It was slow and thorough, inhaling each other's breath, our tongues exploring each other's mouths as if getting reacquainted. His hands followed that lazy rhythm, running over my body, lingering on every curve. Not rushing to any of the places I wanted him to be.

Our movement to the bed was like vines growing across the forest floor. Slow and organic. He pushed me down into a nest of plush silk, unbearably soft compared to the hardness of his body above me. We didn't tear our clothing off—we removed each piece patiently, like petals peeled back from a flower, discarded around us until, between our languid kisses, bare skin met bare skin.

Weaver, I wanted him. Even though this desire tonight was different—not animalistic lust. I wondered if he felt it, too, because his lips trailed so patiently over mine, tasting my mouth, the angle of my jaw, the curve of my clavicle. Even when he lowered his head to my breast, my nipples hard and aching, his tongue working over them in ways that made my back arch and my breath hitch, I wasn't impatient.

I savored him.

And when he finally returned to me, finally kissed me again, finally aligned himself with my entrance, he pushed himself into me slowly.

My thighs opened wider for him, encircling his waist. But unlike our usual frenzied trysts, I didn't urge him harder. I moved with him as he pressed deep into me, allowing him all of me—allowing him to brand the deepest parts of me.

His mouth never left mine, tongue teasing me, lips testing every angle. We moved together as if connected by something deeper than flesh—and indeed, I could feel his presence, his threads, intertwining with mine.

He withdrew slowly and pushed back into me. The pleasure, for the slowness of the pace, was unbearable. Our shared moan vibrated against our lips. My hips rose to meet his.

"Atrius."

I didn't mean to say his name. It was just the only word I could form—the only thing I could think. I was surrounded by him. *Atrius. Atrius. Atrius.*

"Vi," he whispered.

Another thrust. We writhed together, languishing in each other's bodies.

Another. My cries of pleasure grew louder. His grip on my body firmer. We coiled around each other, tighter and tighter, drawing each other closer, wringing shared pleasure from our closeness.

His kiss deepened, fierce and slow and passionate, as he thrust into me, murmuring my name again into my lips.

Weaver, I loved to hear him say it.

I loved to have him this close to me.

I loved being this exposed to him, every part of me.

"Atrius," I whimpered again, my fingernails digging into his back—a plea for him to stay with me, to come with me, to follow me into this oblivion.

"Yes," he whispered, understanding, as always, all that I was saying.

And then he drew back, just enough so that his forehead pressed to mine, and with my eyes wide open I could see him—see his soul, his threads, see the blurry outline of his silhouette, his beautiful eyes, and above all, the confession in them as his hips thrust against mine and we threw ourselves over the edge together.

I clenched around him as I came, pulling him against me. He did the same, the two of us entwined so closely that I could no longer tell where his flesh ended and mine began.

When the ecstasy faded, he didn't move. He just held me. He rolled to the side, pulling his weight off me, but his grip didn't loosen, and I didn't pull away from it.

I would never pull away from it.

A truth solidified in me, an echo of the confession I saw in his eyes then. I wouldn't hide it from him.

Because that's all it was. A truth.

"I love you," I whispered, against the smooth flesh of his shoulder.

The reaction in his presence was immediate and sudden. I felt him stop breathing for a moment, then resume. Felt the skip in his steady heartbeat.

My chest warmed at that.

He pulled me closer and said against my hair, "You like the room then."

I chuckled. "I do."

"Good," he murmured. "Because even though there's no longer a curse, I can't seem to sleep without you."

He rolled to his back, still not releasing me, and I went with him, my head on his chest. I could feel that heartbeat beneath my palm now—slow and strong, and utterly unburdened.

And then he whispered, his fingertips trailing through the whorls of my hair, "I love you, seer."

My eyes closed.

Strange, how being so exposed can make a soul feel so very safe.

We had challenges ahead of us, I knew. A kingdom that would not want to accept us. A human populace struggling with poverty and drug addiction and decades' worth of oppression. A Bloodborn populace still struggling with an ancient curse, even if Atrius's had been lifted. A vampire society that might one day decide to interfere with ours. Gods who may grow displeased at a kingdom led by a vampire and a human.

I was more vulnerable than I had ever been.

But for the first time in my life, I was not afraid. I was at peace with the past, the present, and the future.

"I think," Atrius murmured, as if he was having the same thoughts I did, "the future will be good."

He said this thoughtfully, slowly, like it was a conclusion he had arrived at logically.

"You're lucky I believe you," I murmured.

"I don't lie."

I smiled, recognizing the echo of our past. "Everyone lies."

He stroked my hair. "Not me."

And Weaver help me, I believed him.

THE END

NINE MONTHS LATER

The heat throbbed down at the back of my neck, even though dawn was still hours away. This time of year, the humidity hung heavy in the air, even up here toward the mountains. Then again, maybe it wasn't the heat or the exertion that was making sweat bead. The work wasn't that hard. It wasn't that hot. I'd been jittery lately, something sliding under the surface of my skin.

I dropped my shovel and drew my hand across my forehead. Blurry shapes swirled across my vision. I'd abandoned the blindfold when the sweat had started to soak through it. Not pleasant.

"It's hot," I said. "Isn't it hot?"

"Not that hot." Naro shot me a playful glance as he swung his pickaxe again, breaking up stone to be carted away and make room for more houses. "Tired already, Vivi? Spoiled royalty."

Atrius laughed softly. I couldn't be offended by that, though—I knew he was doing so in an attempt to seem more approachable to Naro, which I thought was sweet. They weren't exactly friends, but they respected each other. That was something.

I scoffed, but secretly I took a moment to appreciate the vivacity emanating from Naro's threads. He'd been working for hours, and he wasn't even winded. It was hard to imagine this was the same man who'd been on the brink of death less than a year ago. The Pythoraseed abuse had damaged his body permanently—he'd be medicating himself for the rest of his life—but he'd worked hard to build his strength up again, and I was proud of him for that.

That was, in a way, an apt metaphor for all of Glaea now.

We were permanently marked by years of abuse and division, and we were far from healed. But we'd been working hard at it, these last months, even if imperfectly. The humans and the vampires were wary of each other. All of us were acutely conscious of the dangers of this arrangement, Atrius more than any. We all knew that the moment a vampire preyed upon a Glaean human, not only would it be a tragedy in its own right, but the shaky goodwill we had built among our deeply distrustful populace would come crashing down.

But the vampires, to their credit, seemed eager to be here. They were respectful of the humans and, above all, deferential to Atrius's command. We expanded housing, taking advantage of the heavily sheltered, mountainous regions the Pythora King had claimed for himself, which were perfect for our new vampire citizens who needed shelter from the sun and space away from the humans.

Still. I sensed their longing every time I was near them. Glaea was not yet their home, and everyone knew it, especially them.

None of us could afford to be picky, though.

I straightened, wincing as I rubbed my back, but then, halfway up the movement, I stopped short. The threads all vibrated at once, as if they'd been struck, and for a moment, I was utterly disoriented. A cold wave passed over me, like a cloud crossing the sun.

When my awareness returned to me, I was on my knees, Naro's hand on my shoulder, all signs of teasing gone. "Hey. What happened?"

His concern vibrated through me, still, after everything, sweet and pure. I stood and shook my head. "Just a long night."

"Vivi—"

"All fine. I promise."

He stared at me, then handed me a canteen. "Drink something."

I did, then smiled at him. "Thanks. Much better."

His face softened, as I knew it would. He was content now that I let him be my big brother. Sometimes it seemed like he just wanted to make up for lost time.

But I could feel Atrius's stare, too. Naro's guilt made him easy to deceive, but Atrius knew me better than that. He sent Naro off to go help the other team of Glaeans down the hill, then pulled me aside.

"Again?" he whispered.

I didn't bother trying to shrug it off. There was no *it's nothing* with Atrius. Besides, I knew that there was nothing to dismiss about the knot of anxiety in my stomach. The threads had grown restless lately, sometimes so tangled that it was hard for me to navigate the world. I wasn't sure what it meant, but it couldn't be anything good. Either the fates were shifting or my hold on the threads was, perhaps punishment by Acaeja for my betrayal. Both possibilities kept me awake in bed.

I didn't say anything, but I didn't need to. Atrius's frown deepened, and he started to speak, but Erekkus's voice came from behind us.

"You have a visitor."

It was nearly dawn. Strange timing for a vampire visitor. "They can wait," Atrius said, without turning. "I'm busy."

"Might not be so simple."

A note in Erekkus's voice—and a sour shiver through his threads— had me pausing. "Why?" I said.

Erekkus's mouth twisted into a humorless smile. "What has Atrius told you of his cousin?"

Atrius dropped his shovel. He straightened.

"Oh," he said. He looked down at his dirt-stained clothes, then remarked to me, begrudgingly, "We should clean up."

"He wanted to meet privately," Erekkus said.

Atrius scoffed. "It is good to want things," he replied, which earned a chuckle from Erekkus.

"He?" I said, intrigued.

Atrius took my hand and together we started toward the castle. "We'll talk as we walk."

THE PRINCE OF the House of Blood had his back to us when we entered the dining room. The scent of cigarillo smoke wafted through the air. The moment I sensed him, the dark depths of his essence startled me—deep burgundy, like vampire blood, elegant and mysterious. I sensed immediately that he was much younger than Atrius, but his soul reminded me of stone smoothed by years of wind and rain. He was staring at a tapestry on the wall—a leftover relic of Tarkan's rule, and a particularly salacious one even by his standards, depicting a tangled mass of naked bodies.

The door shut behind us, and the man turned. He was, I could sense, breathtakingly handsome, the kind of beautiful that even the threads had to bow down to. His mouth curled into a smirk as he pushed a wayward strand of ash-blond hair away from his forehead. He was dressed simply for a prince—fine but plain clothes, though they were impeccably clean. White shirt, white pants, embellished with silver at the folded corner of his collar and at his belt.

"Tasteful," he said, nodding to the tapestry. "No wonder you found yourself a Glaean woman."

Atrius's face did not change. "Not a very respectful way to talk in someone else's home."

The man chuckled, exhaling a stream of smoke, which made Atrius's nose twitch.

"Still on the bad habits, I see," he said.

"Life is short. Though . . ." The Bloodborn cocked his head. "A little less short for you these days, I hear." He stepped closer, slowly, looking us up and down. His gaze lingered on Atrius's horns. "A pity the Mother left those, though."

"Bold of you to suggest they don't suit me, Septimus."

The Bloodborn—Septimus—let out another stream of smoke, and for a long moment, the two of them stared each other down.

Then his face broke into a grin—one that, to my shock, Atrius returned.

Not only returned, but followed with an *embrace*.

"Good to see you, Atrius," Septimus said, clapping Atrius on the back.

"Likewise, my prince." Atrius stepped back and gestured to me. "This is Sylina. She is . . . rules alongside me."

I still felt his little ripple of uncertainty with that description. Atrius and I were not married, though I could often sense him nudging around the prospect of it. It was better, for now, that we weren't. I wanted to steer this country as a member of it in my own right, not as Atrius's wife, and the people of Glaea needed to see me that way, too.

Septimus took my hand and bowed his head to brush his lips across it—an awkward custom that I allowed because it was always useful for me to let someone touch my bare skin. Septimus wore gloves, but still, at his touch, a disorienting wave of tremors crashed through the threads. Like fate was pulling in all different directions at once.

I was careful to keep my face blank as he released me, though the sensation left me dizzy.

"A pleasure, my queen."

"Not queen," I said. "But likewise." I gestured to the table, which had already been set with a mix of human and vampire cuisine. Most of it would be largely ceremonial for a vampire appetite, save for the blood—cow's blood—but as a matter of policy, Atrius and I made all diplomatic meals representative of Glaean culture.

"Please, sit," I said. "I'm sure you have plenty to discuss."

IT WAS FASCINATING to witness Atrius and Septimus reminisce. Neither of them seemed particularly well-suited to that brotherly camaraderie. The conversation was forced and stilted as they spoke of the House of Blood, as if they were going through the motions of what they thought was expected of them. Still, I sensed that this awkwardness wasn't due to their feelings toward each other—on the contrary, I felt clearly that the friendship between them was very real. But all their stories of home were half-finished, with obvious, gaping holes, like healers gingerly working around a necrotic infection.

I thought I knew why.

But my suspicion wasn't confirmed until late in the meal, when Septimus leaned back in his chair and set his wineglass down. A pensive smile twisted his lips as he looked around the room.

"It is magnificent," he said. "You have done well by my brother, Atrius."

Atrius stiffened. I felt his grief—both of their grief—shake the threads at once.

My brother.

Atrius's leader. The prince he had followed to the end of the mortal world. The prince whose head he had brought back as cruel reward for his success.

"I hope so," Atrius said stiffly. "But much better to do right by the living."

Septimus shifted in his seat—his legs uncrossing, his body leaning forward, his long fingers intertwining. So subtle, so graceful, like a panther arranging its body for the hunt.

I knew that Septimus's pleasure in Atrius's company was genuine. But I also knew he had been circling us like prey all night, ready for the perfect opening. Atrius had handed it to him.

"Fitting you should say that." Septimus reached into his pocket. "Turns out I'm here on behalf of the living, actually."

He withdrew a cigarillo, lighting it as Atrius let out a dry almost-laugh.

"I was waiting for this," he said. "It is never just a visit."

Septimus slipped the cigarillo between his teeth before touching his chest. "Your lack of faith in me wounds."

The corner of Atrius's mouth twitched. "I've known you since your first words, Septimus, and those words were silken half truths."

"They're always more than *half* true, my friend." He took a deep inhale and let out a stream of smoke. "I'm here because your House calls upon you."

All levity in both of them disappeared at once.

Atrius straightened. Even without my magic, I would have felt his bolt of hope. Weaver, I felt it in my own heart. How many times had I listened to Atrius whisper in the small hours of the morning of his home? How many times had I held his hand while he spoke of it in such small, tentative words, like he couldn't even bear to give voice to how much he missed it? To how much he wished his men could return?

He wanted nothing—nothing—more than that.

I wanted to seize his hand and throw my body in front of him, a shield against potential painful disappointment.

I turned my awareness to Septimus, wary. Feeling for any sign of dishonesty. But even the sarcasm had disappeared from his demeanor.

"Come back to Obitraes," he said.

Atrius was silent for a moment too long. I had to wonder how many times he had dreamed of hearing those words.

"So my House welcomes me back now."

I could taste the bitterness in his voice. His anger at decades of banishment when he'd needed his home more than ever.

A beat of silence. A wave of something even I couldn't decipher, quiet and pensive, passed over Septimus's threads.

He said quietly, "I never blamed you for what happened to him, Atrius."

A lie, I sensed. Even though I also sensed that Septimus genuinely wished it wasn't.

"We can't leave Glaea now," Atrius said. "It needs us."

We? Us?

But I didn't let my face so much as twitch. As far as Septimus knew, I would take it as given that I would go anywhere Atrius did.

Septimus's brows raised as his gaze flicked to me. "Of course. Glaea needs you *both*."

We all heard the pointed tone of the word.

"Whatever task you're giving me, you'd be fortunate to have a seer, too," Atrius said.

"Task?" Septimus let out a silken chuckle. "What ever did I say about a task?"

Another humorless twitch at the corner of Atrius's mouth. "First words, Septimus. Half truths and tasks."

He sighed, letting out a plume through his nostrils. "But I'm so very good at it."

I was wary. I didn't like seeing Atrius played with like a mouse in a cat's jaws, even if it was by someone who did seem to like him. I decided to poke a little harder. "Maybe not good enough," I said. "I heard about your adventures in the House of Night. It's admirable that you've so easily recovered from such a failure."

Sometimes it took a long time for news of Obitraes to reach Glaea, small as this place was. But with Atrius's men in place, we'd heard plenty in recent months about the House of Blood's ill-fated operations in the House of Night, a rival vampire kingdom. Apparently, Septimus had gotten himself involved in a civil war there, and he'd backed the wrong side.

It wasn't even an especially well-disguised jab. But oh well. I'd been trained as an assassin, not a court lady.

Septimus only laughed. Even the sound of it was elegant and rich. It reminded me of wine.

"Oh, dove. That was no failure. I got all I wanted out of the ordeal, and I have been hard at work since. But I don't blame you for the misunderstanding. We don't know each other very well yet."

He reached into his pocket again and slid his hand across the table. When he withdrew it, it revealed a small, silver box with a black clasp. Its appearance, though, was by far the most unassuming thing about it. I drew in a sharp breath when he placed it on the table. The threads rearranged around it, drowning out everything else in the room.

I had to stop myself from reaching for it, winding my fingers together in my lap.

"A box," Atrius said flatly. Maybe he could feel an echo of the true nature of whatever this was, but if he could, it would be very quiet to him. To me, it was deafening. He had no idea what was sitting in front of us.

I didn't, either. But I didn't need to know the details to feel the way it tugged at fate.

Septimus's gaze fell to me. "Tell us what you feel, Sylina."

I was fascinated by it. And I was terrified of it.

I reached across the table and lay my hand over the box.

A gasp ripped from me.

The Threads tore, tugged, drew taut around my throat. The floor fell out beneath me. I was falling—falling through hundreds of years, thousands of years, backward, forward, both at once. A wound of betrayal opened in my chest, seeped, festered, calcified into fury. I saw countless mangled bodies littered upon a shoreline—human or vampire? Mortal or god? I couldn't tell, except that I was briefly, suddenly, horrifically certain that Atrius's was among them. I saw the sun shattering, a dripping gold inferno like a pierced egg yolk. I saw a thousand years of darkness. I saw clashes of grand power dousing the sky with light and darkness, so beautiful a mortal mind couldn't even conceive of it.

And then, in the next breath, I saw greatness.

Power, strength, towers of marble rising into the clouds, warm hearts and full stomachs. Safety and solace. Wonders beyond anything I could ever imagine—sculptures so elegant they brought tears to my eyes, gardens so lush I could taste the scent of them on my tongue. Above all, the euphoric breathlessness of *possibility*.

I snatched my hand back. I had to put unexpected effort into tearing myself away.

"What *is* that?" The words came out in a single exhale.

Septimus's smirk had disappeared. He was utterly serious now, and I could feel his stare spearing me.

"The gods are preparing for war. And you know what that means for all of us poor exiled souls."

I knew better than most. Unimaginable loss in the collateral damage. "Destruction."

"Maybe," Septimus replied. "Or, perhaps, opportunity. If one has enough vision."

I didn't want to admit he was right. Even if I knew he was.

Atrius's hand was on my back. He eyed the box warily.

"What's in it?" he asked.

"Does it matter?"

"The box is Shadowborn. You stole from the House of Shadow?"

"Stole? You think so little of me. Incredible what you can achieve by making yourself the singular solution to a problem."

He leaned across the table, taking the box back in one graceful movement as he did. "Come back to Obitraes. I'll give you all the resources you need to keep things running smoothly here in your stead. We have an opportunity now. A chance to end millennia of Bloodborn suffering. But only if we act quickly. You know better than any that we do not have time to waste." He extended a hand. "And we need you, my friend. You."

Atrius was silent for a long moment. I ran my mental fingers over his threads, feeling for his reaction. He was torn.

"If I do this," he said, "then that will mean my men can go home?"

Septimus smiled, but there was no joy, not even bitter amusement, in the expression. "If you do this," he said, "maybe they might have a home to come back to."

THE SUN WAS up. It slithered beneath the heavy velvet curtains of our bedchamber. Atrius and I were silent as we walked through the halls. Though we were alone, it didn't feel right to speak of the conversation we'd just had. Though we knew so little of what we'd actually just witnessed, I still cradled it carefully in my chest, like an explosive that might destroy us all with one sudden movement.

It was only when the door was firmly closed behind us that Atrius turned to me. "So?" he said.

He meant: *What do you think?*

He always asked that question with such genuine weight. Atrius valued my expertise deeply. And I knew in this moment, just from the way he said that single word, that whatever I said, he would do.

I wanted to tell him not to go.

I could say that Glaea was too fragile to be left without him, no matter how much magic or manpower we used to close the distance. I could say that Septimus was meddling with powers unfit for mortal hands. I could say that when we already had the gods' teeth so close to our throats, we should keep our heads down and our hands clean. All of these things were true. Maybe they even were the *right* things to say.

But I said, "I think you need to go."

I questioned my own sanity as those words left my lips.

Atrius turned to me, and I felt the surprise ripple his threads, too. It was not what he was expecting.

"You trust him?"

Trust was a funny word.

"I think his intentions are genuine. I also think he'll say whatever he needs to say to meet their ends."

Atrius shook his head. "That was always Septimus."

"But he wasn't lying to you."

He let out a slow breath. Then, "What did you see, when you touched that box?"

I didn't have words to describe it. I was silent for a long moment, trying to find the right ones. But the best I could come up with was, "I saw fates colliding."

"Then perhaps we should leave him to that and run."

Atrius was being half-sarcastic, I knew. He and I both knew what it was like to exist in the forgotten dregs of society. Our people were not the ones who would be able to claim moral piety and wash our hands of these kinds of conflicts. We would be the ones swallowed in the collateral damage. Especially Glaea, which now sat at the tension point of two gods.

The visions racked through me again, and I shivered.

"Glaea will be the first pawn to be swept off the board," I murmured. "He is right that we can't afford to be reactive."

We might not be able to afford to be proactive, either, but I didn't say that part aloud.

I turned to Atrius. He was quiet, pensive, his whole form drawn taut in thought.

"But it was never a debate for you," I said. "You were always going to go."

His eyes flicked to me, surprised. But he didn't argue with me.

Because the moment Septimus had offered him a return for his men, it had been all over.

"You want nothing more than for your men to have the opportunity to go home," I said. "I know you."

He stepped closer. His fingers brushed my cheek, sweeping my hair back. "That's not true," he murmured. "I want one thing more."

Despite everything, a flutter rustled in my heart. Weaver damn this man.

"And you accuse Septimus of silken words."

Atrius's lips lowered to my cheek. "We've discussed this. I never lie."

I hummed my reluctant agreement as he kissed the angle of my jaw. "I'm coming with you, I hope you know," I said. "If there's going to be a divine collision, I don't want to miss it."

He chuckled low in his throat. "Oh, I know."

I let my body melt against his. With all the talk of fates and the end of the world and divine catastrophe, all of it, somehow, seemed more manageable with him beside me.

He pulled away just enough to look at me. Then his mouth fell to my ear, lips skimming the crest of it.

"I never want to go anywhere without you, Vivi. I hope you know that."

I squeezed my eyes shut and tightened my arms around him. I didn't speak over the lump in my throat.

We would, of course, one day be separated. I was a human. He was a vampire. My lifetime would be a blink compared to his. And yet I felt the truth in his words, unshakable. Atrius always spoke in absolutes. He always spoke his truth.

Gods, how I loved him for it.

And I decided in this moment that it was my truth, too. No matter what.

I thought of what I had seen with my hand over that box. The shores littered with bodies. The horrific certainty that Atrius was gone, too.

"You never will," I whispered.

Two words that I seared straight into the Threads. Two words that I vowed would always be true.

No, Atrius and I would never have the luxury of bowing out of the hard conflicts. And I would fight to the end for him, for us, for the people who had entrusted us with their lives.

Even if it meant going up against the gods themselves.

AUTHOR'S NOTE

Thank you so much for reading *Slaying the Vampire Conqueror*! This story and these characters took me by surprise, and I hope you loved reading this tale as much as I loved writing it.

The world of the Crowns of Nyaxia is so dark, twisted, and complex. I absolutely loved getting the opportunity to explore other corners of it with this story. If you'd like to read more vampire goodness in this world, check out the Crowns of Nyaxia series, starting with *The Serpent & the Wings of Night*. While Sylina and Atrius have their happy ending with each other, they still have tons to accomplish in the Crowns of Nyaxia world—they will be making very important appearances later in this series!

If you enjoyed this book, I would truly appreciate it if you'd consider giving a review on Amazon or Goodreads. I can't overstate how important reviews are to authors!

And if you'd like to be the first to know about new releases, new art, new swag, and all kinds of other fun stuff, consider signing up for my newsletter at carissabroadbentbooks.com, hanging out in my Facebook group (Carissa Broadbent's Lost Hearts), or joining my Discord server (invite at linktr.ee/carissanasyra).

I would love to keep in touch!

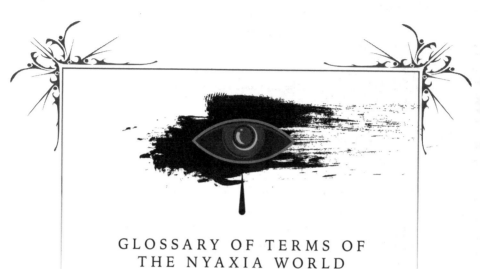

GLOSSARY OF TERMS OF
THE NYAXIA WORLD

Acaeja—The goddess of fate, mystery, and lost things. Member of the White Pantheon.

Alarus—The god of death and husband of Nyaxia. Exiled by the White Pantheon as punishment for his forbidden relationship with Nyaxia. Considered to be deceased.

Atroxus—The god of the sun and leader of the White Pantheon.

Bloodborn—Vampires of the House of Blood.

Blood magic—A type of magic wielded exclusively by vampires of the House of Blood, which allows them to manipulate the blood of living beings.

Born—A term used to describe vampires who are born via biological procreation. This is the most common way that vampires are created.

Extryn—The prison of the gods of the White Pantheon.

HEIR MARK—A permanent mark that appears on the Heir of the Hiaj and Rishan clans when the previous Heir dies, marking their position and power.

HIAJ—One of the two clans of Nightborn vampires. They have featherless wings that resemble those of bats.

THE HOUSE OF BLOOD—One of the three vampire kingdoms of Obitraes. Two thousand years ago, when Nyaxia created vampires, the House of Blood was her favorite House. She thought long and hard about which gift to give them, while the Bloodborn watched their brothers to the west and north flaunt their powers. Eventually, the Bloodborn turned on Nyaxia, certain that she had abandoned them. In punishment, Nyaxia cursed them. The House of Blood is now looked down upon by the other two Houses. People from the House of Blood are called BLOODBORN.

THE HOUSE OF NIGHT—One of the three vampire kingdoms of Obitraes. Known for their skill in battle and for their vicious natures; wielders of magic derived from the night sky. There are two clans of Nightborn vampires, HIAJ and RISHAN, who have fought for thousands of years over rule. Those of the House of Night are called NIGHTBORN.

THE HOUSE OF SHADOW—One of the three vampire kingdoms of Obitraes. Known for their commitment to knowledge; wielders of mind magic, shadow magic, and necromancy. Those of the House of Shadow are called SHADOWBORN.

IX—Goddess of sex, fertility, childbirth, and procreation. Member of the White Pantheon.

KAJMAR—God of art, seduction, beauty, and deceit. Member of the White Pantheon.

NIGHTBORN—Vampires of the House of Night.

Nyaxia—Exiled goddess, mother of vampires, and widow of the god of death. Nyaxia lords over the domain of night, shadow, and blood, as well as the domain of death inherited from her deceased husband. Formerly a lesser goddess, she fell in love with Alarus and married him despite the forbidden nature of their relationship. When Alarus was murdered by the White Pantheon as punishment for his marriage to her, Nyaxia broke free from the White Pantheon in a fit of rage, and offered her supporters the gift of immortality in the form of vampirism—founding Obitraes and the vampire kingdoms. *(Also referred to as: the Mother; the Goddess; Mother of the Ravenous Dark; Mother of Night, Shadow, and Blood.)*

Obitraes—The land of Nyaxia, consisting of three kingdoms: the House of Night, the House of Shadow, and the House of Blood.

Pythora / Pythoraseed—A drug derived from a type of flower that typically grows in the harsh lands of Glaea. The growth, distillery, and trade of Pythora is a thriving market that has given rise to a number of warlords in Glaea and around the world.

The Pythora King—A warlord who built immense fortune and power on an empire of Pythora trade, and then used that power to take over the kingdom of Glaea.

Shadowborn—Vampires of the House of Shadow.

Turning—A process to make a human into a vampire, requiring a vampire to drink from a human and offer their blood to the human in return. Vampires who underwent this process are referred to as Turned.

White Pantheon—The twelve gods of the core cannon, including Alarus, who is presumed deceased. The White Pantheon is worshipped by all humans, with certain regions favoring certain gods within the Pantheon. Nyaxia is not a member of the White Pantheon and is actively hostile to them. The White Pantheon imprisoned and later executed Alarus, the god of death, as punishment for his unlawful marriage with Nyaxia, then a lesser goddess.

ZARUX—The god of the sea, rain, weather, storms, and water. Member of the White Pantheon.

ACKNOWLEDGMENTS

I love this part! The part where I get to be mushy about everything!

As with all of my books, this one was a real effort of love from so many people. Chief among them:

Nathan, I've said it before and I'll say it again, no matter how many times I write these, your name comes first. Thank you for being the love of my life, my support system, my brainstorming buddy, and for solving all my plot issues in like ten minutes flat. You're the best.

Monique Patterson, thank you for being an amazing advocate for the Nyaxia world and for helping this book reach so many more people. To the incredible team at Bramble—including Mal Frazier, Caro Perny, Tyrinne Lewis, Julia Bergen, and countless others—thank you for all you've done to make these books a success! It's an honor to work with such wonderful professionals.

Bibi Lewis, my agent, thank you for being an incredible force in general and for taking my books to heights I never could have imagined! (Also, for keeping me sane. Ish.)

Clare, thank you so much for having the brilliant idea for the series that originally spawned this book and for inviting me on the ride with you! I could not survive this business without you; thank you for being such an incredible friend and "coworker." Candace, Elle, Helen, and Jessica, it was so wonderful being on this journey with you all.

Noah, thank you for being an incredible editor and brainstorming buddy, and above all, thank you for bearing with my even-more-chaotic-than-usual process for this book. You're the best!

Ariella, Deanna, Alex, and Rachel, thank you for being the best beta readers ever and for your invaluable time, support, and feedback!

Anthony, thank you for the amazing proofreading!

And above all, thank you to *you*, for following me and reading my books, for your fan art and reviews and Instagram posts and Book-Tok videos. I owe you everything. You are incredible. Thank you!

ABOUT THE AUTHOR

Victoria Costello

CARISSA BROADBENT has been concerning teachers and parents with mercilessly grim tales since she was roughly nine years old. Subsequently, her stories have gotten (slightly) less depressing and (hopefully a lot?) more readable. Today, she writes novels that blend epic fantasy plots with a heaping dose of romance. She lives with her husband, her son, and one perpetually skeptical cat in Rhode Island.